Mark Greaney has a degree in international relations and political science. In his research for the Armored novels and the Gray Man novels, including *Midnight Black, The Chaos Agent, Burner, Sierra Six, Relentless, One Minute Out, Mission Critical, Agent in Place, Gunmetal Gray, Back Blast, Dead Eye, Ballistic, On Target,* and *The Gray Man*, he traveled to more than thirty-five countries and trained alongside military and law enforcement in the use of firearms, battlefield medicine, and close-range combative tactics. With Marine Lt. Col. Rip Rawlings, he wrote the *New York Times* bestseller *Red Metal*. He is also the author of the *New York Times* bestsellers *Tom Clancy Support and Defend, Tom Clancy Full Force and Effect, Tom Clancy Commander in Chief,* and *Tom Clancy True Faith and Allegiance*. With Tom Clancy, he coauthored *Locked On, Threat Vector,* and *Command Authority*.

Also by Mark Greaney

The Gray Man

On Target

Ballistic

Dead Eye

Back Blast

Gunmetal Gray

Agent in Place

Mission Critical

One Minute Out

Relentless

Sierra Six

Red Metal
(with LtCol H. Ripley Rawlings IV, USMC)

Armored

Burner

The Chaos Agent

Midnight Black

MARK GREANEY

A **GRAY MAN** THRILLER

THE HARD LINE

SPHERE

SPHERE

First published in the United States in 2026 by Berkley,
an imprint of Penguin Random House LLC
First published in Great Britain in 2026 by Sphere

1 3 5 7 9 10 8 6 4 2

Copyright © MarkGreaneyBooks LLC 2026

The moral right of the author has been asserted.

Penguin Random House values and supports copyright. Copyright fuels creativity, encourages diverse voices, promotes free speech, and creates a vibrant culture. Thank you for buying an authorized edition of this book and for complying with copyright laws by not reproducing, scanning, or distributing any part of it in any form without permission. You are supporting writers and allowing Penguin Random House to continue to publish books for every reader. Please note that no part of this book may be used or reproduced in any manner for the purpose of training artificial intelligence technologies or systems.

*All characters and events in this publication, other than those
clearly in the public domain, are fictitious and any resemblance
to real persons, living or dead, is purely coincidental.*

All rights reserved.
No part of this publication may be reproduced, stored in a
retrieval system, or transmitted, in any form, or by any means, without
the prior permission in writing of the publisher, nor be otherwise circulated
in any form of binding or cover other than that in which it is published
and without a similar condition including this condition being
imposed on the subsequent purchaser.

A CIP catalogue record for this book
is available from the British Library.

HARDBACK ISBN 978-1-4087-2436-1
TRADE PAPERBACK ISBN 978-1-4087-2435-4

Printed and bound in Great Britain by
Clays Ltd, Elcograf S.p.A.

Papers used by Sphere are from well-managed forests
and other responsible sources.

Sphere	The authorised representative
An imprint of	in the EEA is
Little, Brown Book Group	Hachette Ireland
Carmelite House	8 Castlecourt Centre
50 Victoria Embankment	Dublin 15, D15 XTP3, Ireland
London EC4Y 0DZ	(email: info@hbgi.ie)

An Hachette UK Company
www.hachette.co.uk

www.littlebrown.co.uk

For Karen Berg Miller, Emma Miller, and Alexa Miller, and for Bruce and Judy Berg.

And for Scott Miller. You were a true legend, and you will never be forgotten.

A person often meets his destiny on the road he took to avoid it.

JEAN DE LA FONTAINE

No tree, it is said, can reach to heaven, unless its roots reach down to hell.

CARL JUNG

CHARACTERS

OLIVIA ANTHONY: director of national intelligence

CHADWICK PHILLIPS: director of the Central Intelligence Agency

WILLIAM "TREY" WATKINS: deputy director for operations, Central Intelligence Agency

ANGELA LACY: senior operations officer, Central Intelligence Agency

JIM PACE: operations officer, Central Intelligence Agency

MATTHEW HANLEY: aka Pilgrim; director of Ghost Town; former deputy director for operations, Central Intelligence Agency

COURTLAND GENTRY: aka the Gray Man, aka Violator, aka Brian Webb, aka Six; Ghost Town asset; former CIA paramilitary operations (Ground Branch) officer

ZACK HIGHTOWER: aka Night Train; Ghost Town asset; former CIA paramilitary operations (Ground Branch) officer

CHRIS TRAVERS: aka Teddy; Ghost Town asset; former CIA paramilitary operations (Ground Branch) officer

ERIN CHILDERS: aka Conductor; Ghost Town assistant to the director

JILL MORI: aka Gumdrop; Ghost Town intelligence analyst

ARNOLD REYES: aka Bricklayer; Ghost Town logistics coordinator

MARCUS MARAGOS: Greek international security consultant

CHARACTERS

MICHAEL "BIG MIKE" SCARDINO: senior operations officer for Gauntlet Group Inc.

JAMES ARTHUR "J.W." WESTWOOD III: director of the Raymond C. Carter Center for Trends in Peace

LEWIS SHAW: IT systems analyst, Office of the Director of National Intelligence

IRENE ORTEGA: mission integration specialist, Office of the Director of National Intelligence

ANDREA "ANDIE" DELANEY: café employee, competitive snowboarder

PETER DELANEY: deputy fire chief, Boulder Fire and Rescue; father of Andie

GAO YUANYUAN: aka Gracie Wu; field agent, Chinese Ministry of State Security

RODERICK "RORY" COYLE: operative, Provisional Irish Republican Army; father of Campbell Coyle

CHARLIE COYLE: security contractor; father of Ronan Coyle

CAMPBELL COYLE: aka Whetstone; father of Charlie Coyle; freelance assassin from Northern Ireland

ALEXI KRAVCHUK: aka Spiral, aka Deep Space; freelance assassin from Belarus

SCOTT KINCAID: aka Lancer; freelance assassin from the USA

ASEM SHABAN: aka Snare; freelance assassin from Jordan

JAMES GENTRY: retired firearms instructor; father of Courtland Gentry

STANLEY "SKIP" ECHOLS: private investigator from Jacksonville, Florida

CATHERINE KING: author, former lead national security reporter for the *Washington Post*

THE
HARD
LINE

ONE

OCTOBER

Faint electronica music pulsed in the air, but the music was shit, much like his mood. His body stood rigid, not moving with the rhythm, his head not bobbing in time with the distant thumps of the backbeat, his face giving off no hint that he derived any pleasure from the repetitious melody.

He did not want to be here. He wanted to be home. More than life itself, he wanted to be home. But he was trying to be a man of principle, a man of honor; he was trying to be a man.

He had made his bed, and he would damn well lie in it.

He wanted a drink. But he'd made a promise to stay sober, and he was determined to keep it.

Three months. Pay bills. Get gone.

That was all that mattered.

The EDM music throbbed in his brain, unrelenting, like the ever-present disquiet in his soul.

He stood at the open top-floor window of the Cabacum Beach Residence, ignoring the cold air blowing in as he gazed down to the swimming pool below that flashed its underwater disco lights, not jarringly out of step with the unceasing music. The crisp autumn evening had brought out hundreds of late-night revelers driving up and down Boyan Bachvarov, the twisty four-lane road beyond the pool: crowds heading to the various bars, restaurants, and nightclubs here in the Chayka district of Varna, Bulgaria.

And Charlie just stood there, a man apart from his surroundings.

Charlie Coyle was not yet twenty-five years old, and handsome, neatly dressed in a blue sharkskin suit only a little wrinkled and just slightly askew on his fit frame, evidence of a long day. He wore a five-o'clock shadow on his chin and upper lip, his skin was fair, and his strawberry-blond hair was curly and only partially tamed with chemicals.

He'd cracked the window here in the suite so that the cold would invigorate him, but as he stood there, continuing his solitary vigil, he found the lively mood at ground level depressing. A party raged all around the hotel and condo complex, and all this revelry stood in contrast to Charlie's dark disposition and his brooding demeanor.

He glanced at his watch, an old Hamilton with a canvas strap, a reminder of his military service days gone by. It was 12:17 a.m. now; a hurried room service attendant had brought him a club sandwich with soggy fries and two bottles of Coke around ten p.m., but otherwise he'd been alone up here since he'd arrived at eight.

The music from below was suddenly drowned out by a voice in his right ear. With a strong Bulgarian accent, the man spoke in English. "Coyle, it is Videv. Boss makes meeting with man in bar, then we come up to safe room."

Charlie furrowed his brow. He knew of no meetings scheduled for tonight. But then again, he didn't really have much of a clue what was going on. He didn't speak Bulgarian, after all, so he might have missed something.

This job is bollocks, he thought for maybe the fiftieth time in the past thirty-six hours.

He reached with his left hand to his beltline inside his coat, his fingers dragging over the spare pistol magazine in a carrier on his belt, kept there should he ever need to reload the Walther PDP pistol he wore on his right hip.

His hand continued on until it found the small radio next to the magazine, and he pressed a button on the top of the device, opening the line to the microphone in his earpiece.

"Copy," he said, his Northern Irish accent toned down so he could be understood by the non-native English speaker, and then he turned away from the window and moved over to a laptop on a table inside the plush suite, taking off his jacket as he did so.

He draped the coat over the chair and sat down, blowing out a long, defeated sigh.

Charlie pressed a couple of buttons on the laptop and then waited while a connection was made. His face hung impassive, a hint of pain around the eyes, but then he shook the expression away, brushed his hair back, sat up straighter, and hurriedly adjusted his tie.

Soon a window on the monitor opened, the screen changed, and so, too, did his visage.

He flashed a wide grin now, his pale green eyes sparkling as a tow-headed baby looked back at him from the computer, drool glistening his lower lip, a onesie with a row of little camels stitched on it, well-splattered with baby food.

Hands under the baby's underarms steadied him in front of the camera.

And with that, Charlie Coyle's immediate predicament was forgotten. In spirit, at least, he was home.

With a bright and powerful voice, along with his now thick natural accent, he said, "There's my big man! Bein' a good lad for your ma, are ya?"

The baby did not respond—he was six months old, after all—but Charlie detected a slight narrowing of his green eyes and the hint of a wet smile, and this was all the proof he needed that his son recognized him.

And all was right with the world.

A beautiful redheaded woman in her early twenties appeared from the right, scooting into view in front of the camera as she put the child on her knee.

Her hair was down, her curls flowing, and Charlie knew Deirdre well enough to know she'd shaken her long locks out of the bondage of a hair tie the second his FaceTime call came through, and she'd done it just for him.

He smiled even wider.

If anything, Deirdre's voice was even more accented than Charlie's. "How ya keepin', love?"

"Hullo, a stór." It was a Gaelic term of endearment that translated to *my treasure*. He added, "It's late. Surprised to see our boy awake."

"Long nap this afternoon. Put him down at eight, but we're just up for a wee feedin'."

"Applesauce, by the looks of his onesie."

"Pears. Managed to get some into his belly, but he spits it out when he's 'ad enough. Just about to put him back down, but I'm glad he was up to see his da."

"Got your tie on, I see. Workin', still, are ya?"

Charlie's smile remained locked in place. It was real. And it was fake. "Aye," he said. "Just 'ad a few minutes free, thought I'd check in."

"Well, we're glad ya did. How's the new job?"

Charlie's bright smile wavered now.

The woman picked up on his unease. "That bad?"

"It's fine." When she did not immediately respond, he said, "It's early days, still."

But Deirdre wasn't having it. "What's going on?"

He gave a shrug and said, "Whatcha think? I got sold a bleedin' bill of goods by Marcus."

The woman shifted the baby on her knee. "The job's not what he said? Again?"

A defeated sigh. "It's bloody gangster shite, love. Same as Macedonia."

The young woman lowered the baby completely out of frame now. "Dammit."

"Aye."

"Drugs, girls, guns? What's Marcus gotten you into this time?"

A pause. Then, "Dunno, to be honest."

"Ferfucksakes, Charlie, I don't believe ya."

"I've been here a day and a half, haven't I? I seen fuck-all so far. The back of a car, a hotel, a couple of nightclubs, a restaurant. And everyone's speakin' Bulgarian other than the one that tells me what to do, so I don't know what the rest are on about half the time."

"Then how do ya know—"

"I *know*, Deirdre. These blokes have the same hard eyes that those blokes I worked for in Macedonia had. Down there it was drugs. Might be the same here, but nobody's tellin' the new lad, are they?"

"Who are ye guarding?"

He waved a hand in the air. "Some wanker. Sasho Minchev. Young fella, for a capo, I mean. Looks like a nepo baby crook. He didn't make his own bleedin' money, that's fer certain."

Just then, Videv's voice came through Charlie's earpiece again. "Coyle?"

Charlie held a finger up to his wife, then tapped the radio on his hip, opening his microphone for a transmission. "Go for Coyle."

The Bulgarian said, "Minchev is talking to an American. Be ready to come down if it is trouble."

Trouble? "What kind of trouble?"

"Boss give me signal. We may have problem. Stand by."

"Aye, sir."

Once he was off the radio, he looked back to his young family on the screen.

Deirdre said, "What's 'appenin'?"

Coyle hadn't a clue, but still, he brushed away any of his wife's concerns. "The principal is meeting with some American, and maybe there's a disagreement. I'm on standby." He shrugged. "Minchev is a hot one; he doesn't like anybody, so nothing new in that."

She looked worried, so he said, "It's fine, love. Regardless of what the boss is into, my part in this is easy. I'm the junior here. They got me securin' the safe room, is all."

"What's that mean?"

"Means I'm sittin' in a suite we took for the night, and I'm talking to you and Ronan." He smiled a little. "The four other blokes are down with the boss in the bar. I'm sure they can manage."

The baby made a few sounds, but Deirdre did not speak.

Charlie noted her silence. "What's wrong?"

She said, "Sounds like you're around a lot of alcohol. You're not on the lash, are ya?"

"I'm dry as a bone, love. We're not going back to that. Those days are behind the both of us."

The young woman didn't seem certain, but she let it go. Said, "Ya think anyone's going to come after your protectee like they did in Macedonia?"

Charlie shrugged. "I'm ready, come what may. One thing I can be sure of is this: anyone who comes at Minchev is bound to be a right big bastard, same as he. I won't think twice about dropping somebody who poses a threat. Down here, it's crook against crook. No good guys to worry about."

"*You're* a good guy, and I worry about you. Look." She hesitated, then said, "Why don't ye just come home? We'll figure something else out for money. This sounds like a bad situation to put yerself—"

"No, love. A man's word's got to stand for something. I took this job, I promised to protect my principal. That's what I'm goin' to do."

After a pause, she said, "All right. I understand. But . . . after this . . . after this, I want you to find honest work."

In his left ear Charlie heard the men on his team transmitting to one another. It was all in Bulgarian again, so he didn't suppose it had anything to do with him.

He turned his attention back to his wife. "I'm down here just ninety days, we'll make what we need to make, pay some bills, and I'll move on to something better." He smiled a little. "And no more takin' work from Marcus bloody Maragos."

"You know," she said now, "there's always another option. Isn't there?"

Charlie cocked his head a little, then made a face of displeasure. "No. No, there's isn't."

Deirdre said, "You could ask your da."

"I'll be makin' my own way, love. Don't need my father's money."

"But—"

Quickly, he said, "Lemme see my son again."

She held Ronan back up. The baby's eyes were softening; he looked like he was about to nod off, but his father wasn't ready to say goodbye.

He feared Deirdre was going to bring up money again, bring up his issues from the past, his relationship with his father, his dirty job down here in the Balkans, all subjects Charlie Coyle was not in the mood to talk about at present, but before she began to speak, he held a finger up, because another call came through his earpiece.

Bulgarian again, but the words sounded rushed, stressed.

A man answered back quickly. Another barked into his microphone.

Deirdre saw the surprised look on Charlie's face. "What's going on?"

He didn't answer her; instead, he pressed the mic button on his radio. "Coyle for Videv?"

On the laptop, his wife said, "Charlie?"

More transmissions in a foreign tongue came through the earpiece, then Charlie again. "Coyle for Videv. What's happening?"

Now the team leader returned the transmission. His words came out quick and clipped. "Coyle. Come down. Escort boss back to safe room."

"Copy that. En route."

Videv added, "Meet us in the back alley, door off kitchen."

The back alley?

Charlie acknowledged the order without question, then ended his transmission. Looking into the camera, he said, "Darlin', I have to go collect the protectee, bring him back here."

"Why don't they just bring him to—"

From the balcony behind him came the unmistakable sound of a gunshot cracking in the night; the crowd by the swimming pool below his balcony screamed, and Charlie Coyle launched to his feet.

Deirdre lowered the baby quickly. "Was that a bleedin' gun?"

"Love you both," he said, and he slammed his laptop shut, grabbed his suit coat, then rushed to the door of the condo. Into his earpiece he shouted, "What's happenin', Videv?"

TWO

Charlie rushed out into the third-floor hall, fighting with his jacket to get it on his trim frame. This done, he reached for the weapon on his hip. Running for the stairs on the north side of the building, he'd just gripped the Walther in its holster when his earpiece came alive again.

It was Videv. "American is in custody. Boss fired shot in air to scare him. We're in the alley. Hurry."

Charlie released his hold on the pistol and began sprinting down the stairs.

When he reached the ground floor he raced through the building, passing hotel guests, partygoers, employees of the restaurant. Some were alarmed by the gunfire, but others were oblivious, the EDM in the air, the booze, or the party drugs in their bloodstream masking the noise. He bladed his body through small crowds in the bar off the main lobby, then raced up a narrow hallway past the lavatories, pushing the drunk and the slow and the unmindful to the side as he moved, and finally he pounded his way into the kitchen.

He ignored the cooks and cleaners and servers, pressed on at speed to the back door, then shouldered it open, finding himself on a raised concrete platform in an alley between the hotel and an adjacent condo tower.

He pulled up and stopped, saw a half dozen men arrayed in the dimly lit space.

At the center, Sasho Minchev stood over a man in a gray business suit kneeling on the wet ground. The stranger faced away from Charlie; a bright smear of fresh blood on the starched white collar of his shirt shone through messy shoulder-length dark hair.

A stainless steel semiautomatic pistol dangled from Sasho Minchev's right hand. Charlie had noticed the gun in a shoulder holster under his protectee's arm the day before, and he'd been concerned about it ever since, because his boss didn't seem like the type to practice safe gun handling.

Charlie had wondered if the pistol on his boss's person might be the biggest danger he'd face on this job; he wondered it even more now, because the son of a bitch had just pulled and fired it, and now it hung in his sweaty clutches, his trigger finger twitching inside the trigger guard.

Charlie's four colleagues stood in various stages of readiness in the alley. Videv, the team leader, had positioned himself directly behind the man on his knees. Big and burly Komitov loomed just to the left, his eyes on the prisoner. Pulev, older and with a mustache that made him look like a Balkan Saddam Hussein, stood a few steps from Charlie by the door, watching the street but not looking particularly alert. Chanev, bright-eyed, swarthy, and a couple of years younger even than Charlie, stood to the kneeling man's right, his hand on the gun on his belt and his eyes fixed on his boss, waiting for orders.

Minchev said nothing. He just stood there, a sheen of perspiration glowing on his forehead, reflecting the light from the soft white sodium vapor lamps that hung over the alley from the rear of the condo tower; more sweat sparkled through little gaps in his dark beard. His normally slicked-back hair hung down into his eyes, and his chest heaved inside his black suit. His neck rippled with sinews emerging from the collar of his burgundy silk shirt, indicating tension in his shoulders.

Charlie hadn't seen any cocaine around in the past day, but he now thought it was likely his boss was on something, or else he was just that damn stimulated from shooting his gun in the air and threatening the man on his knees in front of him.

Videv's left hand rested on the prisoner's shoulder, and he, too, looked to his boss for direction.

It was as if nobody knew what the hell the man in charge had in mind, but they all stood at the ready, prepared to help him do it.

The scene was a shit show in the making, and Charlie's first inclination was to rush to his protectee, disarm him, and then escort him back up to the safe room and put him to bed.

But Minchev held his empty hand out, indicating he had other plans.

In English, the young Bulgarian mob boss spoke to the kneeling man. "You fucked up, Mr. Humphries. And for that you're gonna have to pay a little price."

The man kneeling there said nothing. He did not move; his face remained out of Coyle's view, his head down as if in defeat.

The boss said something in Bulgarian, and then Komitov stepped forward and rifled through the American's jacket, removing a wallet and a phone. He pocketed the wallet, then held the phone up in front of the American's face, thereby unlocking the screen.

Then he handed it to his boss.

Minchev looked over the phone now. In English, he said, "Only two contacts." He grinned at his prisoner. "You don't have many friends, do you?"

Minchev tapped the phone for several seconds, held it back to the man's face, then tapped it again. Charlie knew this move; his boss was changing the password so that he could unlock it any time he wanted.

When he finished, he said, "I'll keep this."

The boss held the phone up to the American a third time, took a picture. "And I'll send this to everybody I know, tell them to be looking out for you.

"And this," Minchev said, "this is for Bogdan." He punched the American in the jaw, a glancing blow, unimpressively executed, though it still managed to echo in the alleyway.

Minchev shoved his pistol into his belt, then began heading towards the door back into the building.

Coyle had no idea who Bogdan was or what the American had done to him to earn the punch to the gob.

As Minchev passed by Videv, he spoke to the team leader of the security detail in Bulgarian; Videv nodded curtly, and Minchev grinned as he climbed the steps and reached Charlie's position.

Coyle wanted to knock the smile off his employer's face with a right cross. He didn't know who the American was. Some thug from a rival concern, no doubt. But it didn't matter.

Minchev himself was a piece of shit.

Everybody around here was a piece of shit.

And all Charlie Coyle wanted to do was go home.

As the capo passed him for the door, Coyle turned and followed him back inside, staying just behind and to his right.

As they moved through the building, Coyle's training took over. A four-month course in executive protection in London just two years earlier, a course he barely passed because he'd spent his evenings in his hotel room downing bottles of cheap Monkey Shoulder blended scotch when he should have been resting up and preparing for the next day's challenges.

But now he was all business. Clocking corners, registering dark spaces, examining the hands and the eyes of the hotel employees, seeking information about any potential threat. His right hand hovered near his weapon, but he affected a guise of calm as he directed Minchev through an employee-only access door.

As they passed through the busy kitchen, Coyle and his protectee walking at a steady pace, Minchev turned to him. The Northern Irishman kept his focus on the path ahead and not the agitated Bulgarian's face. "This asshole shows up," Minchev said, "tells me he knows who I am, what I do. Says he needs to go to Russia, asks me to smuggle him in. I ask him what skills he has to repay me; he tells me about a job he did here in Bulgaria five years ago."

Coyle didn't care. He just took the man by the arm and directed him through a doorway that led to an old utility elevator that would take them right up to the top floor.

Minchev laughed a little now. "He tells me about a Russian spy who turned up floating in the Dambovita River in Bucharest, stabbed in the ribs and the neck. The American says he did it. Asks me if I know about what happened."

As they reached the service elevator, Minchev continued talking, his hyperagitation just getting on Coyle's nerves now. "Yeah, I know about it. Police arrested the wrong man. A friend of mine went to prison for it, for what that American did."

They stepped into the elevator now, and Charlie pulled the door closed, then hit the button for the top floor. The gears began grinding, the doors rattled back and forth in front of them as the pair traveled up a moment, and then Minchev spoke over the noise. "I told Videv to break both his legs and his jaw, then dump him in Priroden Park. Let that fuck crawl out of Bulgaria with his mouth wired shut."

The young mafia man laughed at this, but Charlie did not; then they stood in silence.

To hell with all these assholes, Charlie thought, but he also thought of why he was here.

Three months. Pay bills. Get gone.

Sweat dripped from the Bulgarian's face, and Charlie watched it splatter on the dusty wooden floor of the elevator car.

Finally, the doors rattled open.

Charlie took Minchev by the arm and led him out into the hall, turning towards the safe room, but before he'd made it two steps, he heard a blurted shout in Bulgarian coming through his earpiece.

More shouting erupted immediately after.

Minchev couldn't hear the exchange—he wasn't in direct comms with the security men—but Charlie put his thumb on the push-to-talk button.

A series of muffled pops came through the earpiece just before he pressed to transmit.

Gunfire.

He grabbed Minchev roughly now, began shoving him forward.

"What's wrong?"

Charlie didn't answer. There was a time to let the protectee take charge and a time to take charge of the protectee. As of right this moment, Charlie Coyle was running this show.

As he pushed the smaller man up the hallway, he transmitted over his radio. "Coyle for Videv."

One of the other bodyguards seemed to have his mic open on his radio. All Charlie could hear was shooting, yelling.

Charlie unlocked the door, drew his pistol, and shoved Minchev inside. He tried to transmit again, but whoever was pressing their talk button was still overriding the network.

"Fuck!" he shouted in frustration.

Suddenly, his phone buzzed in his pocket. He snatched it out and answered it, all while holding his pistol on the door, backing up with his protectee through the living room, between the couch and the kitchen island, in the direction of the bedroom.

"Coyle."

Videv's voice sounded nearly frantic, his breathing labored, as if he were running at a sprint. "You have boss?"

"We're in the safe room."

The team leader spoke quickly, words separated by heavy breaths. "Subject has . . . escaped. He has . . . Komitov's gun . . . and radio."

Bloody hell, Charlie thought. "Where's Komitov?"

"He's stabbed, in the alley. Pulev is with me. Subject is fleeing. Chanev is chasing him."

Coyle tried to clarify. "Is the subject in the building or still outside?"

A pause, though he could hear Videv's heavy breathing in the phone. "In building." The background sounds of screaming patrons came over the call now.

"But," Charlie said, "he doesn't know what room we're in, right?"

"Hotel security said he was in building this afternoon. We don't know where he is going."

It was clear to Charlie that Videv didn't have much more awareness about what the fuck was happening than he did.

This was all going so bad, so quickly.

Charlie extended his gun arm even more. Anyone coming through the door to the suite was going to catch a 9-millimeter round to the chest; this he told himself with complete assurance.

Videv added, "Me and Pulev are taking the south stairs, coming up to you."

The building had a main elevator, a larger freight elevator for moving furniture and such, and a pair of stairwells, one on the north side and the other on the south. A lot of directions an attack could come from, so Charlie decided he'd just defend from inside the unit, because there was only one viable access point for an attacker.

Videv added, "We will be there in two minutes. Hotel security is in the elevator; they are also coming up."

"Copy."

The call went dead, but then Coyle heard more shouting in his earpiece. A snap of gunfire was just audible before whoever it was who was transmitting took their finger off the button.

The Northern Irishman turned around to face the bedroom behind him for the first time, and he saw that his boss had his own pistol out again, sweeping it around like a fucking idiot.

Charlie shouted. "Put it down!"

The stainless semiauto shook at the end of the man's hand. "What's going on?" he demanded.

Charlie closed the distance, then pulled the gun from his boss's clutches and tossed it onto the bed up by the pillows. Angrily, he shouted, "You're not shooting *me* tonight!"

Minchev looked up at him, and Charlie suddenly recognized the effects of cocaine or amphetamine or something on his employer's face, now amplified by the terror in his eyes, and he wondered if the man was going to have a heart attack.

Charlie did nothing to lessen the chances of this when he said, "The American is in the building. He has a gun."

Wiping sweat from his forehead with the arm of his jacket, Minchev said, "It's no problem. It's no problem. I . . . I have five guys who will—"

"You have *four* guys," Coyle corrected, and then he turned away and headed back into the living room.

THREE

Charlie went back to the door, listening for more transmissions in his earpiece, frantic for more clarity on his situation.

The gunfire below had stopped; Charlie knew this could mean the American was dead, or it could mean the attacker was well inside the building now, maybe even in the stairwell or on the elevator.

Minchev was shouting into his mobile phone, but Charlie tuned him out because he couldn't understand.

Fuck, fuck, fuck! How can this be happening?

From behind him, back in the bedroom, he heard Minchev shout now, "Videv says the American is on the stairs now, coming up."

"Which stairwell?"

"I . . . I don't know."

"Well, feckin' find out!" Charlie shouted. Minchev began communicating in Bulgarian again, seemingly oblivious to the fact that his junior bodyguard was now screaming orders at him.

A new transmission came through Charlie's earpiece, but it was garbled. The mic of the transmitting radio stayed open; it sounded like it was in a pocket, the scratching noises of someone moving quickly.

Then the boom of a pair of gunshots, fired in nearly impossible rapid succession.

A wave of terror shot through Charlie Coyle's central nervous system as he realized what he was hearing. The person with the radio was the attacker. He'd just shot someone, or shot at someone, with the fastest double tap the young Northern Irishman had ever heard in his life, and the attacker also had the presence of mind to hijack the radio network by keeping the handset locked open as he moved through the building.

This bloke was good.

Behind Charlie, Minchev kept talking into his phone, his plaintive, panicking, coked-up tone and cadence only adding to the insanity of the moment.

Charlie Coyle felt a desire to run. To leave his responsibilities behind and just hoof it the fuck out of there.

He didn't want to die for this criminal in this shit building in this foreign city.

He was only twenty-bloody-four.

His life was a mess, but he had time yet to sort things.

To put things right.

Charlie Coyle's job was to keep his protectee alive, and he had been telling himself that a man's word had to stand for something, but right now, he only thought of Ronan, of Deirdre, of getting the fuck out of here, of getting back home to Derry.

The sound of sirens audible outside the window told him the police were arriving en masse, but he had no illusions that the cops would get up here and control the scene before the American made it up the stairs and found the safe room.

Minchev shouted to him now. "The American was last seen on the southern stairs at the second floor."

Just then, another pair of gunshots came through Charlie's earpiece, as fast as the last salvo.

Minchev said, "Shit! Someone is shooting." Into the phone he said, "Videv? Videv?"

Charlie ran through the living room to the front door of the suite, and he'd just made it to the glass-and-aluminum coffee table in front of the sofa when the lights went out.

Behind him, Minchev gasped.

The outside glow through the window helped Charlie negotiate his way around the coffee table to the door. Opening it, he then pulled a flashlight out of his pocket and wiped his perspiring face with the back of the suit coat of his left arm, keeping his Walther pointed at the door to the southside stairs with his right.

He did not turn on the flashlight; he didn't want to give away his position.

Minchev stepped up behind him. In a whisper that was still way too loud given the circumstances, he said, "Videv isn't responding. It's just one man. Kill this guy, Coyle!"

Charlie whispered back, fighting to keep his voice down considering the tidal waves of adrenaline coursing through him. "Say another feckin' word and you can deal with 'im on your own."

Minchev went silent, and Charlie heard his employer's footsteps retreat back through the living room of the suite.

And then Charlie stood there, looking into the dark, trying to control his breathing because he was as scared as he'd ever been in his life.

The good news was he had some intelligence now. He was still only facing one enemy; his pistol was steady and aimed at where he'd been told the target would be coming from. Also, he had excellent concealment behind the door and the wall of the suite, as only a small portion of his body was exposed to the hall.

The bad news was the fact that concealment, while good, was in no way a substitute for cover.

An enemy could not shoot through cover, but an enemy *could* shoot through concealment.

He heard the stairwell door creak open slowly, just ten yards away from him on the right. Charlie could barely make out the movement, but he lowered to a knee quickly, making himself a smaller target.

A figure appeared.

Charlie clicked on his flashlight, his finger on the trigger of his weapon with enough pressure to take the few millimeters of slack out of it. He just needed to apply a little more force to fire a gunshot.

But the light confirmed it was Pulev, so he relaxed his finger slightly.

And then Pulev's weapon turned towards Charlie.

The Northern Irishman turned off his light as he shouted Pulev's name, along with a few bits of Bulgarian he'd been taught for just such a situation. "Pulev! Ne strelyai! Si Coyle!" *Pulev! Don't shoot! It's Coyle!*

Pulev got the message, apparently, because he did not fire, but then the passenger elevator door opened, just across the hall to Charlie's left.

Videv had told him hotel security was on the way up, but he didn't know if Pulev knew this, so he shouted again. "Ne strelyai!" *Don't shoot.*

This time, however, Pulev didn't listen. He fired three times with his Glock; the flashes illuminated the hall, revealing a man stepping out of the elevator, twisting, and then falling facedown.

Pulev shouted something Charlie didn't understand, and then the Bulgarian shined his own flashlight on the motionless figure crumpled on the carpet.

Charlie recognized the victim immediately. It was the head of security for the beach resort. He'd only met him briefly that afternoon, and he didn't even know his name.

"Fecking hell," he muttered to himself.

Pulev himself muttered something that sounded like a curse, but then a two-round burst of pistol fire, flashing in the hallway from the left, dropped Pulev to his knees.

Charlie launched backwards into the suite, out of the line of fire. He landed in front of the glass coffee table, rolled onto his back, and looked up in time to see another flash of light right in front of the door as Pulev himself fired a round off in response to the person shooting at him. But then Pulev recoiled, his pistol dropped from his hand, and his flashlight went dark.

The thud of a body dropping in the hall told Charlie that his teammate was down.

Charlie rose, stepping around and then just behind the coffee table to create more distance between himself and the door to the hall, his weapon still high in front of him, searching for a target there.

But just as he made it to the other side of the table, he jolted in surprise as fresh gunfire boomed. One round, then two, then three.

He couldn't see the origin of fire, no flashes of light, but with the fourth shot he felt a hard tug on his left thigh, and he knew he'd been hit.

He returned fire reflexively; he had no target in the darkness, but he dumped round after round in the direction of the darkened doorway.

Then he realized what was happening.

The aggressor was not at the door; he was to the left, still in the hallway somewhere, firing through the wall of the suite.

Charlie shifted aim, and as he did so, he took one step to the left, but when he planted his foot, his wounded leg gave out and he fell behind the coffee table.

On his back now, he pushed himself up onto an elbow and began raising his gun again, but before he could sight in on the doorway, a dark figure appeared, sliding into the room like a wraith.

A string of three gunshots flared; Minchev cried out from the open kitchen on Charlie's right, just as Charlie got his weapon up and back into the fight.

The young Northern Irishman centered his aim quickly and fired once at the dark figure as it floated through the living room.

The figure spun, fell, and crashed hard onto the tile flooring on the far side of the coffee table, and through the ringing in his ears Charlie heard the clang of a pistol as it bounced away.

He fired once more as the figure fell, but Charlie couldn't be sure he'd hit his target with the second round.

Charlie realized he'd gotten lucky by falling here on this side of the table; the attacker had not seen him lying on the floor, and he had identified and targeted Minchev instead.

But now the bloody bastard was down himself.

Charlie rose, his gun pointed towards the other side of the table, and he struggled to get an angle to fire an insurance round into the body there. He realized he'd have to stand to see his target, so he used the table's edge to steady himself with his free hand, then pulled up, pushing off on his uninjured right leg.

When he rose to his feet, he peered through the dim light, and he saw the outline of a body lying there, crumpled, unmoving. He could make out no features, but he couldn't ignore the possibility that the man was still alive, so he aimed at the man's head and began to press his trigger.

Then, faster than he could squeeze off a round, the man's legs shot out and his feet slammed into the coffee table, driving the heavy piece of furniture right into Charlie Coyle's legs.

Charlie fell forwards; his gun fired, but he didn't know where the round went. He crashed chest first into the table, the glass shattered, and he fell through, slamming down to the floor.

He kept hold of his weapon in his right hand and flipped quickly onto his back, flinging aluminum and glass as he did so, but just as he began to look for the man above him, the dark figure landed on him.

Charlie felt hands on his wrist, on his pistol; a knee slammed into his wounded thigh, and he vomited from the pain. He threw punches with his left fist, but his attacker was too close for the blows to have any effect.

And then it happened. The American took a hand away from the pistol, drew it back, and Charlie expected him to rain a punch down towards his face. The twenty-four-year-old turned his head to the left so that the punch would hit the side of his head and not his nose, but the punch didn't go for his nose.

It went for his chest.

Charlie Coyle felt a sharp blade slip between his ribs just to the right of his sternum and just below his pectoral. The fist holding the knife punched him in the chest, and then the man on top of him pulled the blade out.

The American rose up to his knees, one hand still on Charlie's gun.

Charlie saw the black knife, not in the American's left hand but rather jutting from under his wrist.

And he knew what it was. Once, when Charlie was in the Foreign Legion and deployed in Ivory Coast, he'd met a Corsican in a bar who showed off his spring-loaded wrist stiletto, a weapon that remained hidden under his sleeve until he flexed his hand up in a certain way, at which point the narrow, razor-sharp blade fired from its scabbard and extended several inches.

He'd thought the weapon to be little more than a gimmick, but he'd just been on the receiving end of it, and he had a new appreciation of its value.

Charlie let go of his Walther because he suddenly felt very tired, and he knew instinctively that this fight was over.

He lay on his back, his feet raised over the aluminum edge of the shattered coffee table, his body covered with broken glass and twisted metal, and the man rolled off him, onto the floor, crunching more glass there as he did so.

How is this man alive? Charlie had shot him; he fecking *knew* he'd shot him.

It made no sense.

The American aimed the pistol with his right hand, not at Charlie but rather in the direction of the kitchen, and then he swiveled it to the front door of the suite, then back to where Minchev had been standing. The knife no longer jutted from under his left hand.

After just a moment, time counted off by the wheezes Charlie could feel in the wound in his chest, the man knelt back down to him, so close Charlie could smell his sweat. He felt a rough hand rifling through his jacket, his pants pockets. He was helpless to resist, weak, but he was able to focus on the man in the soft light above him.

Bearded, maybe forty years old, blood smeared on his neck and shirt collar, a tightness around the eyes that showed Charlie that the man was in a great deal of pain himself.

The American kept the Walther pointed up while he stripped Charlie of his one spare magazine, and then the man looked down into Charlie's eyes briefly.

But only briefly.

Rising slowly, Charlie watched the man look away, then step towards the kitchen with not another glance to Charlie Coyle.

After a few receding footsteps across broken glass, and a few more footfalls on the tile heading toward the kitchen, he finally heard the man speak. "I'm gonna need that phone back."

His voice was strained; he was injured, exhausted, but he somehow nevertheless sounded capable, resolute.

Utterly determined in his mission.

Minchev spoke now, his voice cracked with terror. "It's here . . . sir. Take it . . . please. Just don't—"

There was a quick pause; Charlie just lay there bleeding in the dark, and then Minchev screamed, "No! Please!"

A gun boomed, and an ejected shell casing bounced on the kitchen floor.

Minchev fell silent.

The attacker's footsteps receded into the bedroom. Their cadence was unhurried, though the sirens outside seemed right on top of the location.

It was clear this man had a plan.

But that was the last Charlie thought of him.

He pressed hard into the wound on his chest now, ignoring the one in his leg. He wasn't sure if he was dying. The leg wound was nothing; the chest wound was bad, but help was on the way. He just had to stanch the blood flow and, in all likelihood, he'd make it to a hospital.

The young Northern Irishman felt weak now, but he kept the pressure on.

There was a medical kit in the kitchen, but he couldn't stand, couldn't walk.

Right now, the kitchen might as well have been a hundred miles away.

Charlie Coyle leaned his head back, closed his eyes, and thought of home.

Right now, however, home might as well have been a million miles away.

FOUR

The blue-and-white squad car drove slowly past the small parking lot in front of the youth hostel on Primorski Street, a kilometer and a half west of the mayhem at the Cabacum Beach Residence, and the young officer behind the wheel shined his spotlight on a row of cars parked there.

The cop was disappointed to be relegated to searching outside the perimeter set up by his leadership; the police didn't expect that the culprit of the mass killings a couple of blocks from the ocean an hour earlier would be this far up in the hills. No, their subject would either be hunkered down, in hiding in one of the dozens of buildings close to the action, or else he'd be out of town by now, and for this reason the officer in the squad car performed his duties perfunctorily, whipping the light around for a few moments and then rolling up Primorski to check out a pair of parked vans in front of a paint store long closed for the night.

When the squad car had moved on and out of sight, a man rose slowly up from behind a white Kia Sportage parked in front of the hostel, and he stood there in the darkness a moment, listening for sounds of danger.

Sirens wailed to the east, near the coast, and they'd been doing so for over an hour, since even before he'd climbed out of the suite of the Cabacum, lowered to a balcony, dropped onto a sharply angled balcony overhang a story below, then rolled down, grabbing the gutter before swinging to an even lower balcony. He'd continued like this, eventually making his way down to the ground.

He'd escaped the neighborhood, stumbled along in the dark, his body hunched over in pain.

Courtland Gentry had survived, he'd escaped, but everything had gone wrong, and now the pain, both physical and psychological, threatened to overtake him.

This entire night had been a disaster, and the whole thing had gone to hell about two minutes after sitting down in front of Sasho Minchev.

Court asked himself, not for the first time in the past hour, just how the hell he was supposed to have known that a buddy of the Bulgarian mobster had gone to prison for a killing Court had copped to?

Bad luck for Court.

Worse luck for Minchev.

Court's entire body hurt now, but nowhere more than his chest, where he'd been shot. He'd not really felt it much at first; adrenaline had a painkilling effect that Court had put to good use countless times in his career, but as the adrenaline seeped away, the dull throb in his chest, directly over his heart, had morphed into a sharp and burning sting. He'd spent most of his walk ignoring the vicious pain, focusing instead on getting out of immediate danger, then focusing on lying low while the multiple sweeps of law enforcement passed him by.

He was clear enough for now, he determined, so he retrieved an extra key fob from a small magnetized box in the front driver's-side wheel well, opened his car door, looked around quickly to make sure no one was watching, then took off his suit coat and removed his tie.

His dress shirt came off next, and under it, he ripped the Velcro closures off the thin body armor he wore there, pulled the vest off, and quickly looked at the impact point, high on his chest on the left side. The Hyperline level IIIA armor that had saved his life tonight was the thinnest available on the market, and inspecting it, he saw that the fabric was deformed below the left clavicle, deeply indented, and Court didn't have to feel his chest right now to know he had a nasty bruise that was only going to hurt more tomorrow.

He'd caught the round while entering the suite and engaging the asshole in the kitchen; he'd not detected an enemy lying on the floor behind some furniture in the living room, and if the shot had been about three inches higher and three inches to the left, it would have hit him right in the throat.

But instead, it had struck his soft armor. He'd paid an arm and a leg for the Hyperline in Hungary a couple of months earlier, but at the moment, it seemed like one of his better investments.

But perhaps not his best investment.

The spring-loaded stiletto he'd bought in Tirana, Albania, five months ago for two hundred euros had provided an even better return on investment, in his estimation. He'd sliced an artery of one of the goons in the alleyway, left him bleeding there, snatched a gun, shot a guy, sent the others retreating for cover, and then snagged a radio, dropping another asshole inside the building as he made his way up to the top-floor suite, where he knew he'd find the mobster who'd just stolen his phone with his face on it.

On the way, he'd detonated a remote charge in the building's basement electrical room, plunging the facility into darkness, then he'd moved from the south stairs to the north stairs on the second floor to keep his adversary guessing, fucking with their radio transmissions in the process so that the situational awareness of the guard escorting Minchev would be less than ideal.

He would have liked to have walked away, not to have engaged a half dozen men tonight, but Sasho Minchev had taken his phone with his picture on it, and then he'd told Court to his face he was going to make it so that he could never get into Russia.

Court had to get into Russia, which meant Sasho Minchev had to die, and everyone who got between Court and Sasho Minchev had to be swept out of the way by the fastest means available.

Court Gentry *was* going to Russia; he had a job to do there, and no second-tier Balkan gangster and his goon squad were going to stop him.

He sighed now in the dark, in the cold air blowing against his damp T-shirt, and then he dropped the body armor on the ground.

The Bulgarians had taken his key fob, but he had the spare. He grabbed the key, tossed the box, climbed behind the wheel, and fired up the engine.

As he drove to the north, leaving the Chayka district of Varna, Bulgaria, behind, he thought about his next move.

He'd go to Romania, start from scratch with a new batch of asshole smugglers, see if *they* would be willing to help him get into Russia.

His spirits were low, damn low, and he had a lot to worry about, but he did *not* worry about what had just happened.

Bad men had gotten in his way. Some of them, he'd killed. Minchev for sure, probably the guy in the top-floor hallway, as well. Maybe the first guy on the stairs and the other one in the alley.

But the dude he'd stabbed in the wreckage of the coffee table in the penthouse might live, as would the second guy on the stairs. He didn't really care either way; he only cared that he'd retrieved his phone and his image.

Now all he thought about as he drove north was getting clear, licking his wounds, re-arming, regrouping for his next attempt.

Court Gentry had left dead and wounded in his wake many times in his life.

And there were many ahead of him to deal with.

The Kia drove on, with a killer behind the wheel.

FIVE

St. Malachy's Church sat on the intersection of Carrickcroppen Road and Carrickcloghan Road, on a hill surrounded by a Catholic cemetery that was bathed in rare sunlight on this frigid Sunday morning.

Inside the wooden doors of the church, Father Sean ended his mass with the Concluding Rites, turning to thank the other priests, then raising his hands towards the choir as he gave them a word of appreciation, and finally he addressed the congregation gathered in front of him.

There were fewer than eighty-five parishioners, the pews one third empty today, and this was a disappointment to Father Sean, but such were the times.

He smiled nonetheless, because those who did attend deserved his best.

His accent was strong and his countenance kind. "In your moment of prayer today, I ask you to say a special prayer thanking the Lord for family and for those you love who are not family but nevertheless hold a special place in your heart. Family and friends are the most precious gifts, so remember them in your prayers." He spread his arms and smiled, his eyes tightening behind his thick eyeglasses. "May the Lord be with you."

In the back pew, far to the right side of the sanctuary facing the altar, a middle-aged man in a worn but smart tweed suit, his heavy coat and his herringbone cap in his lap, spoke in cadence with the rest of the congregation now. "And with your spirit."

Father Sean gave the sign of the cross, asked the Almighty God to bless them, then announced that the mass had ended, and that all should go forth in peace.

In the back pew, Jon Jo Sheehan stood, nodded and smiled to a few around him that he recognized from his weekly visits here at St. Malachy's Church, but he spoke to no one. When the recessional was all but complete, he ducked out a side door alone, squinting into the bright blue Sunday sky, and a smile crossed his face.

It was cold, but the air felt crisp and clean, and the sun was welcome. It had been a good mass; Sheehan was as invigorated by the priest's words as he was by the clear weather, and he looked forward to his next stop on this beautiful day.

The pub.

If he were honest with himself, he'd have to admit that his Sunday ritual of going to the Yellow Heifer for a daytime pint and a bowl of fisherman's pie did almost as much to rouse him from bed on the Lord's day as did Father Sean's blessings.

He walked with his hands in his pockets through the hillside cemetery that surrounded the church; he passed the valiant dead of wars gone by, both foreign and domestic, both long ago and more recent, and he paid his respects to all without slowing his gait.

His Irish flat cap formed a shadow across his heavy brow and intense green eyes, but the exposed skin above his reddish-brown beard was like leather. From the neck up he could have passed for much older than his forty-seven years, but he moved nimbly, his pace vigorous; his body, though short and mostly hidden beneath his heavy coat, gave the immediate impression of physicality.

The skin on his face had been weathered by the years, beaten by the elements, but the rest of him moved as if he could handle himself.

He was a blue-collar man, and anyone who looked at him would be able to tell, but no one really looked his way.

Jon Jo installed and maintained security cameras, was a highly sought-after locksmith, and even tended to his own small flock of sheep on his tiny farm, and he felt like he'd met most of the inhabitants of this small hamlet, and those he hadn't met through his profession, he'd likely seen at church or in one of the pubs.

He was known to all here in Camlough, but he was a close friend to none. Jon Jo kept his distance from people.

After a ten-minute stroll, he stepped through the doors of the Yellow Heifer. A bustling crowd waited for tables both outside and in, but he found a single seat at the end of the bar and took it, positioning his back to the wall.

A woman behind the bar looked up from drawing a Guinness and asked him if he'd like the usual, and Jon Jo gave a friendly nod.

His Guinness came first. He waited a few minutes before taking a sip; the pub filled even more, and his eyes flitted around from time to time. He had a phone in his pocket but he ignored it; the pregame coverage of this afternoon's English Premier match between Bournemouth and Nottingham Forest was playing on the television, but he only caught occasional glances at it as he looked around, people-watching, as was his way.

An older couple from church gave him a subdued wave from their table in the dining room past the bar, and he acknowledged them with a nod and a smile.

A young African man who worked at the feed store where Jon Jo bought the grain he fed his sheep was deep in conversation with a woman who must have been his wife at a table in the middle of the room.

Farther down the little bar he clocked a couple of strangers. Men in their fifties. Camlough didn't get much tourist activity, so he found them interesting, but after a couple of minutes they paid and left, and he put them out of his mind.

His fisherman's pie came soon after; thick chunks of fish and vegetables in a creamy sauce, covered in mashed potatoes and baked in the oven. As he ate, the friendly but harried female bartender asked him if he'd like another stout, but he instead ordered a Cidona, an apple-flavored carbonated soft drink.

After lunch, he stopped at a farmer's market, bought some jams and butters and soda bread and a couple of bottles of milk from a dairy farm nearby, and now he carried all his purchases in a pair of cloth bags he'd brought from home.

He left the hamlet behind, and the homes on either side of the lane grew farther and farther apart. He passed a rolling patchwork quilt of farms: barns and outbuildings made of stone that had stood the test of time for centuries. The pastoral land browned as winter closed in on County Armagh, but Jon Jo still found the view to be magnificent.

Chapel Road rose, then meandered to the north, and he climbed it, the exertion along with the sun working together to keep his body just warm enough, though a stronger wind blew than the one he'd encountered on his walk to church a few hours earlier.

And then, at two p.m., he turned up a pea gravel drive in front of a simple white stone cottage set back fifty meters from the lane, just one property from the road's dead end. Last night's rain showers had made puddles in the drive; he walked around them, careful not to muddy his shoes.

This was Jon Jo's farm: four hectares, ten acres, just over half of it pasture, the other half woods.

A fenced rustic sheep pen lay forty meters off to the left; a dozen Scottish Blackface, their wool halfway in its growth stage, stood still as stones, watching their owner approach.

To the right was a utility shed, a broken-down 1975 Land Rover up on blocks alongside it, and directly to the right of the cottage sat a Ford Ranger pickup, black, mud-caked. Stenciled on the side, just legible behind the splatter, it read:

J. J. SHEEHAN, SECURITY SYSTEMS AND LOCKSMITH

This, along with a local phone number.

Jon Jo stepped off the driveway with his two cloth bags full of market goods; he climbed three steps to the door, his legs barely noticing the six miles he'd walked today, his arms barely aware of the ten kilos he'd lugged nearly half that distance.

When his groceries were dealt with, he put the kettle on, started a fire in his fireplace to warm his three-room cottage, then changed into heavy rubber boots and exchanged his Irish cap for a knit beanie. He had some chores around the cottage he needed to tend to, so he stepped back outside to the yard, headed over to his truck, and immediately noticed that the wind had picked up even more. He zipped his coat up all the way and watched his sheep watching him, waiting to get fed.

Jon Jo had just opened the tailgate of the Ranger to get out one of his tool bags when he noticed movement over his left shoulder. A silver two-door Peugeot was just coming over the rise, sun reflecting off its windshield, and this drew his attention.

He did not recognize the car. He recognized virtually every vehicle that came down here towards the dead end.

It appeared that perhaps the driver was searching for an address. Jon Jo let go of his tool bag and rose back up, his eyes tracking the Peugeot as it neared.

The car was a beater, fifteen years old or so. There was body damage on the left rear quarter panel. The engine ran rough; he could hear it from one hundred meters away.

No one was looking at Jon Jo Sheehan at the moment, but if they had been, and if they possessed the training to discern such things, they would have detected a change in the man. In contrast to the solo churchgoer, the lonely man in the pub enjoying his meal, the pleasant solitary pedestrian moving through the market on the autumn Sunday, the man who stood on the drive just steps from the door of the stone cottage now appeared intimidating somehow: his fingers opened and closed, his shoulders came back, his eyes did not blink as they followed the unfamiliar vehicle rolling silently closer.

His breathing slowed; his jaw tightened.

The silver Peugeot arrived at the mouth of the driveway, and then it passed by; a skillful observer might have noticed Jon Jo's shoulders coming down a fraction of an inch, the creases around his eyes relaxing, but only for an instant, because when the car came to a stop, when the transmission clanked into reverse, the shoulders flexed again, the eyes narrowed into slits, and Jon Jo Sheehan moved for the first time.

Just a single side step closer to the front door of his home, but the movement was graceful, skilled, like a ballet dancer gliding into first position in anticipation of the opening notes of the symphony.

The Peugeot reversed a few meters, shifted into drive again, then turned into Jon Jo's driveway and began rolling slowly forward through puddles in the gravel.

Jon Jo took two more fluid sidesteps, and now he stood at the front step of his porch.

The car came to a stop two thirds up the drive, now just fifteen meters or so from where he stood.

The man in the tweed suit and the knit beanie had not averted his gaze since the Peugeot came into view.

He sensed danger, foreboding.

The hard cold wind blew into his eyes, but he ignored it.

There were forces in this world more threatening than the wind, pains deeper than dry eyes, and he knew how to prioritize.

When whatever danger he sensed presented itself, he told himself he merely had to choose the best course of action, and then he would deal with it.

The car door cracked open; Jon Jo was ready to move, either back into the home on his right, behind the grille of the Ranger to his left, or directly at whoever emerged from the car.

But a woman climbed out from behind the wheel; she was small, she seemed to be alone, and immediately her long reddish-brown hair began blowing violently in the swirling wind. She'd seen him already; this was clear, because her eyes were locked on his, even at this distance, and she took a few steps his way.

She wore a thick green anorak with dark jeans, gray boots. The coat was open; a silver cross around her neck sparkled in the sun over her black sweater.

Immediately Jon Jo's head cocked; he recognized the young woman, and he smiled.

It was Deirdre.

His daughter-in-law.

He had not laid eyes on her for over two years.

Quickly he looked to the Peugeot; he expected to see his son climb out of the passenger side.

When he did not, he turned back to her.

Her eyes boiled with intensity. Her face was hard.

He saw unreserved hatred.

His smile faded.

And then, in another instant, somehow, he understood.

Jon Jo fixed his jaw tight but still found a way to speak through it. "Somethin's 'appened to Charlie."

She did not answer for a moment, did not move her body, did not soften her eyes.

Her hair whipped in the wind for several seconds, and then, finally, she spoke one word.

"Aye."

SIX

The driver's license of the man in the tweed suit who lived at 28 Tullywinnie Lane just north of Camlough, Newry, County Armagh, Northern Ireland, displayed the name Jon Jo Sheehan, but the license had been created by forgers in Belfast, the name taken from a child's grave in a cemetery somewhere up in County Tyrone.

The locksmith and security camera installer was not a Jon or a Jo or a Sheehan.

In truth, his da had the surname Coyle. His ma had decided to call him Campbell shortly after his birth in a hospital in Belfast.

And twenty-four years ago, Campbell and his then-wife Annie had named their son Charlie, after her grandfather, because there wasn't a male in Campbell Coyle's own family, himself very much included, that he deemed worthy of commemorating with a namesake.

With his craggy face still impassive, and just a slight crack in his voice, Campbell Coyle said, "Dead, is he?"

Those blue eyes of Deirdre's bore into him like diamond drill bits. She said, "Hung on for eight days. Fought like the devil, he did. But the infection got him."

"Wha . . . what happened?"

"Shot in the leg. Then stabbed in the ribs. But that's not what's done it. What's done it was the shite medical care."

"Where?"

"Bulgaria."

"The feck was he doin' in Bulgaria?" he asked, but deep inside, he knew.

"Whatcha think he was doin'? He was working, wasn't he?"

"Bodyguarding?"

"For a bleedin' gangster. A gangster who got himself slotted, same as Charlie." For the first time, she reached to her face and swept her chaotic hair away from her eyes. "A right proper slaughter."

"When?"

"Some weeks ago. We buried him in your family plot up in Ballycastle. He'd always said that's where he wanted to end up if this happened."

Campbell felt the cold in his bones, deep. He bit the inside of his mouth. He'd somehow known this day was coming, not the particulars, of course, not this soon, of course, but he'd long thought his only child's trajectory could only lead him to one singular fate.

"He had straightened himself out," Deirdre said, as if his daughter-in-law could read his thoughts. "They did blood work. In Bucharest. Not a drop of alcohol. Not a hint of drugs."

When Campbell Coyle did not respond to this, she further confirmed that she was in his head right now. "You're thinkin,' 'Then why the feck was he killed with criminals in Bulgaria if he'd got his life so bloody sorted.' Aren't ya?"

He was, indeed.

"He had some debts, told himself he'd take it back to the knife's edge just one more feckin' time, just to get the money he needed to put everything right, to start fresh. We was ninety days away from a real life, we were."

Campbell nodded, feelings he hadn't allowed himself to feel welling up inside him. He fought his emotions, told himself he was fighting them for the good of Deirdre. "Come in. I'll make some tea. I've already got the kettle on."

But Deirdre did not move. "I won't be drinkin' tea with you, Campbell Coyle. Some gangster brought hell down on Charlie. Some assassin fired the gun and stuck the knife." She pointed at him. "But you was the one what sealed his fate. Your son's blood is on *your* hands, and always will be."

He expected this. He always knew that if his Charlie went off and did something stupid, got himself killed for it, Deirdre's eyes would bore into him, and she would proclaim him at fault. He did not respond to her charge; he only asked a question. "Who did it?"

Her accusatory finger lowered. "An American, they say, but that's all they'll say. One man. Took out eight, five dead, if ya believe that. And Charlie, right there in the way. Doin' a job he didn't believe in for people he didn't like."

She looked back over her shoulder to the car a moment, and when she returned her attention to him, he realized that was the third time she'd done this.

He himself looked to the car but could see nothing save for the sun's angry reflection on the windshield.

Something stirred within him. "What . . . what is—"

She spoke again. "You didn't know. He didn't want you to know."

"He didn't want me to know *what*?"

"You didn't know Charlie was a father. You didn't know that, did ya?"

His knees weakened. He locked them tight. "A . . . father?"

"We had a baby in the spring. Ronan's his name. Seven months old, nearly."

Campbell realized he was a grandfather, and the realization had come in the very same minute he'd learned his son had died.

"Why . . . why didn't he tell me he—"

"'Cause he wanted nothing to do with you." She shrugged. "He didn't love you, you'd done too much to turn him into what he turned into for him to love you. But . . . for some damn reason he could never explain to his own bleedin' wife . . . he wanted to *be* you. Wanted to be just like his da."

A stray cloud passed, the first Campbell had noticed all day long. With it, the reflection on the Peugeot lessened and he caught a glimpse of movement in the back of the car now, and his knees unlocked suddenly, his legs nearly giving out.

He saw just the silhouette of a child's head in a baby seat.

He began to move forward, but she put a hand up. "Not another step out of you."

"But . . . but I—"

"No."

"I can help you both, Deirdre. I have money. I have plenty of—"

"I'm sure you do. I bet you have heaps of blood-soaked money stuffed to the rafters in that wee cottage there. But I won't be takin' it from ya."

"You have to let me help him . . . Ronan, you say? You have to let me help Ronan."

"I wouldn't give you the satisfaction of letting you think you put it all right with Charlie, helpin' out his boy after it was too late to help him."

There was no reasoning with this woman; he knew this. When he'd first met her, he'd been at his son's bedside. Charlie Coyle had been wounded in the Legion; Campbell Coyle had learned and come to a hospital in Marseille. A nineteen-year-old girl had been there, just a waif of a lass, but she'd been strong like an army general, ordering the doctors about, making sure Campbell's boy had everything just right.

Campbell had been impressed with her.

Since that day nearly five years ago, he'd only seen her a few times, but he'd always taken her as strong, and his son needed strength, because his son had issues.

Trauma, addictions. Weaknesses.

Deirdre had no doubt kept him alive, but she'd also done her part to keep Charlie's dad away.

Campbell finally said, "What *can* I do?"

Deirdre all but yelled back at him. "You can go right to hell! No doubt you know your way there."

His body felt weak, unsteady. He felt much older than his forty-seven years, maybe because he'd learned his boy was dead, maybe because he'd learned he was now a grandfather, but maybe also because he felt the weight of all his life's decisions on his back like he never had before.

But something occurred to him. "Why did you even come down from Derry? To tell me that my son died? If you want nothing from me, owe nothing to me, then why do you even care that I know?"

She pushed the shining auburn hair from her eyes. "Because I hope it will eat at you like a bloody cancer. Charlie was half your age but twice the man. He could have been anything, done anything, but your life's what poisoned him." She added, "I pray his death's what poisons you."

Campbell said nothing.

She looked away a moment, towards the sheep pen, then back to him. "One more reason I came."

"Yes?"

"Marcus Maragos."

Campbell cocked his head. "I don't know who that is."

"You wouldn't. He's a Greek. A fixer. A handler of men like you. He's the one that tricked Charlie to go down and work for bloody gangsters."

Campbell was confused. "What do you want—"

Deirdre's eyes managed to find a way to look even angrier as they ripped into the man's soul. She held an arm up, pointed a finger to the southeast. "You might have that wee little village fooled. They might think you are a kind and gentle stranger, a friend to all, a harm to no one.

"But I know what you are, Campbell Coyle. And if there's one person on God's green earth I loathe as much as you right now, it is Marcus Maragos.

"He's in London. That's all I know. I pray you find him." She stared in silence a long time; the wind blew her hair across her eyes multiple times before she spoke. "And I pray you'll do what you do. The only thing you were ever any bloody good at."

At this, she began to turn away, but he called after her.

"You've come all this way. Just bring the baby in, have some tea and—"

"No!" she shouted back.

"But . . . what are you going to do?"

As she faced away, a gust of wind hit, but through it he thought he heard her laugh. She turned back to him, her eyes distant now, blue and shining with tears.

"I'm gonna go home. I'm gonna do my best to raise me boy right. So he doesn't end up dead like his da, doesn't end up broken and empty like his grandda. Doesn't end up murdered in the bloody street for his sins like his great-grandda."

Coyle's fists balled. He didn't want to hit Deirdre. He loved her. He loved her for loving his boy. For doing her best with him.

But he wanted to hit *something*, to pummel *someone*.

He hadn't felt such feelings in a long time, but those feelings were back now, just like that.

The woman with the wild hair raging in the gusty afternoon said, "I've got mighty work to do to accomplish all that, don't I, so I'd best be gettin' to it."

And then she turned away again, made it back to her car. He called after her once more, but his voice cracked as it was lost in another blast of swirling air.

Campbell Coyle stood there in the frigid sunshine, in the whisking wind, looking on as the Peugeot turned around on the driveway. A ray from the sky entered the backseat of the car for the first time, and it shone on a blond-headed baby boy.

He watched the car until it disappeared up the road, certain he would never see that boy again.

Campbell Coyle dug into the cold earth, his sharp spade piercing just a few inches with each violent stab, and then he flung the dirt into the ever-expanding pile next to the hole he stood in.

The half moon glowed through low clouds, giving only the faintest illumination to his work, but when he took little breaks here and there, he could see the steam pouring from his face.

It was past midnight; he worked in darkness, although he did not really think this security measure was crucial. He dug behind his sheep pen; the nearest neighboring home was two hundred meters away, and Campbell doubted eighty-three-year-old Mrs. Brown's cataract-clouded eyes would have noticed if he'd lit a bonfire on his roof and danced in front of it in a clown suit.

Still, Coyle continued digging in the darkness, remaining as quiet as possible.

It had been ten hours since his daughter-in-law left him standing in his driveway, and he'd spent the majority of the time since then sitting at his simple wooden kitchen table, looking out his back window. Past his sheep, out into the neighbor's pasture, into the sunny afternoon, then the evening sky, and finally the darkness.

All this time he thought of his son, of his father, of his grandfather and his grandson.

And now and then he'd even thought a little about his own life.

Young Deirdre had been right about a great many things. Most things. The more he pondered over all she'd said, he wasn't sure she'd been wrong about a word of it.

There was no getting around it. Just as Deirdre had asserted this afternoon, Campbell Coyle was a very bad man.

He was a bad man with a dark history, and he came from a long line of men with dark histories.

Campbell had hoped his dark days were behind him, but somehow he'd always had an inkling that this day would come.

The day when he stopped being Jon Jo Sheehan and once again became Campbell Finley Coyle.

He continued digging his hole, his body using all his muscles for the work but his mind occupied, as well.

Back before Campbell Coyle had moved to Camlough, back before he'd changed his name to Jon Jo Sheehan, back before he'd spent four years living off-grid after ten years traveling the world as a hired assassin, back before his time in Libya and Lebanon, even back before his teens and very early twenties, fighting in the French Foreign Legion.

Back before all that.

Back before he was born, Campbell Coyle was being made into the man he would someday become.

Campbell's father, Rory Coyle, had grown up in Belfast, a member of the IRA. He'd been trusted by Provisional leadership; they trained him, they turned him into a killer, they sent him abroad to assassinate with guns and bombs. He'd worked in London and in Dublin and in Newcastle and in Liverpool. He ran an Active Service Unit—a small team of Provos—was chased across the UK, across the European continent, by the Brits, by Interpol, but they couldn't catch Rory.

In the end, it seemed it was his own people that got him. Called back to Belfast in the mid-nineties, he went to a meeting late one afternoon and did not return.

Campbell was fifteen at the time. He remembered that his father seemed to know and trust the two men who came for him; he went willingly, said he'd be back in an hour, and Campbell heard laughter out in the street as the three IRA men, his da and the two others, bundled into a black hatchback, then drove off.

An hour later his family sat at the dinner table looking at the door; stayed there till evening turned to night.

Rory Coyle turned up dead in an oil drum in an alleyway culvert the next morning.

He'd been shot in the back of the neck.

Campbell told himself he was going to find those who killed him, and he would make them pay.

He joined the French Foreign Legion when he was seventeen; they taught him how to fight and to kill, to live with the utmost austerity, and they gave him an outlet for his rage. In Africa he fought wars. He learned to be comfortable being miserable, and to understand the world as a dark place where primal forces reigned supreme.

He was twenty when he left the Legion; he went back to Belfast and, with some help, he eventually tracked down those who had killed his father.

There had been five of them involved, he'd learned, an Active Service Unit who murdered Rory because of a personal beef having to do with missing money, and Campbell killed every last one of them.

When Campbell was done, he was just twenty-three. By now he had a young wife and a baby; he took work at a factory in Derry, but soon he realized he could not leave his old life behind. He was a fighter. He was a killer.

So he began killing for money. Campbell worked for the British, the sworn enemy of his father, but he didn't care. His da had been killed by the IRA; the British were no better and no worse, and their money spent the same.

He'd continued his training in Libya, in East Africa, in the Middle East, and he'd killed men in Asia and America and Europe.

And then, before he turned forty years old, he'd retired from it all. He had more money than a simple man could spend, and he'd lost his taste for killing.

Mostly estranged from his ex-wife and his young son, he moved back to Northern Ireland, but to a village far away from Derry, down south, where no one knew of his family, and he'd started his life over. His ex-wife died of a stroke, and he'd tried to reconcile with his son, more than once, but Charlie eventually became a Legionnaire himself, now fighting France's international battles, and he'd wanted nothing to do with his da.

Campbell Coyle became Jon Jo Sheehan. Part-time shepherd, full-time security camera installer and locksmith, and regular churchgoer.

Campbell Coyle had been a very, very bad man in his past, but he had worked so hard to put his past behind him, to erase any vestige of what he'd been, that now, now that everything had fucking changed with the murder of Charlie in some coastal town down in Bulgaria, he had to ask himself if he could possibly be a killer again.

Physically, it wasn't a problem. He was still strong from the rigors of his life. His eyes were good and sharp at distance, though he used readers for small print up close.

Small print up close wasn't crucial to an assassin's trade.

Yes, he was physically better than he'd been when he was twenty-five, injured in a gunfight and recovering in a hospital in the Philippines, or thirty, in prison in Senegal and nearly starving on rotten rations. Or thirty-five, in hiding in France and barely seeing the sun and getting no exercise.

Now he was fit, fast, sharp, and capable.

Physically, he was all he needed to be to do what had to be done now.

But mentally? Did he still have what it took to look a man in the eyes and end his life?

The bad news was he did not know the answer to that question, but the good news was he *did* know exactly how to find out.

It took Campbell Coyle another five minutes before his spade struck what he was looking for, and a few minutes more to dig it out.

Three cases, each the size of a roll-aboard, and each covered in electrician's tape and thick plastic tarp to keep them safe from decay.

He'd buried them here years ago, hoped he'd never need to retrieve them, but something that had always been ticking in the back of his brain told him that a day like this might come.

Finished with this stage of tonight's work, he tossed the shovel out of the hole, climbed out with a plastic-wrapped case, and carried it back to a small equipment shed next to his house.

He retraced his steps twice more, and soon he had all three cases on a long simple table in his shed under the light of a single bare bulb.

Casting a long shadow as he worked, he used gardening shears to cut the plastic and tape away, then hung the shears back on the wall and looked at the hard plastic boxes that he had not laid eyes on for such a long time.

They were not numbered; he realized he should have numbered them, but he put that out of his mind and opened the one on the far left first.

It was full of cash. Euros and pounds sterling, U.S. dollars, wrapped in tight plastic bundles.

He retrieved a duffel bag from inside the cottage, then returned, pulled a pack of each, and tossed them into the bag.

He opened the next case and looked down at several handguns packed in foam along with extra magazines and three suppressors.

There were six pistols in all, but he chose only one. A Russian Makarov.

It was loaded with a magazine full of .380 rounds, and he pulled three more mags out of the case and put them on the table.

The gun would need cleaning, the extra mags would need loading. He retrieved the suppressor for the corresponding caliber of the weapon, and this went right into the duffel bag.

In the third case he found ammunition and small gold bars.

He was almost certain he would not need gold where he was going, but he was damn sure he would need the ammo. He took three hundred rounds of .380 ball ammunition and another hundred rounds of .380 hollow-point, and he put these on the table.

It was nearly two a.m. by now, but he had hours' more work to do before the sun rose.

He cleaned the Makarov, screwed on a long suppressor, loaded his mags, and walked outside, again into the cold.

He'd do target practice under cover of darkness. Again tomorrow. During the day he would train in his cottage with his knives. He would run in the hills, pore over his false identities to rememorize everything on them.

He would train with the pistol, train with the knives, work his body as he worked his mind, because though he was still a very fit man, the muscle memory of his past life needed to be refired somehow, and that could only happen if he put himself through the paces of training.

And then, maybe in a month, maybe in two, he would reach out to a neighbor—not Mrs. Brown—about watching over his livestock and his home, and he would map out his plans for the next days, weeks, maybe months.

He did not know what the future would hold, but the drive to fulfill his objective had grown in him from the moment he had looked in the back of that Peugeot in his driveway twelve hours earlier, and each minute since.

He had spent nearly a decade playing the role of Jon Jo Sheehan. A kind man. A simple man.

But now he was Campbell Coyle again.

No longer kind, but still simple.

No longer kind, because he endeavored to cut a bloody swath across this earth to achieve his mission.

But still simple, because his one singular objective in life was to find and kill the man who had murdered his son.

SEVEN

Washington, D.C., awoke to a slushy December morning; the deep gray dawn and foreboding skies warned of more harsh weather to come, but through the curtains of the bay windows on the second floor of the big row house on Dent Place in Georgetown, the man standing in front of the bathroom mirror had already showered, and that after two cups of coffee.

James Arthur Westwood III ran a comb through his thick salt-and-pepper hair, forming the part the same as he had done ever since he was in grammar school in New Hampshire.

He had just turned sixty the week prior, and although he'd forgone the elliptical trainer in his basement this morning because he had an early meeting to get to, he exercised almost every day, with long rides on his bike, in his home gym downstairs, or in his afternoon pickleball league at the club.

Westwood was proud of how he was holding up, but his quest for vitality wasn't just for the sake of vanity.

One also had to look good for the cameras. Vigor conveyed authority, influence, relevance.

He hadn't been in front of the media in a few years; he'd been a man in the shadows, but he held out hope that he'd soon enough be back in the light, and he wanted to be ready.

To that end, he told himself he'd go to the club on Massachusetts Avenue right after work, spend an hour on the free weights, then stretch before his dinner with a couple of senators (Indiana and Vermont) at Fiola, a Michelin-star restaurant in Capitol Hill.

Although Westwood did not presently serve as a member of the U.S. government, he had strolled the corridors of Washington power for nearly thirty years, and dinner with senators was a relatively common occurrence for him.

Westwood's father, James Arthur Westwood Jr., had been a lawyer, a congressman, then secretary of energy in the Ford administration. Westwood Jr. had run for governor of New York in the eighties and narrowly lost, then joined the boards of several Fortune 500 companies, living out the rest of his days on the lecture circuit when he wasn't at home in his Greenwich Village brownstone on West 10th.

James the Third, "J.W." to everyone who really knew him, had been raised in New Hampshire but then moved with his parents to Washington, then to New York. J.W. went to Harvard, then Harvard Law, and then spent a year clerking for a Supreme Court justice.

He practiced law in Concord, then ran for and won a congressional seat. He served four terms, was known as a dealmaker and a moderate, and was well liked by all, back in those days when friendships extended beyond party lines.

J.W. left Congress to move to the executive branch, serving two years as undersecretary of state before being appointed U.S. ambassador to Singapore by the then-president, a close family friend.

That stint lasted three years, and then he left the Department of State to take over as the director of an international think tank based here in Washington, D.C.

But running a think tank was a means to an end for J.W. Westwood. The vehicle that would take him where he *really* wanted to go.

A Senate seat would open up in New Hampshire in just two years, and J.W. Westwood had every intention of running, and of winning.

He'd be a senator in time, of this he was certain.

And then, God willing, he'd be president. He knew he had the right stuff.

And, perhaps more importantly, he knew that if he kept his end of a hard bargain, he would get all the help he needed to make it happen.

Westwood's two children were both at Stanford; his wife had left him a year earlier to no great protest from him, and though their divorce remained unfinalized, he'd been living as a bachelor here in D.C. for a lot longer than he'd been separated, so if anything, his breakup actually facilitated his lifestyle.

He had just pulled a dark gray sweater vest out of his closet and slipped it on over his crisp white shirt and red tie when he heard a noise downstairs. A door opening, male voices.

This was no cause for alarm; a man resided in J.W.'s converted carriage house apartment out back and had the run of the place.

The man's name was Michael Scardino, but most of his friends and coworkers just referred to him as "Big Mike."

Big Mike worked—nominally, anyway—as J.W.'s bodyguard, but Scardino was so much more than that.

Westwood cocked his head now, trying to make out the voices echoing through the two-hundred-year-old home.

Some weekday mornings J.W.'s driver, Hasan, would arrive early to take him to the office, then step in for coffee with Mike, and J.W. assumed that was what was going on, but then the phone in his pocket buzzed.

Looking at it, he saw that Big Mike was sending a text from downstairs.

The shithead is here.

Westwood made a face. At Big Mike, not at the shithead, because he knew a lot of shitheads and didn't know who his bodyguard was referring to.

Just as he was about to ask Mike if he could possibly be more specific, another text came through.

Shaw.

Shaw? *That* shithead.

After a little sigh, J.W. typed back quickly.

B right down

Westwood had had his entire day planned, but with that text, he wondered if his entire day was out the fucking window.

He took his time descending into the kitchen, and when he did so, he was fully dressed, suit and tie and vest and coiffed hair and expensive cologne.

He saw Big Mike in the kitchen; at six-four he was hard to miss. A former army major and then an overseas high-threat security contractor, he commanded attention without even trying.

The other man in the kitchen, sitting at the table, was the polar opposite. Small, shabbily dressed, and bleary-eyed, he looked to J.W. like a college student who'd been out all night on a bender of cheap beer and Jell-O shots.

Though he was, in fact, thirty years old, Lewis Shaw looked nearly a decade younger. Big Mike put a mug of coffee in front of Lewis, and the younger man looked at it.

"Little cream, lots of sugar," he said, and Big Mike flashed annoyed eyes to Westwood.

J.W. sighed, then said, "Indulge our guest, please. We'll warm him up so if I need you to toss him back out into the snow, he won't catch cold."

Big Mike headed for the fridge with a hopeful glint in his eyes.

Westwood leaned against the kitchen island, addressing the visitor. "Well . . . you always look like hell, but today it appears you've visited the ninth circle. That mean you didn't get any sleep last night?"

"What's sleep?" Lewis Shaw replied without batting an eyelash.

The older man himself did not hesitate in his response. "I've got to get to the Center. Have a seven-thirty teleconference with staff in London."

"You might not, actually."

"What does that mean?"

Big Mike poured half-and-half into Shaw's mug, then gave it a long shot of sugar from a pourable container. He put a spoon on the table and Shaw stirred his own coffee.

Though the younger man looked wiped out, he somehow retained an air of confidence. He licked coffee off his spoon and put it down, then tilted his head towards the bodyguard.

"We talkin' in front of the help?"

"I'm out," Scardino said, his voice conveying the loathing he felt for the younger man, and then he left the room before Westwood kicked him out.

When he was gone, J.W. sat in front of his guest, who drank the scorching-hot coffee like it was tap water.

The sixty-year-old said, "Why do you always have to be such an asshole to Mike?"

Shaw didn't hesitate. "He works for Gauntlet Group, what do you want me to say?"

When J.W. just looked at him, the young man said, "I'm a government employee working in the Office of the Director of National Intelligence; he's a contract goon working for you, but the company he really works for has replaced over four thousand positions in the intelligence community, including over three hundred in my building. A lot of our best and brightest have been let go, replaced with those pricks. What am I supposed to think of a Gauntlet goon like Big Mike?

"Plus, that's guy's a bodyguard. I'm data analytics. I'd say we are a different skill set, but what Scardino and the thousands of those Gauntlet security types do isn't much of a skill, in my opinion."

Westwood began to respond, but then he stopped himself, changed course. "Anyone see you come in?"

The young man sniffed out a little laugh. "Before I started at ODNI, I was a DIA field tech for four years. I know how to watch my back."

J.W. moved the conversation along. "What do you have for me?"

"Nicaragua."

Westwood didn't say *What about Nicaragua?* Instead, he said, "You passing over some intelligence?"

"Yes."

"From what agency?"

"*The* Agency."

"Actionable?"

"Very."

Westwood leaned closer, drummed his fingers on the table a moment. "What have you got?"

"It's definitely a 'hair on fire' type of thing on the seventh floor."

The seventh floor of CIA headquarters was where the executive suites were and therefore where the highest-level decision-making happened.

Lewis went on. "There's an asset in Nicaragua who's demanding to be pulled out. Claims to have been burned."

"Related to which operation?"

Shaw downed the rest of his coffee, rose, and poured himself another cup. "I don't know."

"Who burned the asset?"

Shaw shook his head as he reached for the creamer. "Dunno. In this case I only have visibility into the op orders themselves, not the intel that initiated them. I'm spoofing the credentials of a midlevel staffer; she's got some of the raw data but not all. I can make inferences, of course, but there's no explanation about who burned them or what they were working on. Only that it happened.

"I *can* tell you that this came out of nowhere. The CIA is scrambling to put a package together to make the extraction happen. Like, fast."

"Like... *how* fast?"

"Like, tonight. The asset has requested an American present at the extraction, and Managua station says they can't expose their operatives on such a high-risk event. Looks like the seventh floor is considering using either a paramilitary or a trusted contractor." He shrugged. "They'll probably send some Gauntlet asshole down there."

Shaw said, "Gauntlet isn't the only contract group working in the intelligence community."

"No, they're just the president's favorite."

J.W. let it go. He asked, "You have the time and the place?"

"Exact time and place have not been determined. But I'll get it. The lady whose account I'm spoofing will see the seventh-floor decision as soon as it's made. I just knew you were... interested in U.S. government activity in the region, so I figured the sooner I got this to you—"

"You did the right thing," Westwood said. Then he added, "But I don't love you showing up here, in person. Going forward... wait till business hours, wait till I'm at the Center, and then you can impress upon me how I couldn't survive without you to your heart's content."

"That works." Shaw finished his coffee, then stood. "I'll get you the location and time."

As he headed for the kitchen door to the rear garden, Westwood called out. "What I would give to know exactly how you are getting access to this intelligence."

"We have our system, sir. I feed you . . . you feed . . . *them*."

J.W. said, "And I'm sure *they* appreciate what you're doing."

"Then they'll show me their gratitude via my account in the Caymans."

"I'll pass that along with the intelligence you brought me. But no more unannounced visits. Clear?"

The younger man looked out the window by the back kitchen door, making sure no one could see him leave. "As a bell."

And then he was gone.

Thirty minutes later, J.W. climbed out of a black Yukon on Church Street NW with Big Mike Scardino at his side, and as Hasan drove off to the east through swirling snowflakes, the two men climbed the stairs of a redbrick row house twice the size of Westwood's home just a mile and a half to the west in Georgetown.

This building was not much different from a dozen others in the row on this stretch of Church Street. The entire block had been built in the 1880s, and today some were private homes, others had been parceled out into apartments or condos, but a few were owned by foundations.

As they made it to the front porch, they walked past a gold plaque inlaid in the brick wall that read "The Raymond C. Carter Center for Trends in Peace."

The door was held open for the two men by a security guard in a navy sweater with gold-striped epaulets.

In minutes Westwood was alone, ensconced in his office, his headset on his head and connected to his laptop. His laptop was equipped with

FibreNet, a commercial encrypted communications system. He waited just a moment for the call to be answered on the other end.

"Yes." A woman answered and he recognized the voice. She sounded American, her tone businesslike, as always.

"It's me," he said.

"Authentication?"

"Desert Wind."

"Confirmed. My authentication is Harness."

"Confirmed. I have preliminary information about a time-critical event."

"Priority of the information?"

"Ultra."

"Go ahead."

Westwood relayed what he'd heard from Shaw about Nicaragua and a scared agent of the CIA demanding to be extracted, along with the fact that Shaw expected to have specific location and time information in the coming hours.

After the woman on the other end acknowledged that she understood, J.W. said, "Whatever measures they take down in Nicaragua, it has to happen like it was organic, not as the result of obtaining intel up here. We need this source kept safe, in play for our upcoming mission here. I mean, Nicaragua might be important to your people, but it can't possibly be more important than our mission here."

"I'll relay the message, but no one takes strategic advice from you—or from me, for that matter."

J.W. shrugged. "If they want my mission to be a success here in D.C., then they'll do it."

"I will pass your concerns along." The connection ended.

Westwood took off his headset and gazed out the window. The skies looked like they had some more snow in them. Sometimes he liked to walk to work. Often he'd ride his mountain bike. But he'd take the Yukon back home this afternoon, for sure.

Drumming his fingers on his desk, he let the gravity of this moment wash over him, but only for a second.

He had committed high treason this morning, and not for the first time this year.

There had been Tunis, and there had been Addis Ababa before that. There had been Madrid, and there had been Caracas.

And now Managua.

He knew the high treason would continue, he knew the stakes would rise, and he knew that, very soon, the information he passed on would cause actions, lethal actions, not in some far-flung third-world locale where no one mattered and no one cared, but right here.

Right here in D.C.

This is heavy stuff when you stop to think about it.

J.W. Westwood's suddenly pensive mood was not a bout of morality. No, he'd made peace with what he was doing.

It was, instead, the magnitude of his position that weighed on him.

He was changing the world. Not alone. But nevertheless . . . his was no small part.

Treason was only treason if history recorded it as such, and James Arthur Westwood III had faith that history would record him as it did George Washington.

Less as the leader of a rebellion.

And more as the father of the country.

It was true, he admitted to himself, that the world he was helping to create was not entirely the world he would have chosen.

But at least he'd be in it, he would be powerful, and he would be a force for good when the inevitable bad threatened this great nation.

J.W. reached for his coffee, satisfied in the belief that someday he would be richly rewarded for his time in the shadows.

EIGHT

At noon Courtland Gentry pulled into the parking lot of the Bay Point Marina in Virginia Beach, Virginia; parked his rented Altima in a space next to a black Suburban; and looked around.

Court saw a man inside the Suburban sitting alone behind the wheel and talking animatedly on his phone.

The driver was Matt Hanley, a man who had once been his boss at CIA, and Court imagined the call was probably important, so he climbed out of his rental car and strolled down to the wooden dock at the water's edge, just a dozen yards from where he parked.

With his hands jammed inside his black Carhartt coat, his mouth breathing vapor on this cold December day, he saw the gray sky merged with the gray water in front of him. Fully half of the hundreds of boats he could see were covered for the season.

He turned around and looked to the land, just on the other side of the parking lot, and took in what appeared to be several large apartment buildings, all the same design, utterly quiet at this time of day. He wondered who lived here but quickly noticed a sign that offered vacancies for a senior living residence along with memory care services.

He did not know why he was here now. He only knew that he'd been flown here from Charlottesville on a private jet, and then he'd picked up a rental car reserved for him under an alias and followed an order to come directly to this location without delay.

Presuming Matt Hanley had no plans to put him in a home for Alzheimer patients just yet, he turned back to the water and looked over the recreational boats there, but soon his eyes looked past the marina, across a narrow channel of water, and focused on the land. This was, Court knew, a part of Joint Expeditionary Base Little Creek, the major operating base for the Amphibious Forces of the U.S. Navy's Atlantic Fleet.

SEAL Teams 2, 4, and 8 were based right there, just across the spit of water, and while Court had known and worked with men from all three of these teams in his old life in the CIA, he'd never been a SEAL, and he certainly had no connection to Little Creek.

That said, he had worked and lived nearby, in Virginia Beach, a decade ago, as a member of a CIA paramilitary unit called Golf Sierra. At that time, Hanley had been his boss, and now as he looked back towards the Suburban, he knew that Hanley was his boss again.

They weren't Agency now, neither of them.

Now they were sub rosa. Off book. Illegal.

Court Gentry had been doing illegal shit for years, but Matt had always had the safety net of the Agency under him, ready to catch him if he fell.

Court wondered what it felt like for a guy in his sixties to be out in the cold like this for the first time, but he didn't ponder it long, because just then Matt finished up his call, turned the engine off, and climbed out from behind the wheel.

The older man wore a scraggly white-blond beard, with thinning hair of the same color, and it blew in the cold breeze. He sported a blue wool peacoat and khakis, brown leather boat shoes, and sunglasses.

Though the two men hadn't seen each other in some time, Court had known Hanley for over a decade, and he'd never known him to have a beard.

"Dammit, Six." The older man spoke first. "Good to finally lay eyes on you." When Court had first worked under Hanley in the CIA's Special Activities Division—Ground Branch, the younger man had carried the call sign Sierra Six, and half the call sign had somehow stuck throughout the years.

Court extended a hand and Hanley shook it.

"Been a long time, Matt. You operating without security?" Court asked, making a show of looking into the Suburban, although he'd already sussed out that Matt was alone.

"Security? For what? The best gunslinger on planet Earth is standing right in front of me. You're carrying, right?"

"If I've got pants on, I've got a gun on."

Hanley looked down at Court's jeans. "Well then, it's my lucky day, for a couple of reasons." He turned, reached into the backseat of the SUV and pulled out a baby blue Yeti insulated lunch box.

Court said, "You're taking me on a picnic?"

But Hanley did not answer him. Instead, he said, "How are you doing?"

"I'm fine."

"Yeah? Lemme see."

Court understood the request. He unzipped his black coat, then pulled up his gray sweater, revealing a ragged red scar along the right side of his midsection.

When Hanley said nothing, just kept looking, Court said, "That's it."

"Stitches?"

"Stapled me up back in Kharkiv. Got them out a couple weeks ago up in Charlottesville. I'm good as new." He shrugged. "I mean, good as I was before I got shot."

Hanley kept looking at the scar. "AK round, right?"

"I assume so. The bullet was going kind of fast, and it was night . . . so . . ."

Hanley sniffed, shut the Suburban door behind him, and Court lowered his sweater and rezipped his Carhartt. Matt said, "Haven't seen you in a year and a half and you have to be a smartass?"

"I gotta be me."

Hanley gave a little smile. "Glad you are still you. You weren't for a while. Bulgaria, Romania, Latvia, Finland, then Russia. You've been more lucky than smart. Hope you're back to normal."

"Yeah." Court had spent over half a year on a quest, a quest that he had successfully concluded, but only with the help of Hanley, and Hanley himself had been helped by others.

Both Hanley and Gentry had sold a piece of themselves to achieve that objective, and for that reason they were now back together.

"How's Anthem?" Matt asked.

Anthem was the code name for a woman named Zoya, and Zoya had been the objective for which Hanley and Court had sold pieces of themselves to rescue from a Russian penal colony.

Court looked off into the distance. "She's gonna be fine. Not there yet, but doing a lot better than I'd be doing, considering it all." He looked to Hanley. "Thanks for letting me go see her again last weekend."

"I've been running you pretty hard over the last several weeks. I felt like you deserved a little downtime."

To this, Court laughed. "You've had me flying all over the country setting up front companies, buying equipment, establishing safe houses, doing background checks on former government personnel. Considering what I used to do in the past, I wouldn't say that's running me so hard.

"What's the deal, Matt? Am I management now? I kinda prefer being labor."

"You're labor, still. I just didn't have anyone else to do the kind of legwork I needed. I've rectified that, so as of now, you're back in operations."

"Good," Court said, but that went nowhere in explaining why he was standing in the parking lot of a quiet marina on a Monday afternoon.

Hanley looked past him to his rental car. "How much shit do you have with you?"

"Duffel bag and a backpack."

"All your worldly possessions?"

"Pretty much, yeah. I've been living out of hotels."

"Grab everything and follow me."

Court retrieved his bags from the backseat of the car, heaving the duffel. The bigger, older Hanley made no effort to help him; he just held the Yeti, and then the two of them began walking down to the dock.

A Christmas tree sparkled through a porthole in the first houseboat they encountered, but there were very few other signs of life around the marina. The two men passed rigid-hulled inflatable boats and runabouts no more than ten feet long, bowriders, bay boats, and ski boats a little bigger, many covered for the winter, some up on winches, but most bobbing in the water in dozens of slips. As they came to another pier, the smaller craft gave way to larger catamarans, sailboats, and even luxury yachts up to one hundred feet long.

When they reached pier B, Hanley turned and they kept walking.

Court couldn't imagine what this was all about. "What's the deal, Matt? We going for a ride?"

"You'll see," the older man said.

Court saw a large boat docked at the end of the pier.

He recognized it by its shape; it was a sports cruiser, maybe sixty feet in length, old-looking, with a white body and a dull beige stripe running the length of the hull. A beige hard top covered the helm.

Though relatively large compared to most of the other vessels at this marina, it was certainly no luxury yacht.

The name on the bow read *Ship Happens, Two*.

The port of registry was the Hamptons.

The transom was just a step off the pier, and there didn't seem to be anyone on deck.

"It's a 1996 Sea Ray 630 sport cruiser," Matt said as he boarded. "Upgraded in the past couple of years."

"What happened to *Ship Happens, One*?" Court asked as he stepped aboard onto the transom himself.

"Hit an iceberg. Sank in the North Atlantic."

"Really?" Court asked, surprised.

Hanley made a face of disappointment. "No, man. I don't know. Didn't ask."

On the aft deck Court put his bags down, then looked out into the marina, still unsure what they were doing here.

Hanley said, "She's faster than she looks."

"Whose boat is this?"

"My company bought it."

Court laughed. "Which company?" Court had been registering companies up in Delaware just a few days prior.

"TerreCom Industrial Consulting," Hanley said. And then, "Your new employer."

Court had *not* registered a company by this name. "Okay, what do we do at TerreCom?"

"Ostensibly, we facilitate relationships between foreign manufacturing industrial sectors and . . ." He paused. "I don't really know. It's written down somewhere. It's legit, but purposefully boring as shit. TerreCom was a shell company started by the Agency in the eighties. It was run out of a clearinghouse of shells in Delaware for decades, but we bought it legally, and now we've leased a suite in an office park in Norfolk, hired a few staff of ex–intelligence community folks with the right clearances."

"We're a CIA front," Court said.

"Negative. We *bought* a CIA front. We're running it ourselves."

"Bought it with what?"

"CIA money."

Court repeated himself. "We're a CIA front."

Hanley rolled his eyes, feigning annoyance. "Let's go downstairs to the salon. The heater is already on; we can warm up."

Hanley walked off. Court heaved his bags and followed, and soon they were belowdecks in a roomy but simple salon. Both men sat down on couches and Court looked around. The space was not plush or particularly modern; there was a strong smell of cleaning solvents and a faint smell of mildew, but the boat seemed functional.

Hanley explained. "The DEA confiscated this baby like fifteen years ago, a meth distributor up in New Jersey, I think. He'd souped it up, made it deceptively fast. It was in storage for a while after that, but a few years back, the DOJ requisitioned it for an operation they were running in the Chesapeake. They jazzed it up even more.

"That op fizzled, and it's sat in dry dock in a shipyard in Norfolk ever since. I had a broker buy it a couple weeks ago and bring it here, after giving it a maintenance check. It's got a lot of little bells and whistles that you might like."

Court said, "I can guess. Acoustic sensors on the hull so no one slips up from below. An underwater camera or two."

"Or five," Hanley said. "There are more cameras on board. The feds had it wired up pretty good. More importantly, it has a pair of Volvo IPSs, 950 horsepower each. She can make forty-five knots, no problem."

"That *is* fast. What's it for?"

Hanley shrugged. "As you know, we've been staging equipment around the U.S., overseas, too, so it's part of that. It's for whenever we need a boat of this size in this part of the world. But more importantly, I guess, it's for you to live on."

Court laughed at this, but when he saw that Matt was not laughing along with him, he looked around again. "You're serious?"

NINE

"This is your home now." He shrugged. "You don't own it. Pruitt Partners does."

"Wait. Who is Pruitt Partners?"

"A subsidiary of a subsidiary of a subsidiary of TerreCom Industrial Consultants."

"Right." Court continued taking it all in. He hadn't had a fixed residence in many years. He'd lived off grid with Zoya in Latin America earlier in the year, but they never stayed anywhere for more than a couple of weeks. *That* had felt like domestic bliss to a vagabond like Court.

Now he had, from what Hanley was telling him, a permanent address. But he didn't have the girl with him.

Hanley said, "You can sail this up to D.C. in less than a day. New York in two days. But you will be based here. TerreCom's headquarters is just a couple miles away."

"Okay," Court said. "So . . . like . . . I get an office there?"

"Negative."

"A cubicle?"

Hanley shook his head with a laugh. "What are you going to do with a cubicle?"

"I don't know what *anybody* does with a cubicle. I've never had one."

"No, kid. This is where you stay when you're in town, but to be honest, you'll be on the road a lot, and when you're not on the road, much of the time you'll be training."

"For what?"

"For whatever."

"Where do I train?"

"Drum Hill."

Court had trained at over fifty facilities in the United States, but he'd never heard of Drum Hill. "Which is . . . where?"

"In North Carolina, on the VA border. Maybe a forty-five-minute drive from here. There's a farm there, owned by . . . a guy."

"Sounds legit." Court said it sarcastically.

"Legit enough," Hanley replied. "He's an old friend of mine from the army, started a private facility to train PMCs during the GWOT, then lost all his customers a few years back when government funding ran dry. He's retired, but I called him up the other day and told him I wanted to rent his entire facility.

"He was pleased, to put it mildly. Drum Hill has a grass strip, my buddy has a Vietnam-era UH-1, and he can get you from there to here in twenty minutes, and to any airport around D.C. in under an hour."

"Tell me you're restoring his Huey, too."

"That's in the works." When Court did not reply, Hanley looked back to him. "Look, this isn't going to be first class. You'll have gear, you'll have training, you'll have logistics and intelligence coordination, and you'll be supported in the field."

For the first time, Hanley opened his little lunch box and pulled out a pair of beers that had been kept cool with cold packs.

"More importantly than this boat, we've got a contract with a charter air service at Hampton Roads Executive Airport. Bellstar Aviation."

"They're an Agency front, too?"

"No, but a private contractor staffed by ex–Air Force, Navy, and Air Branch pilots. They do government work, but through dummy corps and such."

"So . . . they're an Agency front, too," Court repeated.

"That's not how Washington works these days. Everything is contracted out. It's not a front, it's a . . . relationship."

Court didn't really understand how things worked around here; he had spent a grand total of about a week in the D.C. area in the past decade.

"Anyway, at Bellstar, we have use of a Hawker Beechcraft 800XP, a twelve-seat business jet. Bellstar has crews they can call up in a moment's notice, and we have larger and smaller aircraft that can be rented."

"Kinda like an Agency front."

Hanley sighed. "Like any good company. That airport is thirty minutes from here in traffic, and I have an FBO employee badge for you that gets you right onto the tarmac. And you can forget that Altima you pulled up in. You've got a black Tahoe in the lot here at the marina. It's registered to another shell TerreCom owns."

"Cool."

"And if I need you at the airport quicker than that, there's a rented shed here just off marina grounds with something faster inside."

Court was intrigued. "You gonna keep me in suspense?"

"A motorcycle." Hanley opened up his phone and scrolled through something for a moment, putting on reading glasses as he did so. He said, "I don't know bikes, but I talked to someone who does. Yeah, here it is. A Yamaha YZF. The R1M."

It was a powerful motorcycle Court was familiar with. The sport bike, Court knew, could whip through traffic a hell of a lot better than a Chevy Tahoe.

"Sweet. Registered to . . . ?"

"Brian Webb."

"Who is—"

"Brian Webb is you when you're in the States. We're still getting your legend together, should have that all sorted in a few days, but we do have the bike in that name, at least."

"What happened to Patrick Sanders?" The identification he carried at the moment was fake, as well.

"He just died. Burn those creds, throw the ashes overboard. Forget the name."

"Brian Webb," Court said softly to himself. He'd had dozens of aliases in his life, however, so his attention quickly went back to the motorcycle.

He said, "Somebody's come into some money."

"TerreCom has twenty-five million dollars behind it. Some Homeland Security appropriation that was shuffled out of the light and into the black. Don't know when I'll get more, so we have to be shrewd with our expenses, but it helps that—for now, at least—I've only got one human asset to support."

Court leaned back in the chair. "So, Zack's not healed up yet?"

"Hightower is on injured reserve another week, at least. He has an MRI scheduled, and that will either clear him for service or extend his vacation."

Zack Hightower had been with Court the night in Russia when he was shot, and Hightower himself took an AK round in the back of the thigh, a much more serious wound than Court's. He, like Court and Hanley, had been ordered to start this sub rosa operation by the deputy director for ops at the CIA.

"What's Zack doing now?" Court asked.

"Ignoring my calls, mostly. Sending me texts to keep me happy. He says he's doing PT, but he's also out in Colorado, hunting."

"Hunting what?"

"Dunno. Not humans. Not yet." After a moment, Hanley waved his hand in the air. "Look, before we get to the reason I called you here, I wanted to fill you in about your dad."

Court sat up straighter. "What's wrong?"

"Nothing's wrong. Like we discussed, we have to assume that Russian intelligence obtained your name a few months ago. That could, theoretically at least, put your only living relative at some risk. A few weeks back I found an ex-Unit guy who lives down in Florida and works as a PI to keep an eye on your pop, just to make sure there wasn't anyone snooping around him who shouldn't be."

Court knew this; he'd discussed it with Hanley in their first phone conversation after he returned from Russia. "And?" he prompted.

"And . . . your dad might be a crusty old goat, but he's not an idiot. My guy down there says your dad made him in a hardware store two weeks ago, came up and started talking to him. Asking him why he just showed up in the area, why he'd seen him in a rental with Miami tags on his street, that kind of thing."

"Shit," Court muttered. "Were guns pulled?"

Hanley laughed. "No, nothing like that. But Skip, that's the PI, had to double down to keep his story straight. He told your dad he was buying property there in the neighborhood."

Court raised an eyebrow. "Meaning one of your non-CIA fronts now has a shitty house on a gravel road in northern Florida?"

"Yep, with a sixty-six-year-old former Delta guy in it. A guy who now has a standing invite to meet your dad for coffee every morning."

Court groaned at this. "Some covert surveillance operation."

Hanley shrugged. "It's all good. Echols is doing his job. He hasn't seen anything out of the ordinary. Your pop is fine, and now he has a new friend to bitch to about all his conspiracy theories."

"Sounds like him," Court said. "I appreciate you watching over him."

Hanley waved this away. "CIA has seen no evidence that the Russians are even bouncing your name around in their internal communications. Best-case scenario, the one guy in FSB who knew who you were is now the one guy we have on ice in a black site in Morocco."

An FSB colonel named Baronov had run an operation where he learned Court's name. Court had then, with help, kidnapped the man and brought him out of Russia.

"Fingers crossed," Court said, but he wasn't overly concerned about the Russians having his identity. He switched gears. "So, when you called this morning, you told me to get my ass here on the double."

"Yeah. I wanted to rush you down here today to get you settled in, because I'm about to send you out into the field for the first time with this new venture."

Court leaned forward, his beer still untouched in his hand. "What's up?"

Hanley took a sip of his beer. "You're going to Nicaragua."

Court took a gulp himself, finally, and looked down at the bottle. It was an IPA. He hated IPAs. So much, in fact, that he was more bothered by his beverage than the fact that he'd just been told he'd soon be on a plane to a semi-hostile nation in Central America.

Hanley said, "An asset in their national police is claiming to be burned. Doesn't trust the local station. Wants extraction from the country. Normally, the Agency would tell the agent to pound sand, but this particular agent is claiming to have something big enough to earn the extraction."

Court didn't get it. "The agent doesn't trust the local station, fine. Send a Ground Branch team from up here. Why send me? I thought we were going to be used for big shit that the Agency can't manage."

"This *is* big shit, apparently, because Trey Watkins came to me directly."

Watkins was the deputy director for operations at CIA. The man who'd ordered the creation of this entire enterprise.

"*That* asshole," Court mumbled.

"That asshole who saved your life by helping to get you out of Russia?"

Court shrugged. "Still an ass."

"Anyway... Trey says two recent ops run out of Langley were fumbled badly. Possibly compromised, possibly from within. They haven't identified the leak, or even convinced themselves that there *is* a leak, but they don't want to take any chances on this one."

Court said, "Then fold DIA into this. Get someone at State—"

"They've had compromises, too."

"DIA or State?"

"Both."

Court took another gulp of the beer. The moment seemed to warrant it. "What are you saying?"

"I'm saying that *Trey* says that no one has found any commonality in the exposures. This might be a case of colossal bad luck, but—"

"How could all those agencies be compromised?"

"They couldn't. Nobody knows what's happening yet, but in the meantime, CIA has an in extremis situation in Nicaragua, and Trey wants an outsider to go down and handle it."

Court shook his head. "I don't like the sound of this."

"Unfortunately, Six, you and I have both relinquished the right to say no to Trey Watkins for a while."

Court rose, walked over to the fridge, and opened it, hoping to find it stocked with some different type of beer.

It was empty.

He shut the fridge, then sat back down.

"The asset in Nicaragua?"

"A female. CIA code name is Caprice."

"I'm assuming she isn't to know that I'm *not* with the Agency."

"I don't see the need to bore her with unnecessary details."

"So you want me to lie, basically."

"Nobody does it better."

Court sighed again. "Tell me no one at CIA knows about what we're doing."

"Watkins does." Hanley waved his beer in front of him as he had another thought. "Well . . . someone has to get the information on the extraction location to Caprice, so Managua station has to be at least involved with comms, but otherwise, no one should know."

"You trust Watkins?"

"It's not about trust. It's about mutually assured destruction. He's running us off book. He's given me a long leash. He'd fry if the wrong people found out about this."

"Tell me this," Court demanded. "Is the president of the United States one of the right people or one of the wrong people?"

"I don't think we will ever know the answer to that question, unless and until we find out the hard way that he was one of the wrong people. Look, you've been around a long time, and I've been around for-fucking-ever. We both know that if we get compromised, we'll swing in the wind, and Watkins will look the other way to save his ass."

"What a dick," Court mumbled, and drank down the hoppy beer.

"He's the dick who saved your life."

"Can you just stop saying that?"

"Helping you with perspective."

"Okay. Back to Nicaragua. How are we going to do this?"

"You'll fly to Costa Rica. We'll have something chartered and waiting for you in Tamarindo that you can fly yourself. The local station will leave kit on board for you."

"I'm going to fly myself into Nicaragua?"

"Yes."

"Under radar?" Court swallowed hard, and Hanley just waved a hand in the air.

"Costa Rica station does it all the time. We'll get you the routes and maps. Remind me . . . what's something you fly well?"

"I don't fly *anything* well. I'm not a great pilot."

"But you're good enough."

Court thought a moment. "Get me a Cessna, but something fast. A 210. Make sure it's a Turbo Centurion. Larger gas tank, more powerful engine."

Now Hanley held his hands up in the air. "It's Tamarindo, kid, not Oshkosh. I don't know what my options are down there, but I'll do my best."

"Tell me you've got someone to do this for you."

"Yeah, I do."

Court nodded. "You're the brains of the operation. I don't want you anywhere near the details."

"I think that's a dig, but I'll let it go," Matt said as he finished his beer, then pulled another from the insulated case.

Hanley's phone chirped. He looked at it for some time; he was reading a text, and then his eyes flashed back up to Court.

The men had worked together, off and on, for over a decade, so Court could read into them. "Nicaragua? It's happening?"

"It's happening," confirmed Hanley.

"When?"

"Tonight."

"*Tonight?* I don't even know what—"

"I'll continue briefing you when you're in the air. You'll have to hit the ground running. Extraction will be after midnight; we'll get you in position."

"What about weps?"

"You'll have what you need in Tamarindo."

Court was still thinking over what he'd learned. "If Costa Rica station is involved, who says they won't compromise me?"

"They know you are taking an aircraft into Nicaragua. They don't know the location of the meet with Caprice. Not yet, anyway. Look, there's no way to do this without some CIA involvement, because Managua station has to tell Caprice where to meet you."

"What can we do to minimize the threat of compromise?"

"She's told her handler she will leave the capital, run an SDR. We told her we would give her the location for the extraction one hour before she is supposed to get there. No sooner. We'll make Managua station the last-minute messenger boys for this, nothing more."

"Okay."

"You'll meet with a group of FORNATs that work with Managua station. Trusted guys. They'll back you up at the extraction point." FORNATs were foreign nationals, Nicaraguan agents loyal to the United States.

Loyal in theory, anyway.

Court sighed again. "Another potential compromise. Do I really need them?"

Hanley did not answer, so Court said, "What's the asset involved with?"

"It's a drug thing."

With furrowed eyebrows, the younger man said, "But she's run by the Agency. Not the DEA."

"Yeah . . . from what I understand, there might be Nicaraguan intelligence involvement in some transnational drug shipments."

"From where?"

Hanley held his hands up. "I don't know. Watkins was vague, our conversation was rushed."

Court rose. Mumbled, half to himself, half to Hanley. "Not as rushed as this fucking operation, apparently."

Hanley himself stood. "What's your chief concern?"

"A couple, actually. I don't know what I'm flying into down there. Plus, I'm a little worried about this government-wide intelligence compromise up here that you just mentioned."

"Job security for us, Six. If the DDO doesn't know who inside to trust, he'll look outside. Just go to Nicaragua, do what you do best, get back home, and we'll take it from there."

"You make it sound so easy." Nicaragua sounded like a shit sandwich, but like the older man had said, neither of them was in a position to say no to the deputy director of the CIA.

Hanley said, "I'll drive you to the airport."

Court turned towards the companionway stairs to the main deck. With the motion, the itch and burn in his right hip flared. He said, "Fuck that, Matt. I'm taking the bike."

TEN

Almost *nothing* happens on the streets of London without the authorities there knowing about it.

London has more cameras observing the citizenry than any city in the world, nearly one million by most estimations, and there was little that went unnoticed, but the man in the gray Donegal tweed herringbone cap leaning against the metal fence lining a path running through the middle of Cadogan Place Gardens, in the center of London's bustling Knightsbridge district, knew all this, and he behaved accordingly.

First, TfL, Transport for London, monitors the city's traffic and street cameras at CentreComm, formerly known as the Network Management Control Centre.

Second, the London Metropolitan Police Service piggybacks on the traffic cams and on certain private CCTV cameras, in addition to using their own security cameras, equipped with facial recognition and automatic plate number recognition technology.

The man in the cap knew it would be folly to spend his time in London actively trying to avoid all scrutiny, but still, he walked a circuitous pattern, had done so the past two days in this neighborhood, and now that he was in position here at the edge of the park, he had a pretty good idea where he could move, in any compass point, without having his face picked up by one of the eleven cameras he'd identified on the block.

Not that anyone was actively looking for him. He was a free man, unwanted, this he knew, but he was still careful with his countersurveillance measures.

He wore a raincoat; his hood was up but his beard was wet, and he seemed all but oblivious to the steady shower that had persisted since before ten a.m. It was just past eleven now, and he'd not moved from his position; he just stood there, his bones chilling in the cold rain, his eyes peering down Sloane Street at the traffic there.

He'd stayed in place so long that an incident response technician at the Met, an actual human being, had noticed him on one of his many monitors, and he'd zoomed in.

The name on the technician's screen had read Jon Jo Sheehan; his identity set off no alarm bells, so the incident response technician soon moved on, scanning other camera angles of other areas of Knightsbridge.

But the man under the tweed cap was not Jon Jo Sheehan; he was Campbell Coyle, and Campbell Coyle's history would have raised every single alarm bell in the United Kingdom if the tech at the Met knew the real identity of the man standing in the rain.

At 11:40 a.m. a silver Rolls-Royce Ghost appeared on Sloane Street and pulled to a stop in the middle of the road, right in front of Cadogan Place South Garden, its foliage mostly beaten back by the autumn, though a few persistent trees hung limp in the wet gray.

A large man in a gray suit climbed out of the front passenger seat, popped open a black umbrella, then opened the door behind him, and another big man, his suit dark blue, unfolded from the back passenger seat, then made a show of scanning the area as he himself opened an umbrella.

Both men were young, perhaps under thirty, and they had serious eyes as they looked around, but Coyle noted that they took no more than three or four seconds to scan all the real estate around them, and neither of them locked on him there, forty yards away inside in the garden.

The man in gray walked around and opened the other rear passenger door, and a smaller individual, a man in a blue pinstripe suit under a fashionable black raincoat, emerged and stepped into the street. The silver luxury car rumbled off, and the pair of security men converged on their protectee and ushered him towards the sidewalk that ran alongside the garden.

The man in the center was in his mid- to late thirties; he wore a short beard carefully manicured, a fade cut above both his ears and much longer hair on top, swept back and held in place with product that made his hair shine more than that of any passerby without an umbrella walking in the steady rain.

The man's suit was Savile Row, mostly hidden under his Cucinelli raincoat, and his cherry shoes shone with the luster the sun itself had no chance of mustering on this cold and rainy day.

The three entered the little park with the intent of crossing it to the other side; they walked along the pathway there, and Campbell Coyle pushed off the low metal fence and began walking towards them.

No one noticed him till he was ten paces away, but then it became clear to the two security men that the man in the Irish cap was moving towards their charge and he would reach them before they made it through the small exit gate of the garden. The security man in blue, the closer of the two, switched his umbrella from his right hand to his left, as if he had a gun on his right and was readying himself to access it, and the man on the right held out his free hand, urging the stranger to stop.

Before either of the two bodyguards could speak, Coyle himself called out to the man in the center.

"I beg your pardon, sir."

The security officer with his hand up, his face every bit as assertive-looking as his bodybuilder physique, did the talking. "'S'all right, mate. Keep moving, yeah?"

Coyle realized they thought he was a beggar.

In some fashion, he told himself, they were not wrong.

Coyle halted his advance at five paces, then addressed the man in the middle of the three. "Mr. Maragos, sir. I wonder if I could trouble you for just a moment of your time."

Marcus Maragos stopped, obviously surprised that the stranger knew his name, but one of his guards began ushering him on down the path, away from the man in the simple raincoat and the hood and the tweed cap.

Maragos gave an apologetic shrug towards Coyle, and with a smile, he said, "I'm afraid I'm quite late to lunch at my club. If you know who I am, you can make an appointment with my office." His accent was Greek, but he spoke the King's English with perfection.

"The Special Forces Club?" Coyle said. "Right up on the other side of the garden? Could I walk with you for a wee chat? Please, sir?"

The security officer with his right hand down, perhaps near a weapon, said, "You heard the man, make an appointment."

They passed it through the gate, onto the street, and Campbell Coyle followed along. Just as one of the guards was about to turn around and tell him to fuck off, the Northern Irishman lowered his hood; the rain pelted his craggy face and his thick beard.

"Charlie Coyle, Mr. Maragos. He was my son, sir. God keep his soul."

Maragos stopped suddenly, let out a little gasp, then put his hand over his heart. A car turned onto Sloane Street, and his two officers ushered him back onto the pavement, clearly aware that their boss wasn't going to move on his own.

Coyle moved with them.

Softly, Maragos said, "My God. Poor Charlie. So bloody unfortunate, that. You have my deepest condolences."

The Greek shrugged his security men away, and then he stepped forward to the older man, reached out his hand. Coyle took off his hat, a show of respect, and then he accepted Maragos's handshake. Maragos said, "I am *truly* so sorry for your loss. For all our losses. He was a wonderful lad. He served under me in the Legion for four years, but of course you know this."

"Yes, sir. I know."

Hastily, Maragos added, "I tried to go to the funeral, in that coastal village outside of Derry, I really did. But I wasn't allowed. His wife blames me." He looked into Coyle's eyes now. "Maybe you do, as well."

The older man with his hat in his hands shook his head earnestly. "Not at all, Mr. Maragos. Not at all."

With this, the Greek's hand went back to his heart. "That means everything. I was just devastated." He looked to his two underlings. "We all were."

Neither of the two security officers showed any evidence that they were, or ever had been, devastated.

Coyle fiddled with the Donegal cap a moment more. With a nervous tone in his voice, he said, "I'd . . . I'd just like to know what happened. Anything you could tell me. Maybe you could help me understand."

"Certainly." Maragos looked to his watch; Coyle recognized it as an Omega. "Of course. Look . . . I've got to run. But call my office. Tell Lucy I insisted that she fit you in at *your* convenience. She'll make it happen. We can have tea and I'll tell you all I know, which, I'll warn you now, isn't much." He shook his head. "Not much at all . . . though I can assure you he died doing what he loved, protecting people."

"Do you have children, Mr. Maragos?"

The question seemed to surprise the man. "Not yet. Someday, maybe. Look, again, I'm terribly sorry, but I must rush off for—"

"Certainly, sir. Just one more question."

The man tried to hide his annoyance now, and his security men were already taking him by the arm to force an ending to this conversation. Maragos said, "Yes?"

"Charlie . . . when you were in the Legion together. Or after, maybe. Did he ever mention me? Did he ever say anything to you about his da?"

Now the man appeared uncomfortable. After a time, he said, "Not that I recall. No . . . nothing I remember about you." He added, "I didn't see him much when he worked for me, but when we served together, that's been three years. Plus, we were in Africa most of the time. Mali and such. We were around one another, but in the Legion, there's not a lot of time for chat about family. I'm sorry."

Campbell Coyle saw no sense of deception on the man's face, and this gave him all the information that he'd come for today. "Very well. I should call your office, then?"

Maragos pulled out a business card and handed it over.

"Do, yeah. I've a trip to the Continent planned, but Lucy will fit you in. We'll chat about your boy. About my good friend. Again . . . so sorry, yeah? But I simply must run."

"I thank you for your time."

The men shook hands again. Coyle caught a quick glimpse of Maragos flashing angry eyes at his closest bodyguard; his annoyance that they'd allowed him to drag on this conversation was obvious, and as Campbell put his cap back on and shuffled off through the wet and gray day, the Northern Irishman knew without a doubt that he'd never get that meeting in Maragos's office that he'd just been promised.

No matter, he told himself. The meeting would still happen; it would just happen at a time and place of Coyle's choosing.

ELEVEN

The Toyota pickup turned off the broken two-lane road and began negotiating a washed-out dirt path that led up a gentle rise, scrubby jungle just visible in the moonlight on both sides, and the man in the passenger seat wiped a forearm across his face, trying to keep a measure of the sweat out of his eyes.

He succeeded, but then he caught a thick plume of hot dust in his face as it blew in from his open window.

The dust turned to mud on his forehead and cheek as he wiped again.

"This blows," he muttered, and then he glanced down to his watch, the tritium dial giving him the time.

Ninety degrees, high humidity, at 1:22 in the morning.

In December.

He had been all over the developing world, but this was his first visit to Nicaragua, and so far, he couldn't say he'd found much to recommend it.

In the driver's seat next to him, a younger man turned his way. In a thick Hispanic accent, he spoke in English. "This . . . blows?"

Court Gentry switched to Spanish. "Just an expression, amigo. All good."

The driver looked back out the windshield in time to negotiate a boulder jutting into the road. These were lowlands, vegetation all around, but the massive San Cristóbal Volcano was just a few klicks to the northeast, and volcanic rock lay all around.

Court wore a loose-fitting blue denim shirt and black jeans, his cross-training shoes were black, and he carried a Glock pistol on his hip, with three extra magazines in his pants pocket.

Behind him in the truck was an M4 rifle with an optic and a three-power magnifier, a backpack with extra rifle mags and medical gear, along with binoculars, a thermal imager, water, and a few other tools of his trade.

This was a light load-out for Court, but this was what had been left in the Cessna for him at the airstrip in Costa Rica, and the airstrip had been empty and dark; there was no one to bitch to about getting himself some more kit before this mission.

He looked over to the driver now. He'd read Juan Carlos's file on the flight down today. He'd been a local agent of the CIA for over ten years. An ex-soldier, he ran a team of three other men who helped Managua station down here from time to time.

Juan Carlos was a shooter; he had been deemed reliable by the local CIA station, along with his men, and Court hoped like hell the Agency was right about them, because they were his lifeline on this hastily thrown-together op.

Juan Carlos had a big G3 rifle in the backseat, next to a vest full of magazines and a cheap knapsack and a radio. His buddies were already at the location he and Court now raced to, and Juan Carlos had been in contact with them nearly constantly since he picked Court up from the dirt airstrip to the north of Chinandega a half hour earlier.

Court sighed again, and this time he spoke only to himself.

"What the fuck are we doing?"

He'd been rushed here, given little intel, and he was expected to execute an operation nonetheless.

Once he met up with Caprice, he'd determine if she had performed the duties necessary for her to be safely extracted, and then he would get the asset back to the dirt airstrip sixteen miles to the west, where he'd left his Cessna 210 single-engine aircraft at the end of a darkened and abandoned runway.

Court would pilot the aircraft out of here with the woman, leaving the four FORNAT shooters behind, and then he would head west, out over the Pacific Ocean.

From there he'd turn to a southerly heading and land one hour later in Tamarindo, Costa Rica, where CIA San Jose station would have further instructions for the asset, and Court would head to the international airport to board a private jet back to Virginia.

A lot could go wrong along the way, Court knew, and this, along with the dust and the heat, had him in his current foul mood.

JC looked his way again, however, and said, "Quince minutos." With this came a thumbs-up. *Fifteen minutes.* Court returned the gesture, then returned his eyes to the road.

Forty-five minutes later Court lay on his belly, swatting a mosquito on the side of his neck, probably for about the thirtieth time in the past half hour. He peered into the darkness ahead and wondered if he had time to take a piss before the asset showed up and the show began.

Ultimately, though, he decided to hold it.

His rifle was in the brush next to him, a water bottle next to that. In front of him sat a ramshackle brick roadside restaurant, closed for the night. Picnic tables ran along either side of the little shack, and a clothesline hung between a pair of minquartia trees, a few dishrags swaying in the faint breeze.

Cheap hammocks were strung near the tables, rocking gently back and forth.

A water-filled ditch ran alongside the property; a low metal fence with untreated timber posts separated it from the outdoor dining area. Corrugated metal that showed deep rust even in the darkness ran along the back of the restaurant, and firewood for the oven sat in tall piles.

Beyond the metal fence, a hill rose sharply in the direction of the distant volcano.

On this side of the restaurant, a gravel drive led from the dirt road to the front porch. A single black crew-cab pickup truck was parked there with its lights off, its tailgate backed up to the porch, and the grille facing the driveway and the road beyond, as if ready for a fast getaway.

A trio of redbrick hovels a couple hundred yards away, much higher on the steep hillside, had caught his attention the moment he'd arrived. There were no lights in any of the buildings, no vehicles around them, but they did not appear to be abandoned.

Hillside produce fields staked out around the buildings looked well tended.

He'd determined that someone was living in these homes, but so far, he hadn't seen any movement.

He and Juan Carlos had been lying in the scrub at the edge of the property here for only fifteen minutes, but the other three men who worked with Juan Carlos had been here over an hour already. Two sat in the truck facing the road, and the third had hidden himself behind a pile of firewood at the rear of the property, with a better view up the road that led to Chinandega, ten kilometers to the west.

Court couldn't see this man in the moonlight, but he had picked out his heat signature easily with the help of his infrared monocular, a military-grade Teledyne FLIR Scout Pro that was only seven and a half inches long and two and a half inches wide.

Both lenses of the device kept fogging up in the high humidity, even with the anti-fog spray he'd applied minutes earlier. He wiped off condensation and brought it to his eye.

Both to get a better understanding of the location and to take his mind off the fact that he had to pee, he scanned the FLIR up on the hillside once again, saw nothing but a few chickens scratching the dirt near the three dark buildings, and then he took his eye out of his device and listened.

A rooster crowed, bugs buzzed, and the sound of a poorly tuned bus engine rumbled far in the distance.

It was a calm scene, for the next few moments, anyway; the moonlight illuminated it all, and the noise of bugs in the air told him he and his team were low profile enough.

He examined the jungle on the other side of the clearing for heat signatures, and as he did so, Juan Carlos said, "We could have brought in the asset ourselves. Taken her over the border to the Ticas, in fact. We didn't need you coming all the way down here for—"

"Caprice demanded an American face at the pickup. No offense."

"Well . . . you *do* have an American face."

"Gracias."

"Not a compliment, my friend."

Court liked this guy. He brought the monocular back to his eye and scanned the dark buildings on the hill again. The houses bothered him, because they would make for a good overwatch for an enemy, but he tried telling himself he had nothing to worry about. This extraction location had just been disclosed a short time earlier. Anyone establishing overwatch would need time to get here, to get set up and in cover, and it didn't seem possible the Nicaraguans could have made this happen, even if there was some sort of an intelligence leak.

But just as he was about to put the monocular back down, his eyebrows furrowed as he noticed something he hadn't before.

Whispering, he spoke Spanish to the man lying next to him. "JC . . . that little wooden structure on the far side of building three. Behind the wire fence. What is that?"

He heard the man in the brush next to him bring his binos up to his eyes. After a moment, he said, "Looks like a chicken coop."

"Could it be a doghouse? A pen?"

After a moment, the Nicaraguan said, "Yeah. I think you're right. Most people, if they have coops, don't put them right by the house. That's gross. It's probably for a dog."

Court scanned some more. "Didn't hear a dog barking when we got here. Your boys hear a dog?"

The Nicaraguan made a call on his radio, received an answer. "No sign of dogs present on the hill."

To Juan Carlos, Court said, "There's like . . . no movement in that house up there at all. That look right to you?"

"Maybe the homeowners are out of town."

Court took his eyes out of his binos, turned to the agent. "Like . . . on vacation? South of France, maybe?"

Juan Carlos sighed at the sarcasm. "These are red bean fields all around here. Maybe they go sell their crops at the produce markets in Chinandega or Managua. Must have left their dogs with someone, or taken them along."

"Did your guys check the houses out?"

"I ordered them to stay out of sight when they got here. But they've been watching the windows. Curtains haven't moved. No vehicles." He looked to Court now. "We were given this location about ten minutes before your plane landed, we didn't have time."

"I know, amigo. We've all been handed a shit sandwich here."

Court saw that the curtains were either canvas or burlap or some other type of heavy fabric. His FLIR wouldn't be able to detect heat signatures inside the buildings.

He didn't like it, but he also knew these locals had been rushed into this op much the same as he had.

One of Juan Carlos's men called over the radio, letting them know a vehicle was approaching. Soon Court saw a dark blue Nissan Versa sedan without headlights on pulling off the road onto the drive, heading towards the restaurant.

The pickup facing it flashed its lights two times, and the Versa pulled to a stop ten yards away from it.

The Tacoma's truck lights turned on as the car door opened.

A woman in a gray tank top and dark pants stepped out, and she raised her hands over her head, her eyes squinting into the headlights.

Both Court and Juan Carlos looked her over through their binos, even though they were only twenty-five yards away from her.

Juan Carlos said, "That her?"

Court rose. "Cover me." He moved onto the restaurant grounds, past a few picnic tables, and came up on the left side of the woman, who was still facing the pickup.

He recognized the woman code-named Caprice, and he knew she spoke English, but still, he said, "Buenas noches."

She lurched in fear, not having heard him approach. Quickly, he said, "It's okay. I'm from the USA. Sent down to bring you in."

She turned to him, and he stepped up to her and frisked her quickly. Her body felt unbelievably tense. Muscles tight from head to toe, a slight quiver in her arms and hands, a rocking in her legs. When he was done, he waved to the pickup.

The headlights turned off.

In the darkness now, he said, "You sure you weren't followed?"

"No. I mean, yes, I'm sure."

"Tell me everything you did since you called your case officer last night."

"I took the bus from Managua, changed in León. Arrived in Chinandega this afternoon and rented a car. Went to a movie. Stopped at a restaurant, ate in my car, watching the road.

"I waited two hours, like I was instructed. No one passed. Then I came here."

"Good." Court scanned the road, the hill. "I'm to ask you why you think you are burned."

She said, "Fentanyl. It's coming into the airport in Managua. Direct from Shanghai. From here it's going north."

"From Shanghai?" Court said aloud. So, this had to do with China, not just Nicaragua. *But why isn't this a DEA op?* he wondered. He asked, "How do you know this?"

"I'm Nicaraguan police. Don't they tell you anything?"

He did know that much about her, at least.

"Keep talking."

She looked around nervously. "I conducted an investigation on a man working at the airport. He broke, told me everything. He's working with the Renazco gang . . . a local drug transport organization. He said they are getting the drugs with help from the MSS. That's Chinese intelligence, if you don't know."

Court knew, and now he thought he knew why the CIA was running this. "Did you encounter any Chinese nationals in Nicaragua during your investigation?"

"No, señor. Only Renazco. I don't think the Chinese are working in Nicaragua, but they are involved in sending the drugs from Shanghai."

She went on. "I tried to go to you guys . . . my case officer, I mean . . . Herman. You know Herman?"

Court did not know Herman, but he knew that her case officer worked out of the U.S. embassy in Managua.

"Sure, I do. Good ole Herman. Who do you think sent me?"

"Okay. Anyway, people came to my house. My neighbor told me. Said they were definitely Renazco's men, sicarios . . . I didn't go home. I called my boss, he told me DDI agents were there waiting to talk to me."

Dirección de Inteligencia, Court knew, was the Nicaraguan version of the CIA. Yep, it made perfect sense now why the Agency had taken the lead with Caprice. Chinese spooks working with Nica spooks to bring drugs into the Americas.

Caprice's stress was palpable. "I don't know if they know I'm working with you guys . . . but somebody sent fucking drug gang sicarios to my house, and then DDI shows up at my work! They are all together, and *they* know that *I* know. Why would they send sicarios after me if they didn't know I was working with—"

"Okay . . . calm down." Court was sold on her story. The intelligence she had was enough to get her extracted, and the danger she was in was more than enough to warrant getting her the fuck out of here right now. He said, "You're coming with me."

He had her by the arm and they began moving for the truck facing them; he waved a hand in the air, and the truck lurched forward.

On Court's left, Juan Carlos came out of the darkness, his weapon at his shoulder. Court said, "We'll take our truck. Tell your three to follow us and watch out—"

Juan Carlos's radio squawked, and a man spoke. Juan Carlos looked to Court. "Three vehicles approaching from the west. Moving fast."

"Shit." Court and Juan Carlos had parked their truck over three hundred yards away to the east, higher on the hill behind them and on a road that wound through the jungle, and then they had approached from there on foot. "We'll throw her in the bed of this truck and we'll get in with her."

Juan Carlos waved the Tacoma forward, and then the same voice as earlier broadcast again over the radio. Court assumed it was the man hiding on the other side of the restaurant behind the pile of firewood, because this man would have had the best view down the road.

"Pickup trucks. Men in the back. I see rifles."

The Tacoma skidded to a stop next to the Versa, Juan Carlos lowered the tailgate, and while he did this he asked, "How did they know we were here?"

Court began moving Caprice to the rear of the truck, but as he did so, he lowered his rifle, grabbed his FLIR from where it hung around his neck, and looked through it, pointing its objective lens at the buildings on the hillside two hundred meters away.

He did not know why he took the time to do this; he just had a feeling.

The optic immediately revealed what appeared to be a single heat signature in a window of one of the redbrick buildings.

A thick curtain had been moved, and a warm source was revealed inside the structure.

Before he could say a word, a bright flash flared out his optic.

The first heat signature, Court knew, had been a man hidden in the building, and the second heat signature, Court knew, had been the man firing a rifle.

A gunshot boomed in the night, the rear window of the Tacoma shattered just a few feet to his right, and a man screamed out.

TWELVE

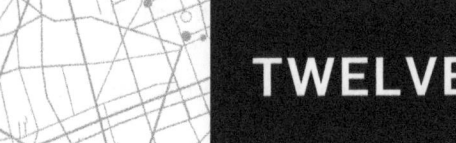

"Contacto!" Juan Carlos shouted, and then he and Court raised their rifles and aimed up the hill. Court flipped his magnifier up in front of his red dot sight, and this gave him a good sight picture at this distance, but he had no illumination to find a target.

Court quickly threw himself between the origin of incoming fire and the Nicaraguan agent Caprice, and an instant later, another flash of light from the building meant another bullet was coming their way.

It zinged again just to Court's right and slammed into the bed of the truck, ripping metal.

The American fired a half dozen rounds in quick succession at the origin of the muzzle flash on the hill. He paused just long enough to shout, "Get in the truck!" and then he fired ten more times, ripping into the building's windows.

When he took his eye out of his magnifier, he was surprised to find Juan Carlos and Caprice still right there with him. But when he chanced a look back over his shoulder, he saw why. The Tacoma wasn't there anymore; it was rolling slowly away down the drive.

The man behind the wheel lay slumped forward against the door. Court processed in less than a second that the first gunshot from the hillside had taken him out, and the shooter up there knew what the hell he was doing.

The passenger rolled out of the moving truck, pulled a handgun from under his arm, and began firing up the hill at the building, but another sniper round hit its mark, spinning the man around dead, leaving him face-first on the gravel, the top of his head a ruined mess of exposed bone, blood, and brain matter.

Court fired his rifle up the hill till it ran dry, and since he was still standing in the open with his agent, and the enemy had the high ground on one side and more enemy were fast approaching from the other, he dropped his weapon down on its sling, grabbed Caprice, and began running with her towards the ramshackle restaurant.

He called to Juan Carlos as he ran. "Come with me! Get your other man to stay in cover, tell him to move through the jungle and get our vehicle. Key is under the mat."

Juan Carlos relayed these commands into his walkie-talkie as he ran, while Court and Caprice raced along next to him. They made it to the restaurant door, where Court pulled his Glock pistol and fired a single round at the padlock.

It blew apart and he kicked the door in, and then they were inside the small shack, just as the first set of headlights swept across the windows.

The three trucks turned onto the driveway.

Another gunshot boomed on the hillside. Somehow the sniper up there was still alive, even though Court and JC had each fired a couple of full magazines in his direction.

While Court reloaded his rifle with another thirty-round magazine he grabbed from his pack, he turned to Caprice. "You can shoot?"

The woman looked terrified, but still, she nodded.

When he finished his reload, he handed her his pistol. "Sixteen rounds. No safety. Understand?"

"I understand." She took it, asked, "What are we going to do?"

Juan Carlos had been on the radio, but he turned to Court now. "Marco is not responding. I think they got him."

Horns began honking out front, and then men shouted, but Court couldn't understand their words. He had taken up a defensive position by a window, but he wasn't yet looking out.

"What are they saying?" he asked Caprice.

"Just . . . shouting. Bad words, mostly. I . . . They are hard to understand."

Court made a face of confusion. The guy on the hill had some serious discipline, some legitimate training. But the dozen dudes honking their horns and shouting curses on the driveway right in front of a building of armed enemy didn't sound like they had much discipline at all.

He pulled his phone out of his pocket, dialed a number on Signal.

The phone rang, and a man shouted out front; his words were in English, and they seemed odd, almost slurred. "Come out, pendejos! Nothing will happen if you come out!"

Other sounds came from the three trucks; Court thought he heard bouts of laughter.

That's fucking weird, he thought, considering the context of the moment.

Then his Signal call was answered on the other side by Matt Hanley. "Go ahead."

Court kept his voice calm but assertive enough to convey the gravity of the circumstances. "Extraction location has been compromised; enemy has opened fire. I have three agents down, one agent and the asset Caprice are with me, but enemy has the personnel to overrun at will. Possibly ten to twenty aggressors on our position at this time."

Hanley did not hesitate. "Notifying Managua station. They have assets in Chinandega and I'll get them rolling your way. Stand by."

Fuck, Court thought. Whatever CIA Managua station had on standby up here in Chinandega would not have been given a heads-up that he would be operating here tonight; it would have been terrible OPSEC to let anyone around here know in advance what was going on. That meant it would be a half hour, maybe more, until reinforcements would arrive, and Court had no idea how effective they would be once they did.

He looked to the two Nicaraguans in the tiny restaurant with him. "You guys have anyone you can call?"

Caprice shook her head. "In Managua, yes. But not up here."

JC shrugged. "Same here. I was told America would have everything under control."

"Well . . . I'm America . . . and for at least the next half hour, what you see is what you get.

"We're fucked," he muttered.

Laughing and shouting continued out in front of the restaurant.

Juan Carlos said, "Those voices out there don't sound like DDI."

Court had been thinking the same. "They aren't intelligence agents. They sound like they're drunk."

Caprice looked over the pistol in her trembling hand. "Renazco gang."

Court said, "Whoever is on the hill is something else, though."

Juan Carlos peeked out the window, then turned in the darkness and spoke to Caprice in English. "You must have been followed."

"No," Court said. "She wasn't. There was a sniper up in that building, probably a two-man team. I couldn't tell through the FLIR. Either way, they've definitely been in position since before your men arrived."

"But how?" the woman asked. "Herman just told me where to come one hour ago."

Both Nicaraguans looked his way. As the American put the phone back in his pocket, he addressed Juan Carlos. "This op was compromised before we gave Caprice the location. Before we gave *you* the location."

"What are you saying?"

"I'm saying we *all* got fucked. Either by Managua station . . . or someone in the USA." To himself he mumbled, "Another compromise." Neither of the other two could hear him.

Court said, "We have to fight these guys from here. We can't win, but we can try to stall for time. Caprice, you don't have a rifle. You go look for a back door, cover it with your pistol. Stay away from any windows, but shoot anybody that tries to come in."

Caprice rose, moved low between a couple of rough wooden tables, around a counter, and then disappeared into a back room that Court assumed to be the kitchen.

Just after she left, a massive volley of fire erupted from the front of the property. Court and his agent dove for the dirty floor of the restaurant, then crawled on hands and knees back behind the small wooden counter, desperate to put something between themselves and the thin walls of the structure.

The American could tell the sound of AK-47s, and he knew they fired a bigger bullet, albeit slower, than his own M4. His weapon was superior in accuracy, and in some types of penetration. Theirs, on the other hand, fired a far superior round for turning a little wooden shack into a pile of splinters.

After what sounded like a couple hundred rounds had been dumped in their direction, the gunfire subsided somewhat, and Court rose and began firing rapidly through the smoke and dust and debris at the light coming from gaping holes in the wall in front of him. He targeted moving shadows, men passing in front of the headlights of the three trucks parked there in front of the Versa and the Tacoma with the dead FORNAT agent inside.

He was banking on the fact that the guys shooting at him were undisciplined enough to where they were all pausing to reload at the same time, but very quickly fresh rounds of incoming fire tore into the restaurant. Glass shattered, simple light fixtures above him fell, and pieces of the ceiling crashed to the ground between the now-overturned tables.

It was just a couple of guys shooting; the rest were probably reloading, but they were executing mag dumps, so a lot of bullets continued pulverizing the ramshackle building.

Next to Court, Juan Carlos fired, as well, emptying his magazine first. He called for cover, then began kneeling back down so he could reload, and Court kept up his own fire until his rifle ran dry.

When it did so, he dropped back down low, reloaded again, and looked over to see Juan Carlos on the floor, blood pouring from his throat, his hands frantically trying to stanch a through-and-through wound that would not be survivable even if they were right next door to the best trauma hospital in all of Central America.

Juan Carlos would live a few seconds more, but that was it, and as harsh as it was to admit it, Court knew he didn't have time for lost causes.

"Fuck!" he shouted out in the dusty room. While more enemy fire raked the building, he hefted JC's rifle and crawled off through broken glass towards the back of the structure, hoping that he could, at least, do something to help save Caprice.

JC's legs kicked, his arms thrashed, but Court left him behind.

Seconds later, he'd moved through the kitchen, now up to a low crouch, and he moved up next to Caprice, who, despite his orders to stay away from the window, was in the process of peering outside. "Just us left," he said.

She nodded in the darkness. The shock on her face was obvious.

"Can you see out the back?" he asked.

"A little bit."

"Anybody moving around back there?"

"Not yet."

It was foolish for the drunk guys in the trucks to forget to surround the location, Court determined, but then he understood.

These were gang members, drunk, not trained soldiers. They wouldn't understand that although the men on the hillside might have had line of sight on the rear of the building, they wouldn't be able to target someone who made it all the way to the base of the hill.

Still, what the Renazco gang gave up in tactical acumen, they intended to make up for in sheer numbers and wild enthusiasm, so he knew he had to move now if he and the agent had a chance in hell of getting out of here.

"Okay," he said, "now that we're not returning fire out front, they'll surround us."

She said, "So we have to run!"

Court raised his own head quickly, then looked out the window. He dropped back down, putting his back to the wall, and she did the same. He said, "If we can make it to that low fence, get on the other side, we can move laterally all the way to the jungle. The sniper in the building above us won't have an angle on us anymore."

"Yeah, but we have to cover thirty meters to get to that fence."

Court reached into his bag and pulled out a pair of smoke grenades. "I want you holding on to my belt for the entire run. We get to that metal fence, we just roll over and fall on the other side."

"What's on the other side?"

"Whatever's there, I'll take it over a bullet in the chest."

"Bueno. Okay."

He opened the back door and stood to the side. Immediately the loud report of a sniper rifle boomed from the hillside. He tossed both grenades out, one farther than the other, and then he dove back into the room, just before another crack of the rifle one hundred meters away echoed, and the wooden wall next to the door, exactly where Court had been standing, splintered.

This sniper had determined in an instant where Court had been when he threw open the door.

Ideally, Court would have liked to give the smoke grenades a full thirty to forty-five seconds to spew the thick obscurant, but he was as worried about the drunk armed wild men at the front of the property as he was about the single weapon operated by the small sniper team at the back.

He counted to twenty in his head, then grabbed Caprice, and they rushed towards the door and into the growing cloud just beyond it.

Wild shooting inside the shack told him the gangsters were just behind them, so he raced out the door, halfway expecting to take a heavy round to the forehead.

There were different schools of thought on how to run through gunfire, even among tier-one-level operators. Some zigzagged, and some preferred the flat-out straight-line approach.

Court was normally a direct kind of guy, but he gave the shooter on the hillside credit for what he'd accomplished so far, and figured that without any new information about where Court and Caprice were, he'd just fire in a straight line along the shortest route to cover.

So Court zigged and zagged with the woman through the dense smoke as booming rifle rounds echoed; Caprice held him from behind and kept up well at first, but then she stumbled right after a shot echoed in the small yard behind the restaurant.

Court thought she'd been hit at first; he slowed and turned to help her, though he could not see her through the smoke, but immediately she crashed into him and he realized she remained on her feet and was still running forward.

The American adjusted, turned back, and ran alongside her, and soon the two of them made it to the rusty corrugated metal fence, only about four feet high.

He went over first, splashing into a low, fetid ditch on the other side; his rifle sling around his neck caught a fence post and hung him up there as Caprice splashed down just behind him.

He unfucked his sling; put the weapon behind him, over his shoulder;

covered the woman with his body for a second; then felt all over her. "Are you shot?"

"No!" she shouted, pushing his hands away. She fumbled with her own weapon; he could just make out her face, and he saw that she remained terrified but alert.

They had cover from the sniper, and some cover from the darkness and the red smoke still billowing from the two canisters at the rear of the restaurant, so they rose to a crouch and began racing, back in the direction of their truck.

Gunfire boomed behind them, but Court heard no rounds zipping overhead or impacting the flora nearby, so he figured the drunk gang of killers at the restaurant were just riddling Juan Carlos's dead body or firing at phantom targets in another direction.

The sniper rifle fell silent, and while this would have been excellent news while they were in the building, now Court found the silence disconcerting. He didn't know where the person or persons were on the hillside, and he was pushing nearly blindly through the thick jungle and did not want to run into them.

After fifteen minutes of slow movement through the foliage on the hillside in the direction of the pickup Court had stashed nearby, he and Caprice arrived at a washed-out road that led down the hill. He knew the truck was probably another forty or fifty meters on, parked along the main road, and somehow he hadn't passed this track when he and Juan Carlos infiltrated the area over an hour earlier. He knelt at the edge of the trees, brought his FLIR to his eye, and scanned to the left and right.

To the left, not more than twenty meters away, a soft glow in his optic told him something registering heat was there. It took a few seconds to focus on it, but when he did, he determined he was looking at a pickup truck, its warm engine cooling quickly, coming down to the temperature of the warm night. In another twenty minutes or so it wouldn't have even registered in his infrared scope.

But it wasn't *his* pickup, and there was no one around it.

A thought occurred to him, so he panned all the way to his right, back up the washed-out dirt road and up the hill. Caprice stirred next to him, but he put a hand on her arm to silence her, because he sensed immediate danger.

He stopped his pan when he found what he was looking for.

The heat signatures of two figures moving in the brush on the other side of the dirt track, struggling down the steep hill. They were picking their way along, not taking the road itself, presumably because they knew, or at least suspected, that squirters had made it out of the restaurant and might still be somewhere in the woods.

But Court noticed something off about the two of them, and for this reason he didn't feel the fear he would normally feel encountering a sniper team in the darkness.

Both figures appeared to be injured.

They were both male, and the man in front had a long rifle on his back and a pistol in his right hand, but the weapon was down at his waist, and his left hand clutched his right elbow. He wasn't exactly stumbling through the thick woods, but he seemed a lot more focused on the injury to his arm than on the way forward, and he leaned against trees from time to time as he passed them.

Just a few meters behind him, a second man had a short-barreled rifle of some sort, and it swung in his right hand, but the man limped, nearly dragging his left leg behind him.

Either Court or JC had hit both of these men while firing up the hill in the initial engagement. They were wounded, the spotter worse than the sniper, apparently.

It was clear to Court that this sniper team was not part of the drunk gangsters who'd arrived in trucks. Obviously both units were coordinating in some fashion, but Court suspected he was looking at Nicaraguan military or intelligence officers.

He didn't give a shit who they were; he was going to kill them.

It would take another thirty seconds for the pair to make it to the other side of the track from Court's position, and by then he knew he'd be able to see them, their silhouettes anyway, without the FLIR. He stowed the scope in his bag, then lifted his rifle and brought it to his shoulder.

Caprice leaned into his right ear. "What . . . what are you doing?"

"What do you think I'm doing? I'm dropping these two motherfuckers."

"No," she whispered, her voice tight and tense. "It will make noise. Those other men will know we're here. Just let them leave."

Court began aiming at the rear target. "We need their vehicle. It will save us another fifteen minutes of moving through the jungle."

"But these men . . . they are not Renazca. They are soldiers. Or else they are DDI. Either way, they are with the Nicaraguan government."

Court spoke as he sighted in on the first man. "They *were*, anyway."

"No," she whispered again. "Let them go. It will be easier that way."

Court ignored her and fixed his sights on the man in the back. He was the most badly injured, but his rifle could get up into the fight faster and cause more stress for Court than the sniper's handgun, so Court decided to drop him first.

Just as Caprice whispered "No" yet again, Court flipped the selector switch on the rifle from safe to semiauto and fired a single round, hitting the silhouette of the man fifteen meters away in the left temple. He rocketed sideways; gear flew out of his pack as he spun, then he slammed into the ground in the thick brush, but Court had moved his sight off him before the body stilled.

The second man spun towards the sound of the gunfire and swung his pistol up, held in the hand at the end of his injured arm, but Court had him dead to rights in an instant.

His rifle boomed again, one shot, and this man took it in the chest and dropped down into a sitting position, his back against a tree.

The American shot him again through the skull, rose, and ran out onto the dirt track. He covered the distance to the two men quickly and arrived to find the spotter lying still on his left side, facing away. The sniper, in contrast, was faceup, somehow still alive, struggling to pull his pistol from the ground on his right side with his left hand.

Court shot the man through the forehead, ending the man's struggle.

One more shot into the back of the spotter's neck as an insurance round, and then Court pulled out his tactical light.

He flashed the beam through the red lens briefly, and then the scene went dark again.

Slowly, he took a step back.

"Oh . . . shit."

The men were not Nicaraguan.

They were Asian. Quite likely, he determined, Chinese.

"Shit," he whispered again to himself.

Caprice stepped up next to him. He'd already turned off the light, so he flipped it back on for her to see.

"Ay dios mío." *Oh my God.*

Court said, "You said you hadn't seen any Chinese involved in this. Now you have."

While she stood there in silence, he stowed the flashlight again, took her by the arm, and hurried back to the road. If he'd had time he would have rummaged through their equipment, looking for the pickup keys, as well as pocket litter or any other evidence of just who they were. He would have photographed their faces for ID checks when he returned to the States.

But he did none of that.

Instead, he pulled her along and began running through the jungle.

"I thought you said we would take their truck."

"We're going back to mine."

She said, "But you only shot them so you could save time in getting a vehicle. That's what you said."

"Yeah, well, I changed my mind."

"Why?"

Court pushed on through the thick foliage, ignoring the woman behind him. He wasn't going to take the time to find their keys. He wanted to be as far away from those bodies as possible.

Whatever had happened tonight was bigger than Hanley had told him. He didn't think Hanley was lying; it was likely the former DDO just did not get all the information from the current DDO.

China was here, likely working with Nicaraguan intelligence and a Central American drug gang, and clearly involved in a kinetic operation to kill CIA assets.

And Court was still certain his operation had been compromised somehow by the CIA.

. . .

Thirty minutes later he bounced his Toyota down a two-lane road leading back in the direction of Chinandega and the airfield nearby.

Caprice had been quiet, but now she said, "You didn't have to shoot those men. You killed them in cold blood."

Actually, Court felt his blood boiling at the moment, but he didn't say that to the Nicaraguan police detective.

"It's a half-hour drive to the airfield," he said.

"So?"

"So maybe you don't talk so fucking much right now."

He could have argued with her, could have made the point that shooting those guys helped his mission, because as long as they were in the area with a vehicle, they could have been a threat to the two of them.

But he did not want to argue. The truth was, she was right. It had not been operationally necessary.

He'd done it out of rage. He'd done it because of the four FORNATs who worked for America who died tonight, and he'd done it because he felt weak for not being able to help them.

He couldn't save JC, but at least he could avenge him.

Court didn't regret what he'd done, but he knew he'd just created a much bigger incident than would have occurred if he'd only come down here to Nicaragua and killed some sicarios from a drug gang.

The fact that an American had come here, killed Chinese military or intel types, and gotten away with that information was going to make this entire event a much bigger deal.

The truck raced along in silence, in darkness, towards a quiet airfield in rural Nicaragua, and away from the death they'd left behind.

THIRTEEN

The Rolls-Royce Silver Ghost that had driven Greek security consultant Marcus Maragos through Knightsbridge earlier in the day pulled up in front of a row house on Colville Terrace in Notting Hill. The street was all but empty at one a.m., so when the two security officers, one in gray and the other in blue, climbed out, their scan of their surroundings was perfunctory at best.

Marcus himself climbed out wearing a leather jacket, a silk shirt, and cream-colored trousers, and then the girl he'd met just ninety minutes earlier at a nightclub off Portobello Road scooted out behind him, dressed in a heavy coat, her coal black hair long and straight, the black skin on her face glistening and shining under the electric lighting around her as if she moisturized it with baby oil.

In her heels she was taller than him, taller than one of his bodyguards even, and this helped to make it an odd grouping when the four of them climbed the steps to his house and the Silver Ghost rolled off.

The bodyguard in blue unlocked the door and led the others inside, and in seconds the door slammed shut, echoing in the narrow road.

Campbell Coyle had watched the entire scene unfold from behind the wheel of a blue work van parked across the street. When the automatic exterior motion light at the door flipped back off, he looked down to his watch.

The light ran for ninety seconds after it sensed the last of the motion at the front door, and Coyle noted this in a little pad he had rested on his knee.

It wasn't this particular camera he was curious about, but the fact that the lighting was set to factory standards on this device told him the same would likely be true on the others around the property.

The notepad in his lap already had hundreds of scribbles: drawings, license plate numbers, street names, descriptions of passersby. Literally pages of data he'd derived from sitting here for the past several hours.

He'd worked out the angles of each camera he spotted in the area, and he'd been around the back of the property earlier, and after that sojourn he'd sketched out a 360-degree diagram of the residence and those around it. He'd figured out what lay behind several of the windows on the property by looking at the vents, the chimneys, and the plumbing he could see, so he felt like he had a decent schematic of the inside of the property, as well.

The little courtyard in back was surrounded by a concrete wall and some vegetation; the motion light back there was the same brand and model as the one in front.

There were two signs on the edge of the property, as well, both giving the name of the security company the homeowner used, so from these he understood the locking mechanism on the doors; he knew how to defeat the alarm and get inside.

Campbell Coyle made his living primarily as a security alarm installer; his work involved protecting people who paid him to do so, but it also gave him the tools he needed to bypass and exploit systems, should the need ever arise.

He sat behind the wheel now, ate a dinner of cold rice and lamb he'd brought with him, washed it down with tea from an insulated mug, and then he waited, his eyes almost never leaving the home across the street.

Finally, at 2:20 a.m., he took one last sip of his tea, put the cup back on, and lifted his neck gaiter over his mouth and the lower part of his nose, all the way up to just below his eyes. He pulled the hood of his jacket over his head, then climbed out of his rented Ford. He headed first for the trunk, and here he retrieved a large satchel full of tools and other equipment.

Closing the back in perfect silence, he then began walking towards the home across the street, but not directly. Instead, he moved in a pattern that would ensure that his face wasn't picked up on any of the cameras.

The twenty-six-year-old French Senegalese woman with the tape over her mouth blinked out tears, clearing her vision, much to her immediate regret, because she now got a good look at the man who'd attacked her for the first time, and she saw that he held a bloody knife in his right hand.

Reflexively she screamed, but the tape over her mouth muffled her cries.

The woman had been in the bathroom minutes before, cleaning up, getting redressed. At the time she'd felt a twinge of regret, but it had been stifled by the bump of MDMA she'd done at the club and the bottle of champagne she'd drunk here in the Notting Hill home. The sex with the handsome Greek who called himself Marcus had been good, not great, and she'd initially planned on sleeping here for a few hours before leaving the charming and handsome playboy's home, but when he'd fallen sound asleep just after the act, she'd taken offense, then stormed into the bathroom, along the way snatching her dress from where it had been yanked off her an hour earlier.

After putting her dress back on, she stepped out of the brightly lit bathroom, more than ready to leave the flat of the man she'd only met tonight at the club. As she'd returned to the nearly impenetrable darkness of the bedroom, her attention had been locked on finding her stilettos, likely somewhere by the side of the bed, but after only a couple of steps in that direction, she'd stopped dead in her tracks, looked at the bed, and saw a naked Marcus, hog-tied, facing down, with a gag in his mouth.

Before she had the time she needed to process all this information and what it meant about her own predicament, she was grabbed from behind, a gloved hand covering her mouth. Then she was yanked across the room like a rag doll.

Her attacker was several inches shorter than the five-foot-eleven-inch model, but he moved her with incredible ease, and she knew her height would give her no advantage now.

She was forced into a seated position in a chair by a tiny table in the bedroom, and her mouth was taped shut; all the while, the person doing this to her was silent, efficient, and almost always positioned behind her.

For a moment she just sat there stunned, her eyes slammed shut, tears breaking through nevertheless, and then, when she blinked the wetness away, she looked up, focused quickly, and took in perhaps the most terrifying sight of all.

The man in the black hooded coat stood feet away in the near darkness, a long stainless steel knife in his hand. The blood on his knife was not hers, and it did not seem to have come from Marcus, because he was very much alive across the room, so she wondered if this man had done something to the two bodyguards whom she'd last seen downstairs.

It was so dark here in the bedroom, and his eyes were all but obscured by the hood, his mouth and nose completely hidden by a scarf.

His clothing was all black, save for the white latex gloves he wore, and his continued silence was, somehow, one of the most chilling parts of this whole ordeal.

Marcus thrashed about on the bed, but he was getting nowhere with it. Now that her eyes had adjusted to the dark somewhat, she saw that the attacker had put headphones over the Greek's ears, and electrician's tape over his eyes.

She watched while the man in the hood lifted her purse from the footstool at the end of the bed, rummaged through it, then walked over to a window to use the light there to examine her ID and then thumb through her credit cards.

She prayed he'd pocket all her cards and just leave.

But he stole nothing; he put everything back inside and looked her way.

Throughout this, the French Senegalese woman was not tied down, not taped up other than her mouth, but she did not consider for one second that she'd have a chance in hell if she tried to run.

The man in the hood moved back over to put her purse on the table next to where she sat, and then, finally, he spoke to her.

When he did, she realized now that the calm manner of his voice was even more chilling than his silence had been a few seconds earlier. The voice utterly belied the violence that he'd already committed. The violence that he still threatened by the knife in his hand.

"Gonna ask you a couple of questions, Aida. I don't need you to speak. Just give your head a wee nod or a wee shake, depending on your answer. Can you be a good girl and do that for me, love?"

He was Irish, so calm and self-assured, as if this was just any night in his life.

She nodded quickly.

"Two men on the ground floor. The man over there on the bed. Yourself. Myself. Have you seen *anyone* else here tonight?"

She shook her head.

He looked at her questioningly. "You're quite certain?"

She nodded again, and then her eyes narrowed, looked off in the distance a moment.

Fresh tears formed and fell.

The hooded man seemed to note the look on her face. He knelt down in front of her, pulled off the tape covering her mouth in one swift motion, and at first, she just gasped for air.

"Something occurred to you. What was it?" he asked.

Through a tremor of terror in her voice, she said, "A man drove us here in the Rolls. I don't know if the driver came into the house. I didn't see him again after we were dropped, but—"

The hooded man gave a little nod. "He did not come in. But I thank you for being thorough."

The young woman forced herself to look into his dark eyes. She said, "Sir . . . sir . . . please. I just met Marcus. I don't know him. I don't know what you want or who you—"

"Relax, love." He said it softly, and again, the calmness in his voice right now scared her, and she began sobbing more; she shut her eyes tight, and she was certain she was about to die.

After a moment, she felt a gentle hand on her forearm, covered in a latex glove. "Oi," he said, and she looked up at the man again. He held her purse out in front of him now, offering it to her.

She cocked her head slowly.

"Go home, dear."

She took the purse slowly, nodded even more slowly. "Thank you."

As she started to rise, he reached out, put his gloved hand back on her, this time, on her wrist. His voice lowered a little, but it was not a threatening tone. "If you go, Aida, and then the police come. Or if you go, Aida, and *anyone* comes. This time of night . . . I'm gonna have to figure it was you what sent them, yeah?"

His voice lowered more, and now there was more than a hint of menace. "Whoever you send . . . they won't get me. I'll get *them*, I'll get away . . . and I'll owe you a wee visit, won't I?"

Clutching her purse to her chest out of fear, she said, "I'll tell no one. I swear it."

"You have kind eyes. I believe you."

"You . . . you have kind eyes, too, sir."

"They are kind now," he said. "But if it should happen that I have to pay you that wee visit . . . you won't recognize these eyes, love. And you won't believe what the mind that sits just behind 'em is capable of thinkin' up."

Tears streamed down the woman's face, rolled onto her throat, continued into her cleavage. She tried to speak, but no words would come.

"Off you go, then, Aida Boucher." She knew he said her full name as a reminder that he could find her whenever he wanted.

She rose and headed for the stairs without a look back at either the man on the bed or the man standing there with the knife in his hand.

Campbell Coyle cut the man on the bed free of his ties, then ordered him to get dressed. The Greek did so, then followed Coyle's order to sit down in the chair the Black woman had just vacated.

Marcus Maragos had tried to speak a couple of times, but both times he was just shushed by the Irishman.

Once he was seated, Coyle stood above him and said, "Now . . . shall we talk?"

"Who the fuck are you?"

Coyle pulled down his hood, lowered the scarf covering his face. "I done told you once, chief. I'm Charlie Coyle's da."

Maragos's face registered astonishment. "The . . . You're the old man. From the street today."

"Apparently I'm not *too* old for what I've had to do tonight."

Maragos looked around the room, then at the bedroom door. "How the fuck did you get in here?"

"Your two men downstairs. They're dead. If you had ten men downstairs, they'd *all* be dead."

"How?"

Coyle did not answer.

The Greek flashed another look to the door, so Coyle reached into his jacket. He pulled out the Makarov pistol, the silencer already attached. "If you're thinking about doin' a runner, if you're thinking you're faster than me . . . you're likely not. But even if you are, I get a muzzle velocity of a thousand feet per second with this pistol, and I don't think you want to race a bullet, not after all the exertion you've already put yourself through tonight with that girl, yeah? She left you knackered enough, by the looks of it."

"What do you want from me? I told you I'd talk to you, all's you had to do was—"

"Make an appointment, yeh? Just call up Miss Lucy, and she'll work me right into your busy day?"

"That's right."

"Bollocks. I could see it in your eyes. No, sir. I'll be having my talk right now. I want to know about what happened to Charlie."

Maragos stopped looking at the door, his gaze turned inwards for a moment. He said, "That was terrible, what the American did to him." With a look up to Coyle, he said, "But why are you here? What are you blaming me for? It wasn't my fault what happened." Quickly, he added, "Wasn't Charlie's fault what happened, either. Not at all. It was the American's fault."

"Aye. And I'll be having a word with the American, won't I? Who was he?"

Maragos shook his head adamantly. "I don't know who he was."

"No matter. Next place I go after you, they'll know who he was. I'll get him sorted."

"Where . . . where are you . . ." Maragos stopped talking, looked at Coyle for a long moment.

He said, "Seriously, mate. Who are you? How did you get through alarms, get past cameras? How did you slot my security boys?"

"I've been around, is all. But I'm askin' the questions. Why did you send Charlie down to work for drug dealers in bloody Bulgaria?"

"That job in Bulgaria was a personal favor to him. I didn't want anything more to do with your son after the last few fuckups, but he made me give him one more chance."

"Whatcha mean by that?"

"I secured him a couple of shit gigs down there in the Balkans only after his first three protection jobs for me ended with his removal. Each time for the same reason."

Campbell Coyle looked out the window at the quiet Notting Hill neighborhood. Softly, he spoke. "Booze."

"Yes, booze is right.

"He got drunk in Belfast and was let go. He showed up to work hungover in Frankfurt and was sacked. And he got caught pocketing a handful of Crown Royal airplane bottles on a private jet in Canada, by the bloody protectee himself, no less, and as soon as they landed in Toronto, he was dismissed.

"You have any idea how embarrassing that was for me? The conversation I had to have? I sacked him then and there, but he did rehab, not for the first time, and he came to me and told me he had bills and he had put himself right. I told him the only job I could get him was down in Macedonia. A gambler needed a bodyguard. He took the job straightaway, did what was asked of him, but he got himself in a shoot-out during a robbery and he had to come home. He did good, saved his man, though he said his man wasn't much worth saving."

Coyle knew nothing about Charlie having been in Macedonia and having been in a shoot-out. But he didn't let on to this. Instead, he said, "And then?"

"He still had bills. I told him I could get him work in Bulgaria, but that was it."

"If he did right in Macedonia, why couldn't you have got him a better job after?"

"Because Charlie was still Charlie; he wasn't drinking, but he had a bad reputation, and I've a reputation to uphold."

Now Campbell Coyle's face hardened. He said, "You've got shite to uphold."

"I'm an important man, Mr. Coyle."

"I've met heaps of men like you. You're nothing."

"You know nothing about—"

Coyle sat down, leaned close to his bound prisoner. "I'll tell you what I know, because I've had time to look into you. You're a bloody fraud.

"That Rolls-Royce you run around in? It's twenty years old, poorly maintained, and you strong-armed it from a pal whose daddy left it to him.

"Your two bodyguards in suits? They were two years infantry, low-end grunts with no executive protection training. Not even that shit school you sent my Charlie to. They were yes-men lads, unarmed, untrained.

"They were just for show. I was going to spare them—I get no pleasure in killing cattle—but then one of them came at me with a steak knife and the other went for my legs.

"They died on the floor of your kitchen, poor blokes put in a no-win situation by Marcus Maragos, and that story sounds awfully bloody familiar to me. Does it to you?"

The Greek said nothing.

"You're not a member of the Special Forces Club here in London, but you tell your clients you are. Your primary residence is in Belfast, but you've let it out to rent this flat. You have lunch at Souvlaki Taverna, a little Greek place near the club, as you lobby for acceptance. You make your Zoom meetings in the car on the way, or on the street outside, being sure to show the neighborhood in the background to make it look like you're part of a society you haven't been accepted into.

"That Omega on your wrist. A Hong Kong knockoff. A good one. Five hundred pounds, maybe, but not the ten thousand you'd need for the real deal.

"You don't get good contracts, but you're trying to pass yourself off in Notting Hill society as a real player. To that end, you send every warm body you can out into the Third World, take any job, accept any risk for your employees, earn a couple dozen pounds a day commission from the worst of them, a thousand a day for the best of them.

"You don't run a private military corporation. You run a fucking livestock farm, and you send your cattle to the butcher to make your money."

"Wait a minute, Coyle. I run—"

Coyle kept talking. "My Charlie probably earned you enough for a decent dinner in Soho once a week, and for you to get that, you sent him off to his death.

"You pushed Charlie off on dangerous job after dangerous job, even though you knew more than most that his head wasn't right. He was doing everything in his power to get his mental health straightened out, but you were more interested in the commission from a fucking Bulgarian mobster.

"So don't tell me how much you loved my son. You did fuck-all for him when he needed you."

The Greek's fury raged across his face. "Yeah? And what did his father do for him? I've known that kid seven years but never even heard he *had* a father till you popped up on the street this afternoon."

"He didn't tell you about me because of what I used to do."

"What's that?" Maragos looked around. The answer slowly came to him. "Kill?"

"Aye." Coyle waited a beat, then said, "I'm going to say a word to you ... I want you to tell me if that word means anything to you at all."

"What is this? A game?"

Coyle shrugged. "Sure. It's just a game. You ready?"

The man in the chair said, "What's the word?"

"Whetstone."

Silence in the room other than a truck rumbling outside. Maragos's eyes went distant; he was thinking, and then they sharpened as something came to him.

After several seconds he spoke softly, "Ochi." *No.*

Campbell Coyle nodded solemnly.

"*You?* You are Whetstone?"

"Was once. Thinkin' might still be, yeah?"

"Charlie never said you—"

"Charlie did not know my code name. He knew I was an assassin for the Irish, for the Brits. He knew I became a killer for hire."

Maragos had lost all the anger from his face; all the fear, as well. He marveled. "You ... well ... your reputation precedes."

"Wait." Marcus seemed to think a moment, and then his face cleared. "There's something going on in America right now. They need men. Not typical security, but the very best operators. Willing to do hard jobs. No questions, no quarter. I've heard of it. I have no one in my stable I can send, not even someone with whom I can bid the contract. The work is now, they're scrambling, but not accepting anyone second-tier. But ... I'm thinking ... how about you? I reach out to the Americans and tell them I have Whetstone, one of the best killers for hire of the past generation ... I mean ... You're old. What? Sixty? Still ... *Whetstone*."

Coyle did not respond.

Maragos shrugged. "You've obviously still got the goods. If others know about your reputation, others can vouch for you, well then, I can connect you. You can make so much bloody money. We *both* can, mate."

"You made the last of your bloody money with my Charlie."

"You ... you need me to—"

Coyle rose, waved a hand in the air. "I didn't expect to get answers tonight. I only needed you to see if I can kill. I don't believe in revenge. I do, however, strongly believe in training. I was worried I didn't have what it takes, but standing right here in front of my next victim, it all feels very natural, very comfortable."

Coyle's lips twitched, a half-second smile, before they relaxed again. "All's right in my world, Marcus."

"Think about this offer. The job could pay you millions. Literally, millions. Nothing will bring Charlie back, and I didn't kill him, the American did."

"You *both* did, and you're both gonna pay."

"You're a talented man, Coyle. You're fucking crazy if you don't take this work I'm offering you."

The Irishman said, "I'm beginning to think I'm the most sane man on this planet, except for the decade I kept my head down and minded my manners like I was bloody mad. But those days are over, chief. Starting now."

He raised the long knife.

Maragos tried to stand, but Coyle just shoved him back down in the chair. The Greek said, "*Please*. Please. I saw how you let that girl go. I know you are a man with a heart."

"Her name was Aida. Did you not catch it?" Coyle sniffed. "I've a heart for a silly girl who met the wrong bloke on the wrong night. I've no heart for the man who sent my son off to his death."

Coyle swept the blade forward, an expert slash across the seated man's throat.

The screams from the man in the chair echoed out into the street, but only for an instant.

Then they were muffled by a hand covered in a medical glove.

And soon, after a deep plunge of the knife into the man's heart, slid expertly between the ribs, they ceased altogether.

A car pulled up out front and three young men leapt out, but by the time they made it upstairs, there was nothing for them to do but survey the horror show of blood and remains.

FOURTEEN

James Westwood's eyes opened in the darkened room; he reached for his phone on the bedside table and checked the time.

It was just moments before his five-thirty alarm was set to sound, so he turned it off, then opened his weather app to check the current conditions.

Thirty-four degrees, cloudy skies.

Next, he scrolled through a couple of websites, looking at news headlines, opened the *Washington Post* app and clicked on a tab that gave him the latest news in Latin America.

His eyes scanned the headlines, but he saw nothing of interest.

A quick review of X failed to show him what he was looking for, either, but he kept scrolling for nearly a minute before a message on his Signal app flashed on his phone.

J.W. sat up in bed; he was alone, as per usual, so he turned on a side lamp and spent the next two minutes crafting and then sending a reply to the text.

He rose for a trip to the bathroom, then dressed for his morning exercise, taking the weather into consideration. He slipped into his running shoes, then made his way downstairs in his Georgetown row house, where he gave a tired nod to Big Mike Scardino, who was already in from the carriage house, leaning against the kitchen counter, sipping coffee.

The Gauntlet operative wore a Gore-Tex base layer and warm-up pants, but his North Face hooded athletic coat hung over the back of a barstool, and this revealed the Smith and Wesson semiauto pistol in a shoulder holster under his left arm.

A pair of extra fifteen-round magazines hung under his other arm.

In a voice revealing that he was still in the process of waking up, Westwood said, "Wesley Heights Trail. Thirty minutes from now."

Scardino did not hide his look of surprise. "Uh-oh. You know why?"

"She didn't say. My guess is Nicaragua, but I didn't see anything in the news."

"Me, either. Not a lot of advance notice, but I can probably get Dunseth and Fields over to the meeting point, scope out the location before we arrive."

J.W. filled his water bottle from the dispenser on the refrigerator door. "No. It's fine. Even if she flexes her muscle, there's no need for us to do the same." He looked at Scardino's pistol hanging under his arm. "Lose the piece."

Scardino sighed, then unfastened his shoulder holster, took it off, and laid it, along with the pistol in it, on the kitchen counter.

Big Mike flung the remainder of his coffee into the sink, put the cup on the countertop, then donned his coat. "Let me grab my scanner and a couple of headlamps," he said, and he left Westwood there in the kitchen as he hurried back to the carriage house.

They left the home on Dent Place and jogged at a steady pace to the north, rising through the narrow streets of Georgetown. They did not encounter a single runner or biker out this early, but they passed a man walking a dog on 35th Street NW, and a small group of workers stood huddled in their coats at a bus stop on Wisconsin.

On Davis Place they picked up the pace a little, running in the middle of the empty road. They continued west, past the elementary school J.W. had sent his children to decades earlier, past the apartment building of one of Scardino's ex-girlfriends, and soon they approached Glover Archbold Park.

At the same time, both men reached to their foreheads, flipped on high-end headlamps, then jogged onto the Wesley Heights Trail that wound through the dense foliage of the park.

Scardino led the way now, his eyes alert, both for people here in the woods and for roots, stones, and railroad ties jutting up out of the ground that could have been a hazard, but they made good time, only slowing to navigate a couple of rocky streams, partly frozen over but shallow enough to be stepped through.

They went up and down hills, feet beating the winding unpaved surface that ran through the thick woods of the 185-acre park, and just as on the streets of Georgetown, they saw no runners out this early in weather this cold.

They had been alone for virtually the entirety of the twenty-five-minute run, but then lights appeared ahead of them, casting crazed shadows in all directions through the mostly leafless trees.

Mike Scardino spoke to J.W., jogging on his left. "Five, six sets. She brought the full gang."

"Yep," the former representative said as he slowed.

They walked down into a gully, navigated another rocky streambed, and climbed the dirt-and-mud track on the far side. Here, a massive felled log just to the side of the trail made a good place for J.W. to sit down, while Scardino remained standing, his eyes on the lights still coming from the west.

The lights converged on the two men, and then, one at a time, they were flipped off. Westwood and Scardino turned off their own headlamps, and in the low light of the predawn inside the dense trees, the men were able to make out the group around them.

Four men and two women, though it was tough to tell because they were all bundled in running gear that included neck gaiters that covered the lower part of their faces.

Some of the darkened figures fanned out on the path, climbing higher to have a better view of the area. Scardino noticed their backpacks, wondered if they were carrying submachine guns in them.

As for J.W., the sixty-year-old regarded the woman next to him in the dim light. Her hair was hidden under a knit cap, her face mostly covered by a wrap. She was short, maybe five-three.

He couldn't see much of her now, but he had met her before in other settings, and he knew she was in her early thirties, attractive, and of Asian descent.

All the others' faces were covered, as well, but Westwood didn't need to see their faces to know who they were. They, like the woman standing next to him, were Asian, young, fit. And they, also like the woman standing next to him, were not American citizens.

These were Chinese intelligence officers. Spies living here, among Americans, using false identities, operating away from the Chinese embassy, existing under the radar.

Westwood unzipped his jacket, took out his phone, and handed it over to one of them. Scardino gave up his device, as well, then pulled a radio frequency scanner out of his pocket, a small device with a retractable antenna on it, and held it away from his body as one of the men wanded both Americans with a handheld metal detector.

He repeated the movements, this time holding a radio frequency scanner, making doubly sure the Americans weren't recording the conversation that was soon to come.

Everyone here on the scene gave off the impression that this wasn't the first time for any of them.

When all the checks had been completed, the woman standing next to the felled tree looked to J.W. "Hello, James." Her English was perfect. To Scardino she said, "Michael."

Big Mike just nodded, but J.W. spoke. "Morning, Gracie. How's the run?"

She didn't answer the question; he'd never known her to engage in small talk, but he needled her with it just for fun. Instead, she said, "Thank you for the information yesterday."

J.W. replied, "I didn't see anything in the news yet. Does that mean nothing happened, or does that mean it was kept quiet?"

"Something happened. It will not remain quiet for long."

"Shit," J.W. said softly.

The woman he'd called Gracie said, "We heard from the Nicaraguan embassy at four thirty this morning. Your intelligence was vital and extremely useful. Unfortunately, however . . . our operation was not executed properly, and there were some unfortunate setbacks."

This was exactly what J.W. had spent most of the previous day worrying about. He sat down again on the fallen tree, put his head in his hands, and rubbed his eyes with his gloved hands. "Keep talking."

Gracie sat down next to him, then leaned forward to stretch her hamstrings, one at a time. "One man from the United States was sent down by the CIA. He linked up with local agents to assist with the extraction. Nicaraguan intelligence set a trap based on your intelligence. They used a group of local gangsters called the Renazco outfit. Heavily armed, but not terribly well trained."

"Never heard of them."

"If you watch the news out of Central America today, you might. Anyway, the American and his Nicaraguan agents killed many of the Renazco outfit, but nobody cares about any of them. It was the other two that are something of a problem."

"*What* other two?"

"A sniper team. MSS operatives." She held a beat, then said, "Chinese nationals."

Scardino was standing in front of the pair, and now he all but shouted in surprise. "Chinese intelligence was there?" Quieter, but with no less intensity, he added, "What the fuck were *they* doing at the scene?"

"They were there to kill the American and the asset, obviously. They didn't trust the Renazco people to do it on their own."

"Why not? It was just one American and some local agents."

Defensively, the woman said, "I don't know why not, but clearly there *was* cause to worry. The snipers' bodies were found near their vehicle a few hundred meters from the extraction site. It looks like they were ambushed by the American after they'd been wounded and were trying to get away."

Westwood wiped ice-cold perspiration from his face with his hand. "Shit. Any comebacks on what I'm doing?"

"As far as the Nicaraguans know, it was just a Chinese operation passed down to them. They have no knowledge that any of this intel came out of the USA. You and your operation are clean." She added, "Managua will just proclaim that its valiant anti-drug officers fell in the line of duty after being attacked by a group of Renazco men. It will all get swept under the rug as far as it being an international incident."

Scardino said, "Like Tunis."

She nodded. "Like Tunis. And like Addis Ababa. And Madrid. And the others." She glanced down at her watch. "Except the Americans didn't send a CIA officer on this job, likely because of what happened in the other places. They sent a contractor so they won't be tied to this publicly."

J.W. nodded at this. "Well, as long as the action is in the Third World, I guess it's going to stay quiet."

Gracie turned all her attention to Westwood now. "We have some concerns about that."

Scardino came closer, indicating to her that she needed to be addressing them both. She rose, J.W. rose, and they stood close together in the darkness. She said, "The American last night might have gotten close enough to the dead snipers to identify them as Chinese. Taking this into account, we have to move forward under the assumption that America will know my country is operating against them."

J.W. said, "What does that have to do with us?"

"A decision has been made in Beijing. You will need to speed up your schedule here. Significantly. Operation Marigold must begin in the next forty-eight hours."

Westwood kept his cool, but Big Mike said, "You've got to be kidding."

The woman hidden behind the neck gaiter stared him down, then said, "Kinetic operations. Coordinated assassinations of all the targets already given to you with their corresponding dossiers. Further targets to be added, if the situation warrants it."

J.W. looked worried, and the woman seemed to take note of this.

"You won't be connected to the American operations, just like you won't be connected to the operations that already happened internationally."

To this, he said, "So far, we've just passed on intelligence to you. But what you need us to do now . . . this is something else."

"It *is* something else. And you have already agreed to Marigold. We thought we had more time to prepare, to bring in resources, but what happened in Nicaragua, on top of the investigations underway in the U.S. intelligence community about the recent compromises, dictates that we act now. Don't forget, James," she said a little patronizingly, "our mission here, your mission here"—she turned to Scardino—"Gauntlet Group's mission here. It is all in furtherance of the same goal."

James Westwood looked off into the darkness, listening to the trickle of the little creek nearby. *The same goal?* His goal was winning that Senate seat; this woman's goal was something else entirely. He imagined Scardino was fuming inside right now, as well.

Still, this plan had been in place for weeks. The Chinese had over twenty people they needed permanently removed from the U.S. intelligence apparatus, and the two Americans in this clandestine meeting with Chinese intelligence had their own reasons for helping.

Scardino said, "We've been seeking tier-one assets across Europe for the operations. We have three in-country now and ready to go."

"The Belarusian known as Spiral? He is here, in the District, now?"

"Yes. Spiral is his Russian code name. American intelligence calls him Deep Space. They don't know who he is, but they will tie him to Russia quickly if he's captured or killed. And as far as he knows, he's working for American contractors tied to Russia. He's already working with his support team. Surveillance on his first target can begin as soon as you give us the green light."

"Then consider this meeting the green light."

Scardino nodded reluctantly.

Gracie said, "You have the Jordanian and the Italian here, as well? They can be operational within two days?"

"Yes," Big Mike said. "Their support teams have been established. But we still need two more assets. We won't be full strength and ready to go in two days."

"We can provide you with one."

"Who are you offering us?"

Gracie answered quickly. "The Havana negotiations have been successful. I only need you to send an aircraft, and you can retrieve the asset in Cuba."

Westwood looked to Scardino and said, "Excellent. That leaves one."

The smaller woman said, "Make it happen."

J.W. leaned forward. "I can't just make—"

Her dark eyes glowed at him, obvious even in the low light. "James, I would hate for you to be under the impression that you and Michael are in charge here."

Westwood bristled at this. This young Chinese woman was just a field agent of her service; she wasn't calling the shots, even though she was his point of contact here in America. He thought about reminding her of this, because clearly she was trying to assert dominance that did not really exist.

But he'd been in and around government a long time. He knew when to posture, and he knew when to kneel. He said, "I am in service of the cause, Gracie."

"Good. Most important is that you obtain the final asset and have him here in D.C. ready for immediate assignment. He will need to be fast and efficient."

Scardino began to say something, but J.W. held up his hand. "We'll find someone. Don't worry."

"Good," Gracie said, and with a nod, the two Americans' phones were returned to them. Without another word, Gracie turned away and ran off to the east, her team of security officers flanking her as she did so.

J.W. watched her until she disappeared on the darkened path, and then Scardino stepped up next to him.

"Call Hasan," Westwood said. "Have him pick us up over on Foxhall Road and take us directly to the office."

"What's the plan?"

"I am going to work on getting one more top-tier foreign agent into the country, and you are going down to Cuba."

The two men began jogging off to the west.

The woman running in the group to the east out of the Wesley Heights Trail had lived in America for nine years, and in all that time, she had worked tirelessly on her accent.

Originally from Hong Kong, she had grown up speaking both English and Mandarin, but there was something about the American accent that made it exceptionally difficult to master, and she often felt as if she were playing a character in a movie when she tried to pull it off.

Her identity to the American James Westwood and his chief of operations Michael Scardino was Gracie Wu, and her cover here in the United States was that she was a research assistant professor of economics at American University, living and working at the sprawling ninety-acre campus just a half mile from where she now ran. But her real name was Gao YuanYuan, and Gao had been an agent of the Chinese Ministry of State Security for eleven years, joining just weeks after her twenty-first birthday.

All the others running along with her on the Wesley Heights Trail were students at universities here in the city: George Washington, American, Gallaudet, and Georgetown. They were also all MSS operatives.

Gracie herself worked out of a safe house in Bethesda, Maryland; she was protected by as many as ten of these agents who lived with or close to her, and she communicated nightly with Yidongyuan, the Ministry of State Security building in Beijing, using a proprietary commo app developed by the Chinese and then infiltrated into the United States for their operatives via computers that, even upon close inspection at the border or by the FBI, appeared to be completely off-the-shelf Alienware gaming laptops.

Gracie ran a human intelligence or HUMINT mission for the MSS by necessity, because *someone* had to communicate with assets such as J.W. Westwood, and there weren't one twentieth of the Chinese-born spies like her in America that there had been a decade ago.

Chinese intelligence had changed its business model in the past several years, after a multitude of high-profile roll-ups here in the United States. So many of their human intelligence operations in America had been shut down by the FBI, their agents arrested, imprisoned, or deported, that the MSS had taken to developing a new strategy. Yes, they were the best in the world when it came to cyber intelligence. And yes, their network of Chinese citizens and permanent residents in the United States provided a steady stream of intelligence about a great many things back to Beijing.

But for the most difficult operations on American soil, the Chinese had learned to employ Americans or other Westerners.

These were the Chinese "cleanskins" in America. People working for China who had no known ties to the nation.

And J.W. Westwood was one of their best and brightest.

They'd gotten to him originally in Singapore, when he was an ambassador there, bitter because he felt the posting was miles beneath his talents and status. He'd wanted to be CIA director, director of national security, or even secretary of state at the time, but instead, the president, an old family friend, had shipped him off to Asia for a mostly ceremonial role.

The Chinese got wind of J.W.'s resentment at the time and identified him as someone who was highly motivated by a personal desire for advancement, status, and power.

And they decided to make their move. The approach by the Chinese security services had been mild at first, deniable by both parties. But then, over time, Ambassador Westwood had shown himself to be receptive to their courting.

The president he considered his best hope of positioning him for a great leap upwards had turned his back on him; the new president barely knew his name, and Westwood recognized that China was now his best hope.

He met with trade delegations from Beijing, was wined and dined by them, even had them over to his ambassador's residence to discuss the opening of a cultural center in Singapore that would highlight the confluence of Western and Eastern art, and then, when he had key people in portions of the residence where he knew no one was listening, the Chinese began making their pitch.

By the time he returned to the United States two years later to run an innocuous-sounding think tank that was, in actuality, a worldwide Chinese front operation, he was in Beijing's pocket. They had money and influence, and he had a desire to become a senator.

Even president someday.

J.W. was an important asset as the leader of a D.C-area think tank that courted high-level elected government officials, to be sure, but he would be even more helpful to the Chinese as an American senator, quietly and deftly helping their interests in return for their political cyber support, financial support, and even physical support against his enemies.

Gauntlet Group Incorporated had, for its own reasons, signed on to support China in this operation, and senior company operative Mike

Scardino had been sent by the home office to run the mission closely with J.W., the American face of Chinese interests in Washington.

Gracie doubted that Westwood and Scardino would have any idea how many cleanskins there were like them, already operating in government and industry around D.C., and they would never know.

Gracie herself did not know. She ran Westwood and Scardino, as well as a couple of sitting congressmen, a half dozen influential lobbyists, and several hotel managers around the city who provided her information about comings and goings.

China, as always, played the long game. They cultivated these assets for one reason, one mission.

Someday, China would take Taiwan. It would be vicious and brutal, and Beijing knew the optics around the world would be bad.

The only reason they had not already invaded Taiwan was the assumed reaction of the West. Not so much the military response China expected out of them; there was little the West could do in the Taiwan Strait to stop China from attacking and winning. Even less they could do to fight China off the island after the fact.

But the diplomatic response would be savage. Sanctions, expulsions, dissolutions of international partnerships and business dealings.

Trade deals would evaporate, and China's strength on the world stage would be eviscerated.

This had been the sole impediment to China reclaiming Taiwan.

But if Beijing had enough intelligence about the West and they had enough agents in positions of power in the West, the response to the attack to come would be blunted, perhaps significantly so. A few sanctions, some full-throated but toothless whining in the UN and the G7, and a few years of annoying but ultimately anemic bad press.

This China was prepared to absorb in order to reclaim the island they had been coveting since it broke away in 1949.

Therefore, people like Gracie Wu were sent out to keep the connections with the cleanskins working in the West, to execute operations beneficial to China's long-term interests.

But nothing had ever happened in America like what was now less than forty-eight hours away.

Operation Wanshou Ju. *Marigold.*

Obviously assassinating nearly two dozen American officials would have started a war under normal circumstances, but the Chinese had a plan to false-flag Russia for the killings. A Russian assassination network was in the United States now; China knew about them, but the Americans did not. The Russians had not done anything of importance yet, and they never would, because China had decided to use them for their own aims.

China planned to conduct its own assassination campaign against the U.S. intelligence community, leave cyber breadcrumbs for investigators that would lead back to the hapless Russians now living in Brooklyn, New York, and then use Gauntlet security officers to eliminate the Russians before authorities could detain them and realize they had nothing to do with the massacre across the U.S. intelligence community.

It was an audacious plan, but the plan could not wait any longer, because China's greatest intelligence asset in the U.S. government was at risk of being discovered.

The Nicaraguan operation had been unrelated to Marigold, but it could easily put the Chinese spies in the American government in peril. Time was short, so Marigold had to happen now if it was to happen at all.

Gracie Wu didn't know how or why Westwood and Scardino came to be working for Chinese interests, but for now, Westwood and Scardino were merely cogs in a machine that Gracie herself was a cog in.

Westwood had been receiving intelligence from someone at the Office of the Director of National Intelligence and passing it to the Chinese, and the Chinese had been using this intelligence around the world to further Chinese aims.

Now the intelligence would be used right here in Washington.

The young Chinese woman ran on through the darkness, her bodyguards all around her, armed and prepared to fight and even die for her to keep her safe, to keep her on her mission.

Her mission was to weaken America, to strengthen China, and to make certain no one in America knew that China was involved at all.

FIFTEEN

Matthew Hanley flew to D.C. from Norfolk on the first commercial flight of the day, arriving at 6:49 a.m. carrying nothing but his coat and a leather shoulder bag.

Once he stepped out of Reagan National Airport, he slid his coat on over his blue blazer and pulled a tie from the front pocket of his trousers. He'd pre-tied it on the plane, planned on just putting it under his collar and tightening it upon his arrival here, but before he got it over his thick neck, three SUVs stopped directly in front of him. The back door of the Lincoln Navigator in the center of the trio opened, while the two Chevy Suburbans rumbled, one in front of the Nav, the other just behind.

Just a couple of years earlier, Hanley himself would have been in that Navigator or one like it, but now he hurriedly shoved his tie back into his pocket and climbed inside, a guest in the vehicle.

There in the backseat waiting on him were one man and one woman. William "Trey" Watkins, deputy director for operations of the Central Intelligence Agency, and Angela Lacy, a senior operations officer in the CIA who worked closely on special projects for the DDO.

Hanley looked back and forth between the two of them, then out the window at the light snow falling in the predawn on this early December morning.

The vehicle rolled away from the arrivals lane, heading towards the exit to the airport; the other two SUVs maintained their positions in front of and behind it. Matt Hanley just sat there a moment waiting for someone to speak. When no one did, he addressed DDO Watkins. "When you set me up as an off-book shop, you made it pretty clear that you and I would not be meeting in person."

"And yet here we are," Watkins replied gruffly. "That give you any kind of a tip-off to how much shit is coming your way this morning?"

After another protracted silence, Hanley quipped, "If you guys are bundling me off to a black site, I might have overdressed."

Lacy looked uncomfortable. Watkins just looked pissed.

Watkins said, "We are debriefing Caprice right now at the embassy in San Jose. She's surprisingly uninjured, considering the carnage that took place just a few hours ago. When does Violator get back?"

"He's in the air, in U.S. airspace but a few hours from touchdown. I haven't seen him, but I texted with him briefly on Signal, just after he dropped Caprice at the embassy. I'll talk with him on Signal this afternoon, meet with him tomorrow."

The DDO rubbed his face now. "That whole fucking thing went to hell down there, didn't it? Just like multiple other intelligence community ops in the past two months."

Hanley just said, "My guy did *not* fuck up in Nicaragua."

"Caprice said he killed two MSS officers who were not posing an immediate threat. That's one hell of an international incident, in my book."

"He didn't know they were MSS."

"And if he didn't fucking shoot them dead while hiding in the jungle, he never *would* have known. The Chinese could have denied involvement, we could have denied knowing this was a Chinese operation, and life could have continued on without a shooting war between the CIA and the Ministry of State Security."

"C'mon, Trey, this isn't going to start a shoot—"

"You don't know what this is going to do!" Watkins shouted back.

Hanley sighed. "I spent ten years in Special Forces, I ran the Agency's Special Activities Division. Then I was DDO, same as you. But I wasn't there, in Nicaragua, so I'm not going to second-guess my agent."

He continued. "You, Trey, on the other hand, spent zero seconds doing *anything* operational—for the military, for the Agency, for the local police of wherever the hell you grew up—and you weren't there in Nicaragua last night, either. Nevertheless, here you are, trying to second-guess Violator and his actions.

"I don't get to make the call on whether or not he fucked up, and neither do you."

Watkins took a few slow breaths, obviously to calm himself down. "I'm not here to dress you or your man down for Nicaragua. I'm not going to think about Nicaragua again."

"Well, *someone* clearly leaked that extraction plan, so you *better* be thinking about Nicaragua."

"I know someone leaked it. Someone up here. Managua station isn't the problem. Langley is. *That* is my focus."

Hanley said, "You know, for sure, that the compromise came from inside the house?"

Lacy answered this. "It's been happening for the last nearly three months. Ops have been blown that couldn't have been blown at the sharp edge; they were blown in Washington. We don't know where or how."

Watkins added, "The problem is, the FBI is making the same claim. State is making the same claim. JSOC had a cell blown a couple weeks ago in Nigeria. Delta Force had to slip out of their safe house just minutes before it was raided by a company of government troops. Nobody outside of JSOC knew where that safe house was."

Hanley thought a moment. "If everyone in the IC is getting hit, then that sounds like an executive branch compromise of some sort. Somebody that's privy to that diverse a set of intelligence."

Watkins said, "Thought of that, of course, but the granularity doesn't lend itself to an executive branch leak. Code words, frequencies, logistics. Our enemies seem to have just what they need, just when they need it."

"And by 'enemies,' you mean the Chinese?"

Watkins shook his head. "No. Last night, two Chinese got smoked by your boy. But we don't know the leak went through China. Could have gone through Nicaragua. In Tunis, there was no hint of Chinese involvement; ditto Addis Ababa. I mean, yeah, China is active in Africa, Central America, pretty much everywhere, but other than the two shooters Violator killed last night, we can't say the Chinese are directly involved in the intelligence leak."

Hanley thought about it a moment. "The ODNI would have knowledge of all operations and might have a more detailed understanding of how they would be carried out."

To this, Lacy said, "One of our working theories is this might be someone at the Office of the Director of National Intelligence. So far, the DNI herself has started an investigation, but she hasn't found any interrelation to the compromises."

"If there is no interrelation to the compromises, then maybe you are looking at multiple compromises."

"And if I'm looking at multiple compromises popping up around the same time," Watkins said, "I am not inclined to see this as a coincidence. It's some player with the ability to cause leaks all across the intelligence community."

Hanley sat up straighter. "You're talking about someone high up the food chain in the American IC passing this intelligence."

"That's the worst-case scenario. It's also starting to look more and more plausible."

Lacy said, "What do you think, Matt?"

He considered this a moment. "Who knew the location of the extraction in Nicaragua last night?"

"Almost no one."

"Almost no one in the IC means fifty, one hundred people."

Watkins shrugged. "It's a bureaucracy. What are you going to do?"

"You need a list. You need to not rule anyone out. You need to investigate this."

Watkins said, "So now I'll circle back to the beginning of this conversation. I don't trust anyone I work with."

"The director of the CIA included?"

"I've discussed this with Director Phillips, of course. He just told me to figure out what the problem was and to tie it off. He doesn't understand the magnitude; he just doesn't want the fallout to affect him."

"Yeah, well, the fallout almost cost Violator his life."

After a pause and a look from Lacy, Watkins said, "I do have concerns about Gauntlet Group. They are everywhere in the IC these days. They aren't supposed to be seeing anything that would have caused these operations to go off the rails like they did, but if you want to talk about commonalities, every single one of the seventeen departments in the IC has Gauntlet contractors doing some work with them. Security, IT, transpo, comms, hardware, whatever. This is new, and this is a problem."

"Gauntlet employees are vetted," Hanley countered.

"Once upon a time, Matt, Denny Carmichael was vetted."

Denny Carmichael had been a former deputy director for operations of the CIA, and he'd been dirty. Hanley himself had been involved in bringing him down.

After a moment, Hanley said, "I get your point."

Watkins said, "I am going to use you and your assets to find where the problem lies, and I'm going to use you and your assets to put an end to this . . . whatever it is."

"Okay," Hanley said, but his voice sounded dubious. He cocked his head as something occurred to him. "What *aren't* you guys telling me?"

Angela asked, "What do you mean?"

To Watkins, Matt said, "You stood me and my team up as an off-book program right around the time this shit started happening. That makes me wonder if you knew this was coming somehow, or if you were setting me and my men up to take the fall for it."

Watkins barked an angry laugh. "A setup? You don't think I'd swing by the neck, same as you, if I was caught setting you up in an off-book program?"

"But . . . but you knew it was coming. You knew there was some sort of compromise of U.S. intelligence, and that's why you needed a small group you could trust, a small group you could run outside the infrastructure."

Watkins shrugged now. "There have been signs that I was losing hold of secrets, that there was a leak somewhere in the U.S. intelligence community. And then there were signs that the leak was bigger than my building."

Watkins took a long breath. "Know this, Matt. I can do a lot to protect you. But I can't protect your assets. They kick in a door in D.C. and put a bullet into a U.S. citizen's brain, and then they get caught by the cops . . . there's not a damn thing I can do for them."

"My guys understand. They'll do their jobs. But frankly, Trey, if I were you, I'd be more worried about the cesspool of D.C. sucking you in than I'd be worried about Violator or Hightower or anybody else on my team getting caught by five-oh."

"Believe me, I am," Watkins said, and then he asked, "What resources do you need to help me?"

"Jim Pace." Pace was a former CIA Special Activities Division paramilitary officer who had moved into a role at the Agency as a case officer. Hanley had worked with the man for years, and he understood his worth.

"What about him?" Watkins asked.

"He's proven himself as an investigator. Have him looking into this, give him carte blanche, tell him to report to Lacy here." Hanley continued, "You know about us, Angela Lacy knows about us. Pace can know about us; I don't want anyone else involved. Lacy can talk to me."

Trey Watkins said, "Agreed. Angela will be your cutout to Jim Pace and his investigation. How soon till Hightower is back with you and ready?"

"He won't be operational for another week, but I'll get him back here and brief him when I brief the other assets tomorrow. I don't need him to run and gun, just to sit and listen."

"Good. I'll get Pace working on this exclusively, and we'll keep you informed via Lacy. Brief your boys about what might be coming down the pike, because I have a funny feeling that when we identify whoever or whatever is compromising our operations, we're going to find a bad actor right here in America, and I am not going to get the FBI involved."

Watkins added. "We'll deal with it ourselves. I'll have you and your boys kill the son of a bitch, whoever it turns out to be."

Matt smiled a little, gave a nod. "Spoken like a man who's finally seen the light."

"I've seen the dark, Matt."

"Same thing."

Five minutes later the Navigator pulled up to the departures lane at Reagan National Airport. Hanley got out and headed inside, ready to get on his 8:20 a.m. return flight to Norfolk. He had to get his team together quickly, and he had to keep them as far away from the real apparatus of the U.S. intelligence community as possible.

Last night Gentry barely had any dealings with the CIA; he'd only been connected to the Agency via the physical extraction of the agent.

But that small connection to the IC had nearly cost him his life.

Hanley told himself he'd stay away from everyone and everything in the community other than Lacy and Watkins, and he'd let Jim Pace figure out where the leak was coming from.

And then Hanley and his men would go and plug it.

When your only tool is a hammer, then every problem looks like a nail.

Hanley's only tool was a couple of assassins.

He would plug the leak by killing the leaker, whoever that turned out to be.

SIXTEEN

Fifteen-year-old Andie Delaney walked the brimful macchiato from the espresso machine to the register, still a little slower than many of the other employees here at Cara's Bakehouse, because this was only her second week on the job.

Andie's mom's best friend owned the place, and she'd been hired for shifts after school and on the weekends. It was tough work at first—this was her first job, after all—but she'd become more comfortable with her duties by the day, even though there were still stressful moments, especially on the weekends, as throngs of locals and tourists ventured in to recharge on coffee here in the attractive Noble Park neighborhood of Boulder, Colorado.

Andie lived just a few blocks away with her mom and her stepdad, both of whom she loved, and her eleven-year-old half sister, whom she occasionally tolerated.

Andie was a bright girl but only a fair student; she had trouble focusing on subjects that didn't interest her. Her true love wasn't academics, it was sports, and she found school so much less interesting than the nearby mountains, especially during the winter. A competitive snowboarder, she'd achieved a national ranking in her age group in both the halfpipe and slopestyle disciplines.

She dreamed of landing a sponsor and even competing in the Olympics someday, and this job here at Cara's would, over time, earn her some money to spend on training and gear.

She also enjoyed the comradery with the rest of the staff here, the sense of responsibility that came along with her first job, and she especially enjoyed meeting people.

Andie Delaney was anything but shy.

She was five-five, pretty, soft-featured, and bright-eyed, and she wore oversized jeans and a black XL Cara's Bakehouse sweatshirt under her apron. She kept her short brown hair back in a ponytail for work today, but more often than not, she kept her hair tucked in a red beanie.

Andie made it to the counter, where she carefully handed the macchiato to a woman who thanked her and headed off to grab some sugar and a spoon, and then she stepped back to the iPad register, spun it back to her, and looked up to see the door open and another patron step in from the sunny but cold afternoon.

He was a regular, at least as far as she could tell as a new employee, and she thought she'd seen him virtually every day she'd worked for the past week.

The man was tall, old—from her perspective, anyway—with short blond and graying hair shaved into dramatic sideburns, a slightly darker beard groomed into a point, and a mustache flecked with even more gray. He wore a thick Carhartt jacket, roper boots, and jeans, and Andie took him as some sort of a cowboy.

He walked towards the counter with a slight limp, locked eyes with her, and gave her a smile.

"Welcome to Cara's. How can I help you?" she asked, although she already knew the answer to this question. Coffee, large, three sugars, and a cheese Danish. She didn't know a lot of people's regular orders by heart, but this big cowboy was such a frequent visitor she had his down.

The big man continued smiling at her, the wrinkles around his eyes deepening. "I bet you can guess."

Andie smiled a little herself. "Coffee, large, three sugars. And a cheese Danish."

The man continued smiling as he spoke. "You got me all figured out."

She nodded as she looked down to the screen to ring him up. "As long as you don't change it, I'll remember."

"I never change. You work every day, don't you?"

She looked back up. "You've got *me* all figured out."

The man grinned, a toothy smile made even brighter surrounded by his beard.

Andie said, "Just about every day. I'm new, but we're short-staffed."

"Must be tough."

"Nah, I like it. Eleven sixty, please."

The man pulled a twenty out of his wallet and handed it to her. As she began making change, he said, "If you don't mind my saying, you look pretty young to be holding down a job."

Andie was surprised by this. This man was the first person to say she looked too young to be working here.

She handed over his change. "I'm fifteen."

"Is that right?"

"My mom is friends with the lady who owns the café, and she gave me a part-time job."

The cowboy nodded, still not taking his eyes off her as he put all his change into a glass tip jar next to the register. He'd given the same gratuity every day, and she thanked him, as always.

"Thanks."

"It's great you're getting some work experience at your age. It will make you stronger." He quickly added, "Mentally tougher, I mean. Ready to take on the world."

She looked at him quizzically now. Unsure how to respond, she just said, "I like it here."

Andie stepped away, poured the man's coffee and put his Danish on a plate, and then walked back to the counter where he stood. As she poured sugar into the coffee, she said, "You don't need the Danish heated, right?"

"Right again." The man took both items from her. "How's school?"

She cocked her head a little. On his earlier visits here, this guy hadn't been so chatty. "School?" she asked.

"Yeah. Having a good year?"

"I guess." She shrugged. "It's school . . . how good can it be?"

"I remember thinking the same thing. Just do your best. No one can expect more out of you than that."

She chuckled. "Yeah? Tell my mom."

The big man said nothing. His eyes were kind but simultaneously intense.

Andie's boss stepped up next to her. With authority in her voice, she asked, "Do you have everything you need, sir?"

The bearded man looked away from the girl and towards the woman. "Yes, ma'am, this young lady has taken great care of me."

"Is there anything else we can do for you today?"

Andie realized Ms. Cara was being protective, and she wasn't trying to hide it.

The old cowboy smiled at Cara now. "Nothing else, ma'am." He held up his pastry and his coffee. "Got what I need." Looking back to Andie Delaney, he said, "Take care. Make it an outstanding day."

"You, too."

Andie noticed that Cara kept her eyes on the man until he headed back to the door and left the café, then stepped around the counter and walked all the way to the windows, as if she were looking to see what vehicle he climbed into.

The young girl picked her rag back up and headed up to the front to start wiping down tables. Cara kept her eyes out at the parking lot, and Andie followed them, seeing the man with the coffee and Danish climbing into a white F-150 pickup.

As the Ford pulled out of the lot and disappeared up the street, Cara stepped over to her. "Was that guy bugging you?"

"No, he's nice. Just a talker, I guess. Every day he leaves like an eight-dollar tip."

"Something's weird about him," Cara said flatly. Then she added, "If he comes back tomorrow, come find me. Let me handle him."

"Okay. Sure." Andie didn't see what the big deal was, but she headed off to clean another table.

. . .

A minute later, the white F-150 nosed into a parking spot in a leafy park across the street from Cara's Bakehouse, just a two-lane road and a sidewalk separating it from the front door, and the driver turned off the engine.

The big bearded man sat still behind the wheel for a moment, and then he grabbed his coffee from the cup holder, took off the lid, and blew on it a moment. He took a sip before reaching into the paper bag; he pulled the Danish out and took a couple of bites while looking across the street at the café.

Andie Delaney appeared in the window, wiping down a table; he watched as she picked up some ceramic plates and mugs and headed back towards the kitchen.

He did not take his eyes off her the entire way.

When she was gone, the man closed his eyes a moment, his hands in his lap, coffee in one and pastry in the other, and his mind drifted back in time, back to another life.

He didn't let his thoughts creep back often, but when they did, they always took a lot out of him.

Zack Hightower slowly opened his eyes again, and his gaze went back to the café as he took another long slow sip.

A sudden pain in the back of his left leg jolted him upright, a nerve tingle that felt like electrified fire ants biting him, and he focused on this so that he could avoid thinking about his past.

The nerve pain subsided, and a dull ache that he'd almost learned to ignore returned.

Zack had been shot six weeks earlier; he was still recovering, and though his muscles were getting stronger each and every day, the pain lingered.

He had prescription medications in a pack in the seat behind him, but he'd forgotten to take them again.

His mind had been on other things of late. Other types of pain.

He saw the young girl through the window of the coffee shop again as she returned to the counter; he closed his eyes again, and the past flashed into his mind with the immediacy of the nerve jolt in his leg.

Thirteen years earlier he'd been an officer in the U.S. Navy, a lieutenant commander in SEAL Team 6. He'd led a counterterrorism hit into Eritrea to kill the head of Al Qaeda in East Africa, and he'd accomplished his mission, gotten himself and his men out alive and unscathed.

A few months after this, however, his name and his role in the op were leaked to AQ by an investigative reporter. Zack was living with his young family at the time outside San Diego, and Al Qaeda sent a cell of three operatives living in LA down to extract some payback.

The big American Navy man was with his wife, Tiffany, and his eighteen-month-old daughter, Stacy, in a shopping mall in La Jolla when Zack detected the trio of foreigners wearing backpacks following him. He separated from his wife and child in the food court and reached into a fanny pack just before the terrorist cell pulled folded stocked rifles out of their backpacks.

As the men leveled their weapons at the American, Zack Hightower drew a Glock 27 and opened fire.

The terrorists got off a few rounds, but Zack's shots had been more accurate.

Two in the chest dropped one man; one in the face and another in the stomach killed the second; but the leader of the cell caught only a single round to the shoulder, dropping the twenty-six-year-old Moroccan to the tile, where he lay moaning on his back between a pair of overturned aluminum tables, his rifle just out of reach.

The Moroccan's wound was survivable with care, but Zack walked up to him, scooped up the terrorist's folded AK-74, stood at his feet, and fired once into the man's crotch.

The Al Qaeda operative bled to death seven excruciating minutes later, long after Zack had left the scene with his family.

After the attack, Zack's relationship with his wife, already hopelessly fractured by his constant absence as he fought in the war on terror, only deteriorated more. Even through the turmoil, however, husband and wife agreed on one thing.

They had to protect Stacy at all costs.

Tiffany wanted Zack to leave the Teams so they could be safe, but Zack countered that the only way they could be safe was for men like Zack to keep doing the job men like Zack were already doing.

It was a cop-out, but he only realized this later. The truth was he loved what he did for a living; he had to keep feeding the beast, killing to assuage his overpowering rage, and home life hardly provided him the outlet he needed to do this.

He'd already accepted a job with the CIA; he would serve as a paramilitary operations officer, and he knew that the danger to his family would only grow with his new position.

In the end there was only one solution, approved by both Zack's employers and, eventually, the Federal Bureau of Investigation.

The United States Federal Witness Protection Program.

He and Tiffany divorced, more amicably than their marriage had been, and then Tiffany and Stacy went into wit-pro, presumably never to be seen again by Zack.

Hightower left the Teams, joined the CIA, worked in the shadows for a decade, and endeavored daily to keep his former life, and the two people who had populated it, out of his thoughts.

He lost himself in his work, and then, almost as soon as he left the Agency, he began reaching out to people in the know in the FBI and the U.S. Marshals Service.

He was older, slightly more mature, and though he knew he could never reunite with Tiffany and Stacy, he wanted to know that they were all right.

Eventually, a friend of a friend of a friend connected him with someone in the Marshals Service Witness Security Program, and he learned where his wife and daughter now were and, perhaps more importantly, *who* they now were.

Zack did nothing with this information for two years, but now he was here in Boulder, watching a teenage kid go about her day.

It had taken him eleven years to find his daughter, and it had taken him a couple of years more to work up the courage to come and see her, just to take a look, but this week he had finally made contact with the little girl he'd last seen just after her second birthday.

The kid in the oversized sweatshirt and the baggy jeans across the street from him had no idea that the big man who came to her new job for coffee every day was her biological father.

And she never would, Zack was determined of that. This was clandestine contact, nothing more.

Stacy was now Andrea—Zack noted that her name tag said Andie—and Tiffany was now Jennifer, and he had learned that Jennifer had remarried three years after Zack went away.

Zack had no idea what Stacy knew about him, or if she knew anything at all. He had no idea what Tiffany's husband knew, or if *he* knew anything at all.

As for Zack, he had no real objective in this. Not really. He'd harbored a vague fantasy about whisking his wife and daughter away from the man who had taken them, but the truth was, no one had taken them.

Zack had given them up.

Furthermore, Tiffany—now Jennifer—had married a man named Peter Delaney. Zack dug into him and found out he was a respected deputy fire chief at Boulder Fire and Rescue, an avid downhill skier, and an enthusiastic churchgoer. Peter had adopted Andie, and then he and Jennifer had a baby girl named Katie. From what Zack could tell, Andie seemed to have an idyllic life, living in a nice part of a nice town with a nice family, working in a nice place with a boss who watched over her like a mother hen.

Andie's life seemed perfect. Jennifer's, too, from what he could tell.

Zack's life, on the other hand, continued to be something of a motherfucking dumpster fire.

He'd left the Agency a few years earlier, then returned as a contract agent, doing deniable jobs for the deputy director for operations.

He'd been shot while taking part in a covert multinational raid into a Russian penal colony, and now his job was to recover enough to go back to work for a new shadow organization.

There was a neurosurgeon in a hospital in town who had once been a surgeon for the Teams, and even though Zack hadn't known the man back then, he'd told Hanley he wanted to come to Boulder to see this doctor for his aftercare following his surgery because the man's reputation was so good.

Hanley had bought the story, though Hanley suspected that Hightower, an avid hunter, actually wanted to come out west to convalesce in a duck blind with a shotgun in his lap.

The truth was, the only thing Zack had come to Colorado to hunt for was his past.

He'd been to Cara's Bakehouse nine days in a row, had seen Andie six times, had spoken to her three. Today he hadn't been able to help himself, and he'd engaged her in a longer conversation. He wanted to keep coming back, he wanted to ask her more about school, sports, boyfriends, plans, dreams... but due to the fact that he couldn't just blurt out that he was her bio dad, any more conversation he had with Andie Delaney was going to make him look like a creep.

His leg hurt, his heart hurt, and his brain was fried.

The pastry in his hand broke apart, and he realized he'd been squeezing it.

"Outstanding," he muttered as he looked down at the cheese squished between his fingers.

Icing streaked across his jeans as the pastry dropped to the muddy floor mat, and he was pissed because even though Cara looked at him like she wanted to have him run out of town, she *did* make one hell of a good cheese Danish.

His phone rang in the cup holder; he struggled for several seconds unfucking his situation with the Danish, putting his coffee down, wiping his hands with a napkin.

On the fifth ring he snatched it up.

"Yeah?"

"Romantic?"

Zack had been given the code name years earlier by Matthew Hanley of the CIA, and he'd hated it every second since.

But he wasn't annoyed right now. He was glad to hear from Matt. He was glad to hear from *anyone* who might break the spell he found himself under.

"Hey, man. What's up?"

"You sound like you're in the middle of something."

"No, boss, all good here."

"Where is *here*?"

"Still in Boulder. Doing some fishing, a little light hunting."

"How are you doing?"

He looked down at the ruined Danish, at the café across the street. "Well, if I had a life coach, he'd probably tell me that I didn't make the team."

"What?"

"Just kidding. I'm doin' okay."

"How's the leg, I mean."

"Which one?"

Matt Hanley gave a little sniff. "You've got to let that joke die, man."

"I thought you liked it."

"Your *injured* leg, Zack."

"Oh. I'm done with PT. I have an MRI next week, should be good to go after that."

"How's your brain?"

"As good as ever."

Hanley sniffed again. "Well, I suppose that will have to do. Can you travel?"

Zack sat up straighter, surprised by the question. "Yeah. Absolutely. What do you need?"

"I need you here, ASAP. I'll get you back to Colorado in time for your MRI."

"Sure, boss. Something's cooking?"

"Or already cooked. Either way, I'm bringing the assets into Norfolk for a meeting."

Zack nodded. "I'll get on a flight this afternoon."

"That works," Hanley said, and then he hung up.

Hightower put the phone down, then looked across the street into the café and watched Andie ringing up a customer.

His daughter.

He shook his head a little, admonishing himself.

Not *his* daughter. Pete Delaney's daughter.

Zack didn't have family.

He had his work.

He forced himself to take his eyes away from Cara's Bakehouse, then fired up the engine of the truck and headed off to his hotel to pack.

He'd be back in a few days, he told himself, and when he got back, he would try his damnedest to just leave Stacy . . . Andie . . . alone.

As before, as was often the case these days, a jolt of nerve pain in his leg gave him something else to focus on as he rolled on through the snow.

SEVENTEEN

The home of Sir Allen Glazebrook was called Greenend Grange; it sat four hundred meters off a quiet country road in the civil parish of Charlbury, just northwest of Oxford and two hours from central London. Positioned on the edge of the Cotswolds, the twenty-room Tudor manor house was first constructed in the 1580s on two hundred acres of gently rolling hills; the stone structure was large and stately by any normal standard, but the property was only twenty acres now. The entrance to Greenend Grange was foliage covered and relatively simple compared to other properties in this area of rural England, and the Cotswolds were dotted with even larger Elizabethan and medieval homes and castles.

Greenend Grange could be passed by on the road without a second glance, though it was an undeniably magnificent place.

The property had been in the Glazebrook family since the turn of the last century, though in both Great Wars it had been handed over to the Crown as a hospital and rehabilitation facility.

Today Sir Allen was the only Glazebrook living on the sprawling property, though ten full-time security staff inhabited outbuildings on the grounds, along with three full-time attendants: a cook, a housekeeper, and a butler.

In his seventy-first year, Sir Allen had served as an officer in MI5, British internal intelligence, for three decades, rising to the post of deputy director general before leaving government to go into the private sector. These days he ran his own international security consulting shop, but not out of the United Kingdom because of his nation's laws about such things. With offices in Frankfurt, Johannesburg, Mexico City, and Jakarta, Glazebrook's company, Advanced Dynamics Staffing Solutions, specialized in assisting foreign nations with staffing their militaries with highly trained advisors.

He offered other services, as well, but the other services he offered weren't advertised.

Glazebrook's wife had died of cancer three years earlier; his daughter was in her thirties, a high-profile solicitor in London, and both his sons were in their twenties, one a major in the Royal Air Force and the other a captain in the Royal Marines.

For this reason, he spent many of his evenings at home, this time of year in front of a roaring fireplace in his second-floor library, reading and enjoying a port or a whiskey.

At eight p.m., he was going through some paperwork at his desk as his butler was setting the logs in the fireplace when a surprise call came for him. An old friend, a colleague from his past, claimed to be in the area and asked if he could drop by for a quick conversation; the tone of the ask was friendly, but Glazebrook detected a distinct sense of purpose to it that the caller did not try very hard to hide.

He also knew this man well enough to know that he didn't just happen to be in Charlbury. He'd come from abroad for the meet, and he'd not set it up in advance.

Despite the obvious deceit in the pretense of the meeting, Sir Allen asked the man to drop by as soon as was convenient. He was bored, to tell the truth; he had a guess or two about what the man might want from him; and most of all, Sir Allen had fought a war with this fellow, and he enjoyed a good war story or two with an old colleague.

The December night was particularly cold and blustery; the guard in the stone shack at the end of the drive checked the arriving car quickly with a flashlight, then let the lone man through. He traveled up the drive and parked as instructed in the forecourt of the manor house, his headlights illuminating two heavily bundled security officers, their black rifles across their chests contrasting with the bright orange of their ski jackets.

Sixty-three-year-old William Tully turned off the engine of his rental and stepped out, took off his raincoat even though there was a smattering of precipitation blowing in the cold wind, and extended his arms.

Tully was Northern Irish, short, with dark hair and bushy eyebrows and a small face that smiled apologetically as the men wanded him and frisked him.

"Cold night, aye?" he said, just making conversation.

"Proper winter, finally, sir," the guard on the right replied as he ran his hands through the raincoat.

His cell phone was taken from him by the other officer, placed in a Faraday cage, a lead-lined bag, and then the officer slipped it into his pocket.

"I'll be returning this when you leave, sir. If you end up overnightin' in one of the cottages, I'll pop right round, give it back to you there."

The Irishman said, "Thanks, mate, but I won't be staying. Just here for a wee chat."

Tully was led to the front door, where he was met by the butler, an older gentleman who took Tully's coat and escorted him through the stately country manor towards the second-floor library.

Here, Allen Glazebrook stood at a scotch bar crafted of African rhino horns and Egyptian marble; he glowed in the light of a massive fireplace as he called across the room.

"Bill. Bloody wonderful to see you."

"You, as well, Sir Allen."

They met in the center of the library, shook hands warmly, but there was no embrace.

"Scotch or port?" Glazebrook said, then quickly added, "This time of night, so close to bed, I usually enjoy port."

"A port would be lovely, thank you."

The butler appeared, as if by magic, and poured the men healthy snifters from a decanter already open and waiting.

The pair sat in leather chairs in front of the fire; both asked after family, about the health of aged colleagues, all the usual pleasantries. It was a polite conversation, but there existed an unspoken but also undeniable lopsided power dynamic between the two men. Tully had been a Northern Irishman working in the Special Branch of the RUC, the Royal Ulster Constabulary, a pro-loyalist force of Irish, mostly Protestant, in Northern Ireland.

Special Branch ran spies against the IRA and its offshoots for decades.

Sir Allen, on the other hand, was British, a top MI5 spook; he ran the mission against the IRA, and men like Tully in Special Branch worked for him. Not as a peer, not as a fellow countryman, but as a local confederate.

Tully had been one of Sir Allen's top local spymasters thirty years ago. In Belfast, in Londonderry, in the little towns and villages of County Tyrone, County Antrim, County Armagh.

There had been no front lines to the war between the Unionists and the Loyalists, but men like Tully worked in the shadows, developing even more shadowy men to spy against the IRA.

Tully had done Glazebrook's bidding for over a decade, but that had been in the nineties, primarily, and since then, Tully had served as a police commissioner in Belfast, but the two men had worked together only on rare occasions until Glazebrook went into the world of international contracting, and then the men hardly saw one another at all.

They sipped port and chatted a few minutes more, and then Glazebrook moved the conversation along. "You sounded rather urgent on the phone."

Tully's face darkened a little. "I did, Sir Allen, and I appreciate your willingness to meet me on such short notice."

Off Tully's change, Glazebrook said, "Is something wrong?"

The Irishman shook his head. "I don't see it as such, and I hope you agree."

"Makes two of us, then. Let's have it, yeah?"

"Did you hear about Marcus Maragos?"

This surprised the Englishman. "A triple homicide in Notting Hill? Indeed, hard to miss *that*. Awful. One imagines he employed someone who was not satisfied with the terms of his contract, or he had a client unsatisfied with the quality of the work done."

"Did you know him personally?"

"No, don't believe I ever met him. Greek lad by birth, raised here, second-tier schooling, but made something of it, I suppose. One of those highly motivated but poorly educated, made a good try but never was able to climb his way high enough up the ladder. Always trying to be too big, too fast. Bypassing the steps one must make in business to build a reputation.

"As a side note, he'd been trying, of late, to get admittance into the Special Forces Club, but we blocked his way. Can you imagine if we'd let him in and then . . . this? Would have been a smudge upon our reputation, I would think." After a look from Tully, Glazebrook chuckled. "I certainly had nothing to do with what happened to him, if that's what you're thinking."

The Irishman exclaimed, "Jesus Lord, no! I certainly wasn't thinking *that*."

"Well, I'll give you my opinion on the matter."

"Please do."

"There are only two types of people in this world, Bill. Winners and wankers. Marcus Maragos, God rest his soul, was a bloody wanker."

Both men laughed a little, and then Glazebrook said, "Wait. Did *you* have something to do with what happened to him?"

Tully did not answer the question. Instead, he said, "The Ulster boy who was killed in Bulgaria back in October. You heard about that, as well, I'm guessing."

Glazebrook took a sip of port. "Only in passing. One of Maragos's armed dolts, wasn't it?"

Tully did not answer. Said, "They say the killer was a lone American."

"I heard that, as well. Then the same American did the thing in Romania. Whoever the bloke was, he was not one of mine, by the way."

"Any guesses who it might have been?"

Glazebrook looked at Tully quizzically. "Why are you asking? What's your connection to this? The Ulster boy? The parents have hired you to find his killer?"

"Something along those lines. Of course, straightaway, I thought you might be the man to speak to. You remain one of the most well-connected geopolitical personalities on this earth."

"Flattery *is* a crude tool, Bill, but often effective." Glazebrook looked into the fire a moment. "You'll only get guesses from me, you understand."

"Certainly."

"There are just a few Yanks who could have caused all that mayhem. A bloke code-named Lancer, he's made a lot of news in the past few years, but I heard he got in a spot of bother and is currently imprisoned in Cuba. There was also a bloke called Dead Eye, a CIA hitter, quite good, but I know for a fact he's been dead some time. Then there's Saga, a killer for hire who worked with me for a spell but is now plying his trade on the dark web, no representation."

The older Englishman thought a moment more, then said, "It could have been Saga. He could have pulled it off, I mean." Glazebrook looked back to Tully. "But it wasn't."

"No?"

Glazebrook shook his head. "No. If the bloke that killed your countryman really was an American, then I believe it was none other than the Gray Man."

Tully let out a little gasp.

"Of course, there's no proof it was an American. Just because the surviving Bulgarians thought it was, how do they know an American accent? I could name twelve other men who could have done it, maybe more, including some from the UK."

Tully nodded slowly, as if the thought had not occurred to him.

Then Sir Allen asked, "Who's your client? What's this all about?"

Tully took a long sip of port, so long Glazebrook made a face of bemusement. The Irishman finally said, "We've been friends a long time. I hope that has bought me a measure of trust from you."

Sir Allen called for his butler to refill Tully's glass. "Jeff? Jeff?" With an annoyed shrug, he refilled the glass himself, then said, "If I didn't have a measure of trust for you, mate, you wouldn't be in my home. Go on, then."

"I want you to think back to the past as I tell you something."

Sir Allen put the bottle back on the table between them, then gave a relaxed little chuckle. "Ah. Something from our shared history, then. Invoking ye olden days. Always gives me a bit of a chill."

Tully hesitated.

Glazebrook prodded good-naturedly. "Well, spit it out, man."

"Whetstone."

Glazebrook's smile faded, and his eyes flicked away, back to the fire. After several silent seconds, he said, "What are we doing here, Tully?"

"We're talking about *him*. About Whetstone." A pause, and then, "We're talking about Campbell Coyle."

Glazebrook's arms crossed in front of his body. "We agreed ages ago, did we not, that none of that ugly business would ever come up again?"

"But it *has* come up again."

"That's a name I had gotten quite comfortable forgetting." When Tully did not respond, Glazebrook said, "Well then, what about him?"

"He came to me."

"He's been quiet a long time. I assumed he was dead."

"I can assure you he is not."

"He came to you in Belfast?"

"Aye."

"When?"

"This morning. The Ulster lad in Bulgaria who died? It was Campbell Coyle's son."

Sir Allen's jaw dropped at this, and then he recovered and said, "Bloody hell. Never heard the lad's name. Just knew he was young."

Now a voice spoke behind Glazebrook, at the door between the library and the second-floor hallway. It was gravelly, low, grave.

And Irish.

"Twenty-four years old, squire."

Glazebrook did not turn around to face the speaker there. He just looked at Tully with wide eyes. Tully, in contrast, shut his own eyes tight, then gave a little nod.

"I'm sorry, Sir Allen," Bill Tully said. "I truly am. Knew he was on the property; didn't know he was going to come in."

Now Glazebrook launched to his feet, turned, and looked at the man standing there. A figure was in the room, out of the light of the fire, in a corner in front of a row of shelves of leather-bound books. He was twenty feet from the hall doorway, twenty feet from Sir Allen.

Half-hidden in the shadows, he was hard to make out. Only that he was not tall, not short. A riding cap on his head, a beard, a raincoat shining wet.

But no other features could be discerned.

With a spin back to Tully, the older man said, "What the fuck have you done, bringing him here?"

Bill Tully responded. "He promises no violence." His voice sounded meek when he said it, as if he did not believe the words he was saying. He added, "Sir Allen Glazebrook, Campbell Coyle. Code name Whetstone. Whetstone, Sir Allen. Code name Juggler. Former deputy director of the United Kingdom's security service."

Coyle said, "How ya keepin', squire? You're looking quite well."

The older man's hands had balled into fists. "You've never bloody met me."

"Television, and such, is what I mean, yeah?"

Still looking at Coyle, Glazebrook raised his voice a little to address the other Irishman in the room. "Tully . . . you have brought this murderer into my home?"

"I murdered for *you*, didn't I?" Coyle said.

"At first," Glazebrook replied. "Yes. And then . . . and then when you'd done what we asked of you . . . you went on killing, didn't you?"

"Man's gotta make a livin'. Seemed right, the only thing I was ever good at. You should know, yeah? For every bastard I put in the cold earth, you ordered the death of ten from behind your desk. Just because you kept those soft hands clean doesn't make you the gentleman here, does it, squire?"

Glazebrook kept his eyes locked on the shadowy intruder, but he spoke to the other man in the room. "William Tully . . . I've always quite liked you . . . for an Irishman. But know this . . . if I die right here where I stand, I've got people who will know you were here. They'll come for you, and they will kill you."

"In old Billy's defense"—Campbell Coyle spoke now from the shadows over by the bookshelves—"I was comin' here whether or not I had a friendly intermediary along with. You might want to thank your old colleague, because our introduction could have happened very differently, and this way seems peaceful enough so far, yeah?"

"I'm not afraid of you."

"If you're not afraid, why is you lookin' at me with a face like a smacked arse? I'd say you are nothing *but* afraid."

"I have my own cards to play."

"Do you, now?"

"I've ten men here who will be on you before you can—"

Coyle spoke over him. "You *do* have ten men. That is true. But they won't be on me."

"Why do you say—"

"Well, for starters, Willis is at the pub with Blake, has been since nine thirty, though they're both supposed to be on duty. They do that a lot, by the way, because you never go outside at night when it's cold or wet to conduct a head count, and you put Whitehead in charge, and Whitehead is afraid of them, because Whitehead is weak. Not a leader. No longer much of a shooter.

"Patel has bronchitis; he didn't come in tonight at all. Barton and Abbott are on duty, but they're old and slow. I could drop them both if I gave 'em ten minutes' warning first.

"Howe is on the grounds, yes, but he's young, untested. He'd hesitate long enough for me to put a bullet through his wee eye."

Coyle continued, effortlessly going down the list of Greenend Grange's site security force. "You sent Kirby to London to watch your girlfriend's cat while she's in Paris. A bloody poor choice on your part. The cat had no history of fucking over assassins, like you do. Anyway, I hear Kirby was SAS. Bet you'd much rather he was here now instead of in Covent Garden tending to a litter box."

"That leaves Powers and Khan. Don't know much about them, but Powers is your dog handler, and I saw the Malinois in the kennel when I came over your fence, so I'm gonna assume Powers is somewhere warm and cozy on this bloody cold night."

Glazebrook and Tully just stared at Coyle in shock at his awareness of the site security force.

"Now," Coyle continued, "if Khan is in the next room, *and* he's God's gift to warriors, if his first name is Genghis, I mean, then I might be right fucked, I'll admit. But I'm willin' to roll those dice because of the sorry state of the rest of your crew. You follow me, squire?"

Glazebrook recovered faster than Tully did.

"Okay, you might have looked into my staff on hand here at Greenend Grange. That's bloody impressive. But don't forget, I sign a lot more than ten paychecks. I literally control armies of private soldiers, mate."

"Yeah?" Coyle looked around the library. "I don't see 'em. Where are they? Bloody Bangladesh? Colombia? Senegal? They're not gonna get here to help you out before I wring your fecking neck, are they?"

EIGHTEEN

"Where is my butler?"

"Your butler has been restrained, but peacefully. In the next room. I even gave him one of his heart pills with a sip of water. He was lookin' a little . . . drawn. 'E'll be fine, though. He's top drawer. I've stared down men half his age who shit their trousers, and he, at least, had the decency to keep it in."

Coyle said, "I don't have to be danger tonight, Sir Allen. You can just think of me as an old associate." He stepped forward, shrugged a little.

"I have cameras," Glazebrook said now; his voice had grown feeble.

Coyle smiled. "I used the distraction of old Billy's appearance to slither in between camera angles. I can talk you through getting your blind spots filled in when we're done here."

Glazebrook nodded slightly. "I suppose I'd like that very much, indeed." His eyes went back to Tully, then back to Coyle. "Look. If we're going to have to talk, come over here by the fire, man, I'll throw out my old neck if I have to—"

Coyle stepped out of the shadows, into the light, and came around to Bill Tully's side of the fireplace. He lowered himself onto the arm of a leather sofa there, and he bade Glazebrook to sit back down.

As soon as he did so, Sir Allen said, "You came to us at what? Twenty-one years old?"

"I was nineteen."

"Two years in the Legion. Said you wanted to kill IRA men for us. Wanted to turn on your own kind."

"I wanted to do the men who killed my da."

"Do them all you did, lad, some after the peace accords were signed."

"*You* lot signed the peace accords. I did not."

"Quite. Then, when we had no more work for you, you turned up in the Middle East. Africa. Asia. Working for someone else."

"Working for meself."

"You got a taste for the killing, didn't you?"

"Had it. Lost it. I'm not here to talk about me, or hadn't you picked up on that?"

"What do you want?"

"You think it was the Gray Man who killed my Charlie?"

"I do."

"Then I want every bit of information you have on the Gray Man. You give me that. Maybe you can give me some names who can lead me to him, and then I will leave, just as quietly and peacefully as I came."

"Did you kill Maragos?"

There was no passion in the response, no reticence, either. "Aye. And I've more killin' to do, but there's no need for any of it tonight."

The decanter of port was on the little table between Tully and Coyle. Coyle took it, stood back up, and walked to both other men, filling their glasses, nearly to the top. It was a faux pas to overfill a port glass, but this wasn't Sir Allen's chief concern at the moment. He took a sip, and his hand quivered a little.

"You're after the man who killed your son," Glazebrook said. "I understand. And you have my sincere condolences. Nothing worse than a parent losing a child."

Coyle held a moment, then said, "But?"

"But . . . I'm afraid I don't respond well to threats."

"Don't you go disappointing me, Sir Allen."

"Look—"

"*You* look," Coyle said. "I'm going to see this through, and until I do, I will consider everyone I encounter as either a help or a hindrance in my mission. Those that help have my thanks, and my leave, and those that hinder... well, God help those that hinder."

"Now," Coyle said, "we was talkin' about the Gray Man."

The older man just sighed. Then said, "He's American."

"Of course he's bloody American."

"Former CIA. A special program, then a para."

"Still not giving me anything useful."

"His code name with the CIA was Violator. Nobody called him the Gray Man till he went into private contract killing."

Tully spoke up now. "See there, Coyle? Sir Allen *is* being helpful."

"How's a ten-year-old code name gonna help me find him? Tell me why you think it was him and not this other knob you mentioned?"

"Lancer?"

"Not the one in prison in Havana. The other. The Saga."

"Just Saga. If I were a betting man, I'd say Violator was the one who did the thing in Bulgaria, then again in Romania in October, then the thing in Russia last month."

Tully looked dumbstruck. "Russia? *What* thing in Russia?"

"The prison raid in Russia. He was there."

Coyle let out a surprised chuckle. "Meaning... what?"

"Yarovoy. The Russians think the Gray Man was already in-country, on the inside, helping with his escape. That's all I know."

"Why was the Gray Man in Bulgaria, then?"

Glazebrook shrugged. "I didn't know he was. Might have something to do with his actions in Russia."

"I need more."

"There is no more to be had from me tonight. I can make some calls. I will do that for you. My nation owes you for what you did back a million years ago."

Tully raised a hand. "There you go, Whetstone. Sir Allen promised to look into—"

"What if I don't believe him?" Coyle said. "I'm supposed to leave now and wait on my phone to ring?"

Tully was adamant, and he was scared. "Now, look here. Sir Allen is shooting you straight. If he says—"

Now Glazebrook interrupted. "You're calling me a liar? You've slipped into my home like a pest, threatened to wring my neck, and called me a liar?"

Coyle said, "Oh, I *know* you're a liar."

Before anyone could speak, Coyle said, "The men you sent me after in Ulster, when I was just a lad. When I was trying to right the wrongs done to my da. Two of them were involved in my father's death. But the others? That was simple score settling with you lot. You tricked me, cooked up bogus proof. I figured it out decades ago. You two lied to me. Had me kill men, women, old touts who'd pissed you off over the years. They'd nothing to do with me, never did me any wrong, and I put a bullet or two in all of them."

Tully said, "I don't know what you're—"

"Fuck off, Tully. Glazebrook is a shite, but he's British. You're a bloody Irishman, turning on your own."

"You turned on your own," Tully said, his voice quivering in fear.

"I turned on those who killed my da. Family is everything, don't you agree?"

Tully didn't know what to say. He hesitated, thinking of a response.

But he never said another word. In a sudden movement, Coyle's left hand came out of his coat, his arm extended towards Tully, a gun with a silencer at the end of it.

It barked once, loud in the library, but quiet enough that the sound wouldn't travel all the way outside.

Tully fell back into his chair. His arm knocked his glass of port off the table; it crashed on the hardwood floor.

The wheezing of a sucking chest wound came right after. Glazebrook launched to his feet in terror, but when the gun was pointed towards him, waving him back into his seat, he slowly sat back down, his eyes bounding between the wounded Irishman and the armed man.

Between victim and perpetrator.

Bill Tully was still alive. Gasping shallowly in the chair, a hole in his chest. Blood trickled from his mouth.

His eyes were wide from shock; the firelight flickered in their wetness.

Campbell Coyle remained standing in front of the fireplace; his shadow danced across the room with the flames, but his body stayed ramrod still.

Sir Allen began to speak, but Coyle cut him off before a single word came out.

"I'm not fucking about, Glazebrook. Don't look so upset. You never gave a toss about Tully, any more than me. You are one of those Brits who thinks he's superior to us Irishmen."

"Of . . . of course not."

Bill Tully slumped forward in the chair, crumpled to the floor. A gurgling came from the heap.

"Why did you do that?" the older man asked.

"I needed him to get in to you. I didn't need him after. He quickly became useless. You see? I want to be certain that you understand this, so that you realize the very second you have nothing left to offer me, your life means fuck-all."

With a little smile, he said, "I won't kill you unless you're useless."

The gurgling stopped. A last breath of air came from the Northern Irishman lying in front of the fireplace.

It went deathly quiet in the room for a bit, and then Glazebrook said, "You made your point. I'm willing to be of service as long as you need me. Longer even, I suppose."

It was a slight joke. British humor, Coyle assumed, though the stakes were too high for it at the moment.

"Right, then," Coyle said. "Who would know about the operation in Russia that the Gray Man was on?"

"CIA. They say they have nothing to do with the Gray Man, but they were definitely involved in that."

"Who ran that raid for the CIA?"

"Matthew Hanley was on the ground in Ukraine, working with the Ukrainians and the Russian partisans. That might mean he was involved with the Gray Man, who was on the ground inside Russia on the same operation."

"Who is Matthew Hanley?"

"He used to be their director for operations. He was ousted, but last I heard, he was still at the Agency."

"Where do I find him?"

"I don't know."

Coyle was about to raise the pistol again, but Glazebrook held a finger up. "I know. I have the answer."

"Enlighten me."

"I can get you work in America."

The Irishman made a face. "Why do people keep saying that? You know what I want, mate, and it's not a bloody job."

"It *is*, Whetstone. It *is*, because the people doing the hiring know everything about what's going on inside the American intelligence community. It's an insider threat. I don't know who or how, but the *what* I have sussed out. Whoever they are, they're connected with the CIA, or at least some facet of the intelligence community. They've come to me, through intermediaries, to try to get hard assets for a series of jobs on U.S. soil. I don't know what jobs, exactly, but the work is all there, *in* America. The men I offered up were good, yet they were still rejected. They are looking for the cream of the crop."

"But—"

"Hear me out," Glazebrook continued. "I just drop the name Whetstone, they will know what you've done. Who you were. They will bring you into their fold. Once you are in with them, you will have resources."

"What kind of—"

"They can get you to Hanley, at least. Maybe even the Gray Man himself." Quickly, he added, "But if you kill me . . . you won't get connected to the right people, and you won't get the information you seek."

The older Englishman smiled a little, then looked at Tully's body on the floor, and the smile went away. "I will make calls tonight. I will get you into the U.S. I have the means to—"

Coyle said, "I will leave you, Sir Allen. I will leave you to clean up this mess." He waved his gun at Tully's body in a heap. He said, "Because I'm not worried about a double cross from you. What I know about what happened twenty-five years ago . . . what I can prove . . . I talk and you go away forever. As do many still in MI5." He thought a moment. "Hell, the service itself would be in jeopardy for some of the dirty work we did together."

Sir Allen paled even more now, as if the thought of having old secrets revealed was even more threatening than the killer now on the loose in his home. Defensively, he said, "You'd go away yourself if you talked."

"Do I seem to you like a man at all concerned about his own self-preservation?"

A pause. The fire crackled. A last wisp of smoke rose from the silencer on the end of Coyle's pistol.

Coyle said, "You have twenty-four hours to get me hired in America. If these blokes there don't have the ability to get me to the Gray Man, I am going to suss it out straightaway, and I will talk and I will talk and I will not stop talking until the British intelligence services hang by the bollocks for the dirty shit you feckers did to a lot of innocent people."

Coyle got the impression Glazebrook wanted to take issue with something he'd said, but the old man held his tongue. Instead, Sir Allen said, "Give me a way to contact you. I will tell my contact in America that he has the world-famous Whetstone on the way to do his dirty work. And I will hold up my end of the bargain here. You do *not* need to go to the press."

Coyle nodded, then said, "Stand up and turn around."

"What? Why?"

"Calm down. I'm going to tie you up so you don't call your jackals before I leave." As Glazebrook turned, Coyle said, "Thought I'd be killing at least a half dozen tonight, maybe more. I was certain Tully and yourself wouldn't live through the night. So . . . good on you, squire, you've made yourself useful."

When Sir Allen's hands were tight behind his back, fixed with plastic restraints, Coyle tapped him on the shoulder with the pistol's silencer, leaned into his ear from behind, and said, "Keep it up. Keep producing. I'll call you this time tomorrow.

"When I kill the Gray Man, you will know that you, and the precious intelligence service you served, are both safe.

"Until that day," Coyle added, "go very carefully with everything you do."

He sat the old man back in the leather chair, putting him right in front of the body on the floor by the fire. As he turned towards the door, Coyle said, "Twenty-five years ago, I was *your* tool.

"Now, ya fecker . . . yer *mine*."

The Irishman became a shadowy figure again when out of the firelight, and then he melted off down the hall.

NINETEEN

Hampton Roads Commons is a collection of four two-story office buildings surrounded on one side by a concrete manufacturing company and on the other by a discount shopping district, all positioned just a half mile east of Hampton Roads Executive Airport in Norfolk, Virginia.

The back side of building three of the commons, making up suite 3107, still had a For Rent banner over the darkened windows, but a tenant had taken possession of the facility a few weeks earlier, and delivery trucks and moving vans had been arriving almost every day since.

There was no other signage identifying the occupant here, but on the other side of the building sat an office annex of the Virginia Department of Health and an independent marketing group that sold small appliances to chain stores in Virginia and North and South Carolina.

The drab parking lot in the rear was wet from an icy morning rain, and only five vehicles were parked in front of suite 3107 at 7:40 a.m.

But then a yellow-and-black Yamaha sport bike growled into view from around the side of the building, kicking up frigid spray as it turned in the direction of 3107, then pulled next to the cluster of vehicles: a black Chevy Suburban, a burgundy Subaru Outback, an old Dodge Ram, and a pair of sensible import sedans.

The biker wore a black helmet with its smoked visor down, and he carried a small gray backpack. He wore an insulated raincoat and blue jeans, brown hiking boots and gloves.

The man parked his Yamaha, turned off the engine, and put his gloves in his backpack, but he left his helmet over his head, the visor still down, as he put the pack back on, kicked off the bike, and then walked to the door of the suite.

Court Gentry never expected he'd find himself at the office of Hanley's new organization, but after returning from Nicaragua and then spending his first night on his boat docked at Bay Point Marina, he'd gotten a text from Hanley ordering him to report to a specific address for a meeting with his new team.

Hanley hadn't instructed Court to keep his face covered here at the TerreCom Industrial Consulting office, but he didn't assume he'd know most any of the other people Matt had working for him, so he wasn't about to stroll around here on full display.

He pushed a buzzer by the door, then looked up at the camera on his right and gave something of a sarcastic "hang loose" gesture with his hand.

A moment later the door below the camera opened, and a woman stepped out. She was in her fifties or early sixties and wore her curly brown and gray hair down and slightly in disarray, but there was both a calmness and a confidence to her that the younger man easily picked up on.

She was professional but placid, easygoing.

"Good morning, sir." She offered her hand. "I'm Erin Childers, Matthew's assistant."

Court shook her hand, but with the gesture came a challenge. "You just open the door to anyone with a covered face and a backpack?"

"I know who you are."

"How's that?"

"The motorcycle."

"What about it?"

"I bought it for you." She smiled; it was a motherly smile, good-naturedly indulging a child who thought he had outwitted her. "Plus, I know what you look like, Brian. I did your papers."

She was telling him she'd forged the identification of his alias, Brian Webb.

He conceded the point, but still, he looked past her into the darkness of what appeared to be a small lobby. He said, "You're the Subaru, right?"

She looked to the car, then back to him. "That *is* my Outback, right."

"Hanley is the Suburban. Who drives the pickup, the Volvo, and the Camry?"

"We just have a few principals in the office today. People who already know what you look like. Matthew is waiting for you in his office. You're the first of the assets to arrive. Follow me, please."

With that, Court shrugged, took off his helmet, and carried it under his arm as he was led into the building by Childers.

Almost instantly, Court saw that there wasn't much to TerreCom's physical office. A plastic fiddle-leaf fig tree covered in Christmas lights in the corner of a little lobby with old furniture, a reception desk behind glass, as if this were a bank or the DMV, the chair behind it unoccupied. Low ceilings, fluorescent lights that were mostly off.

And a door with a keypad lock.

Childers tapped in a code—Court didn't catch the numbers—and then they began walking down another hall, this one much more brightly lit.

Looking around, he realized this place clearly had been some sort of medical suite before Hanley had rented it. He wondered now if he was here to meet with his boss in an off-book spy shop or if he was here for a colonoscopy.

And he wondered if he'd really notice a difference.

A door opened at the end of the hallway, and then Matt Hanley emerged, wearing a blue sport coat, khakis, and black tennis shoes. Childers passed Court off to him, then disappeared up yet another hallway.

"Hey, Six," Hanley said. "Welcome to my humble abode."

Court looked towards the office behind Hanley. It was small and simple. A desk with two chairs in front of it, a couple of monitors on the desk. Paperwork in front of them.

Then he glanced back up the unadorned hall. Almost to himself, he said, "This is it?"

"This is *what*?" Hanley asked.

"I feel like I should get my teeth cleaned while I'm here."

Hanley chuckled. "Close. It's been dormant a couple of years, but it was actually a podiatry office before that."

Court nodded. Again, almost to himself, he said, "This is a small operation."

"Said the singleton," Hanley quipped. Court had begun his career in the CIA as a member of their Autonomous Asset Program, much of the time working completely alone.

Court took Hanley's meaning but said, "Yeah, but the intel, logistics, all that, it was done by others. I was just the dumbass on the pointy tip."

Hanley motioned for Court to step back into the office, but they didn't sit down. He said, "Same deal here. Agency directives come down to us, we evaluate and execute."

"How do they come down to us?"

"Watkins himself makes decisions on what we do."

"You trust him?"

"Not particularly." After a pause, he said, "You know suits."

To this, Court laughed. "Said the stiffest suit of them all."

"Maybe once upon a time. But would you just look at me now?" He waved a hand around, indicating the spartan offices of TerreCom Industrial Consulting.

Court gazed around the room he stood in. "It's a shitty office, yes, but it *is* an office. You're making it out as if you're manning a fucking pillbox on a beachhead."

Hanley shrugged his big shoulders again. "Anyway, that's the job. I'd say take it or leave it, but it's not like I'd let you leave it."

"I'm on board, Matt. I'm just whining."

"I know." He shrugged. "Wish I had someone to whine to."

The intercom on his desk beeped, and Erin Childers's voice came over the speaker. "Lyle is at the door."

Hanley looked to Court. "Zack's alias."

He tapped the intercom. "Take him straight into conference room one. We'll meet you."

"Yes, sir."

To Court, Hanley said, "Follow me. We've got a conference room.

Coffee and donuts and shit. It'll be fun." The older man's sarcasm was obvious, but Court just followed him back out the door.

A minute later Court and Hanley arrived at a conference room with a long table as voices came up another hallway to their right.

Court smiled as Zack Hightower's booming voice filled the space; he was already deep in conversation with Erin Childers, and she was laughing at whatever he was saying.

Zack and Erin came around the corner; she was still chuckling, and then the two men saw each other.

"Six!" he said. "Good to see you."

The men embraced. Court asked, "How's the leg?"

"Okay, considering it caught a 122-grain boat tail just six weeks ago."

"I was there, remember?"

"Barely."

"I was worried it had clipped your femoral."

"The doc in Kharkiv said five millimeters to the left and I'd have probably bled out before I got the tourniquet on. And thanks to you for sealing me up in the transport. Can't say I remember that part, but I've heard accounts."

Court knew Zack would have died in Russia if he'd not gotten immediate medical care. But the man seemed good as new now. He was a big powerful presence, exactly as always.

Hightower now asked, "How's Anthem doing?"

"She's recovering. Taking a break."

"Cool . . . I want a break," Hightower replied.

Hanley said, "You got a break when you got this job."

The intercom on the table came alive again, and Childers said, "Matt, Jason is here."

"Bring him straight in."

"Who the hell is Jason?" Hightower asked.

Court said, "Well, you're Lyle, and I'm Brian, so who knows?"

Hanley did not answer; he just ushered the men into the conference room. Hightower grabbed a donut out of a box on the table, and Court dropped his helmet in a chair, then walked over and poured himself a mug of black coffee from an urn.

He moved back over and began to sit down next to his helmet, but before doing so, he looked up; another figure stood in the doorway.

Hightower was across the table holding the donut in his mouth as he stared at the man; Court was frozen in place a moment himself.

A bald-headed man with a thick beard stood there, a green Patagonia jacket under his arm, a black button-down shirt over his fit frame.

Hightower pulled out the donut. "Travers? Are you kidding?"

Court followed with, "What the hell are you doing *here*?" Court had known Chris Travers for years, as had Hightower. He'd been CIA, was *still* CIA as far as either of the men knew.

The bald man came around the table, shook Court's hand, then Hightower's.

Zack said, "You can't be seen with us, brother. You're Agency." After a pause, he said, "Unless I missed something."

"You missed something," Travers replied. With a deadpan look he said, "I got kicked down into the dirt with Matt and you two jokers."

"Did you fuck up?" Court asked.

"Didn't feel that way to me. My superiors disagreed."

Court flashed his eyes over to Hanley. "Fucking superiors."

Travers laughed a little. To Hightower and Court he said, "Damn good to see you guys. Staying out of trouble, I hope."

"Would we be here if we weren't in trouble?" Court said.

Travers said, "So you guys *were* in that shit in Russia, weren't you?"

Hanley spoke up first. "They can neither confirm nor deny."

"I was just testing them, boss," Travers said.

He poured himself some coffee, found a place at the table, and then all three men sat down as Hanley stood at the head.

"Welcome to TerreCom Industrial Consulting. Let me explain what's going to happen. There are five people inside this office right now other than us. You met Erin; you'll meet Jill and Arnold in a second. Earnest and Doyle are site security; they're in a back office watching over the street via monitors, keeping an eye on the cams all over the office park. You won't meet them, and they won't meet you.

"I wanted to keep the group small today, just because you operators are here, and not everyone needs to know you. But when you guys *aren't* here, we'll have more on staff. Fifteen total. Every single one of them has been vetted by me *and* by the United States government. There is only one employee here I've known less than ten years, and that's only because ten years ago Jill was in middle school.

"All the cameras inside have been turned off for your visit, so don't worry about that."

He added, "Honestly, this might be the only time you three ever enter this building, but I wanted you to see how our operation is going to work."

Hightower spoke up between bites of his donut. "I just want to know when I'm gonna get my teeth cleaned?"

"Violator has already made that joke," Hanley said dryly, without turning to the man who'd said it. "Yes . . . this looks like a medical office. It was. It is no longer. It is where I work."

TWENTY

Hanley went on. "A few housekeeping items. Firstly, code names and code words. This location, and the operation we are all collectively conducting, will not be referred to in any commo as 'Hampton Roads,' 'Norfolk,' or 'TerreCom.' For operational security reasons, this location, this operation, is to be referred to as Ghost Town.

"Each member of Ghost Town will be given a code name; these are in addition to your domestic aliases and any cover for action aliases you will use abroad while in the field."

He turned to the open hallway door. "Come on in."

Erin Childers entered along with a young Asian female and an older Hispanic male. The young woman was dressed in office attire: a pencil skirt, a floral blouse, her hair in a ponytail. The man wore a black suit over a slightly wrinkled blue shirt.

"Meet the team." Court couldn't tell if Hanley was saying it to the three operators at the table or the three office staff just inside the door. The Asian woman smiled and gave a shy little wave, Childers nodded, and the Hispanic man just stood there with his hands in his pockets.

Matt said, "Firstly, my code name is Pilgrim. Erin is my number two. If you need something, logistically speaking or otherwise, and you don't get me, go to her. Her code name is Conductor.

"On the technical side, this is Jill Mori. She is former CIA and will serve as our IT and OSINT expert.

"Jill's code name is Gumdrop." He added, "I know what you're thinking. Jill might be young, but she's one of the top ten best open-source intelligence analysts that I've ever known. I met her when I was DDO; she had just joined the Agency and was already impressing. I got her down to Colombia to work with me there. Earlier this year she was let go, her position was taken over by a Gauntlet contract employee, and I knew it wouldn't take any time for the private sector to snatch her up for her skills, so when I set up Ghost Town, I appealed to her sense of duty and got her to join our outfit."

Jill smiled a little. "He's paying me, too, by the way."

The men at the table laughed, and Jill, Erin, and Arnold sat down, while Matt continued to stand.

He said, "When the CIA sends us on an operation, Jill will use OSINT to make certain you guys have the details you need, not just what comes down from the CIA. She will save all your lives; I'm absolutely convinced of that."

The three assets all thanked her in advance. She said, "I promise to do my best."

Hanley motioned to the older man next to her. "Arnold Reyes here is our logistics coordinator. Code name Bricklayer. He's a civilian, did a few stints as a contractor in Afghanistan, then was brought into JSOC, and finally into Ground Branch." After waiting a beat, Hanley said, "You know you can trust him with your lives, because some of you already have. Lyle and Jason, Arnold has done more for you guys when you were in Ground Branch than you will ever appreciate."

Reyes was deep into his forties and wore his thinning gray hair combed over. He had a slight build, eyeglasses, and a reddening to his face that made it clear he didn't enjoy being complimented, talked about, or even looked at by others.

Still, he was thanked by the three assets, and he nodded, now looking at the table in front of him.

This was all pretty standard stuff for Court and the other two seated at the table. Court rose and refilled his coffee from the insulated decanter,

Hightower finished his donut and licked his fingers, and Travers leaned forward, his elbows on the table's edge.

Hanley said, "The security staff here at Ghost Town are five in number. I've taken to calling them 'the Five Guys.' They're not going to be involved in anything operationally; they are just here for the safety of the building. These are guys I've known forever. You've probably trained with them all at one point or another. Ernie Gamble runs security."

Hightower sat up now. "Gamble from Harvey Point?"

Harvey Point was a CIA training facility in North Carolina.

"That's correct. Ernie was an armorer and a range safety officer there."

"Shit," Hightower said, looking away.

"A problem?" Hanley asked.

"I owe that dude some money. He outshot me once on the range. There was a bet involved."

"I can direct you to the security room after our meeting."

Hightower shook his head. Sheepishly, he said, "I'll catch him later."

Hanley continued. "Now, for the assets. Travers . . . your alias is Jason Reed, and your code name with Ghost Town will be Teddy."

"Roger that."

"Six . . . your alias is Brian Webb and your code name . . . will be Six."

"Creative," Hightower said, and Hanley just shrugged.

To the three office personnel sitting with them, he explained. "It was one half of his call sign on his Ground Branch team, way back when.

"It's secure enough, and three of us know him as that already."

He turned to Zack. "Hightower, your alias is Lyle Hart, and your code name is—"

"If you say Romantic," Hightower interrupted, "I'm walking out that door."

Hanley pointed a finger at the operator now, spoke forcefully. "You are *not* walking out that door, even if I call you Tinkerbell." When his voice subsided, he said, "Your code name is Night Train."

Zack executed a silent and subdued fist pump, but he said nothing.

Hanley said, "Okay, with all that out of the way, let's get to it. As of now, we are now officially active, and I will start by saying, we're in deep shit."

Now Hightower sat up straighter and looked to Hanley. Notably, both Court and Travers continued sipping coffee as if they were not surprised in the least by what their boss had just said.

"The breach in our national security apparatus has continued. So far, the CIA has not been able to determine the location or means of the breach. ODNI, NSA, DIA, State, Department of Defense . . . everyone is running into the same thing. Classified operations are being disrupted in ways that make it seem like someone deep inside the IC is involved.

"We dealt with a leak a couple of years ago, as you all know. That specific compromise was contained to CIA's logistics, specifically air transport. The Agency tied that off back then, so this is something new, and something more pervasive."

"What has been leaked?" Hightower asked.

Hanley looked to Chris Travers. "Teddy? Why don't you start?"

Travers said, "I was in Tunis with my team back in late October. We were blown. Ambushed at a safe house that was not known to the local station, so we think the leak came from stateside. One of my men was killed, three Russian nationals were killed.

"At the ambush, we managed to get two of the Russians. The third squirted. We were ordered home immediately, but I had an idea about where the survivor was heading. I sent my team home with the body of my number three, and I found the Russian eight hours later near the Algerian border."

It was quiet in the conference room till Zack sat forward suddenly, grabbed a jelly donut, and brought it to his mouth. Just before he took a bite, he said, "And you smoked that motherfucker on your own, without special sanction."

Chris Travers nodded solemnly. "I did."

"You got shitcanned from the Agency for that?" Court asked.

"Affirmative," Travers said. "It was payback, what I did. Not operationally necessary, or so they said."

Court examined the man a moment, then asked, "Are you having trouble with your decision?"

"No trouble at all. *That's* what's giving me trouble."

"First thought, best thought," Hightower said, nonchalantly. He was halfway finished with his donut already. "I trust you, man. If it felt right at the time, you did the right thing."

"Anyway," Hanley said, "I snatched him up to work with us. He understands the gist of what we'll be doing."

Changing the subject, Hanley then said, "So that was Tunis. In Ethiopia another operation was compromised. Local ISIS took out several of our indigenous assets. Not a cell of locals, I mean, but men and women walled off from one another. The only way ISIS could have known about them all was a breach from the U.S."

He added, perhaps unnecessarily, "The call definitely came from inside the house."

Hanley looked to Court. "After these disasters in Africa, plus word from other agencies that they were having the same problem, Trey Watkins came to me personally, wanting me to send Six to do an in extremis job down in Central America. The thinking was, it would minimize the number of people at CIA who knew about the op if they contracted it out. Six would go down alone, and since he's not an Agency employee, he might have better luck."

Court corrected him. "Actually, I was sent because they didn't want to lose another Agency employee." He turned to Travers and Hightower across from him. "It was an extraction of an asset in Nicaragua. The fact that I wasn't Agency, the fact that the locals didn't get the information on the location of the extraction till the last minute... none of that mattered." He sighed. "We were most definitely compromised on our end, and we lost four FORNAT agents. I got the asset out, but in the process, I wasted a couple of Chinese MSS officers. The Agency has kept a lid on that, so far at least."

"Someone in the U.S. government gave intelligence to the Nicaraguans?" Travers asked.

Hanley shook his head. "Or Chinese intelligence passed the intel on to the Nicas. Either way, it has to be a leak in America."

Travers said, "So what do we know for sure?"

Hightower said, "Sounds like we know that we're going to have to depend on one another, and no one else."

Hanley said, "Jim Pace, who you all know is at CIA, is looking into these breaches. He got put on the assignment yesterday, and today he already has a target. His orders are to pass what he learns to Angela Lacy, who many of you know. Lacy knows about Ghost Town. She passed the intel to Jill." Hanley turned to her.

"Gumdrop? Fill them in."

"Pace says there is a woman at ODNI named Irene Ortega, who he finds suspicious."

"How so?" Court asked.

"First, she had access to the information about the op in Nicaragua the night before last. But Jim found out that her credentials were used to pull up data on virtually all the affected operations after they happened. He thinks it's strange that after Nicaragua she accessed information about the breaches across the intel community."

Travers cocked his head. "Sounds to me like someone just conducting an investigation on what's going on."

"But that's not her job. She's a mission integration specialist."

"The hell is that?" Hightower asked.

Jill said, "It's her job to evaluate resources to ensure an efficient cross-discipline environment through all the INT regions, specifically when dealing with technological assets."

"The hell is that?" Hightower asked again in the same tone.

The Asian woman furrowed her eyebrows, looking at the much older man like she couldn't imagine how he did not understand what she was saying.

But Erin Childers answered for her. "Ortega is midlevel; she is tasked with making sure each intelligence agency has the data they need from the other agencies." Childers shrugged now. "She shouldn't be investigating anything."

Hanley added, "Pace thinks it's possible Ortega is looking into the past operations to see if she's successfully covered her tracks. She knows all the agencies are conducting investigations into this, so maybe she wants to know what can be found out in the files."

Court said, "Meaning . . . maybe she's the leaker, and she needs to know how worried she should be about a CIA investigator like Pace identifying her."

"That's the concern," Hanley said.

Jill Mori said, "I'm looking into Ortega in open source. She's single, and very private. She works at an ODNI office at the State Department in Foggy Bottom, and lives near Washington Circle, a mile or so away."

"Okay," Court said. "What's our mission?"

Gumdrop spoke as if the answer was obvious. "Go up there and find out if she's the spy."

Hightower made a face. *"Find out?"*

"Yeah."

Hanley started to say something, but Hightower spoke first. "Ma'am, we're not exactly Starsky and Hutch."

She looked to Hanley, then back to the assets at the table. "I don't know what that means."

Court clarified, "We're not detectives. We're not investigators."

Jill said, "Nobody is asking you to decipher the Rosetta stone."

To this, Hightower said, "I don't know what *that* means."

Hanley stepped in. "We will support Jim Pace's operation. Be his eyes and his ears, his black bag team. He'll do the investigating; you'll do the grunt work." He looked to Jill now. "You have to talk to these guys like they're big dumb idiots. It's not their fault. They've all been blown up a lot."

Now he turned to Hightower. "Speaking of which. Night Train, you're not on this op. Go back to Boulder, get your MRI, and get yourself cleared for duty."

Zack looked to the two other assets with him, then back to Hanley. "That's not for several days. Let me go on this. I'll drive the surveillance van or something."

For the first time, Arnold spoke up. "I put a white GMC van on site already in a parking garage on Maryland Avenue. I have four sets of magnetic decals in the back. Different businesses. Three cases of cams, some disguises, other odds and ends. I have a couple other vans and cars in storage nearby. We can rent other vehicles if we need them."

"Weapons?" Hightower asked.

"Shouldn't need them," Arnold said. "But yes. Pistols will be with your ICE uniforms."

"ICE?" Travers said with a tone of confusion.

"You have a few covers. All in the van."

Travers cocked his head. "Wait. You did that all this morning?"

"Loaded the van last night. Dropped it in D.C. this morning."

"It's eight thirty in the morning *now*. That's two hundred miles away."

"*Early* this morning, sir."

"Right." Travers was impressed. "Cool."

Hanley had been mulling over Hightower's desire to join the team. He said, "Zack. Nothing operational. You promise me that?"

"I promise."

"All right. Conductor will stay here. The rest of us will fly up to Reagan on the jet now. It's waiting for us at Hampton Roads."

Hightower said, "It will be good to see Jim again."

But to this, Hanley held up a hand. "You're not going to be interfacing directly with Jim Pace. Watkins's orders. Pace goes to Lacy, Lacy goes to us, we go to you."

Court let out a long sigh.

Hanley heard the noise, then looked to Court. "There's a leak at the CIA. No way Pace is part of it, no way Lacy is part of it, but if you guys are physically interacting with CIA employees, it just puts you at risk. Trust me, Six, we'll get you the intel you need as fast as we can."

The meeting broke up after this, and everyone shook hands again.

As the three assets headed out to Hanley's Suburban for the drive to the airport, Travers shouldered up to Hightower. "You're seeing a doctor in Colorado?"

"Yeah, man. Best in the country."

Travers was incredulous. "The best gunshot wound doctor in the country lives in Boulder?"

"Yeah," Zack answered, but he added nothing more.

Court was walking right behind them, and he picked up on Zack's sudden discomfort.

Travers, however seemed not to. "Shit. I'd have thought the best doc to treat a gunshot wound would be in Baltimore. Maybe East St. Louis, or Memphis."

"Nope," Hightower said, and he climbed in the front passenger seat of the vehicle, leaving Chris and Court to get in behind him.

Court knew exactly why Zack had gone to Colorado. Something Zack had shared a couple of years back, in a moment of vulnerability, about having a kid in witness protection living there. Court wasn't going to bring that up, and he knew Zack didn't want twenty questions from Travers about why he was being treated in Colorado, so Court started chatting away with Travers as Hanley got behind the wheel of the SUV and they began heading to the airport.

TWENTY-ONE

Senior operations officer for Gauntlet Group Inc. Michael Scardino stood on the hot tarmac in western Cuba, looking at a sky speckled with clouds and waiting impatiently for the arrival of the man he'd come all the way from D.C. to pick up this afternoon. Just behind him, one of his company's three dozen or so unmarked Piper Meridian aircraft had finished refueling and sat at the ready. The Meridians were six-seaters that Gauntlet used around the world to ferry small amounts of men or cargo in locations where a jet would not be economical, feasible, or low-profile enough.

This aircraft was a Miami-based 2006 model with a white fuselage and burgundy accent stripes; like most Gauntlet planes, it had been purchased gently used by a shell corporation, then sold off to another front company in an attempt to hide the fact that it was owned by a private security firm.

The five-bladed propeller on this Meridian spun, and the pilot and copilot remained at their controls. The air stairs, which consisted of only two steps, were in the lowered position, and a man stood next to them wearing a baggy white short-sleeve shirt and cargo pants.

Blanchard was one of Scardino's security men, a thirty-year-old former Dallas SWAT officer who joined Gauntlet and moved to Miami to support company operations there and in Central America. He carried a pistol in his waistband, which was absolutely verboten here in Cuba, but this wasn't the only local law that Gauntlet Group was in violation of today. Gauntlet had powerful connections down here, and they'd received approval both for the visit and for the sidearms Scardino and Blanchard were carrying.

Across the runway, a pair of old MiG-21s rested inside two open concrete hangars, reminding Scardino that this was, indeed, a military base and not a regular airport.

Not that he'd needed much reminding.

Base Aérea San Julián was in the far west of Cuba, but still only 150 miles or so from Miami, and there wasn't much here, not even military activity, although Scardino had been promised that would change at two p.m.

He looked at his watch. It was two thirty-six.

Typical, he thought.

Moments later, however, an old white school bus pulled into view around the side of a hangar, coming from the direction of a side entrance of the base. Behind the bus, a Jeep carried four armed soldiers, and Scardino positioned himself to face the approaching entourage.

The bus parked just twenty meters or so from the nose cone of the Piper; Scardino looked back to Blanchard to ensure he was clocking the activity, and the man just gave a little nod, his eyes hidden behind wraparound Oakleys, the afternoon sun shining off them.

Several men in uniforms climbed out of the bus, and then a bearded man in a white prison jumpsuit emerged, his hands cuffed in front of him, chains binding his legs.

As the man neared, Mike Scardino squinted, looked through the thick haze hanging over the tarmac, and positively identified that the man being brought forward by Cuban prison officials was, in fact, the man he'd flown down here to collect.

Scott Kincaid, code-named Lancer.

One of the top dozen or so freelance hit men on planet Earth.

Kincaid had been arrested for homicide in Havana eight months ago, was tried and convicted in weeks, and then he'd been sent down here to the southwest of the nation to serve out a twenty-six-year sentence at the Prision de Sandino, just a few miles from this military base.

When Kincaid and Scardino were just a few feet apart, a Cuban prison guard stopped Kincaid's forward movement by grabbing him from behind, and then the prisoner was unshackled. Scardino just looked on; no words were spoken, and the American in the white jumpsuit just stared blankly ahead.

Scardino noted the man's apparent calm. If Kincaid was confused, excited, suspicious . . . if he felt any emotion whatsoever about being plucked from his dark cell and pulled into the sunlight, driven several miles out into the countryside, and then onto a military base, he did not show it.

And if he was internally bewildered standing face-to-face with another gringo, a man with an aircraft obviously already gassed up and ready to get the hell out of here, Michael Scardino could not detect it.

Kincaid just seemed completely at ease.

When the prisoner's chains had been pulled away and the guards turned around to leave, Scardino stepped forward and extended a hand. "I'm Big Mike," Scardino said. "Let's go."

Slowly, Kincaid shook the man's hand. "Yeah," replied Kincaid. "Let's."

The two men climbed into the small single-engine turboprop; Blanchard followed behind the two others into the aircraft, and then he lifted the stairs and sealed the hatch.

Inside the tight confines of the cabin, Scardino chose one of the two forward-facing seats, and Kincaid sat directly in front of him, facing the rear. Blanchard spoke with the flight crew for a moment, then sat next to Kincaid.

Big Mike noted the heavy tattoos on Lancer's hands, neck, and even behind his ears. Kincaid was a decorated Navy SEAL but had been banished from the Teams for conduct unbecoming: executing a prisoner, shooting unarmed civilians, Scardino couldn't remember the entire list.

He'd returned to the United States and then almost immediately become a white-power neo-Nazi, and Scardino wondered how that had worked out for him in a Cuban prison.

But the man looked healthy, tan, exceedingly fit. He might have been a little underweight, but not that much, and there was a glint in his eyes that gave Scardino the impression Kincaid thought he was in charge right now.

Scardino, on the other hand, was of the opinion that this son of a bitch wasn't in charge of shit. His air of superiority was a put-on, just like his faux nonchalance.

The aircraft began to taxi to the runway almost immediately. As it did so, Scardino said, "You've got a good poker face, man, but you must really be wondering what the fuck is going on."

"Actually, I was wondering something else."

"What's that?"

"Is there a bar on this bird?"

Scardino was surprised by the comment. After looking around a second, he said, "There's a tiny fridge. You want a water?"

"Got a beer?"

Mike Scardino laughed a little. "You don't want to know what the fuck is going on?"

"I'm actually pretty curious. I'm just hoping you'll tell me over a beer."

Scardino shrugged, then nodded to Blanchard, and the young man reached behind him, opened a small fridge, pulled out a Corona, popped the top, and handed it over to Kincaid. He took it with a little smile, then looked back to Scardino. "You're not drinking with me?"

Without speaking, Scardino stuck a hand out to Blanchard, who soon enough passed over a second Corona.

"Got any limes?" Kincaid asked.

Scardino said, "No, but I'll tell you what. Let's get the pilot to taxi back to the hangar and you can run to the market in Sandino to pick one up. That work?"

Scott Kincaid did not answer at first. Instead, he kept his eyes locked on the man in front of him as he took an incredibly long swig, draining nearly a third of the bottle.

Finished, he said, "It's good, just like this."

Now Big Mike said, "The Cubans have handed you over to my company."

"You paid a bribe to get me out?"

"We paid with information that we had and that they wanted. That part doesn't concern you."

"What's your company?"

"Gauntlet Group."

To this, the former Navy SEAL said, "I've heard of you guys. You're taking over up in D.C., aren't you? The president is firing all the federal employees, replacing them with you guys. Saves the taxpayers money, or that's the song and dance, anyway."

"Our footprint and our influence are growing, yes. The current administration appreciates what we're doing. It is our intent to make ourselves indispensable so that any subsequent administration would find it difficult to dislodge us."

"Right. And you want me to come work for you?" He took another few gulps of beer.

"Not officially."

"Meaning?"

"Meaning . . . unofficially."

"A contractor to the contractors." Kincaid polished off the bottle of Corona as Scardino took his first sip. The former prisoner looked to Blanchard, and Blanchard reached for another beer. Kincaid said, "You guys do security projects for the U.S. government, as well as technical analysis, logistics, HR, et cetera, et cetera, for the U.S. intelligence community."

"You got it."

"And you traded me out of prison so I can do . . . what, exactly?"

"My company has access to classified data. This data we have sold to a client, and the client would like to use this data to further their political and strategic aims, geopolitically speaking, in the U.S."

Kincaid accepted the beer from Blanchard with a curt nod, then wiped his face with his tattooed hand, and continued regarding Scardino as he did so. Finally, he said, "You're stealing files, there are names on the files. Spies or informants or troublemakers of some sort, and somebody is paying you to what . . . to *eliminate* those people?"

Scardino did not deny this. Kincaid was a killer for hire. It would be obvious that he was being hired to kill. "Something like that."

"But you don't want to use Gauntlet employees to assassinate people all over the world."

Now Scardino put up a finger. "We don't want to use Gauntlet employees to kill people *in America*. Overseas . . . we can, and we do these sorts of jobs ourselves."

"Roger," Kincaid said. "How does this work?"

"Simple. You will be given names of people you are to eliminate along with dossiers containing their addresses, any relevant training, their patterns of life. That sort of thing. You will then delete your targets. You have any problem with that?"

"Are you paying me?"

Scardino took another sip. "Of course. Your freedom, as well as a bonus of one million U.S. for every target eliminated."

"Then no . . . I don't have any problem with that. How many names on your list in total?"

Mike Scardino laughed a little. "That's not for you to know. It's a big list. You are one of several contract assets we will be using for this operation."

"Send the other assets home. I'll do them all."

Scardino sighed now, and the aircraft began racing down the runway on its takeoff roll.

He said, "You'll just take care of the names we give you."

Scott Kincaid said, "What's your plan? What's your endgame? Who's getting you guys to do this? Some rogue actors in America? Or is it Russia? China? Iran?"

"That information won't be given to you, because you don't need it."

The former SEAL swigged his cold Corona. Said, "Just curious."

"Well, be less curious, because you'll never know. Just do the work. Don't ask questions that aren't of a tactical nature."

As the Piper Meridian climbed into the sky, Scott Kincaid drank his beer and looked out the portal next to him as they flew over hot undeveloped scrubland.

To Scardino, Lancer said, "You're the boss, boss. Where's my first job?"

"Miami. We're on our way there now. You will oversee a team of freelance specialists. You'll have them do any legwork, surveillance work, computer work, whatever you need, but *you* are the trigger puller.

"You'll meet your team and hit your first target in a high-rise condo building in Aventura. When you're done with Miami, you're off to Chicago. A job at a hotel there. Trust me, these are easy targets, relative to some of the others on the list. I'll give you a day for each of the first two, plus a day to set up and a day's travel in between."

Kincaid took yet another hit of his second beer. "Four days from now, two targets will be dead, and I'll be after the third on the list."

"You aren't lacking in confidence, are you?" Scardino noted.

"A lifetime of success will do that to you."

"*Success?* We just pulled your ass out of a prison in Cuba."

"Yeah, it sucked to be there, but by the time I left, I ran that place."

Scardino hid a smile behind his beer bottle. "I'm sure you did."

Now the assassin said, "There's something else I want from you."

"What's that?"

"You just said you have the ability to obtain classified intel from the CIA."

"I did."

"I want you to find someone for me."

Confused, the Gauntlet man said, "Who?"

"The Gray Man."

With a chuckle, Scardino said, "You're kidding, right? That guy's not real."

"He's real to me. He's the one who put me in that fucking prison. I'll work for you, I'll kill for you, but you find out what you can about him."

Scardino said nothing.

"Deal?"

Now Big Mike looked up to the screen on the bulkhead showing the location of the aircraft. They were heading northeast, towards Miami. He said, "We're going to overfly Havana in about twenty-five minutes. Want me to drop you off there?"

"I do not," Lancer said. "Look, I will work for you regardless. But if you really have a lot of targets, you will want me to do them quickly. The longer this takes, the sooner the targets will recognize a pattern, the sooner the targets will realize they might be next. They will go to ground. I know that, and *I* know that *you* know that. I will be more motivated to work more quickly if you and I agree on these terms. My terms are my freedom, which you have already secured. Payment, which you promise me for each successful operation. And information. Get me what the U.S. government has on the Gray Man. I get all that . . . I'll be the best worker bee you've ever seen. Your enemies list will be full of stacked bodies, flies crawling across their eyeballs, that kind of shit."

"What if there's nothing about the Gray Man?"

"There's *not* nothing about the Gray Man. He used to be CIA. There are files on him."

Scardino looked out the window a moment. "Sure, Lancer. I'll put in a request. I don't know what the IC has on this phantom everybody talks about, but if there's anything out there, you can see it."

Scott Kincaid, code-named Lancer, wiped a thin sheen of perspiration from his shaved head, looked out the portal, down at the island he had no desire to ever see again, and smiled, thinking about a future that seemed so much brighter now than it had just a couple of hours earlier.

TWENTY-TWO

The middle-aged man from Northern Ireland stepped out of the cab, looked up at the building in front of him, and read the sign.

KEARNEY AND SONS FUNERAL HOME

At the front door he took off his hat and paused.

This was Boston, South Dorchester, and Campbell Coyle had been in America for less than three hours. The jet lag would hit him later, but he'd fight it, and he'd be fine.

He'd been to Boston before, working, but never had he been to this place, with his hat in hand, asking for a favor from a man he did not know.

He didn't like the feeling of others being involved in his business; he had been comfortable in hiding, using a fake name, living a fake life.

But he'd deemed today necessary, so here he was, standing in the snow, hesitating a moment before opening the door.

But open the door he did, and when he entered, he put a calm smile on his face and lifted his chin.

The lobby was empty, fake flowers in massive urns, a reception desk unattended.

Soft music played, piped over a sound system in the ceiling.

Coyle saw no evidence of a funeral going on right now, so he suspected the somber music was a constant around here. Families came to buy caskets and such, so the music had to remain fitting to the situation.

"Can I help you?" The accent was all Boston.

Coyle tracked the voice to one of a pair of men walking up a hallway on his right. Both men were in their thirties; they both wore dark gray suits that looked off-the-rack but fit well enough. One of the two was slightly taller; the shorter one had a mustache, but otherwise they were nearly indistinguishable, so Campbell Coyle took them to be brothers.

He was expected, so he said, "Jon Jo Sheehan, here for Mr. Kearney."

Both men continued approaching him. The shorter of the two appeared a little older, and he said, "My brother will take your hat and coat, sir."

As the taller of the pair reached out for the coat, Coyle caught sight of the grip of a single-stack Glock pistol in the man's shoulder holster.

Coyle himself was unarmed, which was good, because after his hat and coat were taken, he was thoroughly frisked by the shorter of the two men.

The search of his body was done without comment or ceremony.

Strange behavior for a funeral home, Coyle thought, but all three of these men knew there was much more to this place than met the eye.

Soon he was led out of the lobby, down the hall, and into a back office that telegraphed to Coyle that the occupant of it didn't make his money exclusively by burying the dead of South Dorchester. It was as opulent as it was expansive, with luxurious-looking leather furniture in a seating area, and a long bar across one wall. A man sitting at the bar looking at his cell phone rose and walked quickly to Coyle, with a spry step out of place for the surroundings, and also out of tune with his appearance. The man was well into his seventies, heavyset, bearded, with reddish and gray hair swirled around the top of his head as if he'd just survived a tornado.

He wore a turtleneck sweater that looked expensive, and black suede slippers with the image of dancing skeletons stitched into the tops. His corduroy pants were baggy, but the watch on his wrist, just visible from under the cuff of the sweater, appeared to be a gold Rolex.

The old man shook Coyle's hand with a smile. "Welcome to Boston. We spoke on the phone yesterday. My name is Gerry Kearney." Kearney had an Irish accent to anyone here from the United States, but to Coyle he sounded American.

And Campbell Coyle hadn't needed this man to introduce himself. He was the sole reason Coyle had come to Boston.

"Mr. Kearney, thank you for seeing me."

"Mr. Sheehan, it's a pleasure."

"It's Coyle, of course, as I mentioned on the phone."

The older man smiled, raised an eyebrow. "Is it now? We're about to find out about that."

Coyle felt the presence of the two men who'd led him here; they were now standing very close behind him. Well within striking distance, and the Northern Irishman understood they might get orders to do just that at any time.

"So . . ." Kearney said, "you claim to be the son of Rory *fucking* Coyle, I've got that right, do I?"

"I am."

"I don't know you, and I'm not the type to trust any young fella who saunters into my place of business claiming to be the spawn of the finest man with the biggest balls to have ever walked this godforsaken earth."

"I didn't bring any family photos, and he died when I was fifteen."

Kearney said, "If you're Rory Coyle's son . . . tell me, what years was he at Long Kesh?"

Long Kesh was an infamous prison in County Down, in the southeastern part of Northern Ireland. Originally an RAF base, it had been converted to hold IRA prisoners by the British.

Coyle thought a moment. "He was put in an H-Block right after I was born. Late seventies, that would be. Was there for the hunger strike, did forty-six days before it ended. He got out when I was five, which was the first time I met him." After saying this, Coyle jerked a thumb over his shoulder. "Don't suppose one of these blokes has a calculator in his shoulder holster, but we can figure out the years."

Kearney smiled at this. Coyle knew he'd passed the first challenge. He said, "Your dear mother. Her name?"

"Margaret."

"What did everybody call her?"

"I called her Ma, as did my brother. Everyone else called her Mags."

Now the Bostonian nodded a little. He asked, "Where did Rory meet her?"

"In East Belfast. A pub in Short Strand, or so I'm told. Neither of them talked about that much, so I knew better than to ask more questions."

Kearney smiled at this a little. "Aye. Best you don't. I was there, though I was a wee boy, had no business in a pub myself." He added, "It was young love between them, but it *was* love. I saw it blossom myself. Rory was a tough bastard rendered weak by Mags, if only momentarily."

Campbell Coyle said nothing.

Kearney continued with the vetting process. "Think back now, lad. There was a man with a scar. A ginger. Always ran around with your pop. Quiet, didn't drink, not a drop, unlike the rest of us. You remember anyone like that?"

"Aye. I was young, but that scar was hard to forget."

"From the butt of a British soldier's ArmaLite, taken right to the cheekbone."

Coyle said, "He was missing some teeth, too, if memory serves."

Kearney grinned now. "Your memory serves you well. Now . . . the scarred man's name?"

"Robbie."

"Robbie *what*?"

Coyle thought back. "He was just 'Uncle Robbie' to me. Always brought me and my brother sweets or crisps, he did. If I saw him, I knew I was getting a treat."

Kearney gave a gentle wave of his hand. Coyle was confused by it but quickly felt the men behind him melt back and away, until the door to the big office shut behind them and they were gone. The old man said, "Well, lad, your Uncle Robbie's name was Robbie Kearney, and he was my much beloved brother."

Coyle nodded. "I quite liked him. A gentle soul."

"Not to the British, he wasn't. Rory and Robbie were the terrors of Belfast for a while, they were." Kearney said this with a twinkle in his eye.

"He's still among the living, I hope?" It was said as a question.

"No, no. Died 2008. Natural causes for an Irishman. Smoking, back-breaking labor, fried food." Kearney waved a hand around the funeral home. "The kind of behavior that keeps me in business, even now, even here."

"Right."

Kearney led Coyle to a leather sofa, and they sat down together. The old man said, "You passed the test. An honor to meet you."

"You, too."

"Cup of tea?"

"No, thanks. I can't stay long."

"Your father, quite a legend, he was. He was the best. My brother ran with him for years before your da moved to Derry. I was younger. I only knew your pop a little, you understand, but Robbie loved him, and I loved Robbie."

With sadness in his eyes, he said, "I moved to America when I turned eighteen; Robbie and Rory were in their twenties, fighting the British. I've never forgiven myself for leaving the cause behind."

Coyle wanted to say he wished his da had gone to America and left the cause behind, but he did not.

Kearney said, "Now . . . how can I help you, young Campbell, son of the magnificent Rory?"

This, Coyle knew, was the moment of truth. He said, "I'm here in America to do a series of jobs. I don't know how long it will take. Might be weeks. Hopefully less. I'll be paid well for my efforts here. The work will be dangerous, and the people I'll work for are not to be trusted, if you get my meaning."

Kearney's look gave nothing away. "Maybe I do. Maybe I don't. Go on."

"If you could loan me a small but solid crew of men to watch my back while I work, then all that I am paid, every dollar, I will give to you."

"That doesn't sound like a shrewd business plan on your part."

"I'm not here in America to make money. I'm here to find someone. I'll work for these other blokes, but only until I find who I came for. When I do, I'll do what I have to do, and then I'll go back home."

"You're asking me for men. Why is that? I mean to say . . . most people don't go to a funeral director when they're looking for a crew of soldiers."

"Everyone knows Gerry Kearney runs the syndicate in South Dorchester."

"If *everyone* knew that, I'd be in prison, wouldn't I? How is it *you* know?"

Coyle shrugged. "I'd heard rumors. I asked around."

"Asked who?" Kearney said, a deeper tone to his voice.

"Bill Tully, for one."

The tone remained dark. "Tell me, how is Bill?"

"Good when I ran into him. Not so good when I left him."

"Sent him to the doctor, did you?"

"Only to pronounce him dead."

Now Kearney's eyes narrowed. "You killed him?"

"Aye."

"Who are you, then? Other than Rory's son?"

"You know who Rory was, yeah?"

"I do."

"Well, you might say that I'm a chip off that old block, except I've done it for money, not for a cause; I've done it all over the world, not just in Ulster and London; and I've done it for double the time my da did it before they got him."

Coyle added, "*Nobody's* got me."

Gerry Kearney took all this in. "You're an Irish Republican dissident?"

A shake of the head. "I don't fight for that lost cause."

"Then . . . then you're some sort of a contract killer."

"Aye."

"And you've killin' to do here."

"Heaps of it, or so they tell me."

The old man put his hands on his knees, let out a big sigh. "The syndicate here isn't what it used to be. Twenty-five years ago, we were big. Now we're a shadow of what we once were. If I'd one hundred men, I'd hand them over to you right now, both for being Rory's boy and for fucking up Bill Tully. But the truth is—"

Coyle interrupted. "The two who brought me in to see you just now. They'll do fine. Another pair who look just as keen for action."

"Four men," Coyle said. "Four capable men is all I ask."

Kearney thought a moment. "Those at the front? The Donnelly brothers. Jack and Alfie. They're good, the both of them. They've done dirty work, as I suspect you've figured out. I'll also throw in the Walsh boys for you. Three lads, a little younger, but wicked smart. Able. Can have them here, bags packed, in an hour."

"These Walsh boys can handle themselves?"

"Aye. Gavin, Barry, and Nolan. Nolan's just a lad. Twenty-three, twenty-four. But he's loyal. His brothers are older; they've been heavies for me for years."

"They know guns?"

"It's America, son. We all know guns. I'll outfit them. You, too, if you need it."

"That would be grand," Coyle said. "Pistols only. I can pay."

"Your money's no good here."

Coyle said, "Then . . . what do you want in return?"

Gerry Kearney took Campbell Coyle's hand, squeezed it tight. "I want to go to my grave knowing I did something for the great Roderick Coyle. Even posthumously. My big brother's best friend. And the man I wish I was."

Kearney's eyes misted as he released his grip. Coyle thought this bloke seemed to like his father much more than he himself did.

Coyle said, "The money I make in America is yours, there's no debating that. I'm on a different mission. But we have to leave today. I have a meeting in Washington, and I want those five heavies of yours watching my back, because you can best believe I won't be trusting anyone else."

Kearney agreed, and the two men stood. The older man said, "I wish you all the luck. But . . . whatever you're here to do, if you don't make it back alive, young Campbell, it would be my great honor to handle your burial, free of charge, of course. There's a nice plot at St. Michael, where—"

Coyle interrupted. "Much appreciated, but we've a family plot, up north in County Antrim. Haven't been there in ages, but nevertheless, I've family there, and something tells me that's where I should be planted for the ever after when I go."

Gerry Kearney nodded, then headed to his desk to pick up the phone to round up the five men he'd send out into the field with the son of his dead brother's dead friend.

TWENTY-THREE

Zack Hightower wasn't usually the man sitting in the back of the surveillance vehicle, but here he was, eating a tuna salad sandwich he'd bought at a gas station in Arlington before dawn, and downing it with Gatorade.

It was two thirty in the afternoon; laptops sat in front of him on a table fashioned out of particle board and two-by-fours and attached to the inside wall of the white GMC Savana, and he leaned back in a swivel chair bungeed to the opposite wall.

His boots were propped on a stack of hard-shell Pelican cases and nylon Eberlestock modular bags of various shapes and styles.

His left thigh was stiff, the effects of the gunshot wound still bugging him a little, but it wasn't that bad. He'd taken some Advil this morning and he had more if he needed it, though in typical Zack fashion, the loose pills were mixed in with the lint balls in the front left pocket of his jeans.

Up behind the wheel, Arnold Reyes sat with his head back on the headrest and his cheap sunglasses on, shielding his eyes so that anyone walking by might think he was asleep.

The logistics coordinator of this small team of assets had been drafted to drive one of the two vehicles today, the decision being made hastily this morning when Irene Ortega surprised the team by driving to work from her condo, though it was less than a fifteen-minute walk through D.C.

The team quickly decided to split up, so another vehicle was rented, and now Zack and Arnold, the two non-operational team members, sat in the original van with the equipment, making sure the subject didn't leave her work and either come back here to her car or head out on foot in some other direction.

Zack was dressed in a leather bomber jacket with a knit cap, jeans, and boots. Arnold, on the other hand, was dressed in a coat and tie; his wool overcoat lay on the seat next to him. He wore a suit to Ghost Town every day, Hanley had mentioned, and apparently no one had thought to tell him he didn't need to dress for the office while driving a backup van in the field.

This was the first day of surveillance, and the first day of any surveillance operation was often a mess.

While Arnold watched Irene's car in a parking garage on G Street NW, just a block and a half from the Department of State where she was working at the moment, and Zack watched images from a camera positioned under a bench across the street from a rear exit of Irene's workplace, Court Gentry and Chris Travers had gone to her short-term rental at the Carriage House Condominium near Washington Circle, just a mile to the northwest. The men code-named Six and Teddy were dressed in disguise as telecom repairmen, head-to-toe in blue coveralls, tool belts adorned with the accoutrements of their trade, and shoulder bags over their working-class winter coats that kept them warm as they walked towards the building.

Court held a small ladder, and after slipping through a back door in a rear loading area and into an elevator, they shot straight up to Ortega's eighth-floor condo, picking the lock there just seconds after Jill Mori remotely shut down the woman's wireless service to disable any Internet-based cameras she might have had inside.

The men carried signal scramblers on their tool belts; they were fashioned to look like flashlights but designed to disrupt any recording devices left on in the room, a typical countersurveillance measure, and they swept the unit for bugs with handheld radio frequency scanners just in case someone else was as interested in Ortega as they were.

They found nothing amiss, so they separated and went to work. Moving silently throughout the space, independently from one another, the pair placed three bugs and three pinhole cameras, and they photographed everything they could see lying around. Books, magazines, mail, even the contents of her fridge and freezer and the bottles in her medicine cabinet.

After just a few minutes of searching, Court's phone vibrated, and he tapped the AirPod in his right ear.

Travers did the same, indicating to both men that someone had initiated a conference call with the assets.

Court answered softly, so as not to be heard either in the hallway or in a neighboring unit. "Yeah?"

"It's me, Six." Technically, Zack was supposed to confirm his identity with his code name, Night Train, but it was common for Zack to bend the rules in the field.

"What's up?"

"Subject just exited the rear of her building, might be heading your way."

Court looked to his watch. It was 2:48 in the afternoon, early for her to be coming home from work. He said, "Going out for coffee?"

"There's a Starbucks in her building."

"But she's definitely *not* going for her car."

"Definitely not. She's on foot. Heading away from the garage. We're firing up, going after her."

"Roger, we'll exfil now. Stay on the line, keep us updated."

"Will do, but it's a short walk from her to you, so you better prep to boogie."

"Wilco."

They were packed up and ready to go in no time; Court checked in with Jill to make sure there was no one outside the door in the hallway, and once Gumdrop confirmed this, he and Travers left, heading for the elevator.

They'd made it halfway there when Zack spoke up again. "We've got visual on the subject at this time. She's still on foot, east of her building, turning to the north."

"Still coming this way?" Court said.

"Possibly. Still heading north, in your direction, ten minutes to your poz."

"Leaving her car in the garage? Why would she do that?" Court asked.

"I'm just telling you what I see. You need to get out."

"We're exfilling now."

Three minutes later they were outside; their rented burgundy Chrysler Pacifica minivan was parked on M Street NW, and here they dumped the ladder and the utility belts into the back.

Just as they shut the rear hatch, Zack came over Court's earpiece.

"Be advised, subject is heading into the Metro at George Washington University."

"Okay," Court said. "You close enough to get on her train?"

"Can be." After a second, he said, "This is just on the other side of Washington Circle."

"So?" Court asked, confused.

Travers said, "Meaning she walked almost all the way back home to get on the Metro by her house. Why didn't she bring her car back here?"

"She's going back to work, maybe?" Court speculated.

"Maybe," Zack said. "Or else she's running an SDR."

A surveillance detection route was a tactic used the world over by spies to check if someone was following them.

Court shook his head as he climbed into the passenger seat. "This lady is a desk jockey at the Office of the Director of National Intelligence. What does she know about SDRs?"

To this, Zack said, "I guess I'm about to find out. I'm on foot heading down the escalator, Arnold is topside in the van."

Travers sat down behind the wheel of the burgundy minivan. Court opened a map on the dashboard screen, and Travers began looking to pull out into the heavy afternoon traffic.

Over their earpieces, Zack said, "She's going for the eastbound platform. That's going to put her on the Blue line or the Orange line."

Court had no idea where either of those Metro lines would lead. He knew cities in Russia, in Pakistan, in Mexico, even in rural Brazil or Guatemala, way better than he knew his own nation's capital. He turned to Travers. "You used to live here, right?"

Travers answered, "Heading east, Blue and Orange both go to Farragut West, then . . . uhh . . ." He thought a moment.

"Where?" Court demanded as he began pulling up the info on his phone.

"It's been a minute. There's another station, then Metro Center, then Smithsonian, and L'Enfant, there might be another before Smithsonian."

Court had it up on his screen now. "Federal Triangle is after Metro Center."

"That's right," Travers confirmed.

They pulled out of the parking space now. "Got it. We just keep heading east. Night Train, you're on her platform?"

"Affirmative. There's a Blue line coming in one minute. The Downtown Largo train."

Travers said, "We're going to lose signal down there when you're in the tunnel, but we'll pick you up again at the next station."

"Roger that."

Court and Chris had only gone half a block in the gridlock a half mile north of the White House when Zack spoke again. "We're on the Blue line. Say again, Blue line."

"Copy." Court looked to Travers from the passenger seat. "Where can we intercept them?"

"All depends on parking," Travers said.

"What if we don't park? What if I jump out and you keep going?"

"Forget about the Farragut stations. We won't make it. If she gets out there, Night Train can stay with her. Ditto McPherson Square, we won't get there in time. Let's try for Metro Center."

"Do it."

The minivan raced forward during a break in traffic.

Zack Hightower stood in the train car just forward of his target's car, and he watched while Irene Ortega sat near a doorway near the rear.

The car was half full. Zack was glad it wasn't yet rush hour; he had a good view of her out of the corner of his eye, well enough to see that she seemed alert.

Her eyes flitted left and right, and he got the impression she was checking to see if she was being followed, and she wasn't terribly subtle about it.

If she *was* a spy, Zack decided, then she wasn't a very good one.

He wondered who she suspected was following her right now. Feds? Other people in her agency?

Zack had decades of training in countersurveillance, so he scanned

360, nonchalantly, and saw no one who fit the obvious mold for a countersurveillance agent, but he knew he could not be sure. The FBI used a unit called the Special Surveillance Group, a force of trained operatives, from their late teens to well into their seventies, who worked exclusively on surveillance missions. These weren't feds, spooks, soldiers, or cops, just regular people who worked for the FBI, people who fit in wherever they were tasked to work, so that all the people the Bureau used to tail suspects around the world didn't look anything like central-casting G-men.

But the SSG had been gutted in the last year and replaced mostly by Gauntlet Group contractors. The Gauntlet crew were mostly military-aged males, and even though there were some females, most of the women had military or law enforcement backgrounds and didn't blend in as well as the SSG had.

The train stopped at the Farragut West station; a few people got on and a few got off, and then Irene herself stood, went to the door.

Zack headed to the nearest door of his car, stepped halfway out, and then realized Ortega had not gotten off.

He backed inside, and the door closed.

For a moment he worried she'd outsmarted him, but when he went back to look into the next car, he saw that she was still there.

He did realize that this was a fuckup, however. If there was someone watching her, then they might have noticed the fact that he'd looked down the platform, then stepped back on the train, as if he were trying to anticipate the movements of someone else.

He hadn't expected to do anything more than ride in the back of a van all day, so he'd been caught by surprise when he went operational, but he knew he needed to up his game.

He sat down next to the door, leaned forward a little, and just caught sight of Ortega's boots, fifty feet down the train in the last car.

Quickly, while they were still in the station and before the train went back into the tunnel, he tapped out a quick text on his phone.

Cont past Farragut on Blue. She's def squirrely—6, get to me, ASAP. No sight of counter, but I'm burned if so.

. . .

Court read the text aloud in the minivan as it shot through a yellow light that turned red before they left the intersection.

Both men understood Zack's abbreviated text, but Travers deciphered it aloud, anyway.

"Ortega is nervous about something, and Zack outed himself, not to her but to anybody that he hasn't ID'd that might be watching her."

Court said, "He never was the most low-profile guy out there, was he?"

"Nope," Travers said. "This sounds like a job for the Gray Man."

"Don't fucking start," Court mumbled as he looked at his phone.

A couple of minutes later they were a few more blocks to the southeast when Court received another text from Zack. He read this one aloud, as well.

Continuing past McPherson. She's nervous. Where r u 6?

"Looks like about two minutes to Metro Center," Travers said as he changed lanes.

"Or twenty, depending on this traffic," Court barked in frustration.

TWENTY-FOUR

The Chrysler minivan was still in motion as Court leapt out and began running for the station entrance. He hadn't taken the time to change clothes during the drive, but the heavy coat he'd worn with his overalls was reversible, and he'd switched it from the blue side to the brown side.

He hurried to the escalators on 13th Street and began racing down. Metro Center was a large station with many lines connecting here, so there was a lot of foot traffic, but he wove his way through, then headed to the turnstiles, held his wallet over the reader, and soon he was through.

He slowed to pass a group of Metro Police standing around, then followed the signs to the Blue line and made his way to another escalator, picking up speed again when the cops could no longer see him.

He finally arrived at the platform just as the train appeared, and he looked at his phone and saw another text from Zack that had just come through.

Last car. No counter detected.

He quickly tapped out a reply, acknowledging that he understood the woman was still on the train and Zack hadn't detected countersurveillance.

OK. Get off. Teddy upstairs.

Court headed towards the rear of the train, the doors opened, and he saw Zack exit, heading for the escalators. The men passed within a dozen feet of one another, but there was no eye contact between them. Court was too busy scanning down the platform, making sure Ortega did not leave the train, and looking over anyone getting on.

Soon he was on the train himself, in the same car Zack had just vacated. A quick look at those around him put him at ease; he didn't feel there was anyone here who might be running surveillance on Ortega.

The train left the station; Court moved to a seat where he could see into the last car, and there he saw the woman looking back up in his general direction. He didn't think for a second he'd been spotted, only that she was alert for anyone watching her.

They stopped at Federal Triangle; Ortega kept her seat, so Court did the same.

Irene Ortega rose and moved near the door, and for a second or two, he thought she was about to get off. He held his seat, ready to bolt onto the platform from the next car himself, but then another woman entered Irene's car, moved to a seat, and the door closed again.

Court regarded the new woman, and something about her seemed off. He couldn't quite get a read on her at this distance, but it was in the way she had moved after encountering Ortega. It felt to Court like she'd hesitated a moment when she got on the train and saw Ortega right there by the door, before quickly lowering her head and then passing her by.

It wasn't an obvious tell, but to a guy who had been doing this as long as Court had, it was enough to draw some suspicion.

The new arrival wore business clothes, a nice camel coat, and she held gloves in her hand. A large leather bag hung off her right shoulder, an umbrella jutting out of it, and her leather boots were low-heel and comfortable-looking, but in keeping with something a woman here in D.C. might wear when there was a forecast for snow, like today.

Once the woman sat down across from Ortega, she pulled out her phone.

Quickly, just before the doors closed, Court tapped out a text and sent it to the team of three men and two vehicles somewhere up at street level.

Leaving Fed Tri

The entire way to the next stop, Court split his time between looking at the new woman who seemed to have reacted when she saw Ortega, and looking in his own car, even the car beyond his, trying to spot any other countersurveillance.

Just as the conductor announced they were approaching the Smithsonian station, Irene rose, held on to a handrail, then shifted towards the door. The woman sitting across from her glanced her way quickly, but she did not look for long before turning her attention back to her phone.

The door opened at Smithsonian station and Irene Ortega quickly disembarked. Court left the train himself and headed for the stairs, ignoring the escalator that most passengers took. Once he was far enough away from the crowd, he spoke for the benefit of those connected to his call. "We're off at Smithsonian. Heading up. Both vehicles converge there."

After Teddy and Arnold confirmed, he rushed faster up the stairs, made it to the mezzanine level, then saw that Ortega was already exiting through the turnstiles. He followed the crowd, well behind her, then communicated again with Hightower.

"Night Train, you receiving?"

"Affirm. We're on 14th Street passing the mall, we're about one mike from that station. Bricklayer is in the work van behind us."

"Roger," Court said. "I'll take the eye at street level and inform."

Court stepped out into the frigid gray afternoon and onto Independence Avenue. He followed the woman to the left; she was twenty-five yards ahead when she crossed 12th Street, and here she passed the National Museum of Asian Art.

An icy wind blew in his face; he leaned into it, pulled his knit cap down lower, and walked on, and in moments he saw Travers pass him on his right in the burgundy Pacifica, with Zack in the front passenger seat. They continued east, and Court spoke into his earpiece to let them know where the woman was on the sidewalk.

Arnold passed Court a moment later in the big GMC van; Court told him to turn right on L'Enfant Plaza, drive down half a block, and stop.

Travers and Zack had the eye now. Though they had driven past Ortega, they found a place to pull over in front of the General Services Administration Building, and they could monitor her movements from their vehicle.

Court had just climbed into the Savana with Arnold when Travers's voice came over the AirPod.

"Be advised, she just turned left. She's going into the Hirshhorn Museum."

Court cocked his head as Arnold pulled back out onto the street, still heading south.

The Hirshhorn was a famous windowless building on Independence Avenue, part of the Smithsonian Institution and full of American modern art. It was donut-shaped, with a courtyard in the middle.

Zack said, "This lady's taking the afternoon off to enjoy an art exhibit?"

"Not buying it," Court said. "She's looking over her shoulder for a tail. She's not well trained, but she's definitely up to something."

"A meet?" Travers asked.

"That would be my guess," Court replied, and then he told Arnold to head back to the north to drop him off at the museum.

As Arnold drove, however, Court looked down at his clothing. Blue coveralls, work boots, a heavy brown coat that might fit in in a meatpacking plant but not an art museum. He knew Travers looked almost the same, and Zack wasn't even operational, wearing his typical roper boots and a leather bomber jacket.

He said, "Every one of us is going to stick out like a sore thumb in a Smithsonian museum at three fifteen on a weekday."

Zack replied, "Doesn't matter. She won't pick us up."

"I'm more worried about whoever she's coming to meet, or anyone surveilling her." Court looked at Arnold, saw him dressed in a suit and tie with a camel jacket, and he knew the two men were close to the same size.

He thought about taking his logistics coordinator's clothes so he could slip into the museum, but then he ruled it out. He said, "Guys, we aren't dressed for an afternoon of art appreciation."

It was quiet for a second, and then at the same time, Travers and Zack both said the same thing into his earpiece.

"Bricklayer."

Court understood what they meant, but he was not in agreement. "He doesn't know how to do—"

Zack cut him off. "In one of those Pelican cases behind you, he'll know which one, there is a set of charged video surveillance glasses. He was talking about them earlier. Slap those on his eyes, then give him a sixty-second brief on his mission."

Court looked to Arnold Reyes. "Can you do it?"

"Wear glasses and walk around a museum? Yes, I should be able to do that." Court detected no sarcasm in the man's answer, and he found that a little disconcerting.

He shook it off. "You've got this." To the rest of the team he said, "We're a go. We'll park near the Hirshhorn and he'll go in. I want Teddy to dismount, Night Train behind the wheel and driving around the area. Look for anyone out of place. If someone's followed her in there, then they're just as interested in her as we are. Don't get compromised."

Court crawled into the back of the van, and as Arnold drove, he directed him to the right black Pelican case from the several back there. From it, Court pulled out a set of clear Ray-Bans that felt a little heavy but seemed to be normal in every other way. As he retook his seat, he said, "Okay, try to get close to her, wherever she is in the building; do a sweep of anyone she meets with, but do *not* press your luck."

"Got it," he said, and then he pulled into an open spot almost in front of the Hirshhorn.

Court handed Arnold the glasses and immediately saw that this in extremis plan of his to use the logistics coordinator on a surveillance operation had a couple of flaws in it.

For one, Arnold had never served operationally on a surveillance team. He looked a little bewildered and nervous, though he made no protest to the new plan.

But the greatest flaw with this scheme, it became clear to Court now, was that Arnold *already* wore glasses, and they were clearly not for reasons of aesthetics.

He took off the thick eyeglasses he wore normally, put on the Ray-Bans, then immediately took them off again.

"Problem?" Court asked.

"I . . . I just am used to my own glasses. These don't have my correction."

Court said, "Do your best, man. Just walk around, look at the art, and—"

"I can't see the art. I'll be lucky if I can see the front door."

"Shit." Court rubbed perspiration from his forehead. "Are you legally blind without your glasses?"

"I . . . I don't know. Nobody has ever told me I'm blind, but I definitely can't—"

"Then you're fine." Court patted him on the shoulder. "Just try not to stumble into a Picasso."

With the glasses still off, Arnold said, "I'll try. I have to set these up." For the next thirty seconds he turned on the glasses, made sure there was no light on the frames indicating that the streaming feature was on, then connected the video stream with everyone already on the conference call. Jill came over the call to say she wouldn't be able to run facial recog with the resolution from the stream, but Arnold confirmed that the glasses were also recording in HD, so once he got them back to the safe house, she could get the image quality she needed.

This all taken care of, Arnold put the glasses on, fumbled for the door handle to get out of the Savana, then slid out into the frigid afternoon.

Court climbed out the other side and caught up with Arnold on the sidewalk. "You *can* see a little, right?"

"A little, yes," Arnold said, and then he headed for the entrance to the museum while Court walked off to the left.

Hanley's going to kick my ass for this, Court thought as he headed west on the sidewalk.

TWENTY-FIVE

As soon as Arnold disappeared, Court continued moving back in the direction of the Metro station he'd left minutes earlier, just to look at the vehicles parked alongside Independence, and the people braving the wind and cold on the sidewalk. He saw a few homeless people's tents there in the grass; he'd seen little pockets of tents all over D.C. today and assumed it was like this every day, as it was in most major cities.

He made a right turn, headed up a little footpath in the direction of the National Mall, and checked in with Travers, who was in the process of walking the neighborhood on the east side of the museum.

Zack chimed in, as well, saying that he had parked the Pacifica, and right now he was looking at his phone, watching the real-time video coming from Arnold's glasses as he waited in line to buy a bottled water in the little coffee shop in the museum lobby. Ortega herself was several people ahead of him in line, and Zack thought she was stalling, or continuing her SDR by stopping here in the lobby before her clandestine meet.

Court walked on, passed another cluster of old tents, then got a new call on his phone. He told the others he'd be right back, then accepted the call.

"Yeah?"

Matt Hanley's voice came over his earpiece, and Court knew Matt well enough to know when he was pissed. "Gumdrop tells me you have *fucking*

Bricklayer running point on a surveillance mission against a woman looking for a tail and possibly meeting with a member of the opposition."

Court sighed, turned right on Jefferson Drive. "Well, when you say it like that—"

"What the fuck is wrong with you guys?"

"We're getting live footage inside the Hirshhorn. None of us had time to dress for the Smithsonian."

"I swear to God, if you guys put Bricklayer in any danger, I will—"

"He's doing great."

Court hung up, checked back with Zack, and learned that Irene Ortega had left the line at the café without buying anything, and now she was taking the escalator that led up to the art exhibits.

He ordered Arnold to continue waiting in line so as not to arouse any suspicion, and to let Ortega go up on her own.

Travers checked in that all was clear on the east side outside the museum; Court didn't see anything out of place himself on the northwest side, but then he turned and began walking through the Mary Livingston Ripley Garden, a small park with curved walkways and, at this time of year, next to no living foliage, and here he saw another old tent erected, close to Independence Avenue and next door to the walled garden surrounding the Hirshhorn.

This tent was different from the others he'd seen on this freezing afternoon, in that here the dweller of the tent was visible, sitting inside the open flap, covered in a dirty sleeping bag.

The man wore a beard and seemed to be in his thirties, and he paid no attention to Court as he sat there.

The man appeared to be a typical transient, but Court did what he always did in the field, and he focused carefully.

The tent dweller's hair was matted, his beard long and unkempt.

Right before he walked by the man and lost visual, Court saw a hand come out of the sleeping bag, grasp it at the top, and pull it up closer to his neck, apparently for warmth.

The man's face had been dirty, and his hands seemed dirty, too.

But the man's fingernails looked trimmed and healthy.

Court Gentry had been trained to evaluate fingernails, because although it was easy to change one's appearance in many ways to look like a laborer or even a homeless person, and it wasn't hard to get some dirt on the hands or under the nails, the average transient did not have trimmed nails and most people impersonating one didn't take the time to alter them.

Court turned left on Independence, and instinctively, he flashed his eyes across the street.

Another man was bundled behind a tarp here. He was too far away to see well, but the man appeared to be in his thirties, just like this one.

Court wondered if these two men were working in a team.

He kept walking, but he softly spoke into his earpiece. "Teddy, we've got a problem."

"Whatcha see?"

"Homeless tent on southwest corner of AO is occupied by a possible asset."

"Roger that, I'll see if I can ID others in the AO. Want to consider pulling back?"

Before Court could answer, Zack's voice came over the net. "Bricklayer is on the second floor; he's got Ortega in sight. She's alone but stationary, looking into another room."

"What's your gut?" Court asked Zack.

"She doesn't want to go in there for some reason."

Shit. Court wanted to know what Irene was doing, but the only way to find out was to send Reyes even closer. After a few seconds, he said, "Bricklayer. Go in that room, have a quick look around, then get out of the building."

Arnold did not reply, which pleased Court greatly. He didn't know if he was going to follow Court's instructions, but it was better that he didn't answer him.

Zack, watching the streaming feed through the glasses, picked up the play-by-play as Court walked on past the front of the Hirshhorn, past the GMC Savana, heading to the east.

Zack said, "He's entering a room . . . it's like graffiti on the walls, on the ceiling, on the floor. The whole space is a single piece of art, I guess. Everything's black and white."

After a quick pause, Travers spoke up. "Six, I've ID'd a red Econoline van over here. Two dudes in the front seat. Beardy tough guys."

Travers was a beardy tough guy himself, but Court took his meaning. "Roger, don't get clocked by them, head back to Night Train's vic."

Zack spoke again. "There are just two people in the graffiti room with Bricklayer. You're doing good, man, just keep looking around, and when I tell you, I want you to turn to the right and go out that door on the opposite side. We'll try to get a quick viz on their faces."

Still Arnold said nothing.

Court was barely listening, though; instead, he was making mental calculations. There might have been watchers in the Metro; he had clocked one or two on the west side of the Hirshhorn, and Travers had picked up two on the east. Assuming this was all one team, there would surely be more inside the museum.

Whatever the fuck Ortega was involved in, she sure was surrounded by a lot of interested parties.

Zack spoke to Arnold now. "Okay, man. Just turn right and head out that door, look slowly back over your right shoulder as you do, but don't stop."

Court decided they all needed to get the hell out of here. He was about to order everyone in the vehicles to vacate when Zack said, "Good. Got the image we need of two unknown subjects."

"Everyone, abort," Court said. "Teddy, you're with Night Train. Bricklayer, you're with me, I'll take the wheel."

Immediately Zack spoke again. "Shit."

Court almost stopped in his tracks on the sidewalk. "What happened?"

Zack didn't answer; instead, he said, "You okay, Bricklayer? Just nod if you're good."

"What's going on?" Court demanded now. He was almost back to the work van but had slowed, readying himself to turn and race into the museum in case Arnold had gotten jumped or attacked in some way.

"No sweat," Zack said. Then he added, "Bricklayer walked into a wall when he went into the next room. Shit happens, brother. Now . . . get out of there."

. . .

Five minutes later, Court was behind the wheel of the Savana, driving east on Independence, south of the Capitol Building. Arnold sat next to him; he'd already switched out his glasses and stowed the Ray-Ban video device in their proper case, but he'd said next to nothing, other than asking Court to give him a moment to collect his thoughts.

The guy was scared, still freaking out about what he'd just gone through; his chest heaved under his coat.

"You did great, Arnold," Court said as the man rubbed sweat from his face.

"Thanks," Arnold said. Then he added, "I think Gumdrop is going to have to tell me what I saw, because I barely saw anything. I hit a wall and then, when I was leaving, I almost fell down the escalator."

Court fought a smile. "Usually, our operations run a little more smoothly." He thought about what he'd said for a second, then shrugged. "Usually."

The entire team had been told to conduct an SDR and then rally back at a three-story townhouse Erin Childers had rented for them in Meridian Hill, just twenty minutes to the north in an urban area of the city between Adams Morgan and Columbia Heights.

It was pitch-black by the time they arrived. Travers pulled the Pacifica into the one-car garage, while Court found parking in the alley out back for the Savana.

Once there, everyone climbed out and immediately stepped into the townhouse. Here, Jill sat at a dining table on the ground floor with several laptops in front of her, and Matt Hanley had just finished brewing a pot of coffee in the nearby kitchen.

The small team converged around the table, asset and support member alike, and they talked about the afternoon. Jill began running facial recognition on everyone picked up on both Arnold's glasses and the several camera feeds she'd been able to hack into, both in the subway and on the street outside the museum.

As she did this, Hanley said, "I watched the stream as it came in. I don't think she was there to meet someone. I think she was there to try to spy on somebody else."

"Yeah," Court said. "And whoever *was* meeting in there, at least one of those parties knew Irene was going to be there. A lady was tailing her on the train, and they already had the meet location secure with more bodies." He thought a moment. "If Irene is not the leak in the government we've been looking for, then she could be in danger from whoever is."

Travers shook his head. "I wouldn't say 'danger.' The two men I saw . . . they looked like muscle, like contractors, former soldiers, cops, whatever. But they did *not* strike me as assassins."

To this, Hightower used his coffee mug to motion across the table towards Court. "Does this squirrelly little fucker strike you as an assassin?"

Travers conceded the point. "Not at all."

"I'm five-ten," Court mumbled in frustration.

"Which brings me to my next point," Hanley said. "Today was not how I want us doing things. Making the decision to push Arnold into the eye position for what could have been a critical—"

Court interrupted. "You realize that if Teddy, me, or Night Train were in that museum today, we could easily have been picked up on by countersurveillance. It took sending a guy like Bricklayer in there . . ." He looked to Arnold. "No offense."

Arnold just waved a hand in the air, dismissing his worry, and he sipped his coffee.

Hanley said, "You're the fucking Gray Man. You could have—"

"I was dressed as a telecom repairman. I had a change of clothes in the Pacifica, but I didn't know we'd be going to a museum until after I'd gotten into the Savana."

Hanley turned to Hightower. "What's your excuse? You look like the roadie for an aging death metal band."

Zack's eyes flitted around the room. "Thanks?"

"You're getting a haircut and a shave before you do anything else operational."

"Understood. When I get back from Boulder, I'll look like a choirboy."

Matt sighed. "You don't have to look like a choirboy. You can look like a car salesman, an accountant, whatever. You can*not* look like a professional wrestler."

"Loud and clear, boss."

Jill had been busy on her computer, but now she looked up. "I've got the first match. On Arnold's glasses, the room Ortega *didn't* go into. One subject is Lewis Shaw; he's an employee of the Office of the Director of National Intelligence. He's in IT, not an analyst, he's GS-10, a midlevel government employee."

She raised her eyebrows. "Pretty impressive, actually; he's only thirty years old."

Hanley said, "That's the same agency Ortega works for. Why is she interested in an IT guy in her office? And who is the other person he met with in that room?"

"I've got nothing on him coming up so far."

Hanley said, "Send me the image. I'll get Pace to run it at CIA and see if anything—"

"Oh my goodness," Jill interrupted, leaning close to her screen now. She manipulated an image there, enlarging and then refining it.

"What is it?" Hanley asked.

"This man . . . interacting with Shaw. He's . . . he's not real."

"He's not *what*?" Hanley exclaimed.

"I mean . . . his face isn't real. He's wearing a mask."

Travers said, "A mask? Like a medical mask?"

"No, like a Halloween mask."

Court rushed around the table so he could see the screen. "What the hell are you talking about?"

She cleaned up the image even more. At first to Court, it looked like a man in a black watch cap; his skin was a little pale and he was older, maybe fifties or sixties. But when she zoomed in on his eyes, it was evident that there were slight rings around them, as if there were eye holes in some sort of high-quality latex mask. "I'll be damned. That's good."

Hightower said, "How the hell are you going to walk through a museum with a mask on?"

Arnold hadn't spoken during the entire conversation, but now he said,

"It's the Smithsonian. It's free to enter, but you must pass through a metal detector first."

Hanley said, "The security guards? Were they paying attention?"

Arnold shrugged. "I could barely see them, to be honest."

Jill went back through the video from the glasses, and they watched from Arnold's point of view as he passed by two bored-looking security officers. They never actually looked closely at his face, only at his keys as he put them in a container, then passed through the metal detector.

Travers said, "Here's the problem, though. You might have been able to get past those two dummies in a high-quality latex mask, but you wouldn't have been able to plan that they wouldn't engage you."

Hanley said, "Which means our guy put the mask on *after* he got into the building. Just for the meeting with Shaw. Probably in the bathroom." To Jill he asked, "We have images of people going into and out of bathrooms?"

"Not unless Arnold just happened to catch them doing it," Jill said.

Hanley quickly shook his head. "There's no way of knowing when the other guy came in. He could have been in the building for hours before the meeting."

Court was frustrated. "All that work, and we have no idea who the other guy was."

Hanley said, "No problem. We focus on two people now. Irene Ortega and Lewis Shaw."

Hightower shook his head at this. "We have to wait on Shaw, boss. Gumdrop can dig into him, find out whatever she can so when we can target him, we do it effectively. But right now, with a group this small, we can't split into two surveillance teams."

Court said, "He's right. We've already got Irene's place wired. There's a hotel across the street from her place, and every room in the back of that building is facing every window in that woman's apartment. I say we put up twenty-four-hour physical surveillance on her with an eye to detecting countersurveillance, because we know she had counter on her this afternoon. We see anybody on the street we don't like, we hear or see anything in her unit, and we figure out what they're up to."

"Okay," Hanley said. Then, "Okay, we'll set up overwatch at Ortega's place, and we'll evaluate the situation there. What we *don't* want to do is react impulsively. If whoever is following Ortega is investigating her just like we are, we might end up with a blue-on-blue incident that nobody wants.

"I'll call Lacy at CIA now, tell her to get Jim Pace focusing on Shaw, as well. He'll be able to see what intelligence he had access to, where he's been, who he might be affiliated with inside the government."

The meeting broke up soon after; Arnold headed to the hotel across the street from Ortega's home to get a high-floor rear-facing suite for an overwatch team, while Jill continued looking through both the video feeds and open-source data about other faces at the museum she'd identified.

Court and Zack poured themselves some more coffee, and they stood in the kitchen when Hanley came in. Out of earshot of the others, even Travers, the only other asset on the team, Matt said, "Listen carefully, gents. I am *not* impressed with how today went. That was basic surveillance tradecraft, and still, you almost fucked it up."

Court spoke up in defense of the team. "It's our first day together, we don't have many bodies to work with, and we're just figuring out how—"

"I don't give a damn," Hanley said firmly. "Trey Watkins is acting like the entire American government is some sort of a threat right now, and we're right in the middle of Washington, D.C. You guys have to step the fuck up on your game, and you have to do it now."

The former DDO did not wait for a response; he just left the room.

Zack blew on his coffee, then gave Court a little smile. "We've been operational in this new organization for less than thirty hours and we're already in trouble."

Court shrugged. "No big deal, I'm used to it. Hell, even when I work alone, I yell at myself a lot."

TWENTY-SIX

The Belarusian held the latex mask in his hand, looked it over carefully, and then gave a little smile. The quality of the article was good; he'd tried it on here in the hotel an hour earlier and then stood in front of a mirror. In full light, with his full attention, carefully looking, he could tell it wasn't real. But he was sure that outside, in the night, to a passerby or to a distant security camera, it made him look real enough, if a little ugly.

But he didn't put it on now. He had time, still, and he had other things to do.

He put the mask down, then lifted the squat black suppressor, screwed it onto the barrel of his Belgian-made FN pistol, then loaded the weapon with a twelve-round magazine full of 9-millimeter hollow-points.

He racked the slide, ejected the magazine, then put one more bullet in the mag before reseating it in the grip, bringing the weapon to its fully loaded capacity of thirteen.

There were other magazines on the glass coffee table in front of him, and two more boxes of ammunition, along with his phone, wallet, and passport.

And two lines of coke.

He'd arrange his equipment first, then he would go dress, and only then would he snort the coke. He'd been doing this long enough to know the correct process for optimal performance.

Alexi Kravchuk was forty-three years old, and he'd spent fifteen years of his life as an officer in the State Security Committee of the Republic of Belarus, the nation's version of the KGB.

He now plied his trade in the contract world, working mostly for Russian interests in Europe, but he'd recently taken a private job from a concern in the United States, and now he was here, in Washington, preparing for his first operation.

The passport on the coffee table was legal, given to him by the Slovenian government, and his visa to America affixed inside it was legit. They both named him as Johan Fras, a Slovenian tourist, but in the halls at the FSB, the Russians knew him as Spiral, their word for "helix." Spiral had not used his passport to fly into America; he'd instead been picked up by a private jet in Slovenia and flown in, somehow bypassing customs and border control.

Once he got here, his American handler, a man who called himself Mike, had told him he'd be targeting five different individuals, all in the Washington, D.C., area, over a period of no more than four or five days.

He'd been told that other assassins were in America, and their killings would fall in the same time frame, and the time frame was crucial.

Spiral's first target was to be a forty-seven-year-old woman named Irene Ortega who lived in a condo near Washington Circle. All he knew about her was that she worked for the American government, and someone with money and a crew of support personnel wanted her dead, and she was not thought to have any tradecraft experience or concerns about her safety.

One of the five Americans he had following Ortega called him earlier in the afternoon and told him she'd gone to a museum, the support team had followed her, and though she hadn't detected their presence, she certainly seemed nervous and on alert.

But an interesting thing had happened at the museum. Spiral's support team had bumped into some of their colleagues working a similar surveillance job, because while the Belarusian's team was following Irene Ortega, the other team was following another target who was in the same museum at the same time. Apparently, there was some confusion between the two teams, and Spiral couldn't help but wonder what the fuck was going on in D.C. that there would be so many assassinations in the works that hit men's support personnel were literally stumbling over one another while trying to keep eyes on their targets.

Now that he'd been given a weapon and a disguise, it had been Spiral's initial preference to wait until tomorrow morning and stab Irene Ortega on the street on her commute to work. He'd planned on room service and a quiet night watching TV, but his handler had contacted him an hour earlier and told him the job had to be done tonight, sometime after ten thirty p.m.

Surveillance had followed her to her condo; she was there now, and this meant Spiral had to go into the building, enter her home, and kill her there.

He did not want to enter a building. Much better to eliminate her on the street or, even better, in a parking garage. But according to his contact, some of the other jobs going down needed to happen this evening, and they worried about Ortega being harder to reach if they waited till morning, because she had shown some suspicion to the team surrounding her.

Spiral asked for and was granted an extra one hundred thousand U.S. dollars for doing the job tonight in her residence, and then he asked for and was delivered a few extra items that would make the job easier.

Small C-4 charges that he could put on locked doors if he found himself unable to quickly pick a lock.

Spiral didn't love the idea of the hit in the building, but he wasn't overly concerned about this change to his plan. Compared to where he'd been in Central Europe, the police presence here in the District was minimal, and he had been outfitted with this 9-millimeter CZ P-09 pistol with a Rugged Obsidian9 suppressor. This silencer could be used in a full or partial configuration, and right now he had it pared down to its shortened length to make it easier to conceal. With the subsonic ammunition in the gun's magazine, he knew that firing a pair of shots into Miss Ortega's head inside her condo would go unnoticed throughout the rest of the building.

He looked at the two lines of coke, just waiting for him, and then he looked away. He'd shower now, eliminate some of his loose DNA, and then he would change, put on his gear, and wait for ten thirty.

He'd do the coke, put on his coat, cram the mask into his pocket, and begin walking the four blocks from his safe house to Ortega's condo.

If all went well, he'd be taken by his team straight to target number two, across the river in Pentagon City. There, a lieutenant colonel in the U.S. Army always took the Metro to his job at the Pentagon, and Spiral would stab him on the train, for reasons that had not been given to him.

These Americans were just like the Russians.

Do the job, don't ask questions.

It didn't matter to Spiral. By eight a.m. tomorrow, before the effects of the cocaine even wore off, he could be $2.1 million richer, and then he would rest a bit before the third, fourth, and fifth killings.

These Americans paid more than the Russians, the work seemed easier, the support he got in the field was superior, and America was a weak place, full of the unsuspecting.

What's not to like about this job? he thought as he rose to go take his shower.

Campbell Coyle hadn't told the American he'd be meeting with tonight that he was bringing five body men to watch over him, so there was no small amount of confusion in the parking garage of the Wegmans grocery store in Tysons Corner.

Coyle had been on foot; he came out of the store carrying two bags of groceries and walked through the garage waiting for the meet, giving no tip-off to the fact that two vehicles here in close proximity had Kearney men in them watching his every move.

And when a white Lincoln Navigator entered and pulled into an open space one level below the street, the three vehicles containing Bostonian gangsters were all close enough to notice.

The Navigator's doors opened, three men exited, and they were just steps from Coyle. Two of the three were security men; Coyle knew these guys didn't look like decision-makers, and they took his bags from him, then pushed him a little roughly next to the Navigator for a pat-down.

When they shoved him against the side of the SUV, two vehicles parked close by fired up and raced forward.

A Volkswagen sedan with two men and a Jeep Cherokee truck with three men screeched tires as they closed on the scene. All three American men within arm's reach of Campbell Coyle pulled guns, but the Northern Irishman told them to calm down, then waved off his own security team, telling them to idle nearby but remain in their vehicles.

Then Coyle turned to the one man who hadn't been involved with the frisk. He said, "My mates apparently thought things were getting a wee bit rough. Maybe tell *your* mates that we're all on the same side here, and we won't have any problems."

The man in the middle was big, as formidable-looking as his two goons, although he appeared older and more in charge. He regarded the two vehicles idling close, the five sets of hard eyes watching the situation carefully, and then he reholstered his gun and indicated to his men to do the same. After this, he said, "Would have helped if we'd known about your men."

"Would have helped *you*, I suppose you mean to say," Coyle said.

The two younger Americans finished the frisk, more politely now that they knew they might get riddled with bullets if they misbehaved, then stepped back. The five Kearney men looked on: the two Donnelly brothers in one vehicle, and the three Walsh brothers in the other. They didn't show their weapons, but Coyle assumed their guns were drawn, resting in their laps and out of sight.

Coyle turned away from them and back towards the American who'd been speaking.

Extending a hand, the American said, "I'm Mike. Sorry about that, my boys are a little amped up."

Coyle took it. "Whetstone. No harm done."

"You're something of a legend. It's a pleasure to meet you."

"If it's a pleasure to meet someone like me, chief, then you've taken a bit of a wrong turn in your life."

Mike said, "I'm comfortable with what we're doing and why."

"Fair enough."

"Thank you for getting here so quickly. As I briefed you on your way over, our operation has to start immediately. I need you acting by tomorrow at the latest."

"I believe you said you needed me acting by dawn, yeah?"

"That would be ideal."

Coyle nodded. "I can manage."

"Excellent," Mike said. "I have weapons, ammunition, an iPad loaded with five targets and their dossiers, and a latex mask you can use as a disguise. It's all in a case in the trunk of my car here."

Coyle thought a moment, translating the word "trunk" to "boot." "I'll take the iPad, of course. I've the weps I need already. The mask . . . sure, that sounds like fun."

Mike seemed surprised. "We have full support for you. You only have to—"

"You just met my support. I just need those targets."

The American just looked at him, then at the other men. "Who are your men?"

"They know what they're doing. They all have legitimate IDs, and they have no ties to your group, whatever group that might be. If the other assets you've hired for your whirlwind of killing are using your own support staff, then that's a compromise on you."

"My organization has thought of that already, of course, and has taken measures. I'll worry about my strategy, Whetstone; you worry about your five targets."

"Meant no offense, chief."

Mike said, "One million per. A million bonus for getting all five in a three-day period."

Coyle said, "That's just grand. But there's something else I want."

Mike sighed a little. "Now's not the time to negotiate, friend. You already agreed, Sir Allen Glazebrook told me this himself."

"I'm not renegotiating my price. I'm discounting it."

The taller American cocked his head. *"What?"*

"I'll delete these five individuals for four million total, no bonus, but my price also includes the Gray Man."

"I don't understand."

"Whatever is going on here, you have access to information within the United States government, yeah?"

"We have some access, yes."

"You're sending me, and others from what I hear, out to kill government employees, presumably to cover something up or to keep something quiet."

"Why we do what we do is none of your concern. If you don't understand that, then—"

"I could give fuck-all about that. I'm just telling you I know you can find out about him. I want all the information you have on the Gray Man."

Mike let out an exasperated sigh and looked around the parking garage. An older couple pushed a cart out of the grocery store, but they headed in the opposite direction. "You've got to be kidding."

"What's the problem?"

"I already looked for information on the Gray Man. For another shooter."

"Explain that."

"Another asset he's pissed off, as I understand it." He waved a hand in the air. "If I knew where the Gray Man was, I'd be hiring *him* for this job, not you guys."

Coyle just looked at the man.

"There's nothing in the information we have that says who he is or where he is. There used to be a task force set up to find him, but it was disbanded. It's like he's been erased."

The Northern Irishman thought a moment. "His code name with the Agency was—"

"It was Violator. Yes, I learned that much. Surprised me. I thought he was just a fairy tale. But believe me, Whetstone. My people dug, and that's all they found. I told the other asset that I had no information on the Gray Man. He wasn't happy about it, to put it mildly."

Coyle held a finger up; he had an idea. "There's another man. A CIA man. Hanley. Matthew Hanley."

Mike cocked his head. "What about him?"

"Keep trying to get me information on the Gray Man, but in the meantime, get me intel on Hanley."

Mike didn't hide his surprise now. "Matt Hanley was the DDO. Top operations guy in the Agency, up until a couple of years ago. He's not some denied asset. Not a ghost. Just a very senior-level exec at a desk, or he was until he was demoted. What do you want to know about him, and what's he got to do with the Gray Man?"

"Get me intelligence on Hanley. Where he lives. Where he is now. You get me that, for now, and I'll get started. Keep working on the rest of it. As to the relationship between the two men . . . let's just say there is a rumor I heard."

The American shrugged. "I can get you Hanley's location, I suppose. You'll do your jobs in the meantime, though, right?"

"I'll start immediately. Trusting you to come through."

Campbell Coyle held out a hand; Mike opened the trunk of his car and fished around for a moment, and while he did so, Coyle held his other hand up, telling the Kearney men that whatever was happening was not a threat and they should maintain their positions.

After a few seconds Mike pulled out an iPad and a latex mask. "The code is three, two, three, two, three, one. One of your targets is in Baltimore, two are here in the D.C. area, one is in Chicago, and one will be given to you once you complete the others."

Mike looked at his watch. "The operation will kick off tonight at ten thirty p.m. local time. If you could eliminate target number one by dawn tomorrow, that might keep you on track to complete your task inside of three days."

"And the Hanley intelligence?"

Mike shrugged. "I'll pass it to you as soon as I can. I'll have my contact dig deeper for Gray Man. If we find something, we'll give it to you when you're done with your operation for us."

Coyle shook his head. "When I am done with my operation, I am leaving America. I need the information before."

"What are you planning to do with the intelligence we give you?"

"Nothing that will slow down my operation for you. Nothing that will come back on you. Nothing that will make the news."

It was true that Coyle didn't expect Mike or his operation to be affected by his plan. But as for this not making the news or slowing down Coyle's actions for the American, that was a lie.

The larger man seemed to think a moment, then nodded. "Agreed. But your allegiance is to me. This is a time-critical mission; I can't have you running around on other projects."

Coyle said, "Five targets in three days. I understand my assignment, chief."

Campbell Coyle climbed into the car with the Donnelly brothers, and they followed the Jeep with the Walsh brothers out of the parking garage of the Wegmans grocery store.

TWENTY-SEVEN

The balcony of the ninth-floor corner suite at the rear of the Hotel AKA Washington Circle overlooked L Street NW, as well as New Hampshire Avenue NW, along with parts of 22nd Street NW. On the other side of this intersection sat the Carriage House Condominium, and here Irene Ortega lived in a unit on the eighth floor, also overlooking L Street.

She was home right now, and the blinds in the living room were open.

At ten thirty p.m. the balcony door to the corner suite of the hotel just across the street from Ortega was closed; it was icy cold and misty outside, but just inside the glass, four men sat, looking across the street. Court Gentry and Chris Travers had binoculars on tripods, and they sat on dining chairs moved here from other portions of the suite. Matt Hanley was deeper in the residence, looking across at Ortega's unit with his naked eye, and Zack Hightower was all the way back by the kitchen, his own smaller set of binos in his hand, giving him some magnification, but not as much as the two guys seated closer to the balcony.

This was four people essentially doing the work of one, and a fifth person in the suite, Arnold Reyes, was resting on the king-sized bed in the bedroom, essentially accomplishing no work at all.

But the sixth person in the room was doing more than her fair share.

Jill Mori sat in front of four laptops splayed across a dining room table, monitoring cameras in the condo across the street; she wore a headset that picked up sounds inside the property and watched more images of CCTV in the building. She had a view downstairs at street level through more cams she'd hacked into in the area, and she had an app open on her phone that fed her real-time local police radio transmissions.

Hanley had decided that there would be no attempt to make contact with Ortega, but instead the team would concentrate on looking out for any surveillance. They knew she'd been followed today as she herself surveilled ODNI employee Lewis Shaw, so it was their intention first to find out who else was interested in Ortega.

Were these the good guys or the bad guys? Was Ortega herself one or the other?

So the six people stood, sat, or lay down in the hotel room, all the lights out so that they couldn't be seen by anyone.

They tracked her through the evening, in her living room, her kitchen, and her dining room.

She'd spent the time on a laptop set up at her kitchen bar, she'd ordered DoorDash around eight p.m., and then she'd opened a bottle of red wine and drank a glass while eating ramen.

At one point—Jill marked the time at nine fifty-five—she actually stepped out on her balcony with a glass of wine and looked down through the cold mist at the street.

Her eyes rose slowly, and then she looked across the cold street at the hotel, and Court felt her eyes right on him, though he knew she couldn't see through the glass into the darkened suite.

She went back inside, sat down on her sofa, and turned on her TV, then immediately focused her attention on her phone, and soon after this Hanley pulled his own phone out of his pocket.

"I'll check in with Lacy, see if Pace has learned anything since this afternoon." He stepped out into the hallway of the hotel to take the call, leaving the others to work inside or to continue the vigil.

He'd only been gone a few seconds when Gumdrop spoke up from her bank of laptops. "We've got a vehicle parking on the west side."

There was constant traffic on the streets below, but a car parking on the street next to the target location was definitely worthy of note.

Court rose, moved into the darkened bedroom, and set his tripod up there. Looking down through a window, he called out to the room. "Yep. I'm clocking it. Dark gray four-door Audi."

"Nobody's getting out," Jill said.

"Is the engine on or off?" Hightower asked from the kitchen.

Court couldn't tell from his vantage point, but Jill said, "Appears to be off. No lights, no vapor from the tailpipe."

Court said, "I can see the car where it's parked, but I'd have to go out on the balcony to get a good view of the street. Gumdrop, just keep an eye on it, let me know if anyone climbs out. I'm going to stay in here but watch the street and sidewalks to the west."

Jill did not respond at first, and Court was about to call out again to her from the next room to make sure she heard him, but then she spoke up. "Hey, guys . . . I'm monitoring local law enforcement channels. There's an urgent BOLO in the District on a black motorcycle with a male driver."

Hightower had stepped over behind Jill to take a look at her screens. "Why?"

"D.C. Metro PD has been notified by Fairfax County Sheriff's Office that there's been a double homicide in Tysons Corner."

All heads turned to her.

"Male and female victim in a car stopped at a red light. A lone person on a motorcycle. Witness said they thought it to be a male, but they couldn't make out a face. A pistol with a suppressor. Did it right in the middle of a busy intersection, less than a quarter mile from CIA headquarters. There was no tag on the bike, the shooter got away."

Tysons Corner was in Virginia, just across the Potomac and several miles to the west of them. It wasn't part of D.C., but it was no surprise to anyone in the room that D.C. police would be informed to be on the lookout for the shooter just over the river.

The door to the suite opened back up and Hanley returned. Standing there in the dark and speaking loudly enough for everyone to hear, he said, "Two CIA counterintel officers were gunned down thirty minutes ago in Tysons Corner. Husband and wife. No robbery. Lone assassin on a motorcycle."

"Jesus," Court muttered.

Just then, Travers changed the subject, "Gumdrop, anybody get out of that vic on L Street yet?"

"Negative. Can't see inside, but no one has stepped out."

"Well . . . I've got another vehicle stopped, this one on New Hampshire. I watched it pull up a half block from the Savoy a couple minutes ago, about a block northeast of the Carriage House. It's just sitting there."

Immediately Jill said, "I see it. Black SUV. Could be a Ford Expedition. Can't pick up a tag from my view."

"Me, either," Travers said.

After a moment's silence, Hightower said, "Is it starting to feel like our subject is slowly being surrounded?"

Travers said, "These could be interdiction and isolation elements."

Jill looked up from her computers; in the darkness her brown eyes sparkled wide. "What is that?"

Hightower answered. "Teams brought in to keep the target from getting out, and to keep anyone not wanted at the location from going in. I-and-I elements come first, then comes the strike team." He spoke to Court in the other room. "What do you think, Six?"

"Too early to tell, but not too early to prepare."

"What do you want to do?" Hanley asked.

"I can go solo down to street level. Nobody's going to notice me."

Hanley thought a moment. Then he said, "Stand by for now."

A moment's pause, just long enough for Court to convey that he did not agree with his orders. "Roger."

Hanley's phone buzzed in his pocket again, and he snatched it up, then tapped a button.

"Lacy, you're on speaker."

The female CIA officer said, "There's been a killing down in Miami, had to have been within about ten minutes of the ones in Tysons. A former FBI supervisory special agent, he was downsized last year, has been working for Gauntlet Group for the past few months. Shot dead getting gas at a convenience store in Coconut Grove."

"How do you know about this so fast?" Jill asked.

"Who's speaking?" Lacy asked, defensively.

Hanley answered. "That's Gumdrop. Ghost Town's OSINT analyst. She's one of us."

After a moment of silence on the line, Lacy said, "FBI sends out Agency-wide alerts any time something like this happens to one of their own. The Director of National Intelligence office picked it up and sent out a text to the entire IC."

"Any connection to our subject here in Foggy Bottom?" Hanley asked.

"Jim Pace is looking into that, but so far we have no reason to suspect a connection to the CIA officers killed in Virginia. I did want to alert you as soon as—"

"To hell with that," Hanley said. "They're related somehow. We ran into Gauntlet security men today." To Jill, he said, "What's the status of the two vehicles downstairs?"

"Unchanged. Still stationary, one on the southwest side of the Carriage House condos, the other on the northeast side."

Hanley relayed to Lacy what was going on here in D.C., and while doing so he moved to the balcony glass door, and he looked down at the vehicles, then out, across L Street, towards Irene Ortega, the lights from her TV flashing across her as she sat on her couch looking at her phone.

Lacy said, "Are you starting to think Ortega might be a target?"

"It's leaning in that direction," Hanley said. "I'll call you back if anything happens."

"Boss?" Court said again from the bedroom as Hanley hung up. "Might not have time to react if something goes down fast." He was, once again, asking permission to leave the suite and get downstairs in case everything turned to shit.

Hanley ignored him. He said, "Gumdrop? You picking up any phone conversations?"

Gumdrop said, "She's not talking on the phone, and not texting using her cell provider or Wi-Fi. Must be texting on Signal or some other encrypted app. I can't pick that up. Her TV is muted; I'm not hearing any noises inside her apartment."

Hanley nodded to himself, then said, "Six?"

Court called from the other room. "Yeah, Matt?"

"I want you and Teddy down at street level. Get me a tag number off one of those vics. Be ready to act if someone tries to move on Ortega."

In the bedroom, Court turned to Arnold, who was now sitting up on the bed. "Take over here. Watch that gray Audi parked on the corner. Keep an eye on the street around it. If any more vehicles stop in the area, let us know." He moved quickly in the darkness back into the living room. Travers was already up and moving, pulling on a heavy canvas coat and reaching for a neck gaiter and a ball cap he had lying nearby. Court said, "Chris . . . I'll dress as a telecom repairman again, just in case I have to go into the building and scoop Ortega."

"Roger," Travers said. "Don't forget something to cover your face."

To the room, Court said, "Everyone on the net together."

Gumdrop spoke up, her face glowing behind the monitors at the dining table. "I'll open a group call on Signal to all phones. Everybody get your AirPods in."

Hightower was still in the kitchen, but he moved over towards Hanley while he put in his earpiece. "What can I do?"

"You're not operational," Hanley answered flatly.

"C'mon, Matt. That's three assassinations in the IC in the past twenty minutes, and we've got two vehicles around a woman in the IC who's currently under surveillance by an unknown entity."

Hanley deferred to Court. "Six? What about Zack?"

Court looked to Zack as he zipped up his brown coat and moved towards the door. "Zack, I want you downstairs."

"Hell, yeah."

"Behind the wheel of the GMC in the garage."

"Oh," he said, somewhat deflated.

"If we need a getaway, we'll let you know."

Hightower was already moving, grabbing keys off the counter. Unlike Travers and Gentry, he was unarmed. He was out the door first; the other men were still stuffing pistol magazines into their pockets and getting last-minute instructions from Matt, but a minute later Court and Chris exited the hotel room.

When they were gone, Hanley rushed to the position Travers had held behind the binos on the tripod. Looking across the street, he saw Ortega sitting there on the couch still, tapping on her phone, and he wondered if she was in danger . . . or if she *was* the danger.

The Belarusian assassin known as Spiral walked west on L Street NW, leaning into a cold breeze that blew mist into his eyes. This was a frosty night, but nothing near as cold as Minsk this time of year, so the conditions meant little to him from an operational perspective, save for one thing.

He wasn't out of place at all wearing his wool scarf high on his face, just below his eyes.

Spiral walked alone, armed with his suppressed pistol inside his coat, a couple of extra magazines, and a fixed-blade knife in a sheath hidden below his coat on his right hip. He saw the Carriage House condos straight ahead, walked along with the Savoy building on his right, and sauntered past a couple of slower-moving pedestrians on the sidewalk.

He'd decided against using the latex mask provided to him by his American employer until the moment he hit the woman's condo to lessen any chance of being identified as a threat. He'd move through the lobby with his scarf up, then change into the mask before he made it to the eighth floor.

As he reached the three-way intersection of L Street, 22nd, and New Hampshire, he turned his head to the right, eyed the black Ford Expedition idling on New Hampshire, and knew that three of his American support team would be inside, watching the street, ready to notify him if there were any police or other threats down here. He knew their second vehicle, an Audi sedan, would be straight ahead of him on L, just south of his target location, though he couldn't see past the other cars parked between himself the Audi.

Spiral wondered, not for the first time, about the Americans who had hired him. Specifically, he wondered about their plan; if their intention had been to hire foreign killers to deflect any attention away from their own organization, then what was the rationale for having Americans supporting them, in close proximity to their actions? Couldn't they be identified and linked back to whoever it was doing this in the first place?

He knew he wasn't supposed to involve them in the assassinations, only in his surveillance of the target and the getaway, but he also knew that all these men were armed, and they were damn close to where the killings would take place.

It seemed like a bad plan, but Spiral's plan, to earn over five million dollars U.S. in the next three days, seemed to him like a damn good one, so he trudged on towards the building directly in front of him.

He'd be inside the lobby in just a minute, he'd be done with this target within fifteen minutes, and he'd be out of the area shortly thereafter.

Court Gentry and Chris Travers stepped out the front door of the Hotel AKA Washington Circle together, then immediately split up. Travers went to his right, turned right again at 23rd Street NW, then began heading up to L Street. In the elevator on the way down from the suite, it had been decided that Travers would move behind the Audi, the closer of the two vehicles parked near Ortega's building, and he'd get the tag number and, if possible, get a head count and the disposition of the occupants inside it.

Court went left at the front door, then left again on New Hampshire. This would take him past the entrance to the Carriage House Condominium building, just beyond which there was a covered vehicle entrance and a loading dock. His only mandate from Hanley was to get to street level, but he decided on his own he'd move into this garage. From there he would have a couple of options to ascend towards Ortega if necessary, and he'd also have some cover from whoever was in the blacked-out Ford Expedition across the street.

He'd be in plain view of the Ford for most of his entire movement on the sidewalk, and anyone in the vehicle would be looking right at him as he went down into the darkened loading area between the Carriage House and the Ritz-Carlton, but he liked his chances at remaining covert, as long as he maintained a nonchalant gait to avoid arousing suspicion.

He did his best to move along on the street like any other person out on a frigid night like this, and in so doing he looked around at other pedestrians. There were a couple of dog walkers, a young college-aged person jogging in front of the Ritz-Carlton just beyond the Carriage House, and a lone man with the lower part of his face covered by a scarf crossing the street in front of him and heading to the front door of the Carriage House. Court tracked him as the doorman held the door open for him, then kept it open for a woman leading a rust-colored toy poodle on its leash.

The doorman began speaking with the lady with the dog, and the man by himself disappeared into the lobby of the Carriage House, out of Court's view.

Softly, into his earpiece, he said, "Gumdrop, you get a look at that guy that went in?"

"Negative," she replied. "His lower face was covered, and a hood shielded his forehead. He appeared alone on L Street, on foot from the east, and he didn't seem to be acting weird or anything."

Court turned left into the loading bay between the Carriage House and the Ritz, and he hoped he didn't seem to be acting "weird or anything" himself.

He said, "Try and track him on the cams inside the building."

"I'm watching him move towards the elevators, and the woman with the dog is still talking to—"

"Forget poodle lady. Focus on shady dude."

Hanley's voice came over the net. "You see something wrong, Six?"

"Just being thorough."

"Copy."

TWENTY-EIGHT

Two minutes earlier Zack Hightower unlocked the GMC Savana in the parking garage, climbed into the back, and took a quick inventory of the bags and cases stacked there. Arnold had brought most of the equipment up to the hotel suite, but here in a cluster of padlocked boxes, Hightower knew he'd find what he was looking for. He pulled one Pelican case free from a stack, knocking the others over, and jammed a key into the lock.

Opening it in the low light, he knew he had the right one. Two full uniforms for Immigration and Customs Enforcement, one for Court and one for Travers, along with utility belts, soft body armor, face coverings, and Glock 19 duty pistols with Trijicon sights.

Zack grabbed one of the guns, checked to make sure there was a round in the chamber and the magazine was full, and then he put it to the side while he dressed in the ICE uniform. Once this was done, he put the pistol into the holster on his duty belt, then climbed up behind the wheel.

The van was frigid, but he didn't turn over the engine. Instead, he just spoke into his earpiece.

"Night Train is in position."

His left leg was stiff; he'd done more today physically tailing Ortega and hustling down here to get in the van than he'd done since he'd been shot. It wasn't a sharp pain he was feeling; it was more like a body that needed to get used to work again, so he didn't worry about it.

He did, however, worry a little about Hanley, and a little about the gun on his hip.

Hanley hadn't wanted him armed in D.C. Both Travers and Court would be carrying micro compact pistols on their persons; in Court's case it was a Glock 43, in Chris's case a P365-XL, but until Zack returned to operational status, he wasn't allowed to have a gun. His trusty Staccato P4 was back at his apartment in Boulder, and since he didn't know what the fuck was going on tonight here around the home of Irene Ortega, he'd simply helped himself to one of the G19 pistols the assets had on hand in case they needed to dress themselves to look like ICE agents.

Zack's first choice would not have been the Glock 19, but it was uber reliable, and it was also the new duty gun of ICE, so it did fit his outfit.

He smiled a little to himself now, realizing this had been Court's plan all along. Court had known there were guns in the van, and he knew that Hightower knew. By ordering him to haul ass down here to serve as some sort of potential wheel man, Court hadn't been demoting him, he was surreptitiously telling him to go arm himself and get ready.

Court had put Zack in the operation that Hanley had excluded him from.

Now he just sat here in the low light, focusing on any voices in his headset, listening for action or inaction, whatever the case might be.

Spiral went directly past the elevators to the stairs, and he began climbing. He'd gone less than one floor when a call came through his earpiece. "Uhh . . . Spiral, this is Three on the east side. I have one male subject entering the Carriage House loading dock off New Hampshire. He disappeared inside. He wasn't wearing a hotel uniform, but he looked like he did have a tool belt on."

"Did he have a coat on?" Spiral asked as he kept climbing.

"Affirmative."

"Might have had a uniform on under it. Where did he come from?"

There was a pause. "Unknown. Didn't see him before he entered the property."

Shit, Spiral thought. *Some support.*

"You see any new vehicles on the streets?"

"Negative. Just the one man. A lady with a dog returned to the Carriage House just before this."

Spiral discounted both the lone man with the tool belt and the woman with a dog as any sort of threat. He was more worried about SWAT teams, government cars, massive surveillance operations. If there was a threat to him, it wasn't going to present itself as a lone wolf.

He continued past the third-floor landing, still heading up to the eighth floor. The coke coursing through him now felt good; it made him sharper, stronger, more aggressive.

This job was going to go down quickly and cleanly, he could feel it in his bones.

Court had spent some of the day in and around the Carriage House Condominium building, plus he'd studied blueprints of the other buildings composing the entire block: a couple of restaurants and the massive Ritz-Carlton hotel.

He knew his way around the area: the parking garages, the stairwells, the back employee-only entrances.

As he walked through the darkness of the covered tunnel-like area, he climbed a stairwell entrance to the loading dock of the Ritz, the building connected to the Carriage House. He had taken a look at the lock to the door there earlier in the day and determined he'd need about thirty seconds to pick it if he wanted access to the hotel next to the condo building.

He could even take a back staircase in the Ritz that could put him near a hotel suite with a balcony right next door to Irene's condo.

But he did not move for now. He just positioned himself in a dark corner in the loading area tunnel, out of the dull lights here and there in the cavernous space, and just behind a steel support beam. He watched the Ford Expedition across the street, and he called Travers.

"Teddy? Report status?"

"I'm twenty-five yards from the Audi. I'm at their six o'clock, they don't see me. I think I tally two pax in this vic, but I'll have to get closer to be sure."

Hanley's disembodied voice came over both men's earpieces—"Hold position, all call signs"—and Court and Travers both acknowledged.

Court kept himself hidden in the dark, his eyes back out towards the street and the SUV parked there.

Seven miles to the northeast, a forty-seven-year-old Northern Irishman stood over a thirty-three-year-old American, watching dispassionately as the man on the pavement took his last agonizing breath.

Campbell Coyle was in Hyattsville, Maryland; the victim had come out of a brewpub at eleven p.m., ordered an Uber on his phone, and then lit a cigarette as he waited there on the sidewalk.

The dossier on the iPad that Mike had given Coyle earlier in the evening said his target here in Maryland had military experience but no relevant tradecraft experience, and he worked for the National Security Agency. Other than that, Coyle had no idea why his employer wanted the man dead, and he absolutely did not care.

Coyle had stepped up behind the man as he waited alone outside the bar, a mask pulled down over his face, and then he dragged a four-inch knife across the victim's throat from behind.

The target fell, blood gurgling out of him as he struggled to breathe, and Coyle stood there for ten seconds, making sure the wound was absolutely fatal, taking neither pleasure nor pain from the act. This man—his name was Miles Jorgensen—was a means to an end. Coyle wasn't in the United States for him, but killing him would get him closer to what he *was* here for.

Coyle pulled out his phone as he sheathed his knife; he looked up and down the street and saw no one else around. He took a photo, then turned, slipped the phone back into his pocket, and walked off through the frozen night.

A few moments later Campbell Coyle found himself on Gallatin Street, heading towards a dark blue Jeep Cherokee that idled there in the dark. He climbed into the backseat and sat down next to Nolan Walsh and just behind Jack Donnelly, who sat behind the wheel. Alfie Donnelly rode shotgun; he held a Glock pistol down between his knees, his eyes scanning left and right.

"Wind yer neck in, mate," Coyle said. "Jackie, drive. Calm and cool. Everything's just grand."

The big vehicle began to move, and Coyle pulled out his phone. He sent a Signal text directly to Mike.

Hyattsville job sorted. Standing by for requested information.

With the text he sent the photo of the body; the Cherokee drove through a residential neighborhood, and Jack Donnelly kept within the speed limits.

Behind them, a Volkswagen Passat remained parked a moment, while the two other men from the Boston-based crime group made sure no one was following Coyle away from the scene.

A minute later, the Northern Irishman received a message on Signal.

4008 Meeting House Road, Virginia Beach, Virginia. Home address of M. Hanley. Lives alone. No employer info at this time.

Seconds later, a new text arrived, telling Coyle he needed to get to Baltimore to execute his second operation, killing a man who worked for the NSA. After that was a job in Chicago that needed to happen in quick succession, lest the intended targets go to ground.

They pulled into a parking lot just before a highway ramp; the Passat with Barry and Gavin Walsh pulled in behind them, having hung back a few blocks along the route to watch for followers.

All five Kearney men waited while Coyle looked at a map on his phone, and no one disturbed him.

Coyle had made it clear to all five loaned to him for this operation that he didn't want friends, he wanted employees, and to the Walsh and Donnelly brothers' credit, they kept their mouths shut for the most part.

Coyle climbed out of the back of the Cherokee and the five men stepped up to him. "All's of you. Take the Jeep, start heading to Baltimore. I'll send more information when I have it."

"You're not coming with us?" young Nolan asked.

Coyle shook his head. "I'm going to Virginia Beach."

The Boston men looked at one another. "New target there?" Gavin asked.

"New target there, aye. You lot might have to sort out the one in Baltimore."

Alfie Donnelly said, "If it's as easy as this one, we'll have it done by dawn."

Coyle said, "You'll manage, I'm sure. Know how to fashion a car bomb?"

Alfie shook his head.

Coyle just shrugged. "It's dead easy. Call me when you're on the road, I'll talk you through it."

After moving some bags and equipment between the vehicles, Coyle sat alone behind the wheel of the Passat and took a few seconds to get his head around the fact that he'd have to drive on the right side of the road, something he hadn't done in years.

At eleven twenty p.m. the two vehicles headed off in different directions, leaving the distant sounds of police sirens behind.

Court Gentry watched the Ford Expedition idle across the street, maybe thirty yards away. Still there was no movement around it, and he could make out no figures inside its tinted windows. He hoped Travers could get a better look at the car he was checking out to give him more information, but in the end, it was not Chris Travers who came through with the crucial intelligence.

Over his earpiece he heard Jill's voice; she was calm but nevertheless intense. "This is Gumdrop. Subject who entered the Carriage House condominiums is sighted on the fourth floor at this time; he's moving down the hallway, looks like he's either heading to a unit here, or else to the stairs on the other side of the building. Wait . . ." The pause was brief. "He's pulled down his scarf, we've got his face now."

Hanley spoke from behind the binoculars on the tripod behind the balcony glass. "You running it?"

"Stand by. In the low light of that corridor it's going to take a sec—" She stopped speaking suddenly, and when she spoke again, her voice had completely changed. "Oh . . . oh my gosh."

"Tell me," Hanley said calmly.

"Subject is . . . he is putting on a mask. A mask like the one from earlier today, but not the same mask."

"Oh shit," Hanley muttered as he looked over her shoulder.

"Still running his facial," Jill said. "Wait. Okay, we got a hit. Identity is unknown, but his face is attached to contract killings in Europe. The Agency has code-named him. They're calling him Deep Space." She added, "He's an assassin. He's currently sought for killing a German arms manufacturer last year, and he's suspected of involvement in—"

Hanley said, "He was around when I was DDO. Did other jobs for the Russians. A thing in Rotterdam, another op in Iceland. We caught his face in our files, gave him a code name, but we don't know shit about him."

Court turned to the stairwell door to the Ritz-Carlton Residences behind him and began running for it. He interrupted Gumdrop. "We know he's going for Irene. And we know he'll get to her before I do!"

"What's your plan?" Hanley demanded.

"I'm going to pick a lock, then get into the Ritz residences. I'll have to take the stairs, get into a unit adjacent to her condo, get out to a balcony, and make my way over."

"But . . . from the balcony? How do you do *that*?" Gumdrop asked.

"I'll figure something out," he said, his voice labored as he ran.

"How long is that going to take?" Hanley demanded.

"Five mikes, minimum."

"You *might* have three."

Hanley next spoke over the net to Travers. "Teddy, you reading?"

"Affirm."

"You have a tag number on that Audi yet?"

"Got it." Travers read the tag; Jill typed it into the farthest laptop on her left. "Running it." Seconds later, she said, "It's registered to a Gauntlet Group office in Maryland."

"Of course it is." Hanley sighed, then turned and looked away from the binos, back to Jill. "We need to buy Irene some time. Call her. Tell her to get somewhere safe, to hide, to . . . to whatever. Tell her help is on the way."

"Yes, sir." She grabbed her phone. "I can spoof any number. Make it look like it's her work calling her."

"Do that." Hanley thought a moment. Said, "We have to slow Spiral down somehow."

A new voice came over the team's earpieces. It was Hightower. "I have an idea."

Hanley started to protest. Hightower wasn't officially operational, but he stopped himself because Hanley himself was fresh out of ideas.

Hightower said, "Teddy. Make contact with the driver of the Audi. Act like a cop or something, tell them to get out of the vehicle."

"I don't have my ICE uniform. It's in your van."

"You got a gun and you've got an attitude. Just do it. We need Deep Space to know that the people he has at ground level watching his back are getting jammed up. It might slow him down, or maybe even cause him to break off his attack."

Zack Hightower then spoke to Court. "And Six?"

"Go for Six."

"I'm heading for the Expedition, but you better be hauling ass. This plan of mine sucks, but it's all I've got."

"What are you gonna do, man?" Court asked.

Zack blew out a sigh, then said, "I'm about to do a full immigration check on what I expect to be a truckload of lily-white assholes."

At the same time, Travers, Court, and Hanley all said, "*What?*"

TWENTY-NINE

Irene Ortega felt her phone vibrate on the couch next to her, moments before she was about to fall asleep in front of the TV.

She'd been up for twenty-four hours, hadn't slept well in days, and at first she lamented the disturbance, but when she looked at the number calling, her fatigue was the least of her concerns.

The call came from an extension at the Office of the Director of National Intelligence, although this extension wasn't saved in her phone. She sometimes got late-night calls, so that was no big deal, but considering what she'd actually been doing at work the past few days, a sense of dread jolted her body.

Reluctantly, she reached for the phone. "Hello?"

A woman's voice came over the line, speaking urgently, but clearly. "Irene, I need you to listen carefully to what I am about to tell you. You don't know me, and I don't have time to explain, but there is a man in your building right now, and we believe he is coming to do harm to you."

Irene rose from her couch and stood there in the middle of the room. The TV was on mute; she had Fox News on and she glanced at it. A video of flashing police lights on a street somewhere. Her eyes focused on the chyron running below the images.

DOUBLE MURDER NEAR CIA HEADQUARTERS

Momentarily distracted by this, she heard the woman's voice again on the phone to her ear. "Irene?"

"What?"

"This is serious. Do you have a gun?"

It took her a moment to answer this. "No, I don't have a gun. I live in the District. Is this . . . *Who* is this?"

"There is help on the way to you now, but you need to shelter until he gets there. Can you go to a friend's unit on your floor? Quickly? If you hurry you might be able to—"

"I've only been here a month. I don't know any of my neighbors. Not well enough to bang on their door at eleven thirty."

The woman on the other end of the line sighed, then said, "Lady, you need to find a place to hide."

"No. *You* need to tell *me* what the hell is going on. Is this related to what happened in Tysons Corner?"

"It's related to Gauntlet, Irene. It's related to Lewis Shaw, the man you followed this afternoon."

Irene Ortega's heart pounded so hard she could feel the blood pulsing in her neck. She stood there, frozen in panic.

"Irene?"

Still . . . she did not move. She tried to speak, to lift a foot, to go make sure her door was bolted shut, but she just stood there, looking at the news.

At the murders.

The Belarusian assassin known to the Russians by the code name Spiral and to the Americans by the code name Deep Space passed the sixth-floor landing, ascending at a relaxed speed. The stairwell was empty, concrete, and the building owners had gone cheap with the lights. Dim bulbs widely spaced gave the stairwell an eerie feel, and a damp dusky scent filled the air around him. He'd pulled his FN pistol and screwed on the suppressor, and now he hid the weapon back in a deep inner pocket of his coat.

It bounced around over his right hip as he climbed.

Suddenly, an American's voice came through his earpiece that itself was tucked inside his latex mask. "Spiral, this is One."

"Yes?" One, Spiral knew, was in the driver's seat of the Audi on the west side of the condo building.

"Uh... we've got a guy behind our vehicle on the sidewalk. He's calling out to us; I think he's saying he's with Homeland Security. He's got a gun out and he's ordering us out of the car."

Spiral stopped climbing, held his hand to his earpiece. "What does he look like?"

"He's out of the light. But he's average height, has a beard, a big coat. There's definitely a pistol in his hand."

"Uniform?"

"Not that I see, but some Homeland agents are plainclothed."

"He's by himself?"

"Seems to be."

"That's strange."

"Yeah, that's what we're thinking. I used to be with Homeland, and I'd never make a stop by myself, at least not one I thought I needed my gun drawn for."

"Don't get out of the vehicle."

"We're licensed to carry in D.C., so we're not doing anything wrong, but we don't want to get our names flagged by the cops while you're doing whatever you're doing upstairs. Are you going to call off the op or—"

Spiral spoke into his earpiece. "Three, are you hearing this?"

Three was in the front passenger seat of the Ford Expedition parked on New Hampshire, facing the Carriage House condos, two blocks to the east and a half block north of the Audi.

Three replied quickly. "All quiet over here, Spiral. We can't see the man who went in the loading dock a few minutes ago anymore; he might have gone inside one of the buildings. You want us to go over and support One and Two on the west side?"

"No. But send one man into the loading area to look around. Observe and report only. I want to know if that man is still at street level like the other guy, or if he's in this building."

"Roger."

The back right door of the big black SUV opened. A man in a leather coat and a watch cap climbed out and took a single step into the street, keeping his right arm down to prevent his coat from flying open in the breeze and revealing the pistol on his hip. His number was Five on the Gauntlet team, and as the junior member he knew he'd be the one to climb out into the cold and put himself even closer to what, he assumed, would be the murder of the woman he'd been following for the past day.

A white GMC van approached from the south; he waited for it to pass, but instead it slammed on its brakes right in front of the Expedition, skidding to a stop there next to it.

The man who'd just climbed out of the vehicle froze; the two inside put their hands on their pistols but did not yet draw them.

A lone man leapt out from behind the wheel of the van; he wore a blue coat under black body armor that said "Police ICE" on it, dark blue cargo pants, and a black knit cap. His utility belt held a pistol, radio, and handcuffs. A neck gaiter was pulled up to nis nose.

He lifted a small tactical flashlight with his left hand; his right hovered over his gun.

The man seated next to the driver of the Expedition said, "It's a fucking immigration cop."

The light wasn't bad here on the side of the road, but still the man who climbed alone out of the vehicle shined a flashlight on the three men. "ICE! Let's see some IDs."

All three of these Gauntlet men were white males.

The man standing near the vehicle kept his hands down by his sides. The man in the ICE uniform was just twenty feet away and walking towards the SUV, using the light to mask anything he might be doing with his other hand.

"You've got to be fucking kidding me," the man standing by the Expedition said.

The big ICE officer repeated, "I need to see some papers, motherfuckers."

With no Hispanic accent, the driver said, "C'mon, dude. What the fuck are you talking about?"

"IDs, amigos, and I'm gonna need you two to step out of the car."

The front passenger, call sign Three, said, "Look at us. We're obviously not illegals."

"Obvious to who? Not to me. How do I know you're not illegal Finns, or Swedes? Reach for those wallets, but do it slowly."

Number Three broadcast to Spiral now, speaking softly, cupping his hand over his earpiece. "We've got one man on us at this time. Claims to be with Immigration and Customs Enforcement."

Spiral's reply echoed, likely because he was in a stairwell. "What does he want?"

"He's giving us some bullshit story about looking for—"

The man with the flashlight shined it at the front passenger window.

"Hey. Gustav? Who you talking to?"

The man rolled down his window now. "Look, brother. We're government security contractors, and we're on the job right now. We've got credentials. Green badges. Just get back in your van there and drive off before you blow our op."

In the intelligence world, blue badges signified direct federal employees, while green badges meant contract employees.

"What's your operation?"

"I'm not telling you that, but it's sure as hell not some low-level ICE bullshit."

The man holding the flashlight said, "I need both of you to step out, stand next to your buddy here. If it turns out you're U.S. citizens, then you can go on about your evening."

"What the fuck is wrong with you?" the blond-haired, blue-eyed passenger said.

"Less talking, ese. Get out of the truck. Manos arribe." *Hands up,* the big man claiming to be an ICE agent said, shining his bright light in the man's eyes.

In the building across the street, Spiral did not know what the hell was going on down below, but he wasn't about to bail on his mission because his support crew had been stopped by police. He began hurrying up the back stairs of the Carriage House. He'd need to find a new extraction after the fact, but he wasn't worried about that. In Europe he'd been on his own almost all the time, and frankly, his support team here in America had done little more than get in his way.

He passed the seventh floor, heading for the eighth, taking the steps two at a time.

Court Gentry ran up the fire stairs of the Ritz-Carlton Residences, passing the fifth floor, taking the steps two at a time. He could hear the activity happening at ground level through his earpiece, both Travers and Hightower making police-like stops on the men down there, and although it was a risky move, Court liked Hightower's thinking. He was trying to impede the support team, giving them something to worry about, and he was sure that the assassin moving towards Irene in the building next to this one would be aware that the two vehicles below were in danger of being exposed.

Court himself had been a contract killer, however, and he doubted the man the CIA called Deep Space would just call off his mission this close to his target. There had already been at least three other killings of intelligence community employees in the past hour, and Deep Space would know that breaking off from his objective now would just make it that much harder to pick her back up again in the future.

Ortega would go to ground, Ortega would get protection, Ortega would disappear.

It was now or never for Deep Space, which meant Court had to haul ass.

Ortega was on the eighth floor of the Carriage House, but Court's plan now was to head to the ninth floor of the Ritz-Carlton Residences, so he still had a lot of climbing to do.

He shot up the stairs, praying the assassin next door had been distracted enough by the commotion below to give Court's plan half a chance.

Jill Mori had been holding her phone to her ear, but she tapped it on speaker now and continued looking at the screens showing her Irene Ortega just standing there in her living room, wearing socks, yoga tights, and a sweater.

Jill had called her name multiple times, but she had not reacted. Now the young Asian American woman shouted. "Move your butt, lady!" Jill pleaded. "He's going to kill you!"

Irene finally responded. "Gauntlet? Someone from Gauntlet?"

Before she could answer, Jill saw movement on the laptop screen on the far right-hand side of the dining room table. It showed several camera views from inside the building, and one of them displayed a real-time image of a man coming out of the stairwell on the eighth floor, wearing a high-quality latex mask. He looked left and right, then began heading up the well-lit hall, walking purposefully in the direction of Ortega's condominium.

Jill said into the phone, panic welling in her voice. "It's too late, he's in the hallway."

Hanley spoke into the speakerphone now. "Irene. Get into the bathroom off the bedroom. Lock the door. Help will be there soon, but you have to barricade yourself."

Irene began moving. Jill threw her hands in the air in frustration; it had taken the woman nearly half a minute to respond, after all.

Over the network, Hanley said, "Six, she's heading into the bathroom off the bedroom. Be advised, that bedroom is the closest window to the balcony of the Ritz, only about six feet away. If you can figure out a way to get to that window, you can breach at the bathroom."

Jill spoke with incredulity now. "*Only* six feet? It's eight stories up. How's he going to—"

Hanley spoke over her, calling to Arnold Reyes, who was watching Irene's apartment through the bedroom window. "Bricklayer, we're going to collapse this position. Gumdrop and I are going to stay at our stations until we're clear here; the rest is up to you."

"Understood." Arnold began rushing around the suite, cramming binoculars and tripods into cases.

He had to make it seem like no one was ever here, because it was looking extremely likely that this area was going to be crawling with police in a few minutes.

・・・

The right hand of the man behind the wheel of the Audi was down low, out of Travers's view, and Chris assumed that to mean there was a pistol in it, and it was pointed his way.

"Sir, I'm going to need you to put your hands on the steering wheel." Shining the light on the other man, he said, "You, hands on the dash."

He tried to speak calmly; he knew he couldn't look amped up right now, it would just alert these guys that something else was going on beyond a law enforcement officer checking on suspicious people.

"Who the hell are you?" the driver asked.

"Already told you. Homeland Security. We're investigating—"

"What's your badge number?"

Travers pulled a string of bullshit out of thin air. "Seventy-eight, thirty-nine. Arlington office."

"Nice try, asshole. I was Homeland. Feds don't have to give badge numbers or stations."

"Well then," Travers said, "I can see why you're no longer employed. I was just being courteous. You should give that a shot yourself. Both of you, show me those hands. I'm not going to ask a third time."

The driver's eyes narrowed slightly. To Travers the man looked extremely confident and calm. With a chuckle, he said, "You're *not*? So . . . what? You're going to shoot us if we don't? What kind of traffic stop is this?"

Travers realized these guys weren't buying what he was selling, so he decided to drop the ruse. "The kind of traffic stop that involves detaining the two assholes in a getaway car waiting for an assassin to kill a woman on the eighth floor of this building to my left."

The façade of the driver wavered slightly as his eyes widened back up.

Travers continued. "I know you guys are Gauntlet, and I am assuming you're providing perimeter security to the son of a bitch in there trying to kill Irene Ortega. Maybe somebody told you this was righteous government work, maybe you genuinely don't know what that dude is up to, or maybe you just don't give a shit that a woman's about to die. Don't know, don't care. I can't stop that guy up there, but me and my colleagues down here sure as shit can stop you and your buddies in the SUV on New Hampshire from getting away with your part in it."

The driver bit his lip, looked all around. "Yeah? I don't see your colleagues. I'm thinking you're alone."

Travers said, "Nah, bro. I drew the short straw to come down here and try to talk you out of this. The rest of the team are on balconies across the street, and they've got their scopes on all your foreheads right now."

The man in the passenger side muttered, "Jesus Christ." And he put his hands on the dashboard. To the driver, he said, "I'm not dying for this bullshit, Kyle."

"He's fucking bluffing," the driver said, and Travers saw that the man's cool demeanor was no put-on at all. He did not believe Travers's ruse, and he was *not* going to comply.

Eight floors above, Spiral headed up the hall to Ortega's door; he was twenty seconds away. Softly, he called the Expedition. "Three. Status?"

When he got no answer, he called One in the Audi. "One. Status?"

Again, there was no response.

His support team was dealing with law enforcement on the street, but he had no reason to think law enforcement was aware of him, here, eight floors above.

The Americans would have to deal with their problems. Even if he lost all his support below, he'd be long gone from the scene by the time there was any response up here to Ortega's place.

As he approached the door, he thought about ringing the bell, but he didn't think about it for long. Ortega wasn't going to let a stranger with a Belarusian accent into her condo willingly, at least not without a good story, and he didn't want to take the time to concoct one in case more cops were soon to show up.

This had to happen now, considering the complications downstairs. It was inevitable that this hit would get messy, so he leaned into the mess, made the decision to go loud.

He reached into a pocket and pulled out a small C-4 breaching charge not much larger than a box of playing cards, tore the cover off the adhesive on one side of it, and affixed the explosive between the latch and the doorjamb.

He pressed a tiny blasting cap into the device, unspooled the wire connected to it, and stepped to the side, out of the way of the threshold.

Now he attached the wire to a detonator, pushed himself up against the wall two meters from the door, and pressed a button on the device.

The breaching charge beeped three times, then detonated the explosive, blowing a hole right where the locked door latch had been.

Smoke filled the doorway and the hall. Spiral put his detonator back in his pocket and drew his silenced weapon, then adjusted the latex mask while he waited for the smoke to clear. In five seconds, he'd spin in front of the door and kick it in.

THIRTY

Matt Hanley peered through handheld binos because Arnold had packed up the tripods, and he watched smoke fill the living room of the small condo.

He wished he had a sniper rifle right now; even with a pistol at this distance, he could probably drop Deep Space as soon as he appeared in the living room.

But Hanley hadn't considered for an instant he'd need to be arming himself on an operation to collect intelligence to pass off to a CIA investigator inside Washington, D.C.

This entire surveillance operation had gone insane in the past few hours, and now he was just hoping like hell his three assets—two and a half when you considered the fact that Hightower wasn't even operating at full strength—could control these three scenes and get out with their lives in the next few minutes.

The only lights in the condo on the eighth floor across the street were from the TV and filtering through the windows, so the dense smoke darkened Matt's view momentarily.

Jill watched the same scene from a different viewpoint—the hallway camera—and then she shifted her attention to the cameras Teddy and Six had placed inside the unit earlier in the day, looking for the hit man, somewhere in the darkness, in the smoke.

She spoke into her phone now. "Irene, is the bathroom door locked?"

The woman was in a state of shock, but finally she answered. "Yes."

"And the bedroom door?"

"Shit! No . . . I forgot to lock it."

Hanley called out to her over the speakerphone. "It's okay. Don't leave the bathroom. Get in your bathtub. My man will be there, and he will help you."

Irene whispered. "How close is he?"

"He's almost to you."

Jill looked to Hanley, who looked back to her. He shrugged a little—he had no clue how close Court was—and then he took a few steps away from the speakerphone, deeper into the kitchen of the suite. Cupping his hand between his mouth and his earpiece, he said, "Six, status?"

"I'm on the ninth floor."

"Subject is on the eighth! You know that!"

"Yep. Okay . . . I'm inside the condo next door and one above her. It seems empty."

Hanley didn't give a shit if there was a convention of nuns meeting in that condo, he just wanted Court to get out to the balcony, find a way over and down to Irene's bedroom window, and then save Ortéga. As he was about to respond to his asset, however, Jill spoke.

"Deep Space is in the living room. He has got his gun up, he's moving toward the bedroom. The TV is on, there's half a glass of wine on the coffee table. He's going to know someone is there."

Hanley moved back toward the phone in Jill's hand as Arnold ran by, moving cases to the door of the hotel suite.

Hanley said, "Irene, don't make a sound."

Six spoke up over the network again. "I need a minute to figure out how to get over to—"

"You don't have a minute!" Hanley shouted back.

Jill kept watching the screen in front of her. She said, "He's in the bedroom." After a short pause, she said, "He's trying the bathroom door. It's locked. Irene, get as flat to the ground as you can." She thought Deep Space was going to shoot open the lock, but then he pulled another breaching charge out of his pocket. Jill had a perfect view of Deep Space; a camera

Teddy and Six had placed in a corner vent earlier in the day was pointed right at the bathroom door from across the room.

Calmly, the assassin played out the wire, then stepped to the side of the door. Jill covered her phone and softly said, "He's going to blow the door and shoot her." From the tone of her voice, all was already lost.

Hanley had moved over to the window; watching the apartment with his naked eye, he could see the residual smoke hanging in the living room, but he couldn't see the bedroom from here. Into his earpiece he said, "Six, if we lose Irene, we lose whatever information she has about—"

Court snapped back, "I know what's at stake, dammit! I'm just trying to figure out how I'm gonna fly!"

As he ran through the large hotel suite towards the balcony door, Court felt around in the utility belt he wore around his waist, pulled a hammer from it, then kept feeling around the belt, hunting for something else. He put on work gloves as he leapt onto a white sofa, jumped over the back, then landed on his boots at a run and made his way around a dining table, finding himself at the balcony door of the huge suite.

Soon he had a coiled Ethernet wire in his hand, and then he slid open the balcony door of the hotel room, raced to the railing, and looped the end of the wire over the railing. This done, he climbed up onto the railing, using the wall closest to the Carriage House Condominium building to balance himself, and played out several yards of wire, then wrapped it around his wrist and hand.

There was no way this little computer cable in his hand could possibly hold the dynamic weight of a 180-pound man falling through the air, but Court's life of kinetic operations had taught him an incredible amount about practical physics.

He *thought* this could work, but he was in no way certain.

On the contrary, he was just desperate.

Court heard a loud boom in the adjacent building, coming from Irene's bedroom. This would be Spiral blasting in the bathroom door, and if this asshole had any room-clearing training at all, he would be standing wide of the door, giving the smoke a few seconds to clear. After this, he would just roll into the room with his gun drawn and, as soon as he had a target, he'd shoot until the target was dead.

Nine stories above the ground, Court took a chance on the looped wire.

He leapt forward, out over the sidewalk below, but angled sharply to his left. He kicked his legs, shot several feet away from the building, and then he felt the wire go taut against his hand and wrist.

He began swinging back in towards the structure; Court's momentum had him sailing right at her window, dropping from gravity at the same time. He spun his body in the air, let go of the wire, and flung the big hammer into the glass in front of him as hard as he could, and then, as it shattered right in front of him, he flew towards the window.

He heard the sounds of gunfire booming in the street below as he crashed feet first through the glass and flew into the bedroom, drawing the Glock 43 pistol on his hip as he did so.

The barrel of the small but potent handgun just cleared leather as his boots hit the carpet, the momentum of his swing continued propelling him forward, and he rolled onto the king-sized bed in the center of the room full of smoke.

Fifteen seconds earlier, the man behind the wheel of the Audi still had not lifted his hands to the steering wheel. "Here's the deal, ace. We ain't getting out. We haven't done shit, and we ain't got no idea what potential assassination you are referring to. Now, best you turn around, walk off into the night, go back to wherever you came from, and forget you—"

A muted boom eight stories above the Audi caused all three men to look up at the source of the noise and the sound of shattering glass that came soon after it.

Travers was all but certain the man behind the wheel of the Audi had a gun pointed at him through the door, so as soon as the boom rumbled down here to the street, he rocketed back hard to his right and raised his pistol at the car.

The first gunshot cracked inside the Audi; Travers felt the pressure of the round disturbing the air just to his left.

He returned fire at the driver, but he did it as his feet were retreating as fast as they could move. He had identified his closest point of cover even as he approached the car with the Gauntlet men inside, a corner where the Carriage House building jutted farther out into the sidewalk next to a ramp down to a parking garage at the Ritz-Carlton. The garage door was shut and locked for the night, so seeking cover here would pin Travers into a corner that the two enemy could exploit, but it would also get him out of any potential line of fire and, right now, that was more important.

He headed back towards the corner between the buildings, but he shuffled backwards, not taking his eyes or his weapon off the threat.

The driver and the passenger both opened their doors as Travers backpedaled; window glass from the condo above crashed onto the sidewalk right next to the Audi where Chris had been standing, and this slowed the Gauntlet duo down a couple of seconds, but quickly the passenger stood, spun his gun arm over the roof of the sedan, and opened fire. Chris dumped rounds into the driver's door just as the driver bailed flat onto the sidewalk. Chris fired again; the driver fired his own pistol, but he was still in the process of rolling out and onto the sidewalk and his shots went wild.

It was the third round from the passenger's gun that struck Chris Travers, high on the right side of his neck, spinning him to the ground.

Thirty seconds earlier, Zack Hightower had just cajoled the other two men out of the Ford Expedition, using intimidation tactics he'd called upon many times in his life. They had IDs out claiming they worked for a government contractor and were allowed to carry firearms, but he just kept shining a light on them, doing whatever he could to delay. He had not drawn his gun, hadn't needed to, but his right hand was ready.

Then the low boom came from the building behind him, echoed along the quiet misty street.

The sound of the explosion was soft yet distinct at this distance, and Zack suspected that even if he did not draw his pistol now, these amped-up assholes would probably go for theirs. He started to put a hand out, a warning to them not to move, when a gunshot boomed directly behind him, here at street level.

Glass impacting the road or the sidewalk, probably falling from above, added to the cacophony coming from behind Hightower now.

It was clear to Zack that Travers was engaging or being engaged; he was likely outnumbered, as was Zack, and Zack was ready to kill all three of these motherfuckers in front of him so he could get over there and support the one teammate he actually had a chance of reaching.

Hightower had his Glock 19 out of its duty holster quickly; all three men reached behind their backs and began to separate in front of him, and he knew they were going to engage him on a wide arc, even though they were just steps apart.

These were Gauntlet security men, but he imagined they'd all gotten their training on SWAT teams, in federal law enforcement, or in the military. They would know what they were doing, and all he could do was try to get back around the minivan just behind him for some concealment.

He clicked on the flashlight in his hand, threw it towards the three, and fired his first round from the G19 at the man in the center of the trio.

Return fire came instantly; he heard the windshield of the GMC van shatter next to him, but he kept regressing and firing. Three rounds, then five, then ten before he dropped to a knee at the back of the vehicle.

He knew he'd hit the man in the center, maybe the guy on the left, but he didn't know if either of them was down. This meant he was facing off against somewhere between one and three enemy, and he had no situational awareness as to where they were.

He was deep in the shit here, and behind him, the gunfire from Travers's position suddenly stopped.

THIRTY-ONE

Ten seconds earlier, Court found himself on his knees on the bed in the middle of Irene Ortega's bedroom, smoke swirling around him, and here he took just an instant to get his bearings. Looking through the glass lenses of the holographic weapon's sight on his small pistol high in front of him, he actuated his weapon light and saw through the darkness, through the smoke, a figure standing in the doorway to the bathroom, facing away, waiting for the smoke to clear so that he could shoot the woman who must have been somewhere inside. But the noise of the shattering glass behind him had caused the killer known as Deep Space to look back over his shoulder in Court's direction. Court saw a latex mask covering his face; he barely made out the man's wide eyes reflecting in the light through the eyeholes. The surprised killer began spinning his body, shifting his aim towards the man who'd just appeared behind him from nowhere.

Court fired a double tap, two rounds into the spinning man's torso, and then, not knowing if his enemy was wearing body armor, he targeted the man's head, but Deep Space's body collapsed so fast, Court missed high with his third round.

Court stood up on the bed now, window glass crunching under his boots as he did so, then aimed at the man who had fallen back onto the threshold into the bathroom.

Court fired twice more, both times into the man's head. Blood and tissue splattered into the bathroom, painting the side of the tub.

Court started to broadcast to his team, but then a fresh volley of gunfire echoed up to him from the street directly below, and more gunfire came from the east, from the direction of Hightower and the Ford Expedition.

Both of his teammates sounded like they were engaging multiple adversaries, and there wasn't a damn thing he could do about it up here.

The American leapt off the bed, quickly cleared the rest of the smoky condo with the light on his weapon, then came back and found the woman still lying fetal inside the bathtub, her hands covering her ears.

Court's own ears rang as he grabbed her right arm and helped her up to her feet.

She stood on shaky legs, then stepped out of the tub as he assisted her.

Irene Ortega was in stocking feet; the thick smoke had cleared enough for him to see that much, so he told her to put on her shoes.

But the other complication in a night full of them was that he had no idea what Ortega's involvement in all of this was. Could she have been a bad actor, as well? He realized he'd lost sight of her when she went into her closet, so he pointed his weapon there and shined his light.

The woman's face was drained of color; she was in shock as she stepped into a pair of slip-on tennis shoes, then squinted into the light shining at her.

"What now?" she asked.

He had to get the woman out of here, down to street level, then out of D.C. He prayed the two other assets of his organization would be ready to go with him by the time he climbed into a vehicle, but for now he had to focus completely on his own predicament.

Matt Hanley stood in the darkness of the suite in the Hotel AKA Washington Circle, still wishing he had a weapon, but for now all he could do was try to watch the action in the street and monitor his earpiece for news.

He couldn't see Travers; he was behind the side of a building, but it looked like he had nowhere to go from there. Hightower had disappeared in the distance, somewhere on the other side of his vehicle.

Behind him Hanley heard Arnold quickly zipping bags, clicking closed cases, dragging things towards the door.

He called out to Arnold now. "Bricklayer, how soon till we're clear?"

"Ready to go."

"Okay." He turned to Gumdrop, who stood in front of the last laptop still on the table. "We get to the vic and go pick up the assets."

The three of them rushed out of the hotel room, each one carrying multiple backpacks and rolling more luggage behind them.

Chris Travers found himself back up on his knees, halfway down the ramp to the locked underground parking garage door and facing L Street to the south.

There was no gunfire here, though he heard it echoing against the buildings from the east, and this told him Zack was still fighting there.

At first, that was about all he knew. He found himself a little dazed; he'd pushed himself up to his knees seconds earlier, after being shot and knocked down, disoriented by the spin and the pain and the fall, and it was only now he realized he did not have a gun in his hand.

He looked down and saw it, right in front of him, and he hefted it with his right hand.

And then the pain under his right ear began anew.

Aiming the pistol up the incline and at the street—the Audi was thirty feet out of sight on his left on the other side of the ramp wall—he searched for a target while at the same time evaluating his injury.

He knew he'd been shot in the neck, and that was never good news, but he wasn't dead, and his body seemed to be working, as evidenced by the fact that he was able to wield the pistol. There was blood, of course; no one gets shot in the neck without bleeding. He felt it on the pistol, he felt it running down his upper arm and dripping from his elbow, his forearm, and he worried that fighting with his right hand, swinging his arm around and snapping off rounds with moderate recoil, just might turn a damaged artery into a severed artery. If that happened, he'd bleed out in moments; he knew this, but he also knew he had a job to do.

He reached up with his left hand, put as much pressure as he possibly could on a jagged wound two inches below his ear, and felt blood seep between his fingers.

Chris Travers had been in the Airborne, he'd been in U.S. Army Special Forces, and he'd served in a CIA paramilitary unit, so he knew all about gunshot wounds. The blood he felt was annoying, slightly worrisome because it was coming from his own body, but—in the short term, anyhow—it wasn't life-threatening.

The blood from the wound was not spraying, it wasn't under pressure, and that meant he was still in this fight; he just knew he had to do whatever he could to hasten the end of this fight and get treatment.

He took stock of his physical surroundings now; he had decent coverage here from the little wall between himself and the Audi, but he knew he couldn't hide here, because if at least one of the Gauntlet men was still alive up on the street, and they had an incentive to keep the fight going, it would take just seconds for them to come around from his left, gun or guns barking and belching out lead towards the only tiny piece of cover in the area.

Heavy gunfire continued from Hightower's scene to the east, and Chris wondered how much ammo Zack had with him.

He heard voices off to his left now; this told him both his enemies were still alive, and they were plotting his demise.

Suddenly, a sense of anger welled up in him. He rose from his knees to his feet, the pistol still straight out ahead, and he saw motion now, in the darkness on L Street. A man shifted into view from his left; Chris must have had himself in darkness because the man didn't immediately see him, but when Travers saw the gun in the man's hand begin to swing into the tight corner here, he fired three rounds in rapid succession.

The man buckled, shuffled back a few steps, then dropped dead in the street.

Travers knew there was only one more man from the Audi, and he thought there was a chance the man had been injured in that first close-in volley, just as Travers himself had been. He began creeping forward, ready to engage the man if he was still somewhere by the car on the left, but then he heard the engine of the German sedan fire and the tires squeal as the vehicle began to race off.

For one complete second, Travers thought about letting the Gauntlet man drive away, but then it occurred to him that the Audi driver just might be on his way to go help his teammates up the street in their fight with Zack.

Travers clutched his neck even harder now as he staggered up the ramp, then into the darkened street. Traffic had been incredibly light in the five minutes since he'd come out of the hotel, mercifully so, in fact, but now a single vehicle appeared, slammed on its brakes behind him.

He saw a delivery van, the driver's eyes wide and terrified, and Travers knew this man was no threat.

Turning back towards the danger, he knew he had other things to worry about. Hightower was somewhere beyond his field of view, but he was potentially not out of his field of fire. The black Expedition was two blocks beyond where Travers's gun was aimed, so he knew he had to be careful with his shots.

He ignored the vehicle behind him, kept the pressure up with his left hand on the right side of his neck, and felt himself stumble a little as he slowed to turn, then raised his small pistol with his right hand. He aimed carefully at the Audi heading east on L Street and fired one round directly into the back of the head of the driver at a range of eighty feet.

He did not fire again, did not want to send more bullets downrange, potentially into Hightower's position.

The Audi veered sharply to the right, then crashed into a building on 22nd Street and came to an abrupt stop.

Travers took a few steps in the direction of the continued noise coming from Zack's firefight, then slowed, then stopped. Zack was maybe sixty yards away, but if Travers ran to him, he might well bleed out on the way. He dropped to his knees on the sidewalk and spoke into his mic now.

"This is Teddy. I'm hit."

Matt Hanley responded immediately. "On the way to your poz at this time. Be there in two mikes. Hang on."

"Go help Night Train. I'm good here," he said, and then he sat down, quickly pulled off his jacket, and used it as a larger compress on his neck.

It did not occur to him that Hanley, Jill, and Arnold had no weapons with which they could help Zack. Chris Travers was out of the fight, and Zack Hightower was on his own.

Hightower knelt in the street by the right rear tire of the minivan, and he looked over his right shoulder in time to see the gray sedan crash into the building a block away on his right. He hoped that meant the Gauntlet assholes who'd been in the car and fighting with Travers were dead or otherwise disabled, but he gave little thought to the matter, because just then he heard the sound of a pistol magazine clanging to the street on the other side of his vehicle, telling him one of the two enemy he knew were still up was in the process of reloading.

Zack pushed all other thoughts out of his mind, rolled out from the rear of the minivan, and double-tapped his target just as the Gauntlet man knelt at the rear of the Expedition to reload. The American contractor fell onto his back on the sidewalk; Zack rose to a standing position and shot the man twice more.

There was one more Gauntlet man unaccounted for, so Zack dropped back to his knees at the rear of his vehicle and tuned his ringing ears into the scene, listening for clues. Soon he heard a shuffling on his right. Uncertain if the man approaching up the side of the van had his weapon in position and the skill to use it faster than Zack did his, Zack moved his thumb over on his firing hand, put it on the magazine ejection button, and pressed down.

The half-full Glock mag dropped to the concrete and skittered at his feet.

Quickly Zack lifted his pistol, put it right at eye level at the corner of the vehicle, and waited less than one second.

The masked Gauntlet operative had heard the mag drop and bounce away, took it to mean Zack himself was in the process of reloading, and he rushed around the side of the van to shoot him dead.

Zack fired the one round still in the pipe of his pistol, snapping the enemy operator's forehead back, knocking him out into the street.

The Gauntlet man was dead before he hit the ground. Zack knelt and retrieved his half-empty magazine, slammed it back in the grip of his pistol, and dropped the slide back on a fresh round.

Standing over the dead man, he said, "You don't clear a corner with your face, dumbass."

Zack holstered quickly, checked his body with a blood sweep, and realized to his surprise that he had not been hit in the crazed close-in melee, though it felt like he had. His left leg hurt like hell behind the knee where it had been shot in Russia. Scar tissue there adhered to the muscles of his thigh, and he'd wrenched it crawling and juking around in the gunfight.

Zack's physio back in Colorado had ordered him to stretch every day, and he'd not stretched once, and he was therefore paying the price.

But Zack wasn't thinking right now that he wished he'd been more diligent with his PT; he was thinking about Travers, who had been shot in the street somewhere behind him, and Court, who was somewhere in the condo building, moving downstairs with the subject.

Zack knew his vehicle had probably taken a dozen rounds or more of gunfire right in the grille, so he decided to commandeer the Gauntlet Expedition instead. It would have a radio beacon in it, he was certain, so he couldn't drive it for long, but if it could get him, and maybe Court, off the X a mile or two, they could dump it and then link up with Hanley before Gauntlet HQ could rally a quick reaction force to intercept it.

Zack moved to the driver's side of the Expedition, pushed a dead man crouched behind the open door out of the way, then pulled himself up behind the wheel. Firing the engine and then throwing the truck into reverse, he backed a block down New Hampshire, did a high-speed, reverse-skidding J-turn, and then headed to the left.

He saw flashing red and blue lights behind him, but they were reflections off glass, and any first responders were still some way off.

Racing forward now, he broadcast to the group. "Six, status?"

To his relief, Court answered almost immediately. "I'll be down on New Hampshire in about thirty seconds."

"Okay, that's going to plop you right out into a crime scene. Can you get in the lobby of the Ritz-Carlton Hotel, head out a door on M Street?"

"I'll figure it out."

"You've got Ortega?"

"Yeah, we're both good. You?"

"I'm good, in a black Expedition. No time to lollygag, I'm in an enemy-flagged vic, so shake a leg."

Arnold Reyes drove the minivan down L Street a minute later, slowing just a little as first responders and passing motorists all but blocked the way, and Chris Travers stepped out of the darkness of a cluster of bare bushes, then climbed in the back of the truck, still holding his neck.

Jill shut the door and the vehicle moved on; Hanley took one look at Travers and reached into an already open first-aid kit. He removed a compression bandage, tore it from its green vacuum-sealed bag, and then he applied the gauze-covered end of it to Chris's neck.

Matt pressed the non-adherent cotton pad hard over the wound, and then Travers lifted his bloody left hand high in the air because he knew the procedure. Matt unspooled the elasticized wrapping and tightly wound it around the right side of Chris's neck and then under his left underarm. He threaded the elasticized leader through a hooked plastic device called a pressure applicator, then pulled the wrapping in the opposite direction, nearly as hard as he could, to create the compression needed to slow the bleeding from Travers's neck.

Chris grunted in pain, but he did not protest. The pain he felt was from a treatment that would keep him alive till he got some real medical care, so he sucked it up.

After several more wraps over the right side of the neck and the left underarm, Hanley came to the end of the bandage, where the metal closure bar was attached, and this he hooked over the leader, holding the dressing in place.

"Nice work, doc," Travers said, and then, "I'm good to go. How's Six?"

Just then, Hightower's voice came over their earpieces. "I've got Six and the package, heading north out of the area. Where do you want us?"

Hanley thought a moment. "Any of you hurt?"

"Nothing too dramatic," Hightower answered.

"Okay. I want you three to head to Reagan. We'll get Teddy treated by a doctor I know of near here, and then we'll meet you at the airport."

"How is he?" Hightower asked.

"Lucky," Hanley replied. "He'll need stitches, fresh bandaging, and antibiotics, but he'll fly back with us tonight."

"Roger that," Hightower said. "We'll need to dump this vic first, grab something else. We'll be at Reagan by two a.m. at the latest."

Arnold spoke up on the net for one of the first times of the night, directing Hightower to a rental unit over the Potomac in Arlington where a vehicle owned by a Ghost Town shell was stored in a small garage. They decided they'd dump the Expedition several blocks away from there and then make their way to the cache on foot.

Jill had been watching Pilgrim treat Teddy's wound for the past couple of minutes, and only now did she chance a look down at her phone. She read a text, then opened a link. After a few seconds, she looked up at the three men with her in the vehicle. "There's been another death of an IC official. The FBI supervisory special agent in charge of the New York field office was taken to the hospital after eating in a restaurant in Soho tonight. He died a half hour later."

Arnold called from the front of the truck. "Poison?"

"I wouldn't bet against it," Hanley said. "Was it Doug Holmes?"

Jill looked back down, "Agent Douglas Holmes. Yes."

"Dammit!" Hanley exclaimed. "Doug was a good dude. I knew him what . . . fifteen years?"

Travers winced with pain now as Hanley checked to make sure his dressing was on tight enough to compress the wound. While doing so he asked, "You think it was the Russians?"

"Doug's a rock star," Hanley said. "I mean . . . he *was*, anyway. He ran all counterespionage ops in New York City. That makes for a lot of enemies. Could have been Russia, China, North Korea, Venezuela, Iran. Could have been anybody." Hanley thought for a few moments, then said, "Night Train, you reading me?"

"Yeah, Pilgrim."

"I don't want you and Six talking to Ortega until we get on the plane together. I want to be there for the interrogation. You tracking me?"

"Tracking you one hundred percent, boss."

"I've been working in this town for decades. I'll get the best read on her. If she tries talking, tape her mouth shut; I don't want her crafting a story till I'm the one questioning her."

"Got it, boss," Hightower said.

The black Expedition and the burgundy Chrysler minivan rolled out of the District of Columbia, leaving half a dozen dead bodies in their wake.

THIRTY-TWO

An unadorned gray Chevy Suburban sat in front of the Raymond C. Carter Center for Trends in Peace on Church Street in the Dupont Circle neighborhood of Washington, D.C., and inside sat five plainclothed security officers from Gauntlet Group, each armed with a carbine rifle they kept down low.

The street itself was quiet, but the Gauntlet men watched the flashing lights from nearby Connecticut Avenue, police and medical vehicles heading south, and the Suburban was in radio contact with the security officers inside the row house building it was parked next to.

It was midnight; this crew was due to remain on duty till six, when they would likely be swapped out for another vehicle full of men, but for now they just kept their eyes peeled on Church Street, unaware of any specific danger to their charge, but well aware that something was going on in the area.

Inside, in the third-floor office of James Westwood, there was a lot more information available. J.W. had CNN on mute on the TV on the wall across from him, and the four monitors of his desktop computer were open to various other news and social media sources.

J.W. hadn't been able to hear any gunfire or action at this distance, but D.C. Metro PD was out in force, and sirens filtered through the glass behind him, no doubt keeping everyone in this part of the District awake and annoyed.

Westwood didn't know all the reasons the Chinese had ordered the elimination of all the targets on the list they'd given him, the list he'd handed over to Scardino to pass out to the five assassins they had working in America right now, but J.W. *did* know the reason the Chinese needed the woman who lived in nearby Washington Circle to die.

Irene Ortega hadn't made the news yet, but she would soon, of this he was certain. CNN was already covering the murders in Hyattsville, in Tysons Corner, in New York, and in Miami, and one of their talking heads had just opined that it was still too early to connect the killings, which J.W. found laughable.

Irene Ortega, like the man in Maryland who'd been killed, was on the lower end of the spectrum, not a big player in the community, but they both held secrets about the operation Gauntlet was part of, and for that reason, they were placed high on the kill list. And even though they weren't big players, it was unavoidable that they would be tied to the bigger picture soon enough. One worked for NSA and the other for ODNI, and they were targeted on the same night as several others in the same general profession.

The man Lancer had killed in Miami was a Gauntlet employee. A man Scardino had trusted with information about his company's clandestine work with China.

A man who then told Scardino he was going to report Gauntlet to the FBI for illegally acting as an agent for a foreign power.

Scardino had told J.W. this, J.W. had told Gracie Wu, and then the Gauntlet employee in Miami had been assassinated by the American assassin Lancer before revealing anything to anybody.

A knock at J.W.'s office door came at twelve twenty in the morning, and he did not hear it at first with all the sirens from the police cars still racing through Dupont Circle.

When he did hear, however, he wasn't worried about who it would be.

He kept a pistol in a drawer in his desk, but there was enough security in this row house to where he had little worry of being surprised by someone making it all the way from the street up to the third floor without him at least hearing about it.

"Come in."

Big Mike stepped in. J.W. expected a smile on the man's face; he knew that five of the twenty-one targets had been successfully taken out in the first two hours of the operation, and it sounded like the police heading to Washington Circle meant he was about to learn about the sixth successful job now.

But Mike's eyes were wide, a little unfixed.

This did not look good.

"What's happened?"

Scardino crossed the office, sat at a chair in front of the desk, and leaned forward, his forearms on the desk's edge.

"It's Spiral."

"What about him?"

Scardino seemed confused. Slowly, he said, "Apparently . . . our professional assassin was professionally assassinated."

"*What?*"

"Spiral's dead. His entire fucking team is dead."

J.W.'s ebullient mood of five seconds earlier went up in smoke.

"What . . . the . . . fuck? Your guys, too?"

"All five."

"They weren't supposed to be involved with the hit."

"They were standing watch outside Ortega's building. They were in two vehicles; one was a couple blocks away. Witnesses report a single person stepped up to each vehicle. Two gunfights broke out. This was while Spiral was upstairs. Something happened up there, Spiral blew his way into the condo, then was riddled with gunfire."

"By Ortega?" J.W. asked.

"It wasn't Ortega," Scardino muttered softly. "No . . . there's a professional outfit out there. And they're onto us somehow."

"Any way you slice it, J.W., this was a fucking shit show."

"You have a way of tying off the compromise of losing the Gauntlet men?"

Scardino shrugged his shoulders and nodded. "Yeah. American heroes. Came across a bad actor about to assassinate someone. They tried to help. Fell in the line of duty, or some bullshit like that. We can sell it."

Westwood said, "What if it happens again?"

"Gauntlet is everywhere. It stands to reason that they would be near the scene of another hit around here. We need Gauntlet in this fight. Gracie and the Chinese don't have the assets to support our five hit men." Quickly he corrected himself. "Four hit men."

J.W. said, "Any idea who protected Ortega tonight?"

"No, but we're going to be looking at cameras in the area. We didn't feel the need to bug Ortega's condo . . . she was considered a low-threat target, which obviously was a mistake. But there are other cams in the area, and even a team that good will leave some footprints. Whoever rescued her tonight, whether they were government agents or private forces . . . we'll find them."

J.W. did not hide his concern. "If they have Ortega now, and she's talking, what does she know?"

"She knows that Lewis Shaw used her credentials to obtain intelligence regarding the operation in Nicaragua, and then someone used that intelligence to affect the outcome in Nicaragua. She suspects Shaw used her credentials on the other breaches."

J.W. rose from behind his desk. "He passed that intelligence to *me*, Mike. *I'm* the one who passed that intel to the Chinese!"

"Ortega can't possibly know that. She doesn't know who he disseminated it to, that's why she was trying to spy on Shaw herself."

"What's going on with the other four assets?" J.W. then asked.

"Lancer is on his way up here now; his job in Miami was clean. Snare did Tysons, has more to do in Virginia. Masquerade did New York. Whetstone did Hyattsville already." Scardino smiled for the first time since he came into the office. "I just hired the son of a bitch five hours ago, and he's already crossed one name off his list. He's on his way to Baltimore, then he's off to Chicago after that, I believe."

"You *believe*?"

"Yeah, well, he also has a side quest here in the States. I'm trusting him that he finishes my work before he goes off and does that."

"What's a side quest?"

"Part of his agreement to do the hits was he wanted to know the location of Matthew Hanley."

J.W. cocked his head at this. Of course, he knew Hanley was a former DDO. He'd met him many times when he was in Congress and Hanley was a midlevel CIA exec. "What does he want with Hanley?"

"Beats me. He wouldn't say. Sounded like a personal beef."

"A personal beef?"

"First, he wanted intelligence about the Gray Man. I had Shaw do some digging at ODNI. Did you know Gray Man is a former CIA paramilitary asset code-named Violator?"

"I did not, but I don't see how that's relevant to our operation."

"It's not, but Whetstone wanted Hanley's info, because he seems to think Hanley knows how he can find the Gray Man. Lancer wanted intel on the Gray Man, as well."

"So half the assassins in our stable are more interested in finding the Gray Man than they are in doing their jobs."

Scardino shook his head. "Lancer, for sure, is more interested in the money. I guess there is a lot of rivalry and jealousy in the contract killer field." Scardino added, "Whetstone's still got four ops to do for us; after that, I don't care about Hanley. He's yesterday's news, anyway."

Westwood said, "I'm most concerned about whoever wiped your team out tonight. Aren't you?"

Big Mike said, "We'll figure it out."

Changing the subject, J.W. said, "Spiral had four other missions. Who will do them?"

"I'll talk to Lancer. He seemed very eager. I'll have him do one. Snare is close by, I'll have him do another. I'll get Whetstone and Masquerade to do the others."

James Westwood's phone chirped on his desk. It was a Signal call, and it would be Gracie. She would have heard by now about the five successful operations, but she would have also heard about the shambolic unsuccessful one, and J.W. had no illusions at all about which one this call would be concerning.

Scardino turned and left the room as the older man answered.

. . .

Campbell Coyle sat alone in his Volkswagen Passat, parked equidistant from light poles on Timber Ridge Drive so that he was in as much darkness as possible on this residential street. He'd been here awhile watching a property across the street, and if he'd been shooed away by a passing security vehicle or a nosy neighbor, he'd come back here tomorrow night without a car and use a bit more stealth.

But it seemed he hadn't been noticed by the residents, and no neighborhood rent-a-cop had happened by, so he'd been here most of an hour, examining his target, using binoculars to evaluate access points and security issues at the purported residence of Matthew Hanley.

He had sent all five of his support team to Silver Spring to kill a man. They didn't know why, and they didn't ask, but if they *had* asked, Coyle's only response would have been that they would make a million dollars for the hit, and if they needed more prompting than that, then they'd found themselves in the wrong line of work.

The Kearney team—the Walsh and Donnelly brothers—weren't assassins by trade, but they knew how to kill, and they'd certainly done it in the past for a lot less than a million. Building a car bomb from parts bought from a Home Depot and then stashing it under an unsuspecting man's car didn't sound like it would be too much trouble.

Coyle wasn't worried about them right now; he was worried about the home on the other side of a quiet intersection from him.

And so far, he liked what he saw.

Campbell Coyle had worked for the past eight years installing and maintaining security systems all over Northern Ireland, and he knew the inner workings of both commercial and private systems. He could defeat locks, alarms, cameras, and motion sensors through means both mechanical and high-tech.

He used bolt cutters and iPads, screwdrivers and computer code.

Eyeballing Hanley's home down the street on Meeting House Road, he'd determined that no one was present on the property, and though there was a security system, it was an off-the-shelf variety that Coyle could easily disable.

He was armed with a pistol; zip ties; a wrapped set of tools for picking locks, disassembling cameras, and other purposes; and computer equipment with various peripherals, all stowed in an oiled leather backpack he'd brought all the way from Northern Ireland.

In the bag he also had a burner phone with one number programmed into it, and a handwritten note folded in an outside pocket.

His laptop had been open for most of the last hour, but now he closed the device, then climbed out of the car. His hoodie covered his head and the Irish watch cap he wore on it; he slung his backpack over his shoulder and walked out into the street. Security cameras on people's property were virtually always set to dismiss movement in the road itself, otherwise motion detectors would alert to every passing vehicle, so Coyle began walking down the middle of the street in the direction of Matthew Hanley's house with a gait so calm he likely wouldn't raise suspicion even if someone saw him at this time of night.

The excitement he felt from the action was blunted by the purpose of this mission. He'd killed dozens of times for money, and there had been something of a thrill in that, at least in the very olden days. But now Coyle's actions were for a cause both so solemn and so righteous that he derived no pleasure from them; only his commitment drove him forward, toward the home and, eventually, toward his inevitable meeting with the man who had killed his son.

THIRTY-THREE

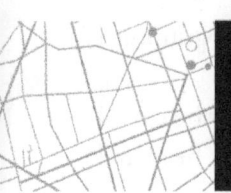

In the twelve-seat cabin of the Hawker 800XP jet flying twenty thousand feet over Richmond, Virginia, Matthew Hanley sat in a comfortable leather chair just behind the copilot, and he looked down at a pair of text messages that just came through on his phone. They notified him that both his home alarm and security camera system had gone down because of a power outage.

Hanley wasn't worried about the power outage at home. He didn't have much food in his refrigerator, and he doubted he'd be back to his house for at least another sixteen hours or so, plus he had much bigger fish to fry, so he dismissed the texts.

The flight was already forty minutes old, and the interrogation of the woman on board who'd found herself at the center of the action tonight had not yet begun. Hanley had been on the phone while Jill Mori sat next to him, completely engrossed with her laptop, and the two had not spoken once during the flight, so focused were they on their own jobs.

Court Gentry and Zack Hightower sat with Irene Ortega on a sofa in the rear of the spacious cabin. A sheet had been rigged to the ceiling of the cabin that blocked off Irene's view of the others, and though Zack and Court were back with her, they wore neck gaiters that hid their faces, so she was pretty much in the dark as to what was going on apart from the fact that she'd been rescued from an assassination by men who themselves appeared rather terrifying. She'd tried to talk to them a couple of times, but both times Court had told her she needed to wait for a debriefing, and it would come soon enough, and for now she needed to just be glad she wasn't lying dead in her bathtub.

Behind Hanley and Jill, Arnold Reyes sat in the center of the cabin next to Chris Travers, whose seatback had been lowered flat. Travers was sedated and he slept soundly, his neck freshly bandaged and stitched. The doctor Hanley had taken him to in the middle of the night had done the job at his kitchen table, then handed over a supply of painkillers and antibiotics. As Jill and Arnold helped take Chris back out to their vehicle, the doctor whispered to Hanley that the bullet had been within an inch of severing the asset's carotid artery, and a severed carotid was a guaranteed one-way ticket to dead.

Hanley knew he needed to get started with the debriefing of Ortega, but he was trying to get as much information as possible about what had happened first, and to that end Lacy had already been very helpful. She'd confirmed that all five men killed at street level had been Gauntlet operatives, and Gauntlet had said this particular team was running a previously scheduled security sweep in the area, and must have just happened to come upon a team of killers.

Both Lacy and Hanley agreed it sounded like bullshit.

Hanley had also learned that the assassin found on the bathroom floor of the condo with four more holes in him than God intended had been identified as forty-three-year-old Alexi Kravchuk, known as Deep Space by the Americans. He had been performing lethal operations exclusively for Russia for the past three years under the alias Spiral, so the inference already running around the intelligence community was that Deep Space was after Ortega on Russia's orders.

This also lent credence to the fact that Russia had been involved in all the other killings of intelligence community personnel tonight, but Hanley had been around long enough to know it was too early to make such inferences.

Lacy was skeptical herself, mainly because Ortega's work at DNI wasn't specifically involved with Russia.

Killing Ortega might provide some benefit to some bad actor, but there were a lot of people who did what she did, so both Hanley and Lacy suspected that Irene Ortega was targeted for something specific that she knew, and not solely because of her job title.

Hanley climbed from his cabin chair, then made his way back past Arnold and Travers to a seat just this side of the fabric partition in the cabin. Calling out through the bedsheet hanging there, Hanley said, "Irene, let me start by saying we are very happy you are alive."

There was a pause, and then he heard the woman speak. "That makes two of us. But I don't understand why I can't see your faces."

"We need to understand what side of this you are on."

"I don't even know what *this* is."

"You know *something*. Why do you think those men were trying to kill you tonight?"

"Who are *you* guys?" she asked again, flatly. Any shock or terror she'd felt earlier in the evening had evaporated. It was as if she were genuinely terrified of the assassination attempt, but the men and woman who'd rescued her and put her on a private jet did not elicit the same amount of concern out of her.

With menace in his voice, Court Gentry said, "Answer the question, lady."

"I don't even know who they were."

"I think you do," Court said.

When she did not respond, Matt said, "You see the predicament you're in, Irene? We saved you tonight; you might not trust us, but you have to ask yourself, Who else *can* I trust?"

"I'll just keep my mouth shut. You can kill me, or you can release me. Your choice."

Hanley said, "We didn't go to all this trouble to save you just so we could then kill you. We will, most definitely, release you, but you might want to think about the ramifications of that. The man who came after you tonight was a contract killer known to the CIA as Deep Space. The other men—some of them, at least—were contractors from Gauntlet."

There was a long pause. Then she said, "How do you know that?"

Hightower answered this question. "We ran tags on one of the vehicles, plus people in both vehicles admitted it. Why is Gauntlet after you?"

"I wouldn't have any idea."

Hanley didn't think this was going anywhere, so he yanked down the sheet between himself and the woman. Zack and Court just looked at him in surprise, but neither of them lowered their gaiters. He said, "Listen very carefully, Irene. We have been surveilling you because we thought you were involved in the intelligence leaks—your log-in was used to obtain intelligence about Nicaragua that was used by the enemy—but we quickly realized there was another group watching you, as well. When they sent a known killer after you tonight, we took it on faith that *you* weren't the real problem, and whoever is causing the compromises in the IC knows you are a threat to them, and they want you taken off the playing field."

Court spoke to the woman, who now seemed fixated on Hanley. "We're just trying to get an idea about who or what is behind—"

The woman's eyes narrowed as she looked at the older man in the cabin chair in front of her. Finally, she interrupted Court. "Mr. . . . Mr. Hanley?"

Matt saw both Court and Hightower lean back now, sharing a frustrated look with each other.

But Hanley said, "Do I know you?"

"No, sir. But I've seen you speak a few times. You came to ODNI for some luncheons, talked about the work of the Special Activities Division—Center, I mean. I still call it Division."

"I still call it that, too," Hanley said. "That would have been several years ago."

"Yes. But then when you became deputy director of the CIA, I saw another speech you made, this one at Langley."

"How were my speeches?"

She faltered a moment. Looked down, then back up at him. "Frankly, you seemed like you'd rather have been somewhere else."

Zack sniffed out a laugh.

Hanley laughed, too. "You're a talented analyst."

Irene looked around at the plane, at Jill and Arnold, at Court and Zack; Travers's stocking feet were just in view where he lay.

"How is he?"

"Took a zinger in the neck. A close call, but he'll be back one hundred percent in no time. More than I can say for the five Gauntlet men and the assassin someone sent to your condo."

She eyed Hanley with incredulity. "You used to be the DDO. Are you on some kind of a . . . a *field* team now?" She said it with a mixture of shock and derision, as if the idea of being in the field and not behind a desk was a fate worse than death.

"Hell of a demotion to be working with these degenerates," Hanley said, and Irene smiled for the first time. He added, "We are working outside the official infrastructure of the intelligence community. I'll just leave it there."

Her eyes cleared a little and she nodded. "That's a good idea. And it sounds like you already have your answer, sir. The people at the heart of this are from Gauntlet Group."

"Why did you follow Lewis Shaw to the Hirshhorn Museum today?"

"I didn't follow him there. I knew he had a meeting. I went to see who the meeting was with."

"And what did you find out?"

"Nothing at all. The person he met with was wearing some kind of a face mask. It looked like a real person, it really did, but it wasn't."

"We saw that. Why were you interested in Shaw in the first place?"

"I realized someone had accessed some files using my credentials, files regarding communications between the CIA station in Managua, Nicaragua, and Langley. Lewis was the only one who had the administrator access to have done it without leaving a record that I could easily find.

"I confronted him, told him I had proof. I was bluffing, I had nothing tangible. He denied everything, of course, but there was something in the way he denied it."

"What do you mean?"

"A threat. An insinuation that he had connections in the building. That I should shut up and not mention anything about the access of those files again. He acted like he was doing me a favor by warning me to be quiet.

"So I thought Lewis was involved, but I didn't think it was just him. Yeah, he could have been pulling the files with his administrator access, but why? Who was he doing it for? He's just some computer geek. I didn't know what to do, but then it happened."

"What happened?" Zack prompted.

"It occurred to me that any investigation would show that it was my log-in that pulled the traffic between CIA and Managua station; it would be obvious that I was the culprit, so I looked back to the other incidents. Tunis and Madrid and Addis Ababa. There is a record of me accessing files for every single one of the breach incidents in the IC. They weren't generated before the incidents; they were generated after, but the dates had been changed to make it look like I'd pulled records *before* each incident."

Hanley said, "He was backdating the searches."

"They weren't there one day. Then after Managua station, they were all there."

"Which means, once he knew you were onto him, he began setting you up."

Court spoke up now. "And once they killed you, they would have blamed you for everything."

Irene turned and looked at the man with the covered face. She seemed to understand this for the first time. "My God."

Hanley said, "When you spoke to Shaw, you said he seemed to threaten you. Did you go to your superiors when you found out?"

She shook her head. "No, I didn't . . . He rattled me, honestly. I was too scared to go to my supervisor, or anyone above him."

She paused, a look of embarrassment on her face, and then said, "So . . . I panicked. I have a friend at CIA, in Science and Technology. About six months ago I thought my boyfriend was cheating. He was, by the way. I asked my girlfriend at S and T what the best off-the-shelf surveillance gear was, and I did my own investigation using it." She smiled. "I still had the bugs I used on my boyfriend. I went to talk to Shaw; he was in a meeting but his office door was open. I put a bug on his messenger bag. That was nine thirty a.m. yesterday. By noon I was listening in on his side of a phone call with someone. He said he'd meet them at the Hirshhorn at three thirty p.m. So I went. I guess they saw me there."

Hightower shook his head. "They were onto you before you got there."

"How do you know that?"

"We followed you on the Metro. You had a Gauntlet surveillance team on you before you got to the Hirshhorn, and there was another one there at the museum. The whole meeting at the museum might have been a setup to see if you were acting alone."

Irene thought a moment. "How did *you* know I was following Shaw?"

Hanley shrugged. "We were told about your access creds being used to pull the Nicaragua files from a CIA officer we trust implicitly."

"So . . ." Irene thought a moment. "What do we do now?"

"We need to protect you, because whoever came at you tonight is obviously scared about what you know."

"Which, as it turns out, is next to nothing."

Hanley smiled at her. "You caused the enemy to react, to show themselves. We learned a lot tonight. Gauntlet is involved, a contract killer most recently linked to Russia was involved, and now we see that a half dozen other people in the IC have been targeted by someone other than Deep Space. Whatever is going on is so much bigger than Nicaragua, or Tunis, or Ethiopia. Someone is enacting their game plan, and they needed you taken out of the mix, right at the beginning, so that you wouldn't reveal what you knew."

Irene was left alone in the rear of the plane, while Court and Zack followed Hanley up the cabin. Jill and Arnold had to give up their seats so that the two assets and the leader of Ghost Town could have a meeting at the front, and they moved back to the couch with Irene.

Hanley said, "First off, let's assess. Ghost Town is two days old, and we've already had our first running gun battle on the streets of D.C. Six dead."

"Yeah . . . but six shitheads," Hightower replied.

Hanley jerked a thumb to Travers behind them; he was sitting up and alert, but his neck was bandaged. "At no small cost." Chris saw the attention on him and gave a glassy-eyed thumbs-up, which Court and Zack returned with a laugh.

"I want what he's having," Court said.

"We can see that you get shot in the neck next time."

Court started to speak, but Hanley held up a hand, because a couple of texts had just come through on his phone, and he pulled it out to check them.

Looking down, he received messages telling him his alarm power had been restored and that his security cameras were back online.

He started to slip the phone back into his pocket, but then he quickly hefted it back up, because it vibrated yet again. This time it was an automatic message from one of his security cameras, indicating it detected movement. At this time of night, he assumed it would have been the cam at his front door, because occasionally it picked up vehicles turning around in his little driveway.

But instead, the camera's name as stated by the text was "Bedroom."

Matt Hanley had cameras all over his house, but like most reasonable people, he did *not* have a camera in his bedroom.

Quickly he opened the app, certain there must have been some kind of mistake. No other camera had registered movement, and he had eight installed both inside and outside on his property.

He waited a moment for a file to load, and then a video began playing and he knew he was looking at a view of his bedroom. The lights in the room were off, but the upstairs hall light was on, and he could see his stairs behind it that led down to his living room.

The image seemed to come from a camera set up on a dresser just feet to the right of where he slept.

A human form silhouetted in front of the light from the hallway stood there, close to the camera.

For several seconds there was no movement from the person, but then an arm lifted, a light came on, and Hanley realized he was looking at the illuminated screen of a Google Pixel phone.

The figure holding the phone waved it back and forth in front of the camera a couple of times, then placed it there, on the dresser. The figure then patted it with a gloved hand. After fifteen seconds, the phone light went out, and the person turned around and walked out into the lighted hallway.

With his back turned, it was impossible to tell much about the intruder.

At the landing the figure flipped off the switch there, extinguishing the light in the upstairs hallway, and then the intruder turned in the direction of the camera and descended, quickly disappearing, heading down the stairs to the main floor.

Hanley's phone suddenly came alive with automated text messages alerting him that cameras had registered movement in the kitchen and in the living room. He looked at the videos, one after the next, as what appeared to be a man in a riding cap walked through the house, out onto the porch, down the driveway, and out to the street.

Each time, only the man's back showed, or his side, the view of his face obstructed by the hoodie he wore.

The pilot came over the PA in the cabin suddenly, breaking Hanley out of his transfixed state watching an intruder leave his home. They were ten minutes from landing at Hampton Road in Norfolk, Virginia.

Court Gentry had been talking to Hightower, kneeling next to him and just behind Hanley, but now he sat down next to his boss and buckled himself into the comfortable leather cabin chair. He said, "Once we get Ortega to Ghost Town, I'll head back to my boat, catch a few hours' sleep, and then—"

Matt Hanley was staring straight ahead, his face as white as a ghost. Clearly Court noticed this now. "What is it?"

"It's trouble," Hanley said, and then he handed his phone over to Court, with the first video from his bedroom cued up.

THIRTY-FOUR

Dawn was still thirty minutes off, putting enough light in the sky on the sleepy suburban neighborhood to make out the homes, the fences, the yards. A dog barked in the distance, and birds stirred in the trees.

A face covered from the neck to just below the eyes appeared over a wooden fence; the eyes scanned the scene ahead, and then a man climbed over and dropped down on the other side. Landing in a crouch, he rose and moved through a backyard full of pine trees. Here he stopped for a moment at the edge of the tree line, knelt, then looked across a swimming pool covered for the winter and towards a small brick home on the other side of a wrought-iron fence.

Waiting, watching. Finally, the man rose again and sprinted forward.

A minute later the same man put a key in the back door of the brick home, drew a pistol from his belt, took a moment to put on a set of black-rimmed eyeglasses over his eyes, then opened the door.

Flowing in alone, he kept his weapon up in front of him.

Court Gentry used the high-lumen weapon light to search for trip wires, and in this he had help. He wore the glasses Arnold Reyes had worn in the Hirshhorn Museum the day before so his scan of the home could be watched in real time by Matt Hanley, who was several blocks away with the rest of the team in a van.

Court began climbing the stairs; Matt was in his ear, telling him to move slowly, to watch for any other cameras the intruder might have set up, attached to his own network somehow.

Fully five minutes after entering the small home, Court arrived at the phone.

He didn't touch the device lying there, but he turned on the overhead light in the room and lowered the pistol. "I'm clear," he said. "There's a folded note on the dresser next to the camera."

"We're on the way," Hanley said.

Court confirmed receipt of the transmission, but he didn't wait on Hanley and company before lifting the note and opening it.

Violator. Gray Man. Call the one number saved into this phone via Signal. Phone password is 00001. I will answer. I can't stop all the killing still to come, but I can stop my part in it. It's now up to you, chief.

Five minutes later, Hanley and Hightower stood in the bedroom with Court, the phone still on the dresser. Behind them, Arnold had just completed his radio frequency scan of the home, making certain no bugs had been placed.

Two members of the Five Guys, the security team at Ghost Town, were armed with AR-15s, and they stood at windows, securing the property.

"What do you think?" Hightower said.

"I think I better get the number off this phone, then use a burner to call it."

Just then, Jill came over everyone's headsets. "It's Gumdrop. Two more killings overnight. One in D.C. and another in Vienna, Virginia. Both current members of the IC. One was DIA, the other Homeland Security office of Intelligence and Analysis."

Hightower said, "That's seven assassinations, eight attempts. In what . . . eight, nine hours? If you had the best hitters in the world, there'd still have to be three, four of them, minimum, doing all this."

Court said, "Let me see the videos again."

They sat on the bed and watched several of the videos of the man in the home, just two hours or so earlier.

Court froze one of the videos and just looked at the darkened image of the man in the hood. "Who the fuck is this guy?"

"Obviously, one of the assassins," Hanley said. "He's close enough to D.C., Maryland, Tysons, Vienna, could have done any of those hits and then come here, or else he hasn't even started yet."

"How does he know about me?" Court asked. "Or about your connection to me?"

"There's a massive intelligence leak under way, or haven't you been paying attention?"

Court rubbed his eyes.

Lacy called again. Hanley took the call downstairs in his den, then met Court and Zack at the back door while Arnold went to retrieve the van with one of the Five Guys. Hanley said, "We've got some new information. Angela told me that Scott Kincaid was released from prison by the Cubans just yesterday."

Lancer, Court thought. The former Navy SEAL turned assassin who Court had come up against in Havana earlier in the year. Softly, he just said, "*That* asshole."

"What's he want with you?" Hightower asked.

But Matt answered. "He blames Six for getting him arrested in Havana. This is probably our culprit."

Court thought back to the video. "That guy . . . he wasn't really built like Lancer."

Hightower said, "Maybe seven months in a Cuban prison changes a man."

The van pulled up and the men climbed in, and Court said, "The rate at which people are dying, I think I'd better call sooner than later."

It was decided by the team that Court would call the number from a computer at Ghost Town and not from the Google phone that had been left for him. That phone was now in a Faraday cage on the outside chance there was a tracker built into it that Arnold's equipment had missed. Jill had assured him it would be impossible for anyone to determine the origin of his call if she used a spoofing app on her laptop, so he now sat alone in the small office that just a year earlier had been an exam room in a podiatry clinic, and he looked at the number on the screen. With headphones and a microphone on his head, the laptop set to record the conversation, he took a deep breath, then ordered the computer to dial the number.

The call was answered on the other end after a short delay. The audio quality was impeccable with the headset Court wore, and almost instantly he heard soft breathing on the other end of the line.

After a time, when the party on the other end of the line did not say anything, Court said, "You wanted a word?"

"Who am I speaking to?" The man was Irish, Court could tell immediately. This was not Lancer, the American hit man he'd run into in Havana.

Court hadn't operated in Ireland in many years.

Confused, he recovered quickly, then answered. "A long time ago, certain people referred to me as Violator."

"Aye," the man said. "If it *is* really you, I *would* like a wee chat. But how do I know it's really you, eh?"

Court leaned back in the chair, put his feet up on the desk. "Well . . . I guess that's *your* problem, dickhead. You broke into a man's house, left a phone and a note claiming to have been part of a streak of killings. You went to a lot of trouble to get this far, and you don't have a plan to identify me?"

Court just heard more breathing on the line. Even though he knew he couldn't be traced, the voice, the tempo of the man's words, and the slow breathing unsettled him just the same. Finally, the man on the other end said, "You are interested in the assassinations taking place in America right now, yeah?"

Court furrowed his brow. He wasn't sure what this man knew about him. He said, "Not really. I'm not in America, and I don't work for the government."

"But my note to Hanley, I said if you called, I could make some of the killin' stop."

Court said, "Hanley reached out to me, and I told him I'd call you as a courtesy. But I'm not involved in—"

"Not buyin' it, chief. This call from you came too quick, didn't it? You're tryin' to help. You're in the middle of all this."

Court did not argue. Instead, he just asked, "Which of the hits was yours?"

The answer came quickly. "Hyattsville, Maryland. Last night. That's all, so far, but I've got work ahead of me yet."

"How do *I* know you—"

"Knife, from behind, straight across the throat. One cut, left to right. Has that been released yet?"

Court didn't have a clue how the victim in Hyattsville had been killed, but there was an authority in the man's tone that left no doubt that what he was saying was true.

"All right, then. What do I call you?"

"Call me whatever you like."

"I'll call you Dick."

"Suit yourself, Gray Man."

Court could hear a searing intensity to the man's words. A derision he did not understand but knew was somehow relevant to all this. To draw the man out a little, he said, "I'm already bored with this conversation. I've got to help a friend move today; he just found out his place has pests, so if you'll excuse me, Dick, I better—"

The Irishman shouted now. "You'll sit right there and you'll feckin' listen to me, yeah?"

Court gave it a few beats. "I'm listening."

"Within the hour there will be another killing. It's my doin', though I won't be there personally when it happens."

"A bomb, you mean?" Court said.

"You'll see."

"Any chance I can talk you into stopping it?"

"None," the man said with finality. "We're not talking about that victim. He's as good as gone. We're talking about the others."

"How many killers are out there?"

"You've done what I do. Did the people in charge tell you everything what was going on?"

"No," Court admitted.

"Nah, mate. You just killed 'cause it's all ya knew how to do. You didn't need a reason."

Court never killed without a reason, but he wasn't going to argue with the man. Yet something in the tone of the Irishman's words bothered him.

Court said, "You seem like you're mad at *me* about something. That this is somehow personal. Do I have that part right?"

"Aye. You do."

"Do we know each other?"

"We've never met. I know your work, though. Intimately."

Court rubbed his eyes now. "What is it you think I did?"

"Don't think. *Know.* And I want you to know that I am comin' for ya, and I will be finding ya, yeah?"

This somehow unsettled Court even more, but he fought revealing it in his voice. He said, "All that, and you're going to be busy killing intelligence professionals across America?"

"The only intelligence professional I care about is you. I just took this job so they could help me find ya, and they're keepin' up their end so far, so I've got to keep up mine, don't I?"

"What's your plan with me, then?" Court asked, genuinely confused.

"I knew you and Hanley had worked together. In Russia, was it? I knew goin' to him would get me closer to you, and I didn't want to chase you around the bloody planet. I would if I had to, yeah, but I didn't want to."

"So?"

"So . . . I want ya to come to me. I'm gonna convince you to do that."

"I've got other things to do at the moment."

"Yeah, you've got to figure out who this bloody cabal is in your government, chief. Thems that want to put an end to the American way, whatever the feck that is."

"Seems like a worthy pursuit on my part."

"And what I'm doin' is worthy, as well."

"Just what is it you are doin'?"

"I've come here to America to kill you, mate, for somethin' you've done."

"Is this the point of the conversation where you tell me what that is?"

The Irishman breathed hard into the phone, then said, "Varna, Bulgaria."

Court let out a long and slow sigh, but he was careful to keep it silent. No, this was not just some horrible misunderstanding. He'd been in Varna a couple of months earlier. He'd done things there. He'd killed people there.

Shit.

He kept his tone even. "Never heard of it."

"You was there. People put you there, then they put you in Russia. Hanley, from what I've been told. I don't care about Russia, I don't care about Hanley, but I care about bleedin' Bulgaria, because there's where you killed me son."

Shit, Court thought again. He stared at the ceiling, his feet on the desk.

"Sasho Minchev," the Irishman said. "You remember the night."

Confused, Court said, "Your son was Sasho—"

"Of course he wasn't Sasho Minchev!" the man snapped. "Do I sound like I'm from the feckin' Balkans?"

"Not really, no."

"You killed and maimed other men that night. One of the dead was my boy."

Court thought back to the night, some two and a half months earlier. A lot had happened since then. Many other violent encounters, other threats, other dangers, other bodies.

Varna. A hotel, a nightclub, an alleyway. He'd injured a man in the alley, another in a parking garage. He was pretty certain he'd killed a man on a stairway, then shot another in a hall.

And then, in a hotel suite, he'd wounded a guard, and then he'd killed the Bulgarian crime boss, Sasho Minchev.

He tried to picture the faces of the fallen, but he could not.

All this thinking took a long moment, and the man on the other end of the line finally interrupted.

"You remember now?"

"I . . . I don't know."

"When we finally meet, I'll be happy to show you a picture."

"If I hurt your son, I did it because he was a threat."

"And you think that matters to me?"

Court took his feet off the desk and stood up now. "What is it you want? You seem like you know this world. You understand this life. You seem like a reasonable—"

"Do I?" the Irishman shouted. "Do I seem reasonable to you? I've killed five men so far trying to get to you, and I'll kill more. As many as it takes. I don't care. I've a job to do, and you're my job."

"What the fuck's wrong with you, dude?" Court asked.

"Many things, chief. Many things. I'm feckin' mad, a lunatic. But this? It's the most levelheaded thing I've ever done."

Court had no words.

The man on the other end of the line finally said, "I've got to go, but each and every hour, know that I'm out here killing them, because I'm not where you are, killing you. Maybe it will weigh on you after a time. Either way, I'll find ya."

"Better yet, mate. Give me a Signal number where I can reach you in the future."

"Why would I—"

"Because I might just say 'fuck it,' and call you up to tell you where you can find me."

Court pulled his mobile, opened his app, and generated an encrypted number. This he passed to the man on the other end of the line.

"Got it," the Irishman said.

Court replied, "Is your plan to keep calling me so you can try to scare me?"

"Today's contact was so you could have time to think on your sins. If I call you again, it will be to see if you've learned anything. I've got people lookin' into your Hanley, lookin' into you, and I know we'll be seein' each other soon."

Court couldn't help himself. "You keep working with Gauntlet, and we'll be seeing each other even sooner."

There was a pause. The Irishman said, "I don't know what you're on about with Gauntlet, never heard of him."

Court couldn't tell if this was true or not, but the man on the other end of the line hung up immediately after.

. . .

Court stood there, the phone in his hand for several seconds, then stopped the recording. He stepped back into the hallway and called Matt, Zack, and a drugged-up Chris Travers in.

He played back the call for them from beginning to end. No one spoke the entire time.

When they were finished, Matt darted away to task Jill, knowing she could find out the names of everyone killed that night in Bulgaria. That done, he came back into the office where the three assets sat around, mostly in stunned silence.

To Hanley, Court said, "He's fishing. He knows that you and I are in contact, but he didn't know my name. He didn't know my voice."

Hanley said, "This has to be tied to the operation in Russia. It's possible someone knew both you and I were connected to it."

"Maybe. But look at all the intelligence compromises going on right now. Someone could, possibly, have gotten some information about me, about my relationship to you, from the U.S. government, and not from the Russian government."

Zack Hightower blew out a long sigh. "So, Six, our situation isn't bad enough that you've now gotten yourself involved in a personal beef with some assassin."

Court sniffed. "He's not some random guy who's after me. He's very much connected with our adversaries now."

Chris Travers spoke up, his hand holding a little pressure on his bandage, because it made talking less painful. "We need to see if what he said about the Hyattsville murder checks out."

Hanley shook his head. "I read details on the flight in. Knife wound to the throat. That hasn't been out in the news yet. This guy is who he says he is. He's an assassin."

Jill knocked on the door and then entered. To Matt she said, "You wanted to know about the bodyguards killed in Varna, Bulgaria. The one you are interested in was a UK citizen, a twenty-four-year-old former French Foreign Legion enlistee named Charles Brendan Coyle. Born and raised in Londonderry, Northern Ireland, he was working for a security company based out of London run by a man named Marcus Maragos. Maragos, perhaps not incidentally, was knifed to death in his own home two days ago. Two security men were also killed with him."

Hanley surprised Jill with the next question. "Do we know anything about his dad?"

She looked down at her laptop, typed a moment. "Father's name is Campbell Finley Coyle. No known address. That's all I have here, but I only ran Charles Brendan Coyle through the database. Need me to dig deeper on the father?"

"Yes, do that. I'll call Lacy, see what she can find out, as well."

Erin Childers said, "Matt, your house on Meeting House Road is now off-limits. We'll have a moving company get your things out of there, put them into storage until this all gets sorted out."

"Okay. But there's nothing tying me to this building."

Childers said, "You could have been followed here from your home."

Hanley shook his head. "I haven't been physically followed by anyone. Here is safe. You all are safe." He looked to Court. "Well, most of you."

Childers nodded. To Hanley, she said, "We've got cots. A kitchen. A shower. Let's keep you here, with the Five Guys. Twenty-four-hour security, for as long as this takes. No more venturing out into the field."

Reluctantly, Hanley agreed.

He turned to Travers. "Teddy, you're out of commission. I want you in the rack recovering, because I need you back in action ASAP. Six, go home, get a few hours' sleep. As soon as Lacy calls with our next target, you're going to be back on the move."

Hightower said, "I'll call and cancel my MRI appointment in Boulder."

Hanley shook his head. "No, you won't. I've been watching you limp around at the airport, my place, here in the office. I want you back in Boulder. Get looked at, then get back here."

"Okay. I'll go back tomorrow, get it done the next day, get back here as soon as I've met with the doctor."

"No time to go hunting, Night Train," Hanley said.

"I'm hunting for *you* now, Pilgrim."

THIRTY-FIVE

Michael Scardino and James Westwood sat in J.W.'s third-floor office watching the midday national news. The vast majority of the airtime was devoted to the spate of killings around the country, mostly in the D.C. region. The media had also tied the death by a second lethal poisoning of an FBI agent in New York to the running death toll, bringing the number, when added to the six in and around the Carriage House Condominium, to a staggering fourteen in the past fourteen hours.

The press hunted for direct connections between the victims; they hunted for sound bites from lawmakers and gave airtime to talking head after talking head, each with less new information and more pointless pontification than the last.

The U.S. stock market had plummeted 820 points since the opening bell; the president had returned to the White House, cutting short a golf outing in Palm Springs, and he made a statement assuring Americans that law enforcement was leaving no stone unturned in finding the perpetrators.

As the two men in Dupont Circle had predicted, the president was careful not to blame a foreign power for the killings—not yet, anyway—but they both assumed Russia would be most everyone's first guess. Russian intelligence activities in the West had been in the news, and the death of the Belarusian assassin, while by no means part of J.W.'s plan, did have the positive benefit of implicating the Kremlin in all of this.

Just as the two men in the office were about to mute the TV and reach out to the individual Gauntlet support teams in the field for updates, Fox broke in from yet another city on the Eastern Seaboard, where yet another murder had just been confirmed.

A man leaving his house for work in Baltimore had started his car in his carport, and then the car ignited into flames. The man staggered out, fully engulfed, and made it back into his home, but died of burns before emergency medical crews arrived to treat him.

It had been a car bomb, and though not a particularly efficient one, it had been successful in its task nonetheless.

Both the men knew Whetstone was the killer they'd assigned to the task of killing Allen Stepanski of the little-known Air Force's National Air and Space Intelligence Center, and this meant two of the assets—Whetstone from Northern Ireland, and Masquerade from Italy—had each managed to kill two of the five targets on their lists within the first twelve hours of the operation. Snare, a hit man from Jordan, had killed the husband-and-wife CIA officers in their car, then killed a third target, a DIA officer in Columbia Heights.

Lancer had only killed one so far, but he'd checked in within the past hour and was setting up for his second hit soon.

J.W. and Big Mike were cautiously optimistic about the way things had been going since last night. Eight killings out of nine attempts in the first twelve hours: it was an extraordinary success, only blunted by the death of Spiral and the Gauntlet men around him.

J.W. rose and told Scardino he was heading downstairs to order some lunch, but before he could leave, Scardino's phone began to buzz on the coffee table in front of him.

Scardino looked down and said, "Signal number. Unknown." J.W. moved closer as Scardino put the call on speaker. "Yeah?"

"It's Whetstone. Checking in, as requested."

The man's voice was so identifiable, Scardino didn't even ask for the agreed-upon code word. As J.W. looked on, Scardino said, "First, let me congratulate you. Hyattsville and Baltimore, within just hours of one another. We're impressed."

Whetstone replied, "I heard about what happened in Washington last night. You lost an entire team. I'm guessing you find yourself now with a lot more jobs that need doin'."

"An unfortunate setback, and yes. But we will adapt."

"You got any more intel for me on the Gray Man?"

Scardino looked at J.W. and rolled his eyes. "Not at this time, no."

"Pity. No worries, though, chief, because I have some intelligence for *you*."

Scardino and J.W. exchanged another look in the third-floor Dupont Circle office. "Okay," Big Mike said. "What do *you* have?"

"This morning, I had a wee chat with him."

"Him? Who?"

"The Gray Man."

Another look between the two Americans. Scardino recovered, then said, "How . . . ? Matt Hanley's address? You were able to—"

"That's right. I dropped in on Hanley, left a number and a note sayin' I'd stop my killin' spree in Washington if he'd call me."

"You'd do *what*?" Scardino demanded.

"Don't get your knickers in a twist, squire. I'm a sneaky bastard. It's all talk. Plus, no matter what I do, I've got five men with me who can keep on killing for ya."

"We hired *you*, not your support team."

"I was in Virginia Beach when that bloke in Baltimore got sent to his maker this mornin'. You can check with the coroner to be sure, yeah, but I do believe he's just about as dead as if I did it meself."

Scardino waved a hand in the air, then said, "Okay. So . . . you said you actually talked to the Gray Man."

"Yeah, and I thought you might like to know that he's knee-deep against you, fightin' on the other side of your mission. Dunno if he was involved in that shite in Washington or not, but he didn't deny he was tryin' to stop all that's happenin'."

J.W. just shrugged at Mike, as if he didn't necessarily buy what Whetstone was saying, or if it even made any difference at all. "How do you even know it was him?"

"We had a professional understanding, he and I. I could hear it in his voice. He's had a bit of my life, I've had a bit of his."

"That sounds thin," Scardino said. Then he added, "So . . . if you left this message at Hanley's place, and the Gray Man called you back, at least we do know now that the Gray Man *is* involved with Hanley to some degree?"

"I'd say they are close. Here's how I put it together. Hanley wasn't at his house at four in the mornin', I can tell ya that, because I was. And Hanley, with all that's going on, managed to make it to his house after I left, get the number I put there for him, get that number to Violator, and have Violator ring me, all in the course of about two and a half hours. Adding the fact that Hanley had to make sure I hadn't filled his home with pipe bombs when I had the run of the place, that sounds like two men in close coordination, damn interested in stopping the killin', wouldn't you agree?"

Scardino definitely did agree. "So, Hanley might be involved in this, and he does have some influence over Violator."

Scardino thought a moment, then said, "That's helpful information. But in the meantime, we need you focused on your next—"

Whetstone interrupted, "Look, chief, I'll take out whoever you want, but right now, you need to be goin' to your people inside the U.S. government and finding me more intel about Violator and Hanley. Where they are now, anyone they might be workin' with. *These* are the enemies to your whole bloody scheme, yeah, and if you've got any interest in self-preservation, I'd be thinking about that."

Big Mike said, "I'm gonna put you on hold." He tapped the key, then looked to J.W.

"We gave Whetstone the Hanley address because we were trying to string him along, feed him something to keep him working on our targets. But we only tasked Shaw with getting some intel on Hanley. We can reach out to him now, tell him to get everything he can get on Hanley, Violator, their dealings, and all their associates. If we find it likely they are with a group working against us, then we give Whetstone what he came for in the first place. The Gray Man."

J.W. wasn't convinced. He said, "We were planning on eliminating Shaw last, so we had access to the information he's getting us out of ODNI. But he's a liability now. Ortega knows about him, and Ortega's in the wind."

Scardino said, "I agree, Shaw needs to die, and we don't want to wait around till the end of the operation, because someone is going to know about him soon enough. But we can't kill him till we have an understanding about what happened last night in Washington Circle. We definitely don't want a repeat of that."

He added, "I've got a Gauntlet team following him wherever he goes. If anybody comes after Shaw, then we'll get him out of there." With confidence, he said, "Nobody is going to get anything out of him, even if we have to put a bullet in his brain from a distance while he's getting arrested."

J.W. nodded, and Mike unmuted the phone. Scardino said, "Whetstone, I am going to appeal to my asset inside the intelligence community to get me everything possible on Violator and all his associates, as soon as possible. I will give you that information the second I obtain it. Stay low in the area until I get back with you."

"Right. But don't take too long. Your operation just gets tougher by the hour."

"I'm well aware. I'll call you back."

The call ended, and Scardino and J.W. looked back and forth at one another for several seconds. J.W. said, "He could be playing us."

Scardino nodded. "Thought of that. He could just want this intel on the Gray Man so bad he's trying to make us think we need to obtain it and task Whetstone to him as a form of self-preservation."

J.W. then said, "But whatever happened last night in Washington Circle... That was a few men causing an incredible amount of damage. So far, we've heard nothing from any of the agencies saying they were involved, and it definitely was *not* D.C. Metro PD. If it was an unknown actor... it could be Hanley, the Gray Man, and maybe a few other assets."

J.W. thought a moment more, then said, "Keep your surveillance team right up Shaw's ass. Do *not* lose access to him when he leaves ODNI. I will reach out to him now, tell him what we need him to find out."

"We've got a long way to go," J.W. said. "Well over a dozen targets left."

"If Hanley has some kind of a field team working against us, then we've got more than twelve targets to deal with."

"Let me bask in our success a second, Mike." After a moment he took a sip of coffee and sighed. "The Chinese better come through with their promises at the end of this."

Scardino said, "Nobody plays the long game like China. We're showing our value to them; we'll both be rewarded when this is all over."

Court climbed off his Yamaha bike, walked it into a storage shed, then locked it up. It was just after noon; the air was cold and the wind was so still that the water here at the marina looked like a sheet of glass.

He walked up pier B with his helmet still on, his backpack in his hand swinging down by his ankle, then climbed aboard his sixty-three-foot Sea Ray sport cruiser at the end of the pier.

He stepped over a telltale, a thin strand of fishing line he'd lightly taped across the passageway between the swim platform and the aft deck. The fact that it was still there, undisturbed, made him confident no one had been aboard in his absence, but still, after he unlocked the door to the companionway down to the saloon, he drew his pistol and cleared the area, flashing the light on the gun a few times, then checked the various holds and rooms belowdecks.

This done, he turned on the stereo, sat at a table in the saloon, and flipped on the monitor that displayed all the camera views around the boat, including two cameras on the hull under the water. He checked for any activity on the cams since he'd left the boat, and saw that all was as it should be.

Satisfied he had no immediate threats to deal with, he put his unholstered pistol on the table next to the monitor, then lifted a seat cushion off a lounger next to him. It came up easily and revealed a stowage area large enough for the twelve-gauge shotgun he retrieved from it. This he put on the table, as well, and only now he felt ready to deal with anyone who might try to board from the dock onto the main deck above.

His immediate needs met, he pulled a burner phone he'd just purchased from his backpack and loaded the Signal app onto the device.

Five minutes after this, he looked down to his Casio G-Shock watch, checking the time, adding five hours to account for the curvature of the Earth, and then he dialed a number he had memorized.

The phone rang several times on the other end, but to his relief it was finally answered, and then a familiar voice spoke.

"Yes?" The accent was British, the tone raspy, with a hint of mistrust.

"Hey, Don. It's me."

Now the man brightened instantly. "Hello, lad. So good to hear your voice."

"You, too." Sir Donald Fitzroy had been Court's handler for years, back when Court was a freelance assassin. They'd been in touch sporadically in the time since, having seen each other most recently in Mexico earlier in the year.

But Court hadn't called the man to talk about Mexico. No, Court was interested in Fitzroy's time in British intelligence, when he'd been a very highly placed MI5 officer serving in Northern Ireland.

"Where in the world are you right now?" Court asked.

"I'm on the Continent. You'd be proud of me. No danger or skullduggery. Too busy healing these old bones up from the last time I saw you, actually."

"That skullduggery will get to you if you're not careful."

"Too true. My life is quite the opposite of the old days, lad. I have beautiful countryside to look at, music to listen to, a home that is small enough that I can almost take care of it myself, though I do have help."

"How are you feeling?"

Fitzroy had Parkinson's disease; he'd revealed this to Court on their last meeting, but Fitzroy had also been all but blown to bits during that same reunion, so the Parkinson's had taken something of a backseat when it came to priorities at the time.

"I'm getting by, lad. Getting by. I must ask, why does it always seem that I only hear from you when the world is on fire?"

"Maybe because the world is always on fire."

"Too true. What can a boring old man do for his dashing young friend?"

"I'm no longer young, and I was never dashing."

"And I'm shite as a charmer. I did try, though."

Court smiled, his eyes on the monitors showing him views around his boat. He was paranoid by nurture, not by nature, but in the past he'd been proven right in his paranoia with such regularity that it usually seemed a safe bet that danger was just around the corner.

He said, "I need to ask you about Northern Ireland."

Fitzroy sniffed. "Vacation plans, have you?"

"For now, I just need a history lesson."

"Well then, if it is ancient history you seek, I'm your man. I was there, right in the bloody middle of it."

"Running MI5 operations, if I remember correctly."

"A step removed from the top, but that was just because my hands had become too dirty, and the effects of my actions too valuable to put me behind a desk at Gower Street or Thames House. I lived most of the time on a military base in Bessbrook, down in South Armagh, or up in Belfast, but I did get out into the field with great regularity, of course."

"I've got questions about a man from back then."

"Our side or theirs?"

"Well," Court said, "that's actually one of my questions. I'm not sure. His name was Coyle."

Sir Donald Fitzroy paused; Court sensed a hesitancy, but perhaps the man was simply unsure. Eventually, Fitz said, "Not an uncommon name there, is it?"

Now Court read the old man's tone. "I hear it in your voice, Fitz. What does that name mean to you?"

Don Fitzroy let out a long sigh. "What have you gotten yourself into with this, lad?"

"You *do* know him?"

There was a long pause. Court scanned the monitors topside now; a sea bird flew by on this gray winter day. "If you know something, it could save some lives."

"Tell me about your sudden interest in an old Ulster ghost."

THIRTY-SIX

"An old Ulster ghost? What does that mean?"

"Back in the Troubles. I knew a man named Rory Coyle."

Court shook his head in the saloon of his boat. "No, this guy would have to be younger, I'm not exactly sure—"

"Let me tell my story, lad."

Court's brows furrowed. "Go ahead."

"Roderick 'Rory' Coyle was head of an ASU, an Active Service Unit, a Provisional IRA cell. Based in Belfast. And he also, for a time, ran a Nutter Squad. They did enforcement jobs, mostly. Targeting other IRA members, killing or maiming them for spying for the British, but when he led the ASU, he assassinated three British police officers in London.

"He was a right bastard."

"Do you know what happened to him?"

Fitzroy hesitated once again, then spoke energetically. "Of course I do. January of 1994, his bullet-riddled body was found in an oil drum in central Belfast, in a little alley called Murray Street, to be more precise."

Court sniffed. "Seeing as how that was thirty years ago, you seem to remember the details especially well."

"Like it was yesterday, lad."

"You did it?"

"If by 'it' you mean put the bullets in him, no, I didn't do it. But . . ." He took a beat, then gave a little sniff before continuing. "You ever roll a two-hundred-pound oil drum out the back of a van by yourself? Could have applied for disability after that. Threw my back out for a week. Old Rory got the last laugh, he did."

Court tried to picture the event. It had nothing to do with him, but he'd always been fascinated with Fitzroy's past. Finally, he understood. "Could this be the father of the guy I'm asking about?"

Fitzroy said nothing. Court registered the pause, noticed it was followed by a shuffle noise and he discerned something from Fitzroy's actions.

"Yes. Rory Coyle, in fact, *did* have a son."

"What do you know about the son?"

"What I know about him has been buried in the back of my brain for a long time."

"Dig it up, Fitz," Court demanded.

"Campbell was the boy's name." Sir Donald Fitzroy added, "Whetstone was the name we gave him."

Court just breathed into the phone for a long moment, then said, "Holy shit. You *ran* him?"

"At first, we did. But at the end of the day, I'd say *he* ran *us*." The older man said, "Rory Coyle's boy was a teenager when his father died, and the lad believed the story that we sold to the media."

"What story?"

"That his father had been killed by a rival splinter Provo unit. Rory had personally ended the lives and livelihood of a lot of Irish Catholics, touts and suspected touts. It was hardly difficult to convince the IRA, and the world at large, that one of their own had a quarrel with him."

"And what did his son do?"

"Funny enough, he came to us. We sent him away at first. He was too young to be of any use. A couple years after, he ran away from home, joined the Foreign Legion.

"He came back our way after that, every bit as eager as before, if not more so. But he'd grown big, strong, smart, trained.

"We ran him as an asset against his own people. He assassinated dissident Irish Catholics, as well as others who'd long since gotten out of the game. Terrorists with English blood on their hands. We sent Whetstone to the continent, and to America. He did jobs in Boston and New York, in Frankfurt, in Madrid. All that in addition to the work he did in Ulster, and down in Ireland. He was an efficient, bloody killer."

Court said, "And he killed because you guys made him think his targets had been involved in his dad's murder, when you guys actually were the ones who killed his father."

Defensively, the Englishman said, "Exactly that. It was the dirtiest of wars. I don't want any moralizing from you on what went on back then, because you weren't there, and you've got your own dirt under your nails, and your own stench on your breath."

"Did I say anything?"

Fitzroy took a beat, then seemed to calm a little. "After a few years, it got tougher to convince him there were others involved in his father's death, and he had no interest in continuing to work for us. He did a couple of jobs we did not sanction. Contract work, including against some of England's friends over there.

"Ultimately, we cut him loose. He went off, trained in Libya, fought across Africa, did work as a hit man all over the world."

"He ever work for you when he was a contract killer? Like I did?"

"Good lord, no! He didn't trust me, and I didn't trust him not to turn on me. Very few people terrify me, lad, but nightmares of the son of Rory Coyle used to scare me out of my bloody wits."

"Any idea where he is now?"

"I haven't heard his name spoken in decades, lad. I'm bloody surprised he's still living, and more surprised you know about him.

"He was young when we ran him . . . still, he's late forties now, I suppose. You think he still has some capabilities?"

"I *know* he does. He's leaving a trail of dead and damaged trying to get to me."

"Bloody hell. How can I help?"

"Put feelers out. I need to know how I can sneak up behind him, should the need arise. Addresses, known associates, methods of operation, whatever you can learn."

Fitz clicked his tongue a few times, as if he were trying to think of something. "I know his da wasn't from Belfast. He was from somewhere north. County Antrim, near the coast, I think. It's been so bloody long, just can't remember."

"You know anything about a mother?"

Fitzroy thought back. Finally, he said, "Rory's wife? I don't. Truthfully, if I ever knew, I've long since forgotten."

"Who *would* know?"

"A little Irishman named Bill Tully. He was RUC, he ran Whetstone up close. He'd know."

Court quickly typed the name William Tully into Google, looking for a photo. Instead, he found a day-old news article about a senior Northern Ireland police official's body turning up in England. "Remember when I mentioned Coyle was leaving a trail of bodies to get to me?"

"Old Bill is lying along that trail?"

"That would be my guess. He was found in a shallow grave outside of Oxford yesterday."

"Oxford? That's strange. Certainly not Tully's normal stomping ground. Wonder why he was in England."

"Any ideas?" Court asked, still scanning the article.

"The MI5 man who ran Tully, back when Tully ran Whetstone. His name is Sir Allen Glazebrook. Back then he was the same rank I was. He's got a place in the Cotswolds. Not far from Oxford."

"Can you ask him about Whetstone for me?"

"Old Allen and I never got on, really; he saw me as rougher, more base, perhaps. Too keen to break the bones of my enemies. I saw him . . . well . . . I suppose I saw him just as he was. An Eton prick, a plugged-in Oxford grad trying to pass his time in Ulster without mussing his hair. He quite failed at that, I'll say. And then, after the service, Sir Allen and I became competitors. Hiring blokes like you, running commercial security services around the globe. But since I've left that game, I imagine that arranging a chat with him shouldn't be a problem. I'll ring a mutual friend and report back."

"Thanks, Fitz."

"This mess going on in America. Is this related to that?"

"It's looking that way."

"Are you back home, then, doing what you do?"

"It won't benefit either of us if you know where I am and what I'm up to."

"That's fair, lad. Word is American secrets are for sale, and whoever's doin' the buying intends on some real damage over there. I hope you get it squared away. America with its house in order is a good thing for the rest of the world."

Court had a camera on the flybridge of his boat, and it faced pier B and the parking lot beyond it. He had noticed a black Suburban pull up a few seconds earlier, and now he saw a group of four men coming up the pier, unlocking the gate with a key as they did so.

Court said, "Rumors around here are that Russia or China is involved."

"Bollocks," Fitzroy said. "America itself is the one you have to fear. Sorry to say, but whether it's China or Russia who's benefiting from what's happening right now, the fact remains there are people high up in your intel community who are happy to let this happen."

Court thought this over; he couldn't argue, especially because only half his attention was going to Fitzroy's comment. The other half was on the group of men heading up the docks in the direction of *Ship Happens, Two*. Matt Hanley was at the center, and the three men around him, Court suspected, were part of the Five Guys, the security team that worked at Ghost Town. Hanley had his phone in his hand, held to his ear.

"Gotta run, Fitz. Glad to hear you sounding good. Please get back to me when you have something."

Court's phone beeped; he looked and saw that Hanley was calling him.

"Will do, lad. Keep ducking those bullets."

"Roger that." Court disconnected from Signal and answered the call from Hanley.

He answered, "Permission to come aboard is granted. I see you brought your backup dancers."

Hanley chuckled a little. "Security. They'll stay up here on deck."

Court hung up, holstered his pistol, and unlocked the door down to the saloon, and soon enough, he and Hanley were sitting on the couch, each with a beer. These were Pacifico Mexican lagers—Court's choice, this time, but Hanley didn't complain.

The music over the salon stereo played a bluesy tune called "Broken Bones"; it wasn't loud, but the first words out of Hanley's mouth were completely predictable to Court.

Hanley said, "Can I get you to turn that down?"

Court moved over to the stereo and lowered the volume, but he let the music play more softly.

"Still with the country music?" Hanley asked.

"How the fuck is *this* country? It's blues. In fact, these guys are from Iceland."

"It all sounds like country to me. When do you have time to listen to music?"

"For every minute I'm operational, there's about a thousand minutes when I'm sitting on a plane, on a bus, in a hide, in a safe house. You have to do all the thinking, boss; I get to decompress once in a while."

"Right."

"What do *you* listen to in your downtime?" Court asked.

"Podcasts about geopolitics, mostly."

"Nerd." Court took a swig.

"I *am* your superior, or have you forgotten?"

Court shrugged. "Superior nerd."

Matt let it go. "You talked to Fitzroy? Did he have any insight?"

"A lot, actually, just as I suspected. It turns out the guy who called me is a second-generation shithead. His dad was Provisional IRA, a straight-up terrorist, killing cops in London, then working as an enforcer, assassinating Irish Catholics who had worked for the British. Then the Brits killed him but put the blame on some splinter IRA faction. A few years later, the son, the guy who called me, was activated by the British to go on kill missions in Ulster, taking out enemies of England because Fitzroy and his minions tricked him. After the Brits were done with him, he went into private practice, working as a hitter all over the world, and then he retired.

"I guess he would have stayed that way if I hadn't killed his kid."

"Unbelievable," Hanley said.

Court said, "The guy's code name is Whetstone."

Hanley thought a moment. "I guess the Brits did a good job hiding that story from us. I've never heard of an Irish Republican asset called Whetstone."

Court took another sip. "Ideally, I think that's how assassins are supposed to operate. Quietly."

"Yeah, well, you wouldn't know, would you?"

"I would not," Court admitted. The legend of the Gray Man had grown in the intelligence and security world to a degree that only made Court's life more dangerous.

Hanley finally took a sip of his beer. "I need you to remain focused on *my* op, Six. In case you've lost count, I am currently an asset down."

"One asset down? Didn't Zack go back to Colorado today?"

"He was on his way to the airport, but something's come up, and I turned him around. I need him here till tomorrow afternoon."

Court put down the beer. "What's going on?"

"Jim Pace has gotten us another lead. From Spiral's mobile phone, he found the names of four other people he planned on killing. The document had an order to delete it once he read it, but Spiral never did. We're hoping the enemy, whoever sent him the document, doesn't know that *we* know his intended victims."

"Who are his intended victims?"

"One of them, next on his list, is a current Gauntlet employee. A business jet pilot named David Rudder."

"Has Gumdrop located him?"

"Not physically. He supposedly lives in the Capitol Hill neighborhood, but cameras there don't show his vehicle in the parking lot of his building. He works at a Gauntlet office nearby when he's not flying, but the dossier Spiral was given says he hasn't shown up to work in the past two days."

"Maybe he knows what Gauntlet is up to, doesn't like it, and that's why he's on the kill list."

"That's my assumption. He's been pilot in command on a pair of flights from Europe into the U.S. over the past two weeks. We can assume that if he's involved with this mess with Gauntlet, then he's been utilized to help bring foreign assets into the U.S. He stopped showing up to work suddenly, Gauntlet realized they had a dangerous situation on their hands, so they're deleting him from the equation."

"But if we can't find him, what do we do?"

"We don't know where he is, but we know where he's going to be. He has a meeting tomorrow in Georgetown, eleven thirty a.m. That's where Spiral was going to hit him."

Court said, "He won't show."

"He might. His meeting is with Catherine King."

Court was astonished. "The national security reporter for the *Washington Post*?"

"*Washington Post*? No, she got laid off from the *Post* last summer. Where the hell have you been?"

"Russia, mostly."

"Yeah, right. Touché. Anyway, she's writing a book about U.S. national security. She's got sources all over town. She even reached out to me, multiple times, but of course I never got back with her.

"Rudder is meeting with her tomorrow, in public. I'm thinking he's passing her information about those flights. We need to assume the enemy will task someone else, and they'll be there at that time."

"Wait," Court said. "You want to use Cathy King as bait?"

Hanley shook his head. "She's not a target, Six. If she were, then she would be there on Spiral's dossier, right along with Rudder. She'll be fine. We'll go there, we'll wrap up all the Gauntlet men following Rudder, and we'll kill whatever assassin they send."

"Who is *we*? Zack with his bum leg, Travers with a neck wound. You going to give Jill a rocket launcher?"

"You have a fair point. Zack will be there; he did one hell of a job in Washington Circle, even with the leg. It's just you and Zack as armed assets." He hesitated. Said, "Unless you think Anthem could be utilized to—"

"Out of the question," Court said. "I just saw her. Trust me. Her heart would be in the fight, but she's weak, slow still. Six months in a fucking work gulag will deplete even the strongest—"

Hanley said, "Say no more. We'll give Anthem more time to recover.

You and Zack will be the only shooters, but Jill will be your overwatch, accessing cameras in the area."

Court thought a moment. "If they send a single asset, like they've done on the other hits we know about, then they will probably employ interdiction and isolation crews again. We know they did that in Washington Circle; Gauntlet has thousands of gunslingers, so it's likely their MO for the other ops."

Hanley said, "So we need to identify whoever shows up for the Rudder meeting with Catherine King. Preferably *before* Rudder gets there." He made a note of it on his phone. "I'll move Jill into the area as soon as we get to D.C. Put her in a rental house there in Georgetown nearby; she can access camera feeds in the restaurant, on the street. I'll have Arnold put a micro drone in the air with a camera."

Court said, "Not good enough. Catherine is a friend; if I'm going to expose her like that, I want to know who's there, ready to do her harm."

"We don't have resources to blanket the whole neighborhood."

The younger man looked up. "You told me Arnold could get me just about anything I want."

"Yeah, I did. I don't know how he does it, but whenever I need something, he just—"

"I need a tow truck," Court blurted out.

"A tow truck? Like—"

"Like a real commercial tow truck. From a towing company, not something all stripped and beat up for sale online. I need a legit wrecker from a legit company that's working the streets of D.C. regularly."

"What are you going to do with—"

Court ignored him. "The truck needs to be parked in Georgetown by nine a.m. tomorrow with the keys in it. Have him put a disguise for me in there. Plus, a short-barreled rifle, but something very compact. Pistol caliber is fine, just make sure it's small . . . and suppressed. An MPX, a Scorpion, something like that. I want an Aimpoint optic, no magnification. I want the weapon loaded with a mag that will fit in the backpack, but I also need two extra magazines, subsonic ammunition."

Hanley took notes.

"You need to get Zack armed and behind the wheel of a getaway car. Something big and heavy but fast, just in case. Jill can monitor all the cams in the area with her facial recognition software. We do all that, and we might be able to pull this off."

"Jesus, Six. It's Georgetown, not Mogadishu. You're not getting in a shoot-out over a lunch date."

"You keep telling yourself everything's going to go smoothly. I'll keep preparing for reality."

Hanley nodded. "I'll call Arnold; if anyone can make that happen, he can. We're wheels up at five a.m. tomorrow. I want you at the airport at four thirty. By noon tomorrow, with a little luck, we will have taken another enemy hitter off the playing field."

Court looked away a moment.

"You're hoping it's this Whetstone guy."

"That would kill two birds with one stone."

"Whoever it is, the assassin who shows up tomorrow is your objective. We clear?"

"Of course, any dead asshole will be a win. But getting Catherine out of this alive is my objective, as well."

He didn't get any pushback from Hanley on that. Instead, the older man said, "Right now, Six, you need to sleep. You look like absolute shit. Don't worry. Tomorrow's going to be fine."

"You make it sound so easy."

"It is easy. I've got you." Court noted the sarcasm in Matt's voice.

Five minutes later Hanley had made it back to the Suburban with his security team, and Court had locked the wooden door over the companionway that led down below deck. His cameras were up, on the app on his phone and on the monitor of his laptop, and they would alert him to any movement above or below the water.

He situated himself in a fiberglass hold along a wall of the main cabin that stored sofa cushions, just across from his bed. It was, essentially, a long low box, slightly curved, and the lid of the hold had cushions on it, serving as a small sofa, as well. The space was cramped, especially because his shotgun and his mobile phone were nestled beside him, but Court was accustomed to discomfort, and he rarely slept in beds or on couches, so paranoid was he that he was always minutes away from someone sneaking up on him in his sleep.

It had happened in the past, often enough that he felt justified in ignoring his bed and making other arrangements. This fiberglass hold wasn't the most comfortable bed he'd ever found, but with the gentle rocking of the sixty-three-foot boat, in minutes he was sound asleep.

THIRTY-SEVEN

La Bonne Vache served casual French fare on Prospect Street, on the corner of a quiet residential strip of row homes just a block north of M Street, the bustling main drag of Georgetown. This morning at eleven thirty a.m. the air was several degrees warmer than usual, just north of forty-five, and the sun shone through the bare trees lining both sides of the quaint street.

Café tables in December in Georgetown weren't common, but the staff had set a half dozen bistro tables and chairs on the brick sidewalk out in front of La Bonne Vache, along with a few gas patio heaters, and already before the real lunch hour had begun a few patrons sat at two-tops and four-tops outside.

Fifty-nine-year-old Catherine King snagged the deuce closest to the corner of the street so she could see both up and down Prospect and Potomac Streets. She sat alone. Her Patagonia coat, knit cap, and two layers of Lululemon pants were slight overkill for the occasion because of the heat coming from the propane flame tower heater right next to her. An iPad sat in front of her; her oversized purse was hooked under her metal chair, a habit she'd learned living and working both in D.C. and in dense and developing cities around the world for much of her career.

As a large white tow truck with a "Big Cheeze Wrecker Service" decal on the side passed by slowly, she ordered a latte from a friendly waitress, then logged in to the restaurant's Wi-Fi to peruse X while she waited for her lunch date. She saw that no new killings directly associated with the intelligence community had been announced this morning, and some in the media were already pontificating that the immediate danger had passed, but Catherine wondered if the slowdown in incidents had more to do with members of the IC watching their backs and less to do with whatever bad actor was out there either running out of targets or dealing with a sudden bout of morality after the dozen or so assassinations in the last day and a half.

The low-hanging fruit had been picked over the last thirty-six hours, and she imagined that those still threatened were taking all necessary precautions.

No one in the media had been endangered, so far, and even though she worked with the IC every day and wrote exclusively about American national security, she didn't think for a moment she was in any danger herself.

Her latte came, and she checked her watch and saw that the man she was meeting was running a few minutes late.

She opened up the *Washington Post* website. She'd been laid off back in the summer; she was still pissed about that, but she didn't take it out on the other writers, and therefore continued to read their work. She perused a new piece about the massive shoot-out in Washington Circle, including the death of a Belarusian assassin named Kravchuk who had been known to work with the Russians, along with the killing of five members of Gauntlet Group. The official word from the U.S. government was that the Gauntlet men had been working on an unrelated surveillance mission for Homeland Security; they happened to be in the area, just a mile or so from the White House, and they had tried to thwart the attack but were instead ambushed by confederates of the dead Belarusian.

The story was already moving down in priority on the *Washington Post*'s website, mainly because of all the other killings that had happened since then, and the consensus across the media that this was a Russian irregular warfare operation running in D.C., and not some sort of abuse of power by a private American security company.

The Russians themselves were denying they had anything to do with what was going on, but they also denied they knew anyone named Alexi

Kravchuk, a provable lie, so they weren't to be believed. Still, the woman sitting alone at the two-top on the sidewalk in Georgetown had her own reason to doubt the official U.S. government line.

Thinking of her doubts about the government and Gauntlet Group's story caused her to check the time on her phone again, and since the man she'd come to meet was almost twenty minutes late, she started to send him a text via Signal. She'd just opened the app when someone appeared from nowhere and stood over her table, his back to the road, momentarily blotting out the meager but welcome sun.

She looked up with a smile, expecting she knew who this would be, but quickly her smile faded. Before she spoke, her eyes flitted left and right.

She swallowed hard. "It's you."

The man she only knew as Six sat down in front of her, facing the bistro. He'd arrived on foot with a small blue canvas backpack that looked like a student's bookbag, and he positioned it under the table between his knees. He wore a black canvas coat, jeans, and brown boots. A dark gray watch cap covered his hair; his beard was dark, with just a few flecks of gray.

He also wore a single AirPod in his right ear.

His face showed deep intensity; his brown eyes remained locked on hers when he said, "I need you to stay very calm. Keep your voice low and make absolutely no dramatic reaction."

A sudden fear coursed through her, but she did her best to hide it. She said, "Well, plopping down at my table with that look on your face and saying all that isn't really the best way to get me to avoid a dramatic reaction."

"A, it's just my face, Cathy. Nothing I can do about that. And B, if I were a people person, I probably wouldn't be doing what I do for a living."

"Fair ... okay. What's going on?"

"Having said all that, you *are* in danger right now."

"*What?*"

She said it with less stealth than the man across from her wanted, clearly, because he shushed her. Then, his voice still low, he said, "Cool as a cucumber, please."

"*What?*" She said it more softly. She put her phone down and reached for her coffee with a quivering hand, trying to appear nonchalant but failing.

The female server came outside; Six ordered a cappuccino, and as the woman turned to go back inside, Catherine said, "Miss? Could I . . . could I have a glass of champagne?" She looked at Six now. "Unless . . . unless we have to . . . to . . . to run."

Six smiled a little. "No. We're fine for a few minutes."

The server acknowledged the order with a smile and retreated to the warmer restaurant.

Catherine said, "Please tell me what's going on."

"We've been scanning the area for the past hour, making sure we know where the adversaries are. We've detected some . . . activity that we find suspicious. At the right time, you and I are going to rise from this table, stroll into the restaurant. From there, we'll go out the back door and into a waiting car."

"There's a car waiting for us now?"

Six made an apologetic face. "At the right time, there will be. To be totally honest, we're still kind of getting our shit together."

"Wow," Catherine said. "That is *comforting*." She made a face of confusion. "How did you know I was here?"

"We picked up some intel."

Despite herself, her eyes flitted around again. This quiet little Georgetown street showed absolutely no evidence that there was some sort of surveillance mission going on. People walked their dogs, delivery people rolled by on bikes. The outdoor café tables were half-empty, and those patrons who were out here spoke in polite, hushed tones. She said, "I don't see anyone around here watching—"

"They're pros," Six replied. "I really have no notes for them. I just drove the neighborhood in a tow truck, looking for them."

"Why a tow truck?"

"Tow trucks have LPRSs. License plate recognition systems. We know, in general, what we're looking for; we have access to cameras in the area, a mini drone overhead, but I wanted to do a better scan. I drove the neighborhood, got the ownership of most every vehicle from the tags. There's a duo in a car directly behind me, I won't tell you where, because you'll just want to look, and my team is not yet in place to get in their way. There are two more vehicles a block away I spotted, but no one is inside either one. We think the folks we're worried about are on foot."

She couldn't help herself now. "On foot? Meaning . . . they could be anyone around us?"

"Everyone around us has been checked out by my associate watching the cameras. There's no one within a block who we've pegged as a threat. We think we've ID'd one person on a rooftop across the street. Can't get a view of the face under their hat, not so far anyway, but they are acting suspicious. No gun visible, so that's good news."

With a tremor in her voice, she said, "I'd say so. Who . . . who *are* these people?"

Six did not answer directly. "We came across a different one of these teams the other day, and there were six people in total. Looks like, for some reason, there might be more than that around today.

"We're still trying to get a picture of what we're up against, so I came here to sit with you. This should slow them down. They won't be able to identify me, not unless they start moving around to get an angle on my face, and that should buy us the time we need."

"Well . . . I'm actually planning on meeting someone here in a—"

Six interrupted. "Would you mind if we held hands a moment? I'm trying to make this look as casual as possible, and I have something I need to tell you."

"You want people to think I'm your mom, or that we're a couple?"

"I don't care what people think. I want to hold your hand because I am going to squeeze it very hard if you react to what I'm about to tell you." He shrugged. "So . . . don't."

Slowly, she extended her arm across the little table. "You are quite the charmer." She said it nervously; she knew bad news was coming.

Six clasped his hand over hers, holding her in place. The champagne came, no words were exchanged, and the female server went to check on a group of three at another outdoor table.

Six said, "Cathy. I'm sorry, but David Rudder was killed this morning. He was staying at a hotel in Alexandria; the enemy found him somehow. Cause of death hasn't been announced."

Her eyes began to mist; her chest heaved in her coat a little. "My God," she said softly.

Six said, "You're doing good. No big reaction."

"I didn't see it in the news."

"I don't think next of kin has been notified, so the police haven't released details." He added, "Here's the thing, though. That killing? It was originally supposed to take place right here."

"Here? Who . . . who is behind all this? Russia?"

"I was hoping you could help us out with that. Everyone who's died has been in the IC, but they've had all sorts of jobs. Different specialties. I'm with a group trying to figure this out, but we always seem to be one step behind."

"If . . ." Her voice cracked a little. "If the people who are here know that David Rudder is already dead . . . then why are they here?"

Six sighed. "You're an extremely smart lady. You can figure that out on your own."

Her eyes widened. "Me? They're after me?"

"That's my guess. The Belarusian who died the other night had a list of five names. Rudder was number two, after Irene Ortega. He had this location and time next to the name. We think he was going to kill Rudder here. When Deep Space died . . . Alexi Kravchuk, I mean. When that happened, it appears that another hit man got the job to kill Rudder. We assumed he would come here today, and it was our plan to stop him before he got anywhere near you. Unfortunately, the bad guys found Rudder before we did, and his body was fished out of the Potomac a half hour ago. We were here already, and that's when we ID'd a surveillance package on you."

"And they came to kill me?"

Court sipped his cappuccino as soon as it was brought to him. "You weren't on Kravchuk's list, but they certainly aren't here to kill David Rudder. You must have been added."

"And I should . . . I should stay calm? That's *really* your advice?"

Court squeezed her hand a little. "I'm asking you to trust me. Look . . . I have some people working with me. We have control of the situation." His eyes flitted left and right. "I mean . . . sort of. We think the people watching you are an interdiction and isolation team. They are in place to support the hitter, to keep you where you are. He, or she, I guess, will likely come at the last moment."

"Why do they want me dead? I'm not in the government like all the others."

"My best guess would be this. Whatever story you've been working on . . . you *aren't* wrong."

With a shaky hand, she brought her champagne to her lips. "That's validating." She sipped, thought a moment. "Are you still working outside the CIA?"

"Yes."

"But . . . you're not with the Gauntlet Group, are you?"

"I'm not." Six chuckled. "I'm one of the few people on the outside *not* working for them these days."

"Right."

Court cocked his head. "Why did you ask about them?"

She sipped her champagne again. "The book I'm writing. It's about Gauntlet. Their overreach, their shady hiring practices, their tight relationship with people in the government who are falling short of their oversight. Their contracts with oppressive regimes in other countries."

"What other countries?"

"They have secret foreign subsidiaries. I have people behind the scenes telling me that Gauntlet-affiliated partners are working contracts for Egypt, Nigeria, even China. They use other names, other bank accounts, but Gauntlet leadership in the U.S., it is my belief, is running it all."

Court said, "Christ. And what was Rudder's connection to all this?"

"David Rudder was a pilot for Gauntlet. He said he was copilot on a flight that flew a woman from Italy to the U.S. last week. They listed her as cargo when they came into the country, landed at JFK. There was no immigration check; the woman just climbed into a Gauntlet minivan and drove away.

"He said he thought it was shady, but Gauntlet does a lot of shady things. It was only when he brought a man here from Slovenia two days later—they landed at Dulles with no immigration checks, then the assassinations started and the Belarusian hit man, Kravchuk, was killed over in

Washington Circle—that he suspected he had brought one of the killers into the country.

"Whether or not the killers are working for Gauntlet, he was sure that Gauntlet brought at least one of them here. Maybe all of them."

Six nodded, as if what she'd said just filled in some holes. He said, "Did he describe these people?"

"He snuck out his phone, took a picture of the man on the tarmac at Dulles," she said. "He'd promised to show it to me today."

Court Gentry's eyes scanned the reflection in the window of the restaurant just next to where he sat, trying to see if he could make any of the pedestrians on this residential street who didn't belong. He was about to address Catherine again when a voice came through his earpiece. Gumdrop said, "This is overwatch. Video canvas shows movement two blocks to your west. A motorcycle just double-parked, and a lone man climbed off."

Court held a finger up to Catherine, and then, to Gumdrop, he said, "Can you get an ID?"

"He's on the sidewalk, heading east on foot. Wait, he's taking off his helmet, putting on a ball cap. Can't see his face yet. He's got a backpack. All Gauntlet elements detected in the neighborhood are holding position. No sightings of anyone else on foot that the software is pinging as hostile. The new arrival will be on you in two minutes."

Court said, "Get me that ID, Gumdrop." He looked to Catherine now. "You might wanna drink up."

"What's wrong?"

"Remember how I said we should be fine as long as it's just the interdiction and isolation element?"

"It's not?"

Gumdrop's voice came over Court's earpiece. "Visual attained. Subject approaching from the east is code-named Snare, he's a Jordanian national who—"

Court spoke over her. "I know that asshole. ETA to my poz?"

"At present speed, about ninety seconds."

To Catherine, he said, "What kind of exercise do you do?"

The question seemed to come out of left field. "Huh?"

"Anything for fitness?"

Confused, she said, "Pilates."

"Yeah, that's not particularly helpful. Anything else?"

"I have a mountain bike. I like to ride the trails here on weekends, or my mom's place up in Maryland when I can get away."

Court nodded. "Excellent. Next question. Do you want to get out of here alive?"

King had consumed almost all the champagne now. She took a few breaths to compose herself, then spoke softly, looking into Six's eyes. "I've always said that I would very much like to live long enough to where my obituary did not contain the word 'untimely' in it."

"Then I hope you are okay with a dine-and-dash."

"What?"

THIRTY-EIGHT

Court said, "Overwatch? How's my exfil looking?"

Instead of Gumdrop replying, Zack came over the net. "I'm pulling up on N Street, one hundred yards north of your poz. Dark gray Yukon. Get inside that restaurant and haul ass out the back alley. Keep moving behind the row houses till you get to me."

Court rose and took the older woman by the arm, and they went inside the restaurant. Quickly, Catherine King fished through her purse; he thought she was looking for some cash to pay the bill, but instead she pulled out a credit card. Handing it to the server, she said, "I'll be back to sign."

Now Court pulled her towards the back; the few patrons inside along with a male server gave him looks of shock, as if they were witnessing some sort of domestic situation. Court ignored them and transmitted to Zack. "Night Train, you see any hint of any oppo in your area, let me—"

"Yep. There's a white Nissan Armada with two men in it. Right in front of me. They haven't locked onto me, but when you two come out of that alleyway, we're going to find out real quick if they're just here to observe and report, or if these motherfuckers are down to clown."

"What's your gut?"

"My gut is we're gonna see some action."

Court and Catherine stepped outside now, hustling past garbage cans, moving through a narrow alleyway past carriage houses and detached garages. Court shuffled his pack from his back and began unzipping it as he walked hurriedly along. To Zack, he said, "You and me are the only shooters today, so we better hope that Snare is the only guy looking for a fight and these other guys are just going to hold back and—"

Zack interrupted. "Six . . . got a black four-door pulling up behind me, close. Gumdrop? Can you ID from a traffic camera?"

"Stand by," Jill said, and Court moved to Catherine's right, held her arm in his left hand so his right hand could hover closer to his pistol on his hip. His blue backpack swung on his left forearm, half unzipped.

Hanley came over the net now. "Six, I'm with Gumdrop monitoring drone footage. I've got two men entering the restaurant you just left, moving with purpose. Cannot confirm they are Gauntlet, but by their actions we should presume they are hostile."

"No argument from me on that," Court said.

Zack spoke up now. "One man exited the black sedan behind me, passenger side. He's approaching my poz, tactical gear, generic police vest, his mask is up. Has *not* drawn his sidearm. Also, the dudes in the Armada are getting frosty. Raising their masks, shuffling their hands below my view. I'm gonna say they *are* about to go kinetic. You two need to find cover in the alley because shit's about to get spicy."

Gumdrop spoke next. "Night Train. Vehicle behind you is registered to Gauntlet Group security division, Falls Church office."

"But of course, it is."

"Fuck," Court said out loud, and then he pulled Catherine behind a wooden one-car garage, out of view of N Street, just twenty-five yards to the north.

"What are you doing?"

He reached into his pack. "Gumdrop, let me know if that pair leaves the restaurant via the alleyway."

"Roger."

"What is happening?" Catherine demanded now.

"Lots of voices in my ear are telling me you and I are about to run for our lives. Take off your coat." She did so, as quickly as the intensity in his voice demanded, and from the backpack he pulled a vest of thin and pliable soft body armor; he hurriedly put it on over Catherine's head and fastened it on the sides.

"Are we about to get into a fight?"

"Dunno, you'd have to ask the other guys."

"What about you? You're not wearing armor."

"I am," he replied, and then he reached back into the bag that was now on the ground. From it he pulled a Scorpion Micro 9-millimeter submachine gun with a short silencer and a twenty-round magazine. It had an extended wire stock, but he left it collapsed, meaning the entire weapon, even with the protruding silencer, was less than a foot and a half in length.

The squat black weapon had a canvas sling, and this he put over his neck, and then he let the gun hang on his chest and zipped his coat about a third of the way up his body, effectively hiding it.

"You can't just shoot Gauntlet officers," Catherine King protested.

"Yeah, but I *can* shoot back," he said, and then he ushered her back out into the alleyway.

They'd taken only a couple of steps when Gumdrop all but shouted over the net. "Two men behind you!"

Court kept walking towards Zack's Yukon, but he glanced back over his shoulder in time to see a pair of men some forty yards back, just outside the rear door of the French bistro. One had a radio to his mouth, held by his left hand, and his right hand reached into his coat at the hip.

The second man was in the process of drawing a pistol, as well.

The man with the radio shouted out, his voice booming in the narrow alleyway. "Federal officer! Stop right there!"

Court did *not* stop right there. He pulled Catherine along, began running, unzipping his coat as he did so, and ahead of him, he saw the man approach the rear of Zack's Yukon. The masked Gauntlet officer raised a pistol at the driver's side of Zack's vehicle.

Gumdrop shouted again. "Snare got into an SUV; he's coming your way. That's at least seven enemy converging on—"

Court couldn't hear anything else that his overwatch said because he drew his Glock pistol and fired twice at the man getting a bead on the back of Zack's head.

He shot the masked Gauntlet man in the right arm with his first shot, and the right side of his knee with the second. The gun flew from the Gauntlet man's hand, and just then, Zack opened fire with his Staccato pistol, dumping rounds through the front passenger-side window glass, past Catherine and Court, and towards the pair approaching them from behind.

Court continued firing at the threat to Zack, while Zack continued firing at the threat to Court and Catherine.

Court yanked the journalist out of the line of fire, pulling her quickly between a construction dumpster and a little carriage house that jutted out into the alley, and then he holstered his small 9-mil pistol and hefted his 9-mil subgun. Leaning back out into the alley, he thumbed off the safety and first fired a burst at the man just behind Zack's truck. He was wounded, but up on a knee on the sidewalk, and he'd retrieved his weapon from the ground. All he had to do was fire into the truck he leaned against and Zack would not have been able to engage him efficiently from the front seat.

Court put a burst into the man's body armor, then a second burst higher, hitting him in the collarbone, shoulder, and right side of his neck. Blood spurted from his body, and the man dropped flat, rolled in pain and in panic, clutching the worst of his wounds and dropping his gun again in the process.

Zack kept firing at the two men over fifty yards away from him, but they'd taken cover behind some concrete steps leading up to the back door of a row house, and all Zack could do from his position was keep their heads down. Court spun and began shooting at the same two men with his subgun, giving Zack time to reload his handgun.

Gumdrop shouted into everyone's ear. "The men in the Armada are on foot with rifles; they are approaching Night Train!"

Zack only had a pistol, though it held eighteen-round magazines. Still, men with rifles firing from just a dozen or so yards away would be able to chew him up in an instant.

Court shouted to Zack now. "Bail out! Bail out! Come to me!"

Gunfire boomed in the quiet Georgetown neighborhood; the windshield of the Yukon shattered, and all Court could do was divide his fire, sending a burst back in the direction of La Bonne Vache and then a burst up in front of Zack's truck, striking the wall of a row house with the intention of impeding the men with rifles who were out of view from where he knelt in the alley.

Suddenly, however, the windshield of Zack's Yukon exploded as rifle rounds raked across it.

Court didn't have an angle to stop the men in the street from shooting Zack, but he kept firing his Scorpion, and soon Zack's passenger door opened. Court blasted a couple more short bursts of fire to keep enemy heads down, and Zack rolled out of the Yukon, onto the sidewalk, and then he rose to his feet and began running down the alley in Court's direction.

Court's Scorpion ran dry; he dropped it on the sling and yanked his Glock out again. As he fired up the alley past Zack, Zack kept running towards him, again shooting his Staccato towards the men in good cover behind the concrete stairs down by the restaurant.

Zack was slow, limping a little on his left leg, so Court's Glock emptied quickly, just as a man with a rifle came into view on N Street.

Zack ducked into the cover next to Catherine and Court as a fully automatic burst of rifle fire tore into the garage wall above them, and then all three of them dropped down low.

Zack reloaded his pistol while Court reloaded the Scorpion with his last magazine, and then, while Zack took a quick peek out in both directions, Court quickly reloaded his little Glock 43.

Court looked to Zack now. "You hit?"

"Not recently, no."

"What did you see?"

"Got one enemy still operational by the restaurant on the south side. Only saw one guy on his feet with a long gun up by the Yukon. A dead guy by the tire; you must have killed him. Don't know where the other dude with a rifle went. Did you hit him?"

"I don't think I ever saw him. Might be trying to flank us."

Gumdrop came over the net now. "Assets, be advised. I think we have a total of ten enemy. Looks like two or three are down now. Others are converging. Two men are on Potomac Street; looks like they've entered a row house one unit to your south."

Zack said, "What about Snare, Gumdrop?"

"He's in a gray GMC pickup and has bypassed your position. He's in the passenger seat; someone else is driving. Looks like they are heading to Wisconsin Avenue. From there they can go north up to N, double back, and cause you trouble. They're . . ." She stuttered her words. "They . . . they're surrounding you."

Zack said, "You have a vector out of here for us?"

Hesitantly, she said, "If . . . I . . . I'm not sure."

Court could hear the young woman panicking. She was an analyst, not a field team controller; this firefight, like the one down in Washington Circle two nights earlier, was completely out of her wheelhouse. "Relax, Gumdrop," Court said. "Just do your best."

Before the young woman spoke again, Hanley came over the net. "Listen up! If you can make it through the crossfire in that alley to the other side, you'll find a row of small backyards running east. There are trees there with some cover. Can't really tell about the fences between the properties from our angle, but you can create some distance from the assholes trying to encircle you, break." A second later, he said, "Yeah, there's a row house about five units away to your east, on the north side of the trees, it looks like it's got active construction or repairs going on. I bet you can get right through it, pop out on N Street."

"Then what?" Court asked.

"Shit, Six," Hanley said. "That's all I've got so far. Move your asses and we'll try to—"

Gumdrop's voice came back in Court's ear now. She sounded more authoritative, as if she'd recovered somewhat. "Six, you left that tow truck right there at N and Wisconsin. It's just a block from where you'll come out. Go for that!"

"Good thinking!" he replied, and then he moved to the edge of his cover. To Zack, he said, "You cover north, I cover south, and we move east. When we get to fences, we go through them, around them, or over them, whatever's fastest. We run with Cathy here between us. You copy?"

Zack nodded as he adjusted the grip on his pistol, readying himself for the run. "Velocity and ferocity. Let's do it."

To Catherine King, Court said, "Cathy, pretend you're mountain biking, and there's a grizzly bear chasing you."

"Can't I just pretend that a bunch of guys in masks want to assassinate me?"

Court nodded. "Yeah, try to picture that."

"Consider it pictured."

"Grab my jacket and don't let go." He took a quick breath, then looked to Zack. "You good?"

"Let's fuck 'em up, Six."

"Go!"

The three of them burst out into the alley; Court immediately saw a middle-aged man in a button-down shirt and slacks ahead to his right, between his position and the enemy nearer to the restaurant. He recognized this man as a civilian, and he started to shout at him to get the hell out of the way, but instead he just sighted through the Aimpoint optic on his Scorpion and fired a three-round burst into some garbage cans next to the man.

The civilian hit the deck just as another burst of fire came from behind the garage near the bistro, and Court returned fire as he sprinted to the east, concerned less with achieving a good sight picture through the optic and more with getting the hell out of there.

Zack began laying down suppressive fire with his pistol towards the north.

This run was all about three things: speed, trust, and noise. Court couldn't shoot terribly accurately at a man forty yards away while sprinting in a different direction, especially while a fifty-nine-year-old woman held on to his coat and pulled him off balance. But the gunfire in the direction of the enemy would give them something to worry about, and that would buy them time. And the speed of the run would shorten the chances that the multitude of enemy around them would be able to aim in and get the accuracy they need.

But it was trust that was perhaps most important. Court had to keep his eyes to the south while running east. He had to trust that Zack would have his eyes and his gun focused on targets to the north, up on N Street. There was no alternative; Court had to fight with his back to at least some of the enemy, and Zack had to protect him while trusting Court to do the same.

They made it to the first fence and Court glanced at it briefly, saw that it was old, weatherworn wood, and he shouldered into it with all his might. The wood snapped and he crashed through; Catherine picked her way through the wreckage more carefully, and Zack backed into the hole, emptying his magazine at the target behind them while he did so.

Court rose, went back to the hole he'd just created, and laid down fire so Zack could get through, and as he did, he announced he was loading his last magazine into his pistol.

They'd just started running together through a cluster of trees in some backyards that were not divided by fences when Zack pitched forward a couple of feet, stumbled, then righted himself. Court could sense the motion from his mate, even though he wasn't looking, but soon he heard Zack shout.

"Enemy on our six!"

It seemed Zack had been shot from behind, hopefully into his vest, but Court knew Zack would need several steps to recover. Court spun around among the trees, shouldered the wire stock of the Scorpion, and immediately saw a man down on one knee on the stoop of a row house one building south of where they'd taken cover. Gumdrop had identified a pair of Gauntlet Group men entering that building, so Court flipped his selector switch to full auto and let his weapon rock.

The man spun, then fell off the stoop and down into some recycling bins.

A second man appeared at the open door, and Court fired a very short burst, sending him back inside.

He turned around and ran again, Zack and Catherine right with him, and they all shifted a little to the north to go through a pass-through gate in the middle of an iron fence between properties.

Once on the other side, they started running again.

Gumdrop shouted into their ears. "That's the property under construction! Go left. Find a way in and get onto N Street."

Zack led the way with his smoking pistol; Catherine wheezed and heaved from the stress and exertion, and Court one-armed his subgun while scanning for targets back to the east, his left hand guiding the former newspaper reporter from behind.

Construction materials were all around the backyard and on the redbrick patio; Zack found the door unlocked, entered the ground floor of a row house, and immediately encountered a four-person painting crew up on ladders working on the molding. The Hispanic crew had stopped working; the intense gunfire outside to their east had been the culprit for that, but none of them had moved from their perches, so frozen were they in disbelief and fear.

Zack passed them by, all business, heading for the front door with his pistol out in front of him.

Catherine shuffled under the ladders next, and Court took the time to shut and lock the door before running himself up the hall, cradling his suppressed firearm in both hands now. He looked up at the crew, two men and two women, gave a little shrug, and kept going.

Seconds later they were out on N Street, a tiny residential tree-lined affair. Zack and Court waved their guns to the left; Zack's shot-up Yukon was there, as was the black Gauntlet sedan parked behind it, but the white Nissan Armada that had been across the street in front was gone.

No one was shooting at them from that direction, at least, so they turned their guns to the east and found themselves just a block from relatively high-trafficked Wisconsin Avenue.

Here Court had parked the Big Cheeze tow truck he'd used to scan the plates in the area just minutes earlier, so he led the others towards it, still at a run.

They were just slowing at the truck, however, when fresh gunfire burst from behind. Court turned to find two men squatting behind parked cars near where Zack had left the Yukon in the middle of the street.

He fired single shots in their direction, desperate to conserve the last few rounds of ammo in his CZ Scorpion.

Zack fired, as well, moving out into the street to get a better angle, and this put him near the driver's-side door of the tow truck.

Court shouted over the gunfire, still aiming in on the targets to their rear. "It's unlocked! The key's under the mat."

"Roger!" Zack shouted back, and then, "King! Get in the passenger side!"

Court hit one of the Gauntlet men right in the pelvic girdle, dropping him writhing on the sidewalk, and the other operator had ducked down to cover either to reload or else to reconsider his career path, but Court took the opportunity to run to the open passenger-side door.

They sat three abreast in the front seat, with Zack behind the wheel. He fired up the engine and then threw the big vehicle into gear.

Just as they lurched forward, however, the white Nissan Armada that Zack had clocked parked in front of him minutes earlier lurched around from Wisconsin Avenue and began racing towards the tow truck, gaining speed.

Behind it, a GMC pickup followed.

Court had just a couple of rounds in his subgun, but he fired them through the window at the oncoming truck, then dropped the rifle and pulled out his Glock again. Catherine screamed, and Zack jerked the wheel to the left in an attempt to avoid a crash, but the full-sized Nissan SUV plowed headfirst into the grille of the tow truck.

Airbags deployed, knocking Court's Glock out of his hand, flinging it somewhere onto the floorboard as the inflating bag shoved Court's hand up into his face.

His AirPod flew from his ear, as well.

Court found himself hopelessly dazed and disoriented with the noise and concussion and the blow of his hand to his mouth, and all this, along with the fine powder from the airbags filling the air of the tow truck's cabin, made it hard to focus on any new dangers.

Maybe five seconds had passed; he heard Zack shout something, and he heard Catherine scream. He tried to push the inflated airbag out of the way, and when he did, he saw a man moving towards him, a pistol high in his hands.

Court recognized Asem Shaban, the assassin who operated around the world under the moniker Snare.

Snare approached Court's side of the truck, a confidence in his movements.

Court reached for the knife he had mounted sideways in front of his belt buckle. It wasn't much, but he knew the Jordanian assassin would kill them all, and he wasn't going to die without some attempt to fight back.

Snare yanked open the door right next to Court and centered his Beretta pistol on him, and Court realized he was out of knife range.

The bearded killer smiled, didn't say a word, because he seemed to recognize that no one here was in a position to stop him. He aimed at the right side of Court's head; he was only eight feet away, and he began to press the trigger.

THIRTY-NINE

A black BMW 3 Series traveling sixty miles an hour appeared from behind Court on his right. It raced along the sidewalk, knocking over mailboxes, and slammed into Snare at the same instant it ripped off the open door of the tow truck, and then it crashed, head on, into the Armada, knocking the bigger vehicle back and spinning it away. The white SUV flew back across N Street, where it sideswiped into cars parked there.

Car alarms rang up and down the street, adding to the concerto of chaos that had erupted in Georgetown.

The BMW came to rest next to the Armada, and only then did Court see the bloody, broken body of what had seconds ago been the Jordanian hit man fall out of the sky, hit the sidewalk, and then roll to a stop.

Court blinked in shock a couple of times. The noise and the violence were almost impossible to take in all at once, but quickly he recovered, leaned down to the floorboard, and scooped up his Glock 43.

Looking at Catherine next to him, he saw that she was unhurt but in an obvious and understandable state of shock herself.

Zack, on the other hand, had already flung his door open. He climbed out, held his Staccato up, and aimed it at the Nissan Armada, which was now nearly fifty feet away. He moved forward without waiting for Court to support him.

Court fell out of the tow truck onto the street because the passenger-side door had been ripped off and flung somewhere else. He climbed to his feet, raised his own little pistol, and began moving forward towards the crashed-out BMW.

As Zack came up on the Armada, he fired several rounds, presumably at someone in the front seat, but Court had to get around the crashed 3 Series, which had come to rest with its grille right in the driver's-side door of the Armada.

Court cleared around the side of the black sedan; the airbags had deployed so it was hard to see who was behind the wheel, but soon a figure began climbing over into the passenger seat, pushing the still-inflated airbag out of the way.

He saw a pistol in the man's right hand.

"Toss the fucking gun!" Court shouted.

The man coughed several times; obviously he'd breathed in the smoke filling the cabin of the BMW, but he did eventually comply, tossing an H&K compact pistol out onto the street.

Court kept his pistol up on the man, even after Zack shouted, "Clear!" on his side, because he didn't know who he was looking at in the smoke-filled BMW.

But then the man climbed all the way out and stood up, and Court lowered his weapon.

The sound of police sirens added to the car alarms and the persistent ringing in his ears as Court holstered his gun, staring at the man who'd climbed out of the 3 Series.

"Holy fuck, dude. You okay?" Court asked, his voice making it obvious that he was having a hard time processing all that had just transpired.

Jim Pace, CIA operations officer and former paramilitary Ground Branch operator, wore a suit and tie; his white shirt was torn and smudged with grease. His eyeglasses were bent comically, his hair a mess.

He did not acknowledge Court at first; he just looked past him.

Court followed Pace's eyes and realized he was checking out the body of the Jordanian hit man lying facedown on the sidewalk. Snare's legs were twisted around each other, almost like a pretzel; one arm was dislocated up over his head, and his head hung at a seventy-degree angle from his neck.

After another cough, Jim finally looked back to Court. "You . . . want to put an insurance round into him?"

Court, still bewildered, shook his head. "I'll save the bullet for someone who needs it."

"Roger that," Pace said.

Zack Hightower came around from behind the Armada now, lowered his gun when he saw Pace, and slapped the man on the back. The three of them all just stood there, disoriented for a few seconds, and then Zack put his hand to his ear. Court saw that Zack's AirPod was still in place, but only barely. "Repeat your last, Gumdrop?"

An instant later Zack's eyes focused. "Cops are on Wisconsin, approaching on foot. A lot of patrol cars are converging, two minutes out."

Pace said, "I can't be here."

To this, Court replied, "And we *can*?"

Pace scooped up his weapon, and the three men met up with Catherine as she climbed out of the tow truck. She retrieved her handbag, and then Court pulled out his empty Scorpion, collapsed the stock, and slung it over his neck.

Following a suggestion from Zack, the four of them separated so they couldn't be picked up on cameras moving together, but they all headed west on foot for a block, then turned to the north.

Matthew Hanley himself picked them all up five minutes later in front of the Volta Park Recreation Center. They climbed into Hanley's rented minivan, and everyone remained silent as the vehicle rolled off to the north.

Eventually, however, Hanley spoke into the car's speakers. "Gumdrop. You with us?"

"I've got you on Wisconsin. Keep heading north and you'll miss all the first responders converging in Georgetown. I see no more Gauntlet assets near you. I'm bringing the UAV back, so I can only see you on traffic cams."

"Roger that." Now Hanley turned to Pace. "Nice going back there."

Pace said, "I don't know what you're talking about. I was never here."

"Understood."

Pace directed Hanley to pull over at a corner, and he climbed out. Once on the sidewalk, he leaned back in, and looked to King. "We're taking you at your word, ma'am."

"Mr. Six and Mr. Hanley here have both taken me at my word in the past, and I hope they agree with me that I've never violated their trust."

Both men nodded.

"But," Cathy said, handing a business card to Pace with a shaking hand, "if you ever want to grab coffee, I am working on a book about—"

Pace interrupted. "I'm going to have to pass. Glad you're okay, Ms. King, but since I don't exist and all, I won't be able to have coffee with you." He disappeared down a side street and Hanley continued north on Wisconsin, leaving Catherine holding her business card.

They drove towards the safe house in a roundabout way, and the heavy breathing from everyone in the vehicle—including Hanley, even though he hadn't been directly under any threat—steamed the windshield so bad they had to roll the windows down.

Court pulled a fresh pair of AirPods from his pack so he could listen to Jill as she flew the drone back and broke the safe house down with help from Arnold.

It had been like this when he worked in CIA's Ground Branch as a paramilitary operations officer. Short bursts of almost unimaginable stress followed immediately by the mundane. They'd pack gear, climb on a jet, take a short flight, undergo some sort of after-action briefing, and then Court planned on heading back to *Ship Happens, Two* to clean his weapons, charge his communication devices, and hopefully get some rest while he waited on Pace and Lacy and Hanley and Watkins to give him his next orders.

Tomorrow, he imagined, it would be another surveillance op, perhaps another kinetic op, followed by another decompression cycle.

They were still on the D.C. side of the Potomac when Catherine King said, "What about me?"

Hanley answered, "Where can you go where you'll be safe?"

"Tahiti sounds nice," she replied. The team looked at her a moment, then she said, "But I have a girlfriend in Taos, she's always trying to get me to visit. This might be a good time."

Hanley shook his head. "Gauntlet no doubt has the ability to get into your credit cards, see where you are and what you're doing. We have a safe house a few hours away; we can put you in there until this is all settled."

Court said, "You might see someone you know there."

"Who?"

"I'll keep it a surprise."

King seemed to take a moment to choose her words, and then she said, "You guys were the ones the other night in Washington Circle." It was a statement, not a question, and for Court's part, he was temporarily too tired to protest. She followed it up with, "If Gauntlet is behind the assassinations, then it's a safe guess they are behind the intelligence leaks somehow. They are going to be incredibly focused on figuring out who you all are, considering how you've disrupted two of their operations so far. If they are able to obtain unlimited quantities of intelligence, then I hope you will all be very, *very* careful."

The comment hung there in the air a moment, amid the heavy breathing and the steamed windows, as the minivan took the Chain Bridge over the river, heading into Virginia, on their way to Reagan National.

Had James Westwood stayed home from work, he would have been able to hear the majority of the action in Georgetown. The unsuppressed weapons at the scene would have sounded like soft pops, the screeching of tires would have made its way up to him, and perhaps even the car alarms that went off near the scene would have been audible.

He would have also found himself just a few blocks north of where Hanley picked up the two Ghost Town operators, the CIA officer, and the intended assassination victim in Volta Park.

But instead, J.W. was in his office at the Carter Center more than a mile to the east, so he had heard nothing but racing fire trucks and ambulances and wailing police cars, all heading towards Georgetown.

Despite the fact that he wasn't there, however, he still had a pretty good picture as to what was going on, because he'd been getting near real-time updates from the scene. Mike Scardino had laptops on the coffee table in J.W.'s office to use as a sort of war room for the series of assassinations planned for today. He'd been there with a headset on, linked to Gauntlet

Group operators present at the killing of former Gauntlet pilot David Rudder less than two hours earlier, and he'd heard the reports from a Gauntlet surveillance team getting into position for another assassination in McLean that was due to happen later in the afternoon, and of course he'd been listening in to the chatter as two support teams, ten men in all, converged on a restaurant in Georgetown for what was supposed to have been an easy hit.

When it was reported to Big Mike that the woman they were following this morning, Catherine King, had chosen a table outside on the sidewalk, the already easy-sounding job just seemed like it was going to be that much easier.

But somehow it had all gone to hell.

Five Gauntlet men were dead. Two more were injured. Snare's shattered body would be identified by authorities soon enough, and the media would learn that a Jordanian assassin active for years in Europe had been killed by unknown parties in the heart of one of the most exclusive portions of Washington, D.C., on a sunny morning.

The gunfight in Georgetown had happened four hours earlier, and only now were Mike and J.W. about to get the answers they'd demanded the day before from Lewis Shaw.

The young man had insisted on coming into the Carter Center. He had been picked up by a Gauntlet team in Tysons Corner, near his office at Liberty Crossing, and driven here. Security on Church Street out in front of the Center was heavy as he was shuffled out of a van with a hat and a hood on, holding a backpack with an iPad inside, and then he'd come up here, set up in the war room, demanded coffee, and drunk a full cup before he was ready to talk to the two older men.

Shaw looked like shit, as always, J.W. noted, but the young man retained his air of superiority, less towards J.W. and more towards Big Mike, whom he still only knew as a bodyguard.

Now, the thirty-year-old cracked his knuckles, made eye contact with J.W., then nodded towards Scardino. "We talkin' in front of the help?"

Westwood did not break eye contact with the young man. "No time for your cute shit today, Shaw. We need you to tell us both everything you've got. Now."

Shaw looked back and forth between the two men. Finally, he glanced down and unlocked his iPad, then said, "You told me you wanted everything on Hanley and his associates. This shit was damn tough to get; let me start with that. I'm going to want more money from our friends; they—"

Westwood all but yelled now. "Fucking *talk*, Lewis!"

"Jesus, dude. Okay. First... Matt Hanley left his employment with CIA seven weeks ago; he has no official job, but he's been handed access to Agency black fund accounts totaling well over twenty million dollars."

Scardino looked to J.W. "Just what I suspected. He's running an off-book program. I assume with the knowledge of Phillips or Watkins at CIA, maybe Olivia Anthony at DNI. Maybe all three."

Shaw made a face at the Gauntlet man, a look of surprise, as if he couldn't believe the dumb bodyguard could figure something out on his own. But he shook his head. "It's gotta be one of the CIA guys. Olivia Anthony is *my* boss. If she were involved with Hanley, I'd know about it, because I know everything that's going on over there." He then looked back down to his iPad. "Anyway, seen with Hanley recently is this joker." He held up the screen, which was completely taken up with a full-page image of Zack Hightower's official U.S. Navy photo.

J.W. said, "A sailor?"

Shaw shook his head. "He was a Navy SEAL. One of their Team Six guys, way back. An officer. He then joined the CIA and worked in Ground Branch. Snake-eater stuff.

"His name is Zachary Paul Hightower. He was in Kharkiv with Hanley in November. He was wounded in Russia. Treated at a hospital in Germany. Doctors there thought he was a JSOC operative, but in actuality, he was a... well... he was a nothing. A private civilian. Obviously, he was working sub rosa with Hanley at that time, and it stands to reason he is still doing so. That makes him part of this outfit."

Shaw moved some pages around on the device, then held up a new picture. A man on a street, crouching behind a van, a pistol in his hand. His neck gaiter covered his face below the eyes. He said, "In this image, the computer matches the eyes, the separation of the eyes, the bridge of the nose with Zack Hightower."

"Where is this?"

"This was the other night in Washington Circle. He killed three Gauntlet men in close-quarters battle, right there on New Hampshire Avenue."

Scardino sat back in his chair, a smile widening on his face. "That's one of the assets, then. Is it the Gray Man?"

"No," Shaw said. He scrolled to another page, then held it up. A high-up view down into the windshield of a black Yukon. Looking down, it was the image of a man with a neck gaiter pulled up to his nose. "This was four hours ago, on Reservoir Road, very near the disarray in Georgetown. The facial recognition algorithm says it's the same guy. Hightower. This very Yukon was left at the scene. Shot to shit. Dead Gauntlet men lying around it." He glanced at Big Mike, who only stared back at him.

J.W. said, "This is one of Hanley's operators, obviously. But how do you know it's not the Gray Man?"

"Because . . . *this* is the Gray Man." Shaw found another photo on his iPad, held it up. It was a picture of a man walking down a hallway in a building with a woman.

"That woman is Irene Ortega, and that man is Courtland Gentry."

"Who is . . . ?" J.W. prompted.

"Who is the Gray Man."

Both men leaned in, looked more carefully. "How do you know?"

"There was an ad hoc team set up at CIA a few years ago—the Violator Working Group—and its sole mission was to find and kill a CIA asset code-named Violator, who had turned into a freelance assassin and was referred to as the Gray Man. The group was disbanded a couple years ago. No one knows why, but I found some scuttlebutt that said Violator did a job for the Agency in Germany and the sanction on him was removed as a thank-you. Not sure how true that is, but the dates work out.

"Anyway, this picture." He showed yet another photo of a man with dark hair in wire-rimmed glasses, seated and facing the camera in a sport coat. It looked like a slightly wider view of a regular passport photo, "This is Courtland Gentry, and this is, according to the Violator Working Group, the Gray Man."

He swiped a couple of times back to his left. "Here is the same guy rescuing Irene Ortega in the same incident where Zack Hightower was outside shooting up a team of Gauntlet dudes." He looked to Scardino.

Big Mike said, "The Navy guy . . . he looks like an operator. But this guy . . . he looks like—nothing."

Shaw agreed. "That passport photo looks like a bus stop ad for a real estate broker. Of course, that was several years ago; he probably has changed in some ways."

J.W. said, "Okay, this is all fine. But where are they now?"

Shaw smiled. "Hightower has no known next of kin. No wife, kids, nothing. But we do know where he is at the moment."

"Where?"

"Hightower is on a Delta flight to Boulder, Colorado. He's flying under the name Lyle Hart, but the facial recog there at Reagan shows him to be the same man.

"Lyle Hart has a return flight from Boulder tomorrow evening."

Scardino rose quickly and headed out of the room, pulling out his phone as he went.

Shaw watched this, and J.W. spoke up. "What's he doing in Boulder?"

The younger man shrugged his narrow shoulders. "*That* I don't know. You got any killers working in Boulder?"

"That's not your concern. Just dig, find out if there are connections between Hightower or Hart and Boulder, Colorado."

Shaw said, "I guess I can see if he's been there before, get into credit cards and whatnot. That's not really what I do, that's more like PI work. I'm sure somebody at Gauntlet can—"

J.W. interrupted. "Events have escalated, Lewis. We need everything you can get us right now. All your efforts. I want to put a Gauntlet team on Hightower while he's in Boulder. If he has a vehicle there, either a rental car waiting for him or his own vehicle, like if he lives there, I want a Gauntlet operator in that city to put a tracker on it before the plane lands, so work fast."

Shaw nodded. "I'll get on that."

"What about Gentry?" J.W. asked.

"For Gentry, he had a brother who died several years ago. His name was Chancellor, went by Chance; he was a cop in Jacksonville, Florida. Shot while making a traffic stop. But Gentry does have a father, still there in northern Florida, outside of Jacksonville. I have no idea if there is any communication between them. Apparently, Court Gentry lives like a ghost. CIA blames a couple dozen hits around the world on him, and that was before the working group disbanded. Who knows what that fucker has been up to since."

Westwood said, "He's working with Hanley, obviously."

Shaw nodded. "Yeah . . . there is some evidence he was on the ground in Russia a couple months back, and that was definitely Hanley's op."

Westwood looked at the image. "So he's a ghost, but he's taking part in gunfights in D.C."

"Against your buddy's company," Shaw said, referring to Gauntlet Group.

Scardino reentered the room and immediately addressed Shaw. "I've got a Gauntlet man in Boulder ready to run surveillance. I'm sending Lancer there, too. He says he can get a team of locals, non-Gauntlet guys, to support him there."

"What locals?" J.W. asked.

Scardino flashed a look to Shaw. "We talking in front of the help?"

To this, Westwood chuckled, then said, "Let's discuss details after young Lewis leaves."

"Right," Scardino agreed.

J.W. looked back to Shaw. "Where's Hanley working out of?"

"I don't know. What I just gave you is all I have for now, but I'm still digging. Once I got the ID of the Gray Man, I figured I needed to come to you ASAP."

Scardino said, "Good. Go back to Liberty Crossing. Keep at it. We need physical locations for these people. Vehicle information. License plates. It does us no good if we can't find—"

Shaw interrupted. "I don't take orders from you."

Big Mike turned to J.W., who then looked directly at Shaw. "All that."

"Fair enough, boss." Shaw packed up his things and headed for the stairs.

When he was gone, Westwood said, "We'll give Whetstone the information about the father down in Florida. It will probably lead to nothing, but at least we can keep the trickle of information going to the Northern Irishman. He has a lot of work to do yet. He's in Chicago now; supposed to be, anyway."

Scardino said, "Two of five hitters are off the playing field. We still have a long way to go."

"Yeah. We have to assume that Hanley's people will show up at all our targets now, and plan accordingly."

Scardino said, "I've lost ten men already. I have the men to lose, and we have help in the government so that we can spin their deaths, make it look like they were trying to stop the hitters, but this can't keep happening."

J.W. nodded. "Hanley is fucking everything up. As soon as we have location intel from Shaw, you need to send a full strike package down on him."

"Agreed," Scardino said, and then he left the room again to check in with his forces in the field.

FORTY

Court Gentry lay on the sofa in the salon of his boat in Marina Bay, a sweating bottle of Mexican beer all but untouched on the little side table next to him. He listened to a soft rain outside, glancing occasionally at the monitor with all the security camera images displayed across the room by the table with the radio set, as he fingered the trigger guard of the pump shotgun propped up on the sofa next to him.

It was nearly midnight now. He'd lain here for hours; he imagined he'd eventually get the energy to climb up and head into the cabin, climb into his box with his shotgun, and catch some sleep, but for now he just tried to relax.

He'd talked to Zoya tonight over Signal, told her everything that had happened, not because he'd wanted to but simply because he knew she'd pick up on the fact that he was lying if he tried to keep info away from her to prevent her from worrying. As soon as he told her what happened in Georgetown, she'd wanted to return to the field, to come help; she'd even reached out to Hanley directly, but he'd told her her services were not required and would not be accepted. Physically, Court knew, she had a long way to go until she was one hundred percent, and mentally . . . well, who could say how she was doing mentally? The woman was tough as nails, but she'd been through so much.

Court had been happy talking with her, though. He'd seen her just days earlier, but he didn't see her enough, and already the longing was getting to him. For much of his life he'd wondered what it was that made people settle down in one place, but he did not wonder about that anymore. Now he wondered why there were people out there like Whetstone, people who struggled to find a home.

Court had a home now.

This boat wasn't it, but this boat was good enough for tonight.

There had been two killings today related to the intelligence community. A Department of Energy officer in the Office of Intelligence and Counterintelligence was murdered at a conference in Chicago. Shot nine times in front of his hotel by a man in a latex mask. No one had thought to give the Department of Energy officer security protection, his agency was so little known. But Russia's energy-related raw materials were its lifeblood, and Russia spied on the American energy sector, as did the Chinese. The man killed today had set counterintelligence protocols at nuclear, oil, and gas facilities, and from what Hanley had told Court, he was something of a legend in his field, so it made sense that whatever bad actor was doing all this would want to take him out.

At roughly the same time, a DEA operative who ran several international investigations in Latin America was killed at his home in Landover, Maryland. The cause of death had been a crude but effective car bomb, and it was a slap in the face of the U.S. government that they still weren't protecting their own.

First, the layoff or forced resignation of thousands of intelligence officials as a cost-cutting measure, to be replaced by a private company run by a billionaire friend of the president.

Then, a spate of murders of intelligence officials, on U.S. soil, perpetrated by assassins from abroad.

Court was glad he was in the private sector.

He'd also spoken with Sir Donald Fitzroy tonight. His former handler told Court he'd spent the past day trying to track down Sir Allen Glazebrook, but the man had suddenly fled the Cotswolds, and even his butler Jeffrey didn't know where he'd gone. Jeffrey, worried about his employer, did admit to Fitzroy that two men from Northern Ireland had come into the home several nights earlier, and only one left alive.

It seemed to Court like Coyle had cajoled Glazebrook into making connections here in America with whoever was behind the assassinations, only so that Coyle could find out more information about Court.

Fitzroy promised to keep feelers out for Glazebrook, but the man seemed so scared he could be anywhere in the world right now, simply hiding out from Whetstone lest he return unsatisfied with the services Glazebrook provided him.

Court sat up slowly now, was about to head to his hidden sleeping quarters, and then the FibreNet secure communications app vibrated on his phone. He looked down, did not recognize the number, but answered it anyway, waiting until the tenth ring to do so.

"Yeah?"

It was the Northern Irishman again. His voice was gravelly but a little jovial. "Someone's been a busy boy, eh?"

Court wasn't in the mood. "I don't know what you're talking—"

"Of course ye do, chief. I've been watchin' the news. Startin' to recognize your handiwork."

Court took a few breaths. "I imagine you've been busy yourself. I'm guessing the car bombs were yours. You IRA guys love a good car bomb, don't you?"

"No, mate, I took the day off. Sharpening my blade. Yours is the next neck I'll be sinking it into."

"Why is it I don't believe you?"

"Because neither of us was raised to be the trusting type. Don't worry, though, you'll believe me soon enough."

"Not soon enough," Court said. "I'm in the mood to deal with you right now. You and your friends are killing a lot of innocents."

"Right. Better I get back out there, go kill someone important, perhaps you'll show up like you and your mates did in Georgetown today."

"Why do you think I was there?"

"Snare, the Jordanian, was quite good, I hear. Not a contemporary of mine, really. I never knew of him, but I am hearing he'd done some good work back in Europe."

Court said, "I've looked into you."

"Woulda been surprised if you hadn't."

"I know your name is Campbell Coyle. I know you're forty-seven, son of a terrorist named Roderick Coyle. I know you were in the Legion, then you assassinated for the British, and then you turned into a killer for hire. I know you went dark for a long time, only came back into the light to kill a guy in London along with two of his bodyguards."

Coyle said, "Very good, but you left out one thing. I was father to a lad named Charlie. And *that's* the only thing that ought to matter to you, because that wee fact is why you're dying at the end of all this."

"I've thought back to that night. I killed a couple of men, injured several more. I don't know which was your son."

"One of the injured. I did some digging myself. He was pulled off the living room floor of a suite."

"Right," Court said. He of course remembered the man who shot him in his bulletproof vest.

"He died in the hospital a week later," Coyle said.

"You going after the doctors next?"

"No. Yours will be my last killing. I've got this big, long to-do list from those that employed me here in America, but I'll chuck it and go home once I've dealt with you."

Court said, "You know you're working for the Russians, or maybe the Chinese. You feel okay about that?"

"I'm working for meself."

"You're working for Gauntlet, a private military company with ties to China."

"Maybe I am, I have no idea. But I couldn't care less who they're tied to. They are bringing me to you. That's all I wanted out of them."

"And what did they want in return?"

"They know you're one of the ones tryin' to stop them, so they want you done, as well. I came here to kill you for free. I'd have paid all my money to do it. Now there's those that actually want to pay me to do it. Ain't life grand?"

Court thought this over a moment. Finally, he said, "I went to Bulgaria to ask that mob boss for some help. I had no ill intent. Then he ordered his men to beat the brakes off me, maybe even kill me, and he took a photo of me that he was going to send to some people, and that could just not happen."

"So?"

"So if the situation had been reversed, you'd have gone through his security team to get to him, just like I did."

"Again . . . so?"

"So . . . you have to acknowledge I was just doing what I thought was right. You have to acknowledge your boy was in the wrong place at the wrong time."

"What difference does that make?"

"You could just let this all go."

"Unfortunately, chief, I just can't do that."

"*Why* can't you? You sound like a man who's been around long enough to know that vengeance never produces the satisfaction that one—"

"This is not about vengeance. I've no need for that. Charlie lived in a world where this was the only outcome."

Court looked down at his phone a moment, then brought it back to his ear. "Then why the fuck are you—"

"Because Charlie himself had a child."

"Charlie had a . . . What does that have to do with anything?"

"Family is everything. Would you not agree?"

After a moment, Court spoke softly. "I wouldn't know."

Campbell surprised Court with a little laugh. "To be fair, neither would I." But then he added, "But 'ere's the problem, chief. Twenty years from now, Charlie's boy, my grandson, might not see it the same as me. Family might be everything to him. So much so that maybe he'll take it on himself to avenge his father. Just like I did."

"You're saying some kid is going to come after me?"

"Might do. Except he won't be a kid."

Court understood now. "You're telling me that if you kill me, you might be saving your grandson's life in the future?"

"Could be just that, yeah."

Court dropped his head into his hand. Still holding the phone to his ear, he said, "Fuck, dude. This isn't the twelfth century."

"Like hell it isn't," Coyle said. "We humans have not progressed; you and I are God's living proof of that."

Court now said, "The problem is, you have to know that if you come after me now, there's a chance *I* could kill *you*. What's your grandson going to think about that?"

"Doubt he'll ever know that I was alive."

"But isn't there someone who cared about your son who would care that they lost you, as well?"

The pause was brief. "As a matter of fact, no, chief. No man, woman, or animal would care if I died."

Court sighed. *Shit.* "Well then, maybe we should just go ahead and get this over with."

"Pragmatism. *That*, I can respect. Problem is, I don't believe you. You give me an address, and you'll hold all the cards there. We're going to have to meet out there on the field of battle, won't we? You're goin' through those Gauntlet lads like butter. But I have my own team. When I see you out there, I'm going to—"

Court cut him off. "When you see me, Coyle, it'll be too late."

Both men breathed into the phone.

Finally, it was Court who spoke. "I think you are calling because you don't have anyone else who can understand you, except the man you want to kill."

"I don't *want* to kill you."

"You could have fooled me."

It was quiet a moment, and then Coyle said, "What I do, what you do . . . it's not about what we want. It's about what we are."

"You can decide to do whatever you want, Coyle."

"Just like you did? Just like you decided to put a knife in my boy? To kill those men in Georgetown?"

Court did not respond.

Coyle said, "Ya know, mate . . . I've a brother in Belfast who has a wee shop, sells school uniforms. An uncle there, he's dead now, but from cancer, not a bullet. Lived to be sixty, worked his life for the phone company, never missed Sunday church. I've an aunt who became a financial advisor. Took in stray kittens. Not a dangerous bone in her body. Not an ounce of her that wanted anything more for her life than peace and love.

"Got a cousin, we're the same age, he grew up on the same streets as me. He's a fecking' florist in Derry. A *florist*."

Court sighed. "What on earth does this have to—"

"You have siblings?" Coyle asked.

Taken aback, Court responded honestly. "I had a brother."

"Yeah? Bet he turned out, didn't he?"

Court shrugged. "He was a cop. He died."

"What kind of cop was he?"

"He was a good cop, as far as I know."

"Ya see? Some family . . . the bloodlines, they're not all bad. Some are soft. *Most* are soft. Good. You and me. We're from the hard lines. The thorny leaves in the family tree is what we are. We can't help it. We can't change it. We can wish it weren't so, but you, me, Charlie, my da. His da. We're part of the hard line."

Court took this all in, then said, "But why would your grandson be one of us? Maybe he'll be a florist. A cop, a doctor."

"Dunno that he would be like us. Dunno that he wouldn't. All I can do for him, all I can *ever* do in his whole life, is right now, stoppin' any chance he goes after the bloke that took his da from him.

"I've a bloody righteous mission, mate. And the man with the most righteous mission, nine times out of ten, is the man who's gonna win."

"*Win?* You're not going to win, Coyle. Whatever happens to me, you're working for some people who aren't just going to let you walk away when you're done."

"I'm thinking you're right, mate. But I've made peace with that. I help my grandson stay off the hard line, and then everything that comes after will be what it will be."

"Well then," Court said. "I'll see you out there. In the meantime . . . go fuck yourself."

He hung up the phone, feeling angry and depressed and tired.

He climbed to his feet and headed into his cabin to get some sleep.

FORTY-ONE

A steady, icy rain pelted the Noble Park neighborhood of Boulder, Colorado; the spray that kicked up from the all-season tires of the white F-150 had just settled back on the parking lot as Zack Hightower opened the door of his truck and rushed through the precipitation, entering Cara's Bakehouse just after nine a.m.

His heart pounded. It felt like the world was falling apart right now; he'd dealt with so much danger and discord in the past couple of days, but somehow the opportunity of seeing his daughter again had his heart in his throat in ways that pitched battles on city streets in Washington, D.C., did not.

She was here this morning; he saw her as soon as he came through the door, her hair pulled back and her black sweatshirt, cut off at the neck, and baggy jeans billowing around her green apron like she'd stolen the clothes of a grown man. She had a line of people at her register and he joined them, did his best to glance left and right, even pretending to check his phone from time to time as he waited, working like mad to make himself appear like a normal human, when right now, he was anything but.

He listened to her voice as she talked to the customers and the other employees behind the counter; she laughed a couple of times, and Zack himself fought a smile.

His MRI was at ten a.m., and his doctor's appointment directly after.

The imaging center was a thirty-minute drive from here in traffic, so he was glad the line moved quickly, and then, with the same slight quiver in his knees he'd felt every other time he'd been in the presence of Stacy Hightower, aka Andrea Delaney, he made it to the counter.

Andie smiled when she saw him, then flashed a quick clandestine look to her right, in the direction of Cara, who was across the room stocking a shelf with bottled water. Zack read it as if Andie were a little worried that the proprietor of the store was going to see him, and equally worried about what Cara might say or do when she did.

"Morning," Andie said. "What can I get you?"

He'd been gone four days; he hadn't expected her to remember his order, but when he started to speak, she said, "The usual?"

"Uh, the usual. Exactly."

"Cheese Danish, unheated, coffee, cream and sugar."

"You got it." He loosened a little. "How's your day goin'?"

As she rang him up, she said, "Busy but awesome." With a wide grin, she said, "I'm off at ten thirty, then I'm going snowboarding at Eldora Mountain."

Zack had no idea where that was, and he'd never been on a snowboard in his life, but he found himself pleased that she was pleased.

He looked back over his shoulder, past the long line and towards the windows. "In this weather?" he asked.

She made a face as if it didn't matter. "Nah, this'll turn to snow any minute. Going down to the twenties. Gonna be some sick ice up there on the slopes."

"Sick ice," he said softly. Then, "Outstanding."

He watched her pour his coffee and get his Danish, and he chastised himself for being so fucking proud of her.

He paid in cash, left a big tip. As he turned to walk away, he said, "Have fun out there."

"Have a good one," she said as she smiled at the next customer.

Zack Hightower left without Cara noticing him, which was another win for him.

Five minutes later he sat across the street, the grille of his truck facing the café, and he sipped his coffee, ate his Danish, and stared through the window, lost in his thoughts. He had to fly back to Vah Beach tonight, was sure the doctor would sign off on his full recovery today after the MRI, especially if he could hide the big purple bruise on his knee from where he banged it during the first D.C. shoot-out three nights ago.

Once the doctor told him he was good, then he had no real reason to ever come back here again.

He was needed elsewhere; people were dying back east, and he was part of the group that was killing the killers, but he honestly just wanted to come here every day, have ten seconds of conversation with that kid across the street, and then sit right here in his truck and enjoy his breakfast.

Part of him was angry that he would settle for this, and another part of him felt like this didn't seem like such a bad life at all.

Eighty yards away, a dark blue Jeep Wagoneer with Utah plates was parked between a couple of smaller vehicles, and inside the Jeep, three men used the zooms on their iPhones to filter out the water on their windows and to enlarge the distant image of the man in the truck.

They watched him eat a bite of food, drink from a paper cup, and stare across the street, through the rain and into the café.

"The fuck does he keep looking at?" The comment was made by the twenty-seven-year-old behind the wheel. Todd Voorhies was tall, broad, and muscular; he had his razor-short hair covered by a knit cap, but the tats running up his neck revealed to any who knew the signs that he was a member of a white nationalist group based in Ogden, Utah. The man in back, a twenty-two-year-old with similar tats, was his younger brother, though at six-four, he was an inch taller than his sibling.

"Something in that restaurant," Lee Voorhies answered.

"That's not a restaurant. It's a café," Todd corrected.

"What's the difference?"

"Dumbass."

Another man sat in the front passenger seat; he was older, head to toe in the camouflage gear of a hunter, and he'd been silent while the brothers jawed back and forth, but now he turned his head a little to the right, focused on Cara's Bakehouse.

"Bennett's sure as shit taking his time."

"He's probably eatin' a donut," Todd said. Then, "Hey, Kincaid. Why don't we just do it right now? I'll walk right over there and pop that old motherfucker in his truck, three in the back of the head, and we can be out of here before it starts snowin'. Back to Utah by this afternoon."

"Not yet," Scott Kincaid, code name Lancer, said in the front passenger seat. "This guy's trained like you wouldn't believe."

"Yeah," the younger Voorhies brother said from the back. "But he's sure as shit not payin' attention right now."

Lancer looked back to him. "He's *not*? Really? What are you, a fucking genius? Right now he is sitting behind the wheel of a parked vehicle. Do you even understand what that means when you're talking about a guy like that?"

The man in the backseat looked to the truck, then back to Lancer. "Doesn't mean shit other than the fact that I can walk over there and—"

"It means, not only does he have windows that look out in all directions, but he's got three mirrors that are showing him angles other than the direction his head is facing. He's more situationally aware than in almost any other setting. Sneaking up on someone behind the wheel of a parked car is harder than it fucking looks, and I should know, because motherfuckers have tried it on me.

"Now, what do we know about this fuck? We know he's spent about thirty years fighting people or training to fight people a hell of a lot more impressive than the fuckin' Voorhies brothers from Ogden, Utah. You walk up on his car and he's going to know it, and no matter what he's got in his hands right now, he's going to have a pistol in them before you can get close enough to shoot him."

Todd muttered, "I've also got my hunting rifle in the back. I can pop that dude from here, no big—"

"I don't give a shit if you have a Javelin missile system," Kincaid said. "Everybody just calm down and wait for my instructions."

No one spoke for half a minute, and then Lancer let out a sigh. "He's distracted. I'll give you that. Might not be checking his mirrors, but normally, a dude like him? Former DEVGRU operator, former CIA paramilitary. No chance in hell you big motherfuckers are gonna catch him napping behind the wheel. And you fire from this vehicle, and this vehicle is gonna get stopped as soon as we get back on the highway. We have to catch him at a time that's to our advantage."

The three of them watched a man step out of Cara's Bakehouse with a paper cup of coffee in his hand, cross the street in front of them, then move to the back right door of the Wagoneer. The driver unlocked it, and he climbed in, dripping with cold rain.

Lancer said, "Target is eighty yards off to our left. He pulled in there after he left the café. He's looking at the café now. Why?"

The new man in the Jeep was in his thirties, burly, burlier still with his camo-green cold-weather hunting gear on. He was bearded, and his black ball cap dripped icy rainwater. No tattoos showed on his neck, but if he'd not been wearing the coat, the ink would have been evident on his arms. He said, "The little chick behind the register. Young kid. They knew each other somehow. She remembered his order, she said something about Eldora Mountain and snowboarding, I couldn't pick it all up, but they acted like family or something."

"You sure he didn't clock you?"

"I was in the back of the line. He had no idea I was even there. I'm just that good."

Scott Kincaid thought about this a few seconds, then said, "If he didn't notice you, it wasn't because you were good, it was because his head was somewhere else." Looking at Bennett now, he said, "You get a picture of the kid behind the counter?"

"A picture?"

Lancer sighed. He reached back and took the coffee out of the man's hand. "Go get another coffee. But don't come back without a picture of that girl at the register."

Five minutes later, Lancer's man was still in the coffee shop when Hightower's F-150 rolled out of the parking lot; the three men left Bennett behind with orders to text the photo as soon as possible, and they followed the truck at distance out of Noble Park.

The image arrived on Kincaid's phone a minute later; he sent it via Signal to the Gauntlet team back in D.C. tasked to help him, and then he called in. "We need to find out who this girl is, stat."

The Gauntlet analyst asked why; Lancer told him that the girl might be family or just someone Hightower knew, but whoever she was, she might be leverage.

Lancer had two more white nationalists on his team, both in a black Bronco with Utah plates, rented the night before when the team arrived. After a call from Kincaid, the two vehicles switched positions on the highway; the Wagoneer dropped back half a mile and the Bronco edged up closer.

They didn't need to get too close; Bennett had put a tracker in Hightower's F-150 in the airport garage early the evening before, just minutes before he landed, so they could follow the truck's movements on Kincaid's phone. That was what led them to an apartment complex last night, then the bakery this morning, and then, just before ten a.m., to a medical office park.

Here they found the F-150 parked in a busy lot in front of the Boulder Imaging Center.

Both vehicles continued driving around the block, and then they pulled into different entrances of the same parking lot. The Bronco reported to Kincaid that they saw their target enter the imaging center doors.

Once the Wagoneer parked, Todd Voorhies turned to Lancer. "If he's getting an MRI, then we should do it now."

"Why?"

"You ever get an MRI?"

"Like a half dozen."

"So you know. The MRI is a big magnet. You can't have any metal on you in there. You make this dude out like he's some kind of badass. Is he gonna be a badass wearing a fucking hospital gown, no gun, no knife? We get in there, hang out in the waiting room, let him go back to the dressing room. We find a back way in, catch him in his underwear before they turn on the MRI. We use knives, keep it quiet."

Lancer thought about the situation, and he also thought about the kid in the bakery. He wasn't sure taking Hightower down in a medical office was going to work out, but it was worth a shot, especially since he hadn't heard back from his Gauntlet support yet about the girl.

Just then, his Signal app notified him he had a call coming through.

Snatching the phone off his lap, he said, "Tell me you have something on the girl."

The person on the other end of the line was not his Gauntlet support lead; it was Mike himself. "Get ready for this. They kicked your request up to me, and I reached out to my guy on the inside. Took him a minute, but he just learned that Zack Hightower had a kid who went into wit-pro twelve years ago. She now lives in Boulder. Name is Andrea Delaney and she works at Cara's Bakehouse. The image you sent the team matches a picture of her on a website for junior national ranked snowboarders."

"Oh, shit," Kincaid said. "Old Hightower is here spying on his biological kid."

Mike said, "You going to snatch her? Use her to get to him?"

Kincaid looked at the front door of the building on the other side of the parking lot. "Another opportunity has presented itself. We're going to try this first but use the girl as a backup plan. Either way, I'll let you know when the job is done."

"Good. Don't fuck it up."

"I don't fuck up."

"Says the guy I pulled out of a Cuban prison."

Kincaid ignored the comment and said, "What do you have for me on the Gray Man?"

Mike hesitated, then said, "Still looking into that. Hope to have something soon."

"Bullshit. You can get me the identity of somebody in witness protection in under an hour, but you can't find out anything about the Gray Man?"

Mike said, "We don't know how our guy has access. Certain data is available to him, other data is not. Like I said, he's on it, and we'll let you know if—"

Scott Kincaid hung up on Big Mike, then looked to the brothers. "Get in there. Get to him before he goes into the MRI. Knives only. I'll pick you up from any door you exit from, just text me."

Both men stepped out into a freezing rain and began walking towards the building.

When they were gone, when Scott Kincaid was all alone in the Wagoneer, he moved to the driver's seat, then drummed his fingers on the wheel a moment. After just a few seconds, he snatched up his phone and dialed the two other men on the other side of the parking lot in the Bronco.

Ronald Winter and Carl Maybus were in their forties, and they'd been involved in the white nationalist movement since they were children. They had been brutes their whole lives, and unlike the other three men on Lancer's team, he'd known them before this week.

Carl answered the phone. "Yeah?"

"Get back over to the bakery. Pick up Bennett and park the Bronco. One of you goes in and lingers, the other waits in the truck. After forty-five minutes switch out, but don't lose sight of the girl. If she leaves, follow her, see where she goes. We might need to grab her. Hightower's her biological dad. Also, rent us an out-of-the-way place near Eldora Mountain, just in case we need to bolt. Don't use your credit card. Find someone else's card you can use, something the feds won't trace back to your group." He thought a moment. "And I'm gonna need a couple more men. You know anybody up this way wants to make five grand for an afternoon's work?"

Carl showed no excitement or even great interest in this enterprise. He just said, "Yup. I'll make some calls," and hung up.

Angela Lacy spoke with urgency. "We've had another breach."

Matt Hanley had been meeting with Erin and Jill in his office just after noon when the call came through. When he heard Angela's words and her unmistakable tone, he tapped the speaker function on his device so the others could hear.

"What's happened?"

"It's not good," she said. "Someone with a specific CIA credential set spent most of last night digging into the personnel files of yourself, Zachary Hightower, and Courtland Gentry."

Hanley sat on the edge of his desk. Erin looked at him with wide eyes. Hanley said, "Not Violator? Not Agency intel on the Gray Man? But Courtland Gentry? By name?"

"All three. They got into information on something called the Violator Working Group that was running a few years ago, apparently there was—"

"Yeah, I know all about that. All traces of that were supposedly purged from the system."

"They weren't. His name was mentioned in a meeting, notes were taken and recorded, though it was a code-worded file."

"And someone got the code word yesterday?"

"It seems so."

Hanley looked to the ceiling, shaking his head. "What else did they learn?"

"Some known associates information, next of kin of Six . . . apparently he has one living relative, a father, down in—"

Hanley said, "I'm calling you right back." He hung up the phone and dialed Court.

Court raced down the highway on his Yamaha, heading from his boat in Virginia Beach down to the southwest of the state, to Drum Hill, Ghost Town's private training facility forty-five minutes away in North Carolina. He had a backpack full of gear, and it seemed like Ghost Town was standing down for the day since Zack and Teddy were inop, so he'd decided to spend a cold afternoon heating up some guns and testing some new ammo.

His earpiece rang; it was his Signal app, and he opened it by touching the phone that was mounted on a chest rig on his jacket. Through the headphones he wore, he could make and take calls even while riding his motorcycle. "Yeah?"

"Six, we have a problem." It was Hanley, and Court wished he had a dollar for every time Hanley called him and began with this line. Then he said, "How soon can you be at the airport?"

The exit to Hampton Roads Executive Airport was less than a quarter mile in front of him. "Under ten minutes. Where am I going?"

"Court," Hanley said. "It looks like you're going home."

"Home?"

"The enemy knows about your dad. I have no idea if they will try to exploit that or—"

"Fuck!" Court said into his helmet. "Yeah. Whetstone most definitely will. I'll go down and pull him out."

Hanley replied, "I've already called my guy watching your dad down there and told him to be extra vigilant. This information was just disseminated last night. Obviously, the assassins have other targets, so we don't know—"

"Matt. What about Teddy and Night Train?"

"Teddy's at home. Lacy didn't say anything about him getting pinged in this. Night Train is in Boulder; he has no next of kin, so I assess him as less of a threat to—"

Court interrupted. "Call the pilot. Now! Tell him to file a flight plan for Boulder."

"*Boulder?* What about your dad?"

"Just have your guy down there keep eyes on and a phone ready to call the local five-oh. I'm heading to get to Night Train."

"Okay, stand by." A few seconds passed. "Erin just called him; his phone went to voice mail. I think he's in his MRI appointment about now, might not have his phone on him. We'll keep trying."

There was a brief pause. Court figured Hanley was about to ask what it was he wasn't telling him, but then Court just said, "Trust me on this, Pilgrim. If I'm wrong, I'll never explain. If I'm right . . . I'll tell you more."

Hanley took a beat, then said, "Let me call Bellstar and have them file that flight plan. We'll keep trying Zack."

Court said, "Tell Bellstar I need whatever aircraft will get me to Boulder fastest."

"Roger that."

Court was already on the off-ramp leading to the airport. He thought of his father; he hadn't spoken to the man in nearly twenty years, although he did actually lay eyes on him a few years back. But then he thought of Zack. Court had no idea if the enemy that seemed to be so good at getting secrets out of the U.S. intelligence community could manage to get secrets out of the famously secure FBI Witness Protection Program, but if they could, then Zack needed all the help he could get.

Zack Hightower sat alone in a small room, on a bench in front of a row of four wooden lockers. He wore a paper gown, his black boxer briefs under it, and patient-mandated footie-socks with little grippers on the bottom on his feet.

The leg was stiff today, but it didn't hurt. He massaged the wound as he sat there, and he wanted to hurry this process up, talk to his doc, and get his ass back to Ghost Town.

As ordered, he'd removed his watch and any other metal objects on his body. He'd answered a questionnaire given to him by the technician ensuring he had no bullet fragments in his body, and that he wore no other jewelry. The only other metal objects he'd brought into the hospital with him were his phone, which he'd turned off, his backup pistol, and a knife. His primary concealed weapon, a Staccato HD P4 9-millimeter, was currently in a lockbox in his truck, but he also carried a tiny Ruger LCP MAX micro .380 pistol in his boot, and this was in the locker, right next to his Ka-Bar Ek Commando fixed-blade knife.

His phone and keys were locked up, as well. He had a key to his locker in his hand, hanging from a string, and he swung it around. He felt naked without his weapons, felt extra vulnerable at the doctor, but he was used to this.

Zack had been injured more times than he could count in his career; this was just another MRI, another doctor's visit, another day.

He looked at the clock on the wall. It was ten thirty a.m.

The Voorhies brothers entered the imaging center a full minute apart, and each man immediately pulled a disposable mask from a dispenser by the door to cover his face. They took seats across the busy lobby from one another, then spent a couple of minutes there, getting a feel for the layout of the area and texting back and forth.

These two guys were not exactly strangers to this sort of thing. Two years earlier the brothers had partnered with four older and more experienced men in their organization to go on a three-month crime spree. They hit a pair of sporting goods stores in Coeur d'Alene, Idaho, for guns and ammo, and three credit unions outside Portland for cash. Todd had shot and wounded a security guard at one of the credit unions, and Lee had pistol-whipped a clerk reaching for a sidearm in Coeur d'Alene, so the duo had blood on their hands, and from the older members they'd learned how to quickly register patterns in a business. The attentiveness of the employees, what parts of the building were busy, which parts were idle and accessible. These and many other factors went into casing a location before committing a crime, and the brothers used this hard-earned knowledge today.

Within moments of arriving in the busy medical office, they had both noticed that a side hallway was quiet, and a doorway at the end of this hall had a trickle of patients exiting through it. This showed them that the patients to the imaging center, when finished with their procedure, were not led directly back through the doors in the lobby they'd entered through, and this gave Todd, the older brother, an idea.

Without a word to his brother, Todd rose and began heading down the hall, and as Lee followed, the older brother rushed to catch a door opened by a departing vending machine attendant.

Once inside the inner portion of the facility, Lee found a map on the wall that showed them the location of the MRI suites, down past a row of X-ray machine rooms and right before a CAT scan area.

The map also indicated the small waiting room for the MRI center, along with two dressing rooms adjacent to it.

Both men could feel the weight of the pistols under their shirts, but they'd decided they'd do this with knives, catching their unsuspecting target outside the MRI scanning room. Each man carried a fixed blade mounted to his belt under his coat.

Todd whispered to Lee just as they neared an area with a pair of nurses standing at a table and typing on laptops. "Spread out. Patients don't walk around together." Lee nodded, lagged back.

They passed a medical technician who gave them a nod without really looking, and then, when they were alone in a hallway on the way to the MRI suite, they passed shelves of storage, then walked by an elderly patient heading for the exit.

They entered a door that was marked Zone 2: MRI. There were computers, a desk, and a few chairs, and the men saw doors marked Dressing Room 1 and Dressing Room 2. No one was around at the moment, so each man pulled his knife, and after a quick look and nod between them, they yanked open the two doors.

Both rooms were empty. Lee came to Todd, and they looked in the little room he'd just entered. Stacks of gowns in plastic bags, socks with grippers on the bottom, and hair nets lay on shelves next to a row of four lockers. Three of the lockers had keys in the locks with strings hanging on them, but the fourth locker had no key. The men rushed over to the only other door in the room, then read the sign there.

Zone 3: Control Room. There were various caution signs on the wall, but the Voorhies boys were too amped up to read them. They knew MRIs could be dangerous, but they'd gotten back here quickly, and they figured they'd either kill Hightower before the procedure started, or else they'd put a knife to the neck of the technician and get them to turn the machine off so they could stab Hightower where he lay, vulnerable inside the big cylinder.

Todd started to reach for the door, but then he saw that he needed a key card to get in.

"Fuck," he whispered. Quickly he began looking around the desk, opening drawers.

He found a white key card in one of the drawers, but it didn't work on the lock. While he went back to continue looking, his brother stepped to the door out of the room, then pulled his Smith and Wesson pistol from under his coat. Cracking the door open, he looked out, saw a nurse alone at a computer monitor on a rolling stand. She wore several ID badges and cards on a lanyard around her neck.

She didn't see him, but he hid the pistol behind his back and called to her. "Ma'am... the technician told me to change, but I can't get my locker open." He laughed a little. "I think it's stuck."

The woman had a slightly confused look on her face, but she helpfully came to the door; he held it open for her, and she moved a few steps in before noticing Todd, still behind the desk.

She said, "You can't be back there, sir." It seemed to occur to her, at just this time, that there was no reason two patients would be back here at the same time, so she began to turn back to the man behind her, but before she did so, Lee Voorhies slammed the butt of his pistol into the back of her head.

She crumpled to the ground, and then he tore the lanyard off her neck.

FORTY-TWO

Todd rushed around the corner, flipped a lock on the door out to the hallway of the MRI suite, then converged with his brother at the Zone 3 door.

One after another, Lee hurriedly tried the key cards; none worked, so then he began scanning the badges, hoping one of them had been coded to let the woman into the MRI control room.

The third badge did the trick. A red light to the left of the door turned green right above the keypad and sensor, and Todd pulled the door open.

The room had an operator's control desk, with a large window in front of it, and above it was an illuminated sign that he didn't bother to read.

To the right of the control desk, directly in front of the two brothers at the Zone 3 door, was another door that was marked Danger—Zone 4: Scan Room.

Both men ducked down so they couldn't be seen through the window, but before they did, they'd looked inside and saw their target being moved, legs first, into the machine by the technician, who operated a lever on the side of the scanner that controlled the patient table motor.

Behind her was a computer, and soft fluorescent lights glowed from the ceiling above her.

Todd leaned over to Lee. "When she opens the door to come back in here, you hold your gun on her, and I'll go in and slit his throat."

Lee nodded. "I like it."

. . .

Zack wasn't claustrophobic, but he didn't love being shoved into a little metal tube.

Over his career he'd probably had close to a dozen MRIs, either at the VA, at some far-flung military base, or, more recently, at private facilities like this when he worked for the CIA.

The good news about today, and the MRI he'd received a month and half earlier at Ramstein, was he'd gone in feetfirst, and his head and much of his torso didn't have to go into the tube for the procedure. It was his leg that was being imaged, after all, so at least he'd not have his head in there for the half hour to forty-five minutes it would take for the scan.

Zack had made some small talk with the attractive technician, and then she'd given him headphones to wear, because MRI machines are notoriously loud when they're scanning. She asked him what type of music he liked, he'd told her whatever her favorite was, was *his* new favorite, and she rolled her eyes playfully before telling him how much she loved Taylor Swift.

Zack had heard the name; he had a feeling he should have said Chris Stapleton or somebody more to his taste, but he just smiled while she turned on some sugary pop music.

She headed out the door back to the control room; he couldn't see her because he was on his back, facing up, staring at a fluorescent light and the outside rim of the scanner, with a red emergency button on it.

He knew he'd be hearing the technician's voice over the music in a few seconds, letting him know the procedure was about to begin. He indulgently listened to Taylor Swift but wasn't paying close attention; he was mostly thinking about Stacy, or Andie, and how much he was going to miss stopping by her bakery for coffee in the mornings.

It had been a minute; Taylor was singing something about being young and reckless, Zack couldn't really relate so much to the young part, but the tune was catchy nonetheless. Then, while focusing on the fluorescent lighting above him, he saw something suddenly flash by, right over his face, missing it by not more than a foot.

The item flew towards the machine, an impossibly loud bang followed, and Zack quickly threw off his headphones.

Sitting up, he looked down and saw a fixed-blade knife stuck to the inside wall of the MRI machine, right above his knee. A wooden hilt had shattered and bits of it lay across Zack's legs.

And then he saw the blood.

Blood grew on his gown, six inches above his left knee. The wound there didn't even hurt yet, but he knew the pain would come soon enough.

He looked at the knife and saw it was the kind often used for hunting or even self-defense, and *not* some piece of medical equipment.

Quickly he struggled to shimmy the lower portion of his body out of the machine. A gunshot cracked behind him right as he rolled off the table and down to the floor to the far side of the patient table, and only then did he truly understand he was under attack.

There was only the one shot, and just as he chanced a look over the table to see where his attack was coming from, he saw a black semiautomatic pistol fly across the room, slam into the side of the MRI tube, then bounce around the inside, like a wild bird in a cage, fighting to get out.

After a few loud strikes the polymer grip of the weapon shattered, the magazine exploded, and cartridges bounced all around, whipping this way and that.

Zack went flat on the floor now, still unsure how badly he'd been hurt, feeling only the effects of fresh adrenaline.

Chancing another quick look back over the table, he saw the technician in the operator's window; she was being held at gunpoint by a man with a surgical mask, and the man stared at him through the operator's window from inside the control room.

A second man stood at the open door; he was apparently the one who'd lost both his gun and his knife in the last few seconds. Now he screamed at the woman to turn the magnet off.

Apparently Zack knew something this would-be assassin did not. An MRI machine's magnet could not be turned on and off with a press of a button. It remained on—Zack had noticed numerous warning signs to this effect in the control room—but apparently the idiots trying to kill him right now weren't big readers.

The man who held a gun to the technician now shouted, "Turn it off!" over the PA system that broadcast into the room. Zack looked at the machine, saw the red emergency button close to where he crouched, but he knew the button just stopped the scan; it didn't remove the magnetic charge from the massive device.

"You can't turn it off!" the woman shouted back at the man holding the gun to her head.

She tried explaining to the man that MRI machines' magnetic fields are always generating, and this particular machine was a powerful 3 Tesla model, so any magnetic metal in the room, even at the open door, would come sailing towards the scanner at high speed.

Zack knew that the room he was in now was encased in copper shielding, and the window itself contained a fine copper screen, and the glass would be more than thick enough to stop any bullets fired from the men's pistols.

There were metal tools, instruments, and other items here in this room, but they were all made of material that would not be attracted to the magnet.

The open door with the unarmed man at it was twenty-five feet from him; he began running for it, immediately felt the sting of a long cut on his leg, felt blood running down his shin, but he just ran faster, his blue gown flailing with the motion.

The man at the door held it open, but when he saw the man nearing him, he shut it.

An open toolbox sat on a table next to a computer monitor. Zack assumed the tools were made of titanium or some other non-ferromagnetic metal, and he grabbed a wrench from the box, kicked open the door from the inside using the emergency handle, then threw the instrument overhanded, hitting the unarmed baldheaded man with the mask in the chin at ten feet.

The man fell back into the room by the door to Zone 2.

The armed man by the control booth spun in Zack's direction and aimed at him, but Zack made it back into the door of the scan room before the man holding the tech could get a shot off.

Over the speakers in the scan room, Zack heard the man with the gun shout at him again. "Come out, or I shoot this bitch!"

Zack chose another weapon. It was a long screwdriver, and again, it was titanium, so it was not pulled into the machine like the knife or the gun. He turned and ran back towards the MRI machine. He said, "Unless your bosses are paying you to shoot an MRI technician, you aren't going to achieve anything by killing her. You're going to have to come in here."

"I'll fucking do it! I'll—"

"I don't even know her, asshole."

Zack used the screwdriver to try to pry the knife off the MRI scanner, but it wouldn't budge. Giving up, he turned to head back to the door, and he saw a trail of bloody footprints.

Shit.

He looked through the window and saw the armed man hit the technician over the head with his pistol.

Tossing the gun on the control panel table, he turned away for a moment, and when he turned back, the masked attacker himself held a titanium hammer in his hand.

His comrade had stood back up; his face was bloody where Zack had hit it, but he wasn't down for the count.

He armed himself with the titanium wrench Zack had thrown at him, and the two men rushed to the door.

Their plan, Zack realized, was to burst in, two on one, and try to beat him to death.

A blaring siren went off in the medical center now; Zack didn't know if the woman was still conscious on the floor and had reached a button, or if just the noise of the shooting and the screaming fight in the MRI suite had caused someone else to raise the alarm, but Zack ran towards the door himself, meeting the attackers just after they came in.

The first man was wearing thick rubber snow boots, and he slipped on Zack's blood and fell onto his back, and Zack leapt over him, swinging at the uninjured man carrying the hammer. Blows were exchanged; both men managed to control the weapons in the other man's hands, but they butted heads, sent knees toward groins, threw shoulders into each other's chests right there in the doorway.

It was an ugly, bloody brawl between Zack and this skinhead with tattoos on his neck. Zack got the man's medical mask pushed up over his eyes for a moment, then knocked him down to the floor, back over the threshold and into the scan room.

Once inside the copper protective barrier of the walls, the attacker climbed to his feet but then grabbed at his own neck, dropping his weapon as he did so. Zack didn't understand what was happening at first, but his opponent stopped fighting him and began clutching his throat.

Soon the big man began backpedaling towards the MRI machine. His own feet slipped in Zack's blood, he stumbled backwards faster, and only when the man fell back on the patient table and slid into the scanner did Zack realize the man must have had some sort of a large chain around his neck.

He was effectively being strangled inside the 3 Tesla scanner.

Zack had no metal on him at all, however, so he quickly left the room, returned to the control room, and saw the technician pulling herself back to her feet.

He shouted to her. "What's the biggest piece of magnetic metal in this room?"

Her eyes widened, but she understood. She pointed to a single oxygen tank in the far corner from the door to Zone 4. Zack ran to it, looked through the operator's window, and saw that the man with the chain had managed to break free before he was strangled, and the one who'd been on the floor was now back on his feet, rushing to help the other man.

Zack hefted the heavy steel tank and ran towards the open door, and before he passed the threshold, he threw it up and into the air.

The tank dropped to the floor but immediately began skidding through the scan room, faster and faster and faster, towards the two men in front of the cylindrical Tesla magnet. The tank then flew through the air, slammed into the patient table, and hit both men on its way towards the bore of the machine.

The tank struck one of the men in the face hard enough to kill him instantly, and Zack grabbed the gun off the control table, moved back to the door, and fired a single round into the scan room before the pistol was wrenched from his hand.

Looking again through the safety of the operator's window, he saw both men dead, blood everywhere inside the scan room.

He knew that some of it was his, because even here in the control room he'd smeared the floor red.

The technician was back on her feet, but Zack turned away from her and raced back into the dressing room. He made it to his locker; the key was somewhere in the control room but he just grabbed the top of the wooden door and pulled with all his might.

The door snapped open easily, and he retrieved his clothes.

The technician entered, bringing him a pressure bandage and a roll of tape.

He spent twenty seconds bandaging himself, and then he looked up at her. "You have a side door out of here?"

"No. Just the one entrance."

"Look. I kind of need to *not* be stopped by the police right now."

She took one look at him, gave him a curt nod, then said, "Put your clothes on, wait in here one minute, then just go. I won't point you out to security."

"Thanks," he said, and he put his injured leg into the leg of his jeans with a wince.

Minutes later Zack calmly unlocked his truck and climbed in. Police were everywhere, so he took a chance that if there were more attackers around watching for him, they wouldn't act at least until he got out of the parking lot.

He drove to a nearby convenience store, climbed out of his vehicle, then dropped down to look under it. Using the light of his iPhone, he found the tracker on his car in under thirty seconds. He removed the magnetized device, walked over to a Land Rover at the gas pump, saw that the owner was inside the store, and slapped the tracker on the rear of the vehicle.

Zack was back on the road in his own truck in under a minute, and seconds after that, his phone rang.

He saw that it was Hanley, and he answered quickly. "If you're calling to tell me I'm in danger, then you're too late. I just got hit. Two enemy down. I'm clear. A little banged up but mobile."

"Jesus Christ," Hanley exclaimed. "Were these guys Gauntlet, you think?"

"Negative. Looked like a couple of skinheads. Not as professional as the

Gauntlet Group goons we've run into. Tatted necks. Muscles, though they didn't really have the brains to know how to use them."

"If they're nationalist dudes, then they're probably working with Lancer. They're dead?"

"Somebody's gonna have to shovel them into body bags."

"Any way law enforcement can link you to what happened?"

"For sure. I was getting my MRI. My name, insurance, everything. I wasn't using Lyle Hart; I was still Zack."

Hanley said, "I'll talk to Lacy. We can make that part go away; my concern is Lancer. He's probably still out there. If he just sent a couple of flunkies after you, and didn't do the op himself, then I expect he had some other play in mind."

"Yeah, I just cleared a tracker they put on my truck, so they won't be able to . . ."

Zack stopped talking, so Hanley said, "Night Train?"

A wave of panic washed across Zack. He'd been so hyped up on adrenaline that he hadn't picked it up, but Hanley was absolutely right. Lancer was out here, in Boulder; he'd tracked him to the imaging center, and he knew where he'd been right before the imaging center.

The bakery.

Andie's bakery.

Court Gentry's voice came over the line now. "Hey, man, I'm en route to Boulder. There was a breach of personal information about you and me out of CIA yesterday. I'll be there in three hours."

Zack still did not speak.

"Hey, brother? You with me?"

Zack's meaty hands clutched the steering wheel so hard he thought he might rip it off.

Finally, Court said, "Hey. It's okay. I just told Matt about your little girl out there. He knows. If she's in some kind of trouble, we're going to—"

Hightower finally responded, his voice even more intense than usual. "Her name is Andrea Delaney. Get Gumdrop working on this. Right now, she's supposed to be at Eldora Mountain snowboarding. I don't know who took her there. She's fifteen, doubt she's driving. I don't know what she'd be wearing or where she'd go when she got there."

Jill Mori came on the line; her voice was all business. "Parents' names? We can try to track phones."

Zack hesitated. He wasn't supposed to know this information himself, and he sure as hell wasn't supposed to blab it to anyone else. If she was *not* in danger, this could screw up her world over here.

But then he thought about Lancer, about the guys he'd just dealt with in the MRI center, and he relented. "Father is Peter Delaney. He's deputy fire chief out here. Mom is Tiff"—he caught himself—"*Jennifer* Delaney. I'm heading to my apartment now to get some gear. Help me find Andie before they do."

Court said, "I'm kitted up with guns, ammo, and body armor. Got equipment for you, too."

Hanley said, "Gumdrop will be in touch."

Zack hung up. He was on the highway heading back to his apartment; the snow was picking up.

Just like Andie had said it would.

A minute later, his phone rang. It wasn't his Signal app, just his cell service, and the number didn't show up on the screen, but he decided he'd better answer it.

Nervously, he tapped a button on his steering wheel and said, "Yeah?"

An unfamiliar voice came over the line. "Dude . . . I've been listening to the police scanner. Some crazy shit! It sounds like you left a fucking mess back there, didn't you?"

"Who is this?"

"This could have been so simple. Not involve anybody but you. But I know your type, Hightower, and I had a funny feeling you were going to weasel your way out of that somehow. You kill those guys in your underwear? That's impressive, but it wasn't exactly unexpected."

Hightower wasn't sure, but he took a chance. "This is Kincaid, isn't it?"

"Is it?" the man replied, but Zack heard something in the voice that told him he was right.

Zack said, "I always heard you were a piece of shit. You didn't have the balls to come at me yourself? Why is that not a surprise?"

He pulled his pistol from his now-open lockbox, held with his free hand between his knees as he drove. It felt comfortable. Soothing, somehow.

He squeezed the grip tightly, wishing he was aiming in on Lancer's brainpan right now.

Lancer said, "Honestly, I would have liked to be there myself, but I was a little busy. I was so sure those two dipshits were going to make a mess of things at the clinic that I was already on plan B, and I couldn't be there for the fireworks."

Zack was doing sixty miles an hour in the heavy snow. He said nothing.

Kincaid himself paused a moment, then said, "My plan B, if you haven't guessed, was to grab your kid."

A wash of panic coursed through Zack Hightower. The wipers swept snow and ice and water off the windshield in front of him; he blinked once, twice, said nothing.

"C'mon, fucker!" Lancer shouted. "Say it. Say, 'What kid?' I fucking dare you."

Zack wasn't going to give this man what he wanted. Right now, all he wanted to do was figure out where Andie was. Desperately, he tried to think of words to say that could elicit this.

After a moment, Kincaid said, "Does she know? Does she know you're the dude who gave her up? I guess I could ask her."

"If you fucking touch her, I'll—"

"Don't pretend to give a shit now, Hightower. If you cared about her back then, we wouldn't be here, would we?"

"You kidnapped her?"

"I did."

"Let me talk to her."

"You don't make the rules, asshole."

"What do you want?"

"I want to trade."

"Me for her? You got it. Me, *unarmed*, for her, *unhurt*. Let's do it right now." Zack was serious. He would toss his weapons and meet up with Lancer to save Andie.

But Lancer had other plans. He said, "Nope. That's not the trade I want."

"What . . . what then?"

"You have until five p.m. to get the Gray Man here. I imagine he's across the country. I don't give a shit. Feed him a story, get him on the way. You give him to me, I give you Andrea. If I even smell a hint of the cops in that time, and believe me, I know the smell of cops, that kid will die, and I'll be gone."

"Wait," Zack said. "Hang on. Just . . . just hold on a second. How am I supposed—"

"My employers know everything, Zack. We know Courtland Gentry and you and Matthew Hanley are working together. I know you can get Gentry here. Tell him whatever you want. I'll give you a location, you tell him it's you he'll meet there. He shows up, the girl walks free. It's her only fucking chance, man."

Zack's mind raced. The stinging in his leg was forgotten. "Look . . . what about me? You sent those guys after me at the clinic. Obviously, your bosses want me, just the same as—"

"It's not what *they* want that matters. It's what *I* want. You, Hightower, you don't mean shit to me. Court Gentry is the man who put me in prison in Cuba, and he's gonna pay, or your kid's gonna pay."

It was quiet between them, Zack trying to think of some other way to bargain. Then Kincaid said, "You turned your back on that girl a long time ago, bro. Don't do it again."

"Wait."

"I'll wait. I'll wait five hours, twenty-eight minutes. Get Gentry to Boulder, I'll call you back at five p.m. and give you a location. It will be in the mountains, within thirty-minutes' drive time of the airport.

"If Gentry shows up, you and your girl walk away from this."

Scott Kincaid ended the call.

Hightower tried to control his emotions, to come up with some kind of a plan.

He didn't have much, but after a few seconds, he did have *something*.

He did not know where they'd take Andie, but at least he knew where they grabbed her from. He put Eldora Mountain into his navigation system and saw he was forty minutes out if he drove the speed limit.

He'd make it in a half hour despite the snow, he told himself, and he called Hanley back.

FORTY-THREE

Among Scott Kincaid's many peccadilloes, lying was hardly one of the most severe, but he had just told Zack Hightower an outright lie.

At this moment he did *not* have Andie Delaney. He had his eyes on her, but they were through binoculars, and she was several hundred yards away, high above him on the ledge of a snowy mountain.

No, he didn't have her, but she'd be down here soon enough, one way or another, and he was determined to get her when she came to him.

His men—Bennett, Maybus, and Winter—had followed her from the bakery at ten thirty, when her mother picked her up, all the way to Eldora Mountain, twenty minutes west. Here her mom had left her with her snowboard and her gear, she'd met up with some other kids, and they immediately headed for the Corona chairlift.

Andie wore a distinctive yellow coat with a red helmet and black pants with white kneepads, making her easy to spot from a distance. Winter and Maybus stayed down at the base while Bennett followed her up, watched her separate from her friends and then go solo to the far-right side of West Ridge, a double-black-diamond slope that ran along and then through a thick wood of pine trees.

Winter had a set of binoculars in the Bronco, and he watched her descend. She wiped out a couple of times; he saw her spend a couple of minutes halfway down recovering from a particularly bad spill, but she seemed determined, and eventually she got back on her board and continued on.

Scott Kincaid had called with the news about the Voorhies brothers, and then he arrived alone in the Wagoneer a few minutes later. He kept Bennett at the top of the hill but sent Winter and Maybus up the mountainside through a foot trail in the trees, told them to snatch the girl when she was alone on the slopes, put a gun in her ribs, and tell her they'd shoot her if they all didn't walk down through the thick woods together.

Scott Kincaid remained in the Jeep Wagoneer. Just as he doubted his men would get Hightower in the MRI center, he also doubted his men trudging up the mountain would capture the girl. It was possible, of course, but if she came back down with a story of dangerous men in camouflage on the hill, he'd be here to throw her in the SUV at gunpoint before she alerted the authorities.

Andie Delaney took a deep breath, looked through the heavy snowfall, down the double-black-diamond course in front of her, and prepared herself for another run.

There was almost no one on the right side of West Ridge right now; even her friends had left her for some easier slopes. The freezing rain hardening under the fresh snow here had made this run almost impossible, but Andie loved a good challenge.

Her backside and right arm still ached from her last run, but she was indomitable, and she was determined to give it another go.

She'd started well on the first run of the day but acknowledged now that she had grown a little overconfident in the top half, and when she hit the full shade between two banks of trees, she'd shifted her weight wrong on her board, lost her balance, and tumbled off, slammed chest first into hard-packed snow.

Another wipeout just forty yards down the slope, still in the trees, just pissed her off; she'd sat there on her butt, her board still on her feet out in front of her, for nearly a minute, slapping the hard-packed snow in frustration with a gloved hand.

She told herself to shake it off, just like her dad always told her to do, and finally she did, recovered from a brief bout of doubt and self-pity, then got back up and finished the run beautifully.

Now her goal was to do the whole thing without landing on her chest or on her ass. She took a couple more slow breaths, closed her eyes to mentally visualize the toughest part of the entire course, and then dropped her snowboard over the ledge and took off.

Just like the first run, the top half felt great. Even more snow had fallen in the thirty minutes since her last try; she had the friction she needed on the turns, even when she felt rock and ice below the packed precipitation.

She made it down to the chutes between the trees; the gray day and heavy snow building on her goggles made the visibility poor, but she knew the line, and she stuck to it.

Her speed was good, her knees and low back working as shock absorbers, her mind still visualizing what was just ahead.

The pines around her were heavy with fresh snow; this track of the slope felt narrower than it had when she shot by a half hour earlier, but she concentrated on the icy patch just ahead, the area that had been her undoing on her first run.

Squinting through her goggles, she was surprised to see a pair of men in camouflage, directly ahead, standing between trees. It was weird to be dressed for hunting here on Eldora; she'd been coming here since she was four and couldn't remember ever seeing anyone halfway up the slope who wasn't a skier, a snowboarder, or a member of the ski patrol, and the ski patrol always wore easily identifiable jackets.

These men in front of her were right at the icy patch; they held their hands out like they wanted her to stop, and she thought they must have been with Eldora Mountain Resort, trying to stop her for her own safety.

This was dumb of them, she was fine, but she slowed up anyway.

She came to a stop just ten feet away from the men, immediately knelt and flipped the levers on the bindings holding her boots onto the board. She kicked out, hefted the big board, and leaned against it.

"Hi," she said.

One of the men spoke to her, "You're the Delaney kid?"

Her guard went up instantly. "Who are you?"

She noticed that these guys didn't have any skis, and there was no tracked vehicle in sight. They must have walked up through the trees all the way from the parking lot, and she couldn't understand why.

The other man said, "We're friends of your dad. He wanted us to come get you. There's been an emergency. We'll explain in the car."

She cocked her head. "How come I don't know you?"

"We work with him. Don't think we've met."

She looked back and forth between the two men. "What . . . what emergency?"

"Nothing to worry about. Look, we have to hurry."

She took off her left mitten and reached into her jacket, pulling out her cell. This was a bluff; she was never able to get cell service on the mountain unless she was at the very top or the very bottom, but she wanted to see how these guys would react, because she suspected they were full of shit. She said, "I'm gonna call him and—"

"He's in the hospital," the guy on the left blurted out. "We have to take you to—"

"What hospital?"

The two men glanced at each other; now she was *sure* they were full of shit.

"What's my first name?"

"Your name? It's Andrea," one said.

"Yeah, right." Everyone called her Andie.

Immediately, she realized she'd made a mistake. She'd proved the men weren't who they said they were, but that only forced their hand in this.

They had no choice now but to come after her.

The closest of the two reached into his coat, and she just saw the butt of a pistol when she swung her snowboard at them. They both lurched back, and the man with the gun slipped on the ice and fell back into the snow, hitting his head in the process.

Andie used the momentum of swinging the board to thrust it out in front of her; she let go and it hit the snow about ten feet down, just at the far edge of the icy patch. She ducked under the standing man's arms as she ran for it, then she leapt into the air.

Her boots landed perfectly in the bindings; with a pair of loud clicks they snapped tight to the board, and she took off, streaking towards heavier pines and thicker snow below.

As the two men behind her struggled to find their footing, she weaved through trees, heading down the mountain. They wouldn't catch her in a million years, this she knew with certainty, and once she made it to the base of the mountain, she'd alert the ski patrol that a couple of creeps in the trees had just tried to accost her.

But how the hell did they know her name?

Five minutes later, she ran through the parking lot, her phone in one hand and her board in the other. She hadn't seen anyone with the resort standing nearby, so she concentrated on trying to get bars on her phone.

She'd been so deep in concentration doing this that she missed the Jeep Wagoneer that was following just behind.

Finally, she had a signal. She thought of calling her mom, then her dad, but then she landed on calling 911, because she knew her dad was twenty-five miles away at work and her mom wasn't supposed to pick her up till five, and she'd said something about taking her little sister for a haircut and then going by Costco.

Just as Andie started to dial 911, she sensed motion right in front of her, and then she felt an arm wrap around her neck and she was lifted into the air.

The cell phone fell to the ground; someone knocked her big board from her hands and then dragged her backwards, onto her heels. She tried kicking and screaming, but a gloved hand went over her mouth, and she bit down hard but caught nothing but quilted insulated fabric between her teeth.

Another set of hands lifted her legs and she was thrown into the backseat of an SUV; the vehicle launched forward soon after, and a big man pushed her down to the floorboard, his feet on top of her.

The man behind the wheel spoke for the first time, shouting over the young girl's screams. "Calm down! Nobody's going to hurt you!" He then chuckled. "Although my associates up on the mountain would probably like to." She looked up and saw that the man looking down at her had a beard, like the others.

"Her phone?" the man behind the wheel asked.

"It's in the parking lot."

"Check her for anything else."

The man rummaged his hands through her coat and pants pockets, unzipping and unsnapping to do so. She was too terrified to scream. As he pulled out items, he announced them. "Wallet. Ski pass. Lip balm. Sunscreen. That's about it."

"Toss it all out the window."

The SUV made it out onto the highway, she could tell by the speed, but she had no idea what direction they were traveling.

From the front seat the driver said, "We're going to go somewhere and get you warmed up. Then you'll sit there and wait. We don't want you. But I need you in order to get the guy I'm after."

Her voice cracked as she spoke up from the floorboard. "My . . . my dad?"

The man laughed a little. Started to say something, then stopped himself. Finally, he said, "No . . . somebody else."

"Who?"

"Just shut up and lie there."

Andie Delaney did as she was told.

Thirty minutes later, the vehicle stopped; Andie was pulled out by the two men and taken into a small cabin. She didn't recognize this place but knew there were vacation cottages all around Boulder available for rent, so she could be anywhere.

There were no other cabins around, however, so she wondered if she might be in some lesser-known, lesser-traveled area.

Each minute that this had been going on, she'd found herself less afraid and more pissed off. She had no idea who these guys were, what or who they wanted, but she told herself she needed to escape.

She was put in a bedroom by the two men she'd first encountered on the mountain. They'd arrived in a Bronco at the same time she did with the other pair, making a total of four different men here at the cabin, all involved in her kidnapping. The guy who fell on the ice had a bruise on his temple, and the guy who seemed to be in charge was thin with a bald head and what Andie thought were crazy eyes.

Two of the men pulled everything out of the bedroom while she stood there watching, her arms crossed in front of her. The bed, shelves, floor lamps, it was all removed and taken somewhere else, leaving her in an empty space. The windows were checked; they'd been painted shut and wouldn't open, and the tiny window in the bathroom was too small for anyone larger than a cat to pass through.

The one in charge showed up while they were doing this; he brought her a bottle of Sprite and a protein bar. When Andie didn't take them from him, he just dropped them on the floor in front of her.

"That's yours if you want it. Consider that lunch and dinner, depending on how long you're here. I'm not running a boardinghouse.

"In the meantime, you can sit in this room and stay fucking quiet. It's your job right now to not be any sort of an inconvenience to me, because I do not like to be inconvenienced when I'm working."

She looked around. "Working . . . ? This is your job?"

"As a matter of fact, yes, it is."

"Kidnapping kids . . . is . . . your . . . job?"

He smiled a wild smile. "Killing men is my job." He looked to the man who had been standing on her in the back of the SUV for the entire trip. "You searched her, right?"

"Yeah. I mean, she was on her back, so I might not have gotten to—"

The thin bald man sighed. "Okay, Andrea. Take off your coat, any outer layer of clothing. Your boots and socks, too. Keep on your pants and base layer."

She did as instructed, and the boss went through her pockets on his own.

"Who do you want to kill?" she asked as he did this.

"Somebody you don't know, honey. So don't stress about it."

"But I've seen your face. I've watched TV. I know what that means."

"You've watched TV?" He laughed, going through her belongings. "I don't care if you know who I am. The feds are going to know it was me, anyway." He looked up at her. "Not my first rodeo, if you know what I mean." She took off a boot, handed it over, and he began feeling around in it. "I'll be out of the U.S. before you get the chance to squawk to anybody about what happened to—"

He stopped talking and looked up at the girl, his crazy eyes widened.

"What?" she asked. She was genuinely confused.

"Yo, Bennett! Get your ass in here!"

The boss kept his hand inside Andie's boot until the man who'd searched her earlier returned to the room. "Yeah?"

Slowly, the boss took out the insole of the boot, threw it on the ground. He then took out the liner under the insole, ripping it clear of the boot.

Finally, he brought his hand out holding a small silver Apple AirTag.

He held it up to Andie, who had no idea that had been in her boot. "Who's going to come looking for you?"

"I . . . I . . . I don't know."

"Your dad? Your *real* dad?"

"I . . ." Confused by the wording of the question, she said nothing else.

The one called Bennett said, "We can be out of here, but it's going to take a—"

The boss cut him off. "Where are those other guys?"

"I've got two more; they'll be here in a half hour. They're good. They know the area. They're armed." He added, "And they want that five grand. They'll do whatever you need."

Kincaid handed the AirTag over to the man. "Take this a few miles down the road, then throw it in the trees. Get back here in twenty minutes, get the rifles out of the truck, and get ready. We might have company."

Bennett took the AirTag and ran out the door.

Andie started to cry now. "I swear to you, sir. I've never ever seen that—"

"I believe you. But that's not gonna save your daddy or your mommy if they come up that driveway looking for you."

"No!" she cried, and she charged at him, her fists pounding his chest. He shoved her off, down to the floor. The man with the bruise on his face entered the room, and the boss looked to him. "If she tries anything like that again, tie her and gag her."

The boss left the room without another word.

FORTY-FOUR

A half hour after Zack put in the coordinates for the ski resort, he was on the mountain, just minutes from the entrance.

He'd spoken to the team at Ghost Town twice in that time, and during their last conversation, ten minutes earlier, they told him they had looped Angela Lacy and Jim Pace at CIA into this because they had access to methods that Ghost Town did not.

The Signal line rang again. It was Court; he told Zack he would be flying into Boulder Municipal Airport. It was closer to where Andie was last seen, and there would be a vehicle waiting for him so he could meet with Zack wherever he was.

Zack instructed Court to make sure the vehicle was four-wheel drive—the roads were shit and getting worse—but he did not tell his friend that Lancer had demanded Court's neck in exchange for his daughter.

The conversation was brief; Zack was busy fighting the elements and concentrating on the road, and after Court hung up, the former Navy SEAL began winding his way up the mountain.

Just minutes later the Signal app chirped again; Zack answered it with the press of a button on his steering wheel.

"Yeah."

Hanley said, "Night Train, you've got everybody on conference here. Lacy, Gumdrop, Teddy, and myself. We've got intel for you."

"Give it to me."

Jill said, "The two dead men at the MRI center have been identified. Brothers, Lee and Todd Voorhies, out of Ogden, Utah. They are... *were*... members of a small white nationalist group. We ran car info on them; Todd owned a blue Jeep Wagoneer.

"From cameras around Boulder I accessed, I see a blue Jeep Wagoneer parked across the street from Cara's Bakehouse and in the lot of the MRI center at the same time you were at both places.

"I then have several images of what appears to be the same vehicle entering Eldora Mountain Resort. I see one person in the vehicle.

"But there is also an image from when it's leaving the ski slopes, and I see two figures. One in the front seat, one in the back. Both are large, presumably male, but with the snow and shadowing, I can't tell more than that."

Zack said, "That's probably going to be Lancer and an accomplice. A full-sized man in the backseat sounds like somebody controlling someone down on the floorboard."

Teddy spoke up now. "That's what I'm thinking. But it's not just the two dudes. One of the images Gumdrop got shows the Wagoneer parked next to a black Ford Bronco. Can't see inside either vehicle, but a man from Ogden named Carl Maybus owns the same make, model, and color vehicle. He's a known associate of Todd Voorhies, and a member of the same nationalist organization."

Zack said, "Okay, that's three enemy, minimum, in addition to the two DRTs at the clinic."

Gumdrop spoke up now. "What's DRT?"

"Dead right there," Hanley answered. "Don't worry about it," he immediately said. "Night Train, there's more."

Hightower said, "I only need to know where they went after they snatched her."

Angela Lacy spoke up now. "I tracked the cell phone of Andrea Delaney, and it is still showing at the resort. We've got to assume they tossed it when they took her."

Zack said, "Yeah, that's a dead end."

Lacy continued, "And I tracked credit cards of the brothers and Carl

Maybus, didn't get anything in the area, but then I ran a very wide net. Had a team here at Langley check the credit card usage of every name in the group, and then every known associate of Maybus, Lancer, and the Voorhies brothers. Some one hundred thirty individuals in all. Finally, a woman named April Winter came up. She's not in the nationalist movement currently, but her cousin is Ronald Winter, and he is in the group. He did two years in the pen in Idaho for armed robbery. Anyway, April's credit card was used about two hours ago to rent a vacation cabin online that's ten miles northeast of Eldora Mountain Resort." Lacy added, "She lives in Utah. Who rents a vacation home the same day they're going to use it?"

Zack almost shouted into the phone. "That's it! Get me the address!"

Hanley said, "I don't want to give you the address till Six gets there. You can't hit that place alone."

"I won't. I'm only armed with a pistol, and I've got a fresh knife wound to my already shot-up leg."

Teddy said, "Wait. You got stabbed? At the clinic?"

"Not a big deal. I can do what I need to do, but I won't be taking on four or more guys by myself. I'm not a fucking idiot. Give me the address."

Hanley relented. "Okay, Gumdrop will give it to you, but answer this. Did Lancer say why they were going to call you back in a few hours? If they're trying to swap you for the girl, why didn't they want to meet up right then?"

Zack shut his eyes a moment. Held in a sigh. He said, "They probably want time to fortify their location. They wouldn't have known about Andie till I went to the bakery this morning, and they probably thought they'd kill me without having to use her. They figure I've got a few tricks up my sleeve, so they're going to get that cabin ready for me."

Hanley said, "You are not making a trade with them, are we clear? There's no way they're just going to set her free after killing you; don't let your judgment be clouded by—"

Zack yelled into the phone now. "My judgment is fine! I'm going to the area, I'll stay out of sight, and I'll get a plan together for when Six arrives."

"Okay," Hanley said finally, and Lacy passed on the address.

. . .

Thirty-five minutes later, Zack's F-150 was virtually the only vehicle rolling along a snow-swept two-lane mountain road. It was two thirty in the afternoon now, three hours into the five-hour countdown, and he slowed a little, because instead of focusing on the road, he had turned his attention towards a winding, narrow, snow-covered drive on the left that disappeared up a steep slope into thick pines.

This was the address Angela Lacy had provided, and as he passed, Zack saw multiple fresh sets of tire tracks going up the drive.

He continued on the two-lane paved road for a couple of minutes, passing several other driveways, all, he assumed, leading to individual secluded cabins up on the same hillside. Finally, he slowed and pulled into a turnoff a couple of miles past where he suspected Lancer was keeping Andie, deciding that he would go back the other way and make one more pass by the target before stopping at a gas station three miles to the east.

But just moments after turning back in the other direction, he saw a vehicle approaching, its lights on in the already fading afternoon light. As he neared, he realized it was a white pickup, and quickly he noticed it had an orange stripe on the side and a light rack on the roof.

He passed the truck seconds later and saw an emblem on the side and the word "Fire," also in orange.

The vehicle rolled by at speed, but he got a quick glimpse of the driver, and he also noticed that the vehicle's emergency lights were not flashing.

Zack slowed, his heart pounding even more than it had been, and then he turned around in the road and began following the emergency vehicle, because somehow he had a feeling that he knew what was going on.

Soon the emergency vehicle pulled off the road onto a drive and parked, flipped on its hazard lights, and a man got out. Zack pulled straight in behind it and climbed out in time to see the driver as he stood outside his vehicle. He wore a heavy black coat, black pants, and black work boots, and he held his mobile phone as he moved up the driveway, looking at the device as he hiked up into the trees.

The man hadn't noticed Zack yet, and for a brief second, Zack thought about backing out and driving off, but he forced himself to stay. He was certain he was looking at Pete Delaney, Andie's dad, and he knew he needed to talk to him to see why he was here.

His voice cracked a little bit when he called out, just as the man in the firefighter's uniform and the heavy coat leaned forward and picked up something out of the snow.

"Sir?"

Delaney spun to him. Zack had seen pictures of the deputy chief of Boulder Fire and Rescue online, but he never expected to be standing face-to-face with him.

The man seemed agitated. He looked down at something in his hand, then back up at the man standing there. "Help you?"

Zack didn't know where to start. Telling the truth seemed like a terrible idea right now, but he didn't have any brilliant ruse in mind.

He held his hands out in a nonthreatening manner. He was about to speak, but then the man's eyes widened suddenly.

"Shit! You okay, fella?"

Zack tracked the man's eyes, looked down, and saw the blood on his left leg. It had made its way through the bandages, through his jeans, and it covered them from the knee down.

"It's . . . it's okay. It's nothing."

Pete walked over to him, momentarily sidetracked from his primary mission by the injured man in front of him.

"You're bleeding pretty good, there. What'd you do?"

Zack saw what was in the man's hand now. It was an Apple AirTag, and suddenly it all made perfect sense.

The men were just feet apart. Pete noticed Zack looking at the AirTag, and his helpful demeanor seemed to change, as if he sensed danger somehow.

He said, "You live here?"

Zack shook his head.

"What . . . do you want?"

"It's about Andie. Did she have that AirTag on her?"

The man looked down at it, then back up at the bearded man in front of him. Suddenly he pulled a radio off his belt.

Zack said, "Wait! Listen. You don't want to call anybody till I talk to you." He paused, "It's for her own good."

"What the fuck did you do to her?"

"Nothing. Swear to God. I'm here to help. But *somebody* has her, and you and me are going to have to work together to get her back."

"Fuck that." Delaney brought the radio to his mouth.

And then, more reflexively than anything else, Zack Hightower reached under his coat, pulled his pistol, and leveled it at the man.

The radio lowered. Delaney stared at the gun. "What's going on?"

Zack said, "Brother, I know it's gonna be a hard sell for me convincing you of this . . . but I'm on your side here. I just need to talk to you a second."

Snow fell all around them. Delaney said nothing. Finally, Zack said, "Sit in my truck with me. I'm going to explain everything and then you'll understand what's going on."

"Talk, then. Right here, because I'm not getting in your fucking truck."

"Yeah . . . okay. Well . . . Andie has been kidnapped by some people who will know immediately if you report it. They're professionals, they'll be listening to all the emergency frequencies. If you get on that radio, or call someone in the police and it gets out over traffic, then they will move her somewhere we can't find her. Or they will . . . they will do something worse."

"What do they want with her?"

"It's . . . it's nothing she's done. It's—"

"Of course it's nothing she's done!" Delaney snapped. "She's fifteen, what could she have done?"

"It's . . . I guess the truth is . . . it's something *I've* done."

A momentary look of utter confusion on Pete Delaney's face melted away, slowly but obviously to Zack. He had a feeling he knew some version of what the man was about to say before he even said it.

Delaney said, "Jen swore this day would never come."

Zack nodded slowly.

"You're him, aren't you? You're . . . the guy Jen was married to before. The CIA guy."

Hightower nodded again now. He had no idea what Tiffany had or had not told her second husband, but it didn't surprise him at all that she'd told him everything.

"And you're pointing a gun at me now?" Delaney said.

Zack lowered it immediately. "Andie's life depends on you taking a beat and listening to me. I'm just trying to do what's right."

"Okay." Delaney put the radio back on his belt. "Talk."

Zack holstered his weapon, then moved to the front of Delaney's emergency vehicle and leaned against it, taking weight off his injured leg. "Tiffany and Stacy. Jennifer and Andrea. Their names got out."

"Fuck. *Fuck!*" Delaney stomped the snow-covered ground. "To *who?*"

"An enemy. A dangerous enemy. I can't tell you any more than that."

"*Your* enemy, you mean."

"Well . . . I guess he's yours now, too."

"So . . . why is anyone after *my* daughter?"

"I . . . It's complicated."

"Well, why don't you try simplifying it for me?"

"Their mission is to get to me. We've tracked them to a cabin about a mile back to the east. She's there, I'm sure of it, and I've got assets inbound that are going to help me take care of this situation."

"Assets inbound? The fuck are you talking about?" Before Zack could answer, Delaney said, "How did they even find her?"

Zack looked up at the snow falling all around them. Said, "That's, unfortunately, on me. I found out what happened to Tiffany and Stacy. Their new names, where they were living. I found out and I came here, not to see my ex-wife but to see . . . I went to Cara's. I got tracked by the opposition. From that they must have figured out that—"

"You motherfucker," Delaney said, balling his fists and moving closer. "I'm going to beat the shit out of you."

Pete was big, but not bigger than Zack. And Pete looked like he could handle himself, but Zack knew, even with the knife wound to his leg, the deputy fire chief was not going to take him down in hand-to-hand combat.

But he understood the man's sentiment. He said, "I get it. But can you do that *after* we get your daughter back?"

Delaney stopped his advance. He seemed to think it over a moment. He said, "And . . . if I pull out my radio or my phone to call the police, you're saying . . . they'll kill her?"

"The guy who has her. His name is Scott Kincaid. He's an assassin. A good one. And an absolutely ruthless one. He's got at least two other men with him. Their names are Maybus and Winter. I don't know much about them. We also think there might be more.

"Kincaid wants my neck, and the neck of an associate of mine, an associate who is on the way here right now. I promise you that if I thought for one second that if we drove up to that cabin and traded ourselves for her that she would walk away, we would both do it, but that's not how this kind of thing works."

Delaney gave Zack a long, hard look. "You know how this kind of thing works?"

Zack sighed; steam poured from his mouth. "Intimately, I'm afraid." He brightened a little. "But Kincaid doesn't know that we know where he is, and that's to our advantage. When my friend gets here, we're going to go up there and we're going to get Andie out."

"How are you going to do that?"

"You might not want to know."

Delaney stared at him a long moment. "Oh, I most definitely *do* want to know."

"My friend and I are going to kill the people holding her."

Delaney put his hands on his head. Turned and walked away a few steps. It was a lot to take in, Zack understood.

He turned back to Zack. "Can you show me some kind of ID that says you're CIA? Something so I know you're not just bullshitting me right now?"

Zack shook his head. "My real name is Zack Hightower. I can show you ID that says my name is something other than Zack Hightower, so that's not going to help." After a second, he said, "The killings at the MRI center?"

Pete cocked his head. Of course he would be aware of the double homicide just hours earlier. "What about them?"

"That was Kincaid's plan A. It didn't work. I killed the two men who came after me this morning. Andie . . . she is plan B."

"Christ." He did not move.

Finally, Zack said, "I can't be standing out next to this road any longer. I saw a driveway a little closer to their cabin. Maybe there's another cabin up there, seven or eight hundred yards to the west of where Andie is. I saw no tire tracks in the snow, so I think it's abandoned. Maybe we can go there to stage for this."

Delaney said, "Jennifer told me what you did. How you did some mission you couldn't tell her about, but then Al Qaeda found out about you. How you saved her and Andie down in San Diego. Killed a bunch of terrorists."

Zack said, "Just three."

Delaney continued staring Zack down. "Just tell me that you can do it again."

"I can. With help, I definitely can."

Delaney nodded, then moved towards his vehicle, but Zack said, "Hey, what do you carry in this truck?"

"Just first aid, rescue equipment, my turnout gear, stuff like that."

"What's turnout gear?"

"Fireproof jacket, boots, stuff I need to wear to respond to a fire."

Zack thought a moment. "You have a tank? A mask? That kind of thing?"

"Of course. Two of each. Why?"

"Just trying to figure out a plan. What about weapons?"

"Not unless you count bear spray."

Zack nodded slowly. "I've got some in my truck, too."

Delaney was confused. "You don't have any other weapons?"

"I have a pistol, and my friend is bringing more. I'm just thinking things through. Kincaid is going to be taking measures. We might have to get creative here." Zack began to climb into his truck, and then he pointed at Delaney. "Listen, I promise you . . . we can fix this, but the second Kincaid and his people hear that their location has been discovered, it's over."

"You said that already," Delaney responded angrily. "I'm not going to communicate this to anybody."

The two men climbed into their vehicles, and Pete Delaney followed Zack Hightower back in the direction of the cabin holding his daughter.

FORTY-FIVE

Zack and Pete commandeered a small dusty rental cabin, just under one quarter mile west and on the same heavily wooded hillside as the one Kincaid held. From Google Maps, Zack could see that there was only one more cabin in the woods between the two structures, and he had no idea if it was inhabited or not.

To be safe, the two men drove to the cabin they commandeered with their lights off, and they did not use the electricity inside, in case Kincaid sent out a patrol to check the woods or the neighboring dwellings.

Zack called Court and directed him to take a different route to the target than he had. It was shorter, shaving off a little time, but it also meant twenty minutes of difficult driving, navigating down a steep decline and three-foot boulders covered in ice.

It was just past four p.m. when a black Jeep Wrangler turned onto a small utility road, wound its way up and up a hill, and then through thicker and thicker trees and deeper and deeper snow.

Sunset would officially come at four thirty, but gray skies and consistent snowfall, along with the higher mountain peaks all around, made it effectively dark, so the headlights of the Wrangler bounced across the foliage and the precipitation as the vehicle picked its way through.

Court arrived before dusk, climbed out of the Jeep, and then grabbed a pair of thick duffel bags, heaving them out of the backseat. He thought he was going straight into the cabin, but Zack met him outside on the front porch.

"Delaney's inside. I wanted to talk in private first," Zack said.

Court dropped the bags as snow fell in fat flakes in the darkening light off the porch. He said, "Easy day, man. We're gonna get her back."

Zack did not respond to this; instead, he said, "What can you tell me about Kincaid?"

"What do you need to know? Tactically sound. Crazy as an outhouse rat."

"Yeah, I picked up on that." He sighed. "Six, here's the deal. Don't know why I didn't tell you this already. He's offering to give me the girl back if you go up there unarmed. You for her."

Court nodded, looked through the trees. "I wondered if that would be the deal."

Zack said, "But you and I both know how that would play out."

"He kills me, then kills the kid. Probably goes after you anyway, for the money."

"Yep," Zack said. "No doubt. So we're going to have to hit that place."

"You able?" Court asked.

Zack sniffed out a little laugh. "Don't see we have a choice. It's that or get local SWAT out here, and that's just going to get Andie killed. I hear SWAT here is top-notch, but Gauntlet is going to get word of it before they can muster, and that can't happen."

Court pointed down to Zack's leg. Even in the poor light, the blood on his jeans was obvious. "I meant *that*. Can you operate on that leg?"

"Pete just rebandaged me, actually. This is mostly dried. It will slow me down, but I can still do some damage."

Court turned to look in the window of the darkened little cabin. "Pete? You been making friends?"

"He's a good man, actually. He fucking hates me for putting his family through this, I'm sure, but I can't say I blame him."

"Let's fix it, then," Court said. "How far to the target?"

"Seven hundred yards due east. The target is in a clearing in the woods, right next to a sheer hillside that goes all the way down to the road. Lots of trees. There's a trail a couple hundred yards east of that, leads down to the road. Looks like a good exfil route for after. The trouble is going to be getting into that property undetected and getting the girl."

Court scoffed at this. "We're going to be detected, all right. We hit that house, we own that space, we get that kid, we get the fuck out."

Court then said, "The guys with Lancer. Jill is guessing there are probably three, maybe four. How good are they?"

"The two I met? Dangerous, but nowhere near tier one," Zack said. "One thing's for sure: Lancer only gives a shit about Lancer. He'll let all the other dudes with him die, and he'll grab Andie to use as a bargaining chip if he's outnumbered."

"Understood."

Zack put a finger up in Court's face. "Andie is the objective. Not Kincaid. And not me. If it comes down to it, your job is *not* to watch my back. Your job is to get *her*. Are we clear?"

Court nodded. "Same rules apply for me. You, me. One of these days, we're gonna get what's coming. That's just the way it is. But that girl doesn't deserve any of this bullshit. The girl is mission critical, end of story."

Court pulled his neck gaiter up over his nose, essentially masking himself, then picked up the two bags. Zack opened the door to the cabin. Here, in the low light of a single flashlight pointed at the ceiling, he saw a man in his forties wearing a firefighter's uniform, a black sweater with an emblem, black cargo pants, and black boots sitting nervously on a barstool at a kitchen island.

As a way of introduction, Court said, "Hey, man. Everything's going to be fine."

"That's what I keep hearing," Delaney said.

Court turned to Zack as he dropped the bags. "I've got two subguns, two pistols, three sets of soft body armor, medical equipment, extra mags. A couple of nine-bangers, too."

Delaney said, "What the hell's a nine-banger?"

"It's . . . it's a disorientation device. Like a flash-bang grenade."

Zack said, "I've got my piece and a knife." He looked to Delaney. "Pete's got a big-ass can of bear spray, fire extinguishers, breaching tools, and a blowtorch."

Delaney said, "And I've got two face masks and two oxygen tanks."

Court nodded. "I like it." He thought a moment. "We know anything about the layout of that structure?"

Again, Delaney spoke up. Reaching for his phone on the island, he opened it and then handed it over. "Got about thirty photos of the inside of the cabin." Court took the phone, utterly confused, until Delaney said, "It's for rent online. You can see every room of the place, the area outside, too."

Zack added, "We think they'd be holding her in one of the bedrooms upstairs. We can't be sure." He looked to his watch. "Okay, Kincaid is going to call me in forty-five minutes."

Court nodded slowly. "When he calls, I want to be looking at that property." He turned to Delaney. "We need your help."

"She's my kid. I'll do anything."

"Let's start by getting some useful shit out of your truck."

Scott Kincaid, code name Lancer, looked at the watch on his wrist, saw it was nearly five, then looked outside as the last light of dusk gave way to darkness.

He headed for the stairs to grab the girl before calling Hightower. The man was going to want proof of life, so he'd have to put her on the phone, even for just a moment.

It was wild to Lancer that this fifteen-year-old didn't even know the man she'd be talking to was her real dad, and he thought about blowing her mind with that information, just to be a dick, but he decided he had enough to worry about without this kid freaking out.

Lancer's plan was simple, and it was variable. If Hightower said he had Gentry along with him, then Lancer would tell them he'd meet them at the gas station up the road, and then, when Winter drove by in the Bronco and saw them there, Lancer, Bennett, and Maybus would be following along to do a drive-by in the Wagoneer, all three men pouring rounds into the two men right there.

They'd have the girl in the Jeep and they'd shoot her at the scene, kick her body out into the street. Lancer didn't particularly love that part of the operation, but it didn't bother him, either. He'd killed kids before in war, and some of them had been unarmed. He'd even gotten court-martialed for it, though he eventually received a pardon.

What was one more dead body?

But if Hightower said that Gentry was not with him but *was* on the way, Lancer would just direct Hightower up here to the cabin, wait with him at gunpoint for Gentry to arrive, then kill them both and shoot the daughter right there in the bedroom.

Maybus had gotten two more local nationalists to join them, so there were five other armed men on the property, and Kincaid felt very comfortable in his plan.

Maybus sat on the front porch of the cabin; he had Todd Voorhies's hunting rifle, a Savage 110 Switchback in 7-millimeter, and a .357 Magnum pistol on his hip. Bennett was in the room with the girl, but it was also his job to keep looking out the window. There was a sliver of the road visible from there, many hundreds of yards down the hill and to the east, so any cars approaching from Boulder with their lights on could be seen well in advance.

Bennett had a Glock and a hunting knife, same as Lancer himself.

The two new guys had been introduced to Lancer as Dog and Rausch; each had an AR-15, and they sat in a Chevy Silverado behind the cabin, watching the trees and waiting for orders.

The last man, Ron Winter, sat in the living room on the couch, trading time outside with Bennett. He had a pistol-grip 12-gauge shotgun in his lap, loaded with five shells of double-ought buckshot, along with a Smith and Wesson semiautomatic pistol under his coat.

Lancer had been moving from room to room, looking out the kitchen window at the trees in the back, then out the open garage back to the west, but now, as he walked along the mezzanine that looked over the living room, he told himself it was time to get down to business.

He opened the door to the upstairs bedroom where he'd been keeping the girl for the past few hours and saw Bennett standing by the window in the empty room, looking out into the darkness.

The girl was nowhere to be seen.

Just then, the toilet flushed in the en suite bathroom.

Lancer addressed Bennett. "How long was she in there?"

"Like two minutes. I checked the bathroom beforehand. Got everything out of there that she could use as a weapon."

"Good. Eyes on the road. I'm making the call."

"Got it, boss."

Lancer heard the water running in the bathroom sink through the door right next to him, and then he pulled out his phone and dialed Hightower at exactly five p.m.

The phone rang once, twice, and then, on the third ring, it was answered.

"That you, Kincaid?"

"Yeah, man. You got the Gray Man?"

"He's in a car right behind me. I'm heading west on 119, just leaving Boulder. I told him I've got a staging area; he thinks we're heading there now."

Lancer was pleased but still suspicious. He put the phone on speaker as the door to the bathroom next to him began to open. "Good. I'm going to let you talk to the kid, just so you can—"

Lancer let go of the phone and brought his right arm up to protect his face, just as he was hit hard by something flying down at him. It was the porcelain lid of a toilet tank; it banged his elbow and the side of his head, but his reflexes were good, and he collapsed his legs just at the point of impact, and this had blunted the force. He went all the way down to the floor, clutching his elbow in pain.

Andrea Delaney jumped over the boss and ran towards the man standing by the window, who had been looking in the other direction. She yelled wildly as he turned in surprise, and she swung the ten-pound lid again, striking the man on his left shoulder and knocking him off balance. The man extended his right hand to brace himself, but he put it straight through the glass window, slicing his hand in the process.

Andie still held the lid; she turned back around to swing again at the boss back by the bathroom, but as soon as she turned, she found him up and running across the room, closing on her fast. He drew a pistol, but she swung at him anyway, missing.

He grabbed her by her hair, yanked her so hard she dropped the toilet tank lid, and threw her across the floor. She rolled several times, almost all the way back to the bathroom.

When she came to a stop, she looked up through the hair in her eyes and saw him charging towards her, his eyes wild with rage.

"Fuck you!" she shouted.

And then it happened.

A single gunshot cracked outside, somewhere on the property. Then another.

Then came the crashing of glass downstairs.

Another shot came from outside at the front of the cabin.

Andie began to crawl towards the bathroom, but the boss was on the floor behind her; he had hold of her ankle, and he pulled her back.

In the living room, a series of incredibly loud explosions went off, one after another after another after another. It sounded like a war down there, and then the lights of the cabin went out.

Andie kicked at the man who had her; she got him up on the shoulder and his cheek, and she brought her snowboard boot back to stomp down again, but before she did, she heard the click of a pistol, then felt the barrel of a handgun jammed into her stomach.

More shooting came from below. The man who she'd pushed into the glass window staggered past the two on the floor; he held a gun in his hand and blood dripped on Andie's forehead as he passed.

The boss leaned into her ear. "Your dad just got you fucking killed!"

He began yanking her to her feet, but before they'd gotten all the way up, she heard a scream from the man with the cut wrist, now in the doorway. Andie started to scream herself, then realized she could not breathe.

Her eyes began to sting.

The man at the doorway began coughing, but he fired his pistol down at something below him in the living room at the same time.

The boss who was holding her coughed, as well, dropped down to his knees, then dropped low and began crawling towards the door, out of the room. He passed the man standing there shooting down into the living room and disappeared in the direction of the stairs.

Andie remained in the empty room, now lying on her back, covering her face with her coat. She didn't know what was happening, but she couldn't see, couldn't breathe, couldn't think.

She was sure she was about to die.

FORTY-SIX

Court Gentry shattered the already broken window with the silencer on the end of his Scorpion submachine gun, all but leapt off the ladder, then landed on the floor of the room where someone had smashed the window out just twenty seconds earlier.

He'd placed the ladder at a second-floor window to another room on the east side of the building and had begun to climb, but when he heard the commotion one room over, he dropped off the collapsible ladder he'd taken from Pete Delaney's truck and carried through the forest for hundreds of yards, then hurriedly moved it twenty feet to the right and climbed back up to the damaged window.

He moved fast, but he would have moved a hell of a lot faster without the gear he wore. In addition to his body armor and his weapon, he had an oxygen tank on his back and a mask on his face, and another mask was hooked onto his belt and connected with a hose to the same tank.

Now in the room, he swept for targets, but the bear spray Pete Delaney had deployed through the garage door downstairs had already made it up here and it was only adding to the darkness and confusion of the smoke from the nine-banger Zack had thrown after shooting the man on the porch.

Court shined his weapon's light and immediately saw a target in front of him, an armed man facing away. He pressed the trigger on his subgun and shot the big man three times in the back. He pitched forward, flipped over the railing of the mezzanine, and disappeared.

But Court noticed one more figure in the middle of the small and empty bedroom, a small girl with a beanie on her head, writhing on the barren hardwood floor, covering her face and eyes with her coat.

He ran to her, pulled the secondary mask from his belt and put it on her, then lifted her back up to her feet.

She seemed to recover quickly; Court kept his weapon on the doorway as he waited for her to do so. She looked towards him in the low light, and Court thought she might have been expecting to see either her father or some other firefighter she knew.

Instead, he saw confusion on her face, looking through her mask at him.

He wanted to move out to the landing with his weapon, to help Zack, who was down there fighting God knows how many people, including Lancer.

But he was tethered to the girl, the girl was the mission, so he pulled her back to the window. She coughed and staggered, but she followed along nonetheless.

As soon as he got to the window, however, he saw that the ladder had fallen over.

Shit.

Over the past half hour, Zack, Pete, and Court had been moving through thick woods; Court had used a compass on his watch because they weren't getting consistent signals on their phones, but eventually they'd found the cabin. The lights were on; the Wagoneer and the Bronco were parked inside a garage with the door open. Court tracked around the back of the property, carrying a small folding ladder and an oxygen tank, and here he had stumbled upon a pickup truck with two men inside.

He couldn't make noise by shooting them; even with the suppressor on his weapon, the report would be audible inside the cabin, so he'd given them a wide berth, stayed out of the lights, and gone around to the eastern side to access the cabin from one of the upstairs bedroom windows.

Zack had stayed on the western side, in the trees but within view of the front of the cabin, right across the steep driveway. He carried a subgun and a pair of flash-bang grenades, and he immediately set his sights on a man standing on the porch.

Pete Delaney had been given a hands-on job, as well. He had a firefighter's crowbar for accessing locked doors easily. He knew that the breaker switch to shut off power to the entire cabin was in the garage. And he had the two cans of Sabre Frontiersman bear spray, one from Zack's truck and one from his, and each with fourteen ounces of propellant that would shoot the powerful chemical irritant forty feet.

The three men had determined from the online photos of the cabin that the garage door opened into the dining area, which itself looked straight over the living room. The living room was surrounded by a second-floor landing that ran in a U shape, which meant applying the spray straight through the garage door into the unit would, effectively, cover the entire building.

Pete had been reluctant to use the bear spray, not because he was afraid for his safety prying open the door of a building full of armed men but because he didn't want to hurt his daughter in the process.

But Court had assured him that he would have a mask on Andie within just a few seconds of the beginning of the attack.

Pete had been waiting to hear Zack's first gunshot, to take out the man they'd seen through the trees standing on the porch, and then he was to wait even longer, till Zack got a pair of nine-bangers through the front windows, before prying open the door, then standing to the side and deploying both cans of the spray, one at a time.

But before either Zack, Court, or Pete were quite ready, a window broke on the east side of the cabin. Not knowing what this meant but assuming it to mean Andie was in danger, all three men decided individually to begin the operation instantly.

Zack shot the man at the door, then ran as fast as he could across the slippery driveway towards the front window to throw in the nine-bangers.

Pete ran across the driveway through the open garage, threw the breaker to shut off power, then raced to the door, just past the Bronco. As the nine-bangers began going off inside, he slammed the hook of the thirty-inch pry bar into the door. He ripped it free of the doorframe, using a foot to kick it open farther, then stood to the side just as a burst of gunfire came his way from inside the cabin.

He got the bear spray out just as the second distraction grenade began going off, and then he blasted the potent chemical into the building.

Zack was at the front door now, and it had been his worry that any enemy trying to escape would go through the garage and not towards him. He'd given Pete his Staccato pistol, but Pete wasn't well trained, and he would have his hands full with the two large cans and the crowbar.

But the men had seen no alternative to this plan. Zack told Pete to just continue blasting the spray, sweeping it up and down and back and forth, and hopefully it would drive any enemy squirters *away* from the garage door and not towards it.

In the end, that part of the plan had worked.

One man came racing out the front door just seconds after Zack tossed the grenades. The two men were just six feet apart on the porch when Zack shot the man, but his momentum took him right into Zack. They slammed together; Zack took a blow to the face from the barrel of a shotgun, but then the enemy staggered off the side of the porch. The man tried to get his weapon up and pointed at Zack, but Zack was faster; he blasted the Scorpion a half dozen times, the enemy dropped his shotgun, and then the forward momentum of his stumble off the porch caused him to tumble farther out into the snow, and he slid down the hill into the trees, painting it red with blood as his lifeless body slowly descended.

On the second floor, Court looked out the window at the long drop to the uneven ground. He didn't like it, but he could do it. His worry, however, was that Andie would balk and he'd have to waste precious time coaxing her.

He shouted into his mask, "We need to jump! It's soft down there! You good?"

Without saying a word, she climbed past him on the windowsill, squatted, and pulled off the oxygen mask. Then she leapt out, away from the house, and disappeared in the darkness.

Court was pleasantly surprised, but he recovered quickly, held his breath, removed the tank and let it fall to the floor, then leapt out, keeping the subgun away from his body so it didn't strike him when he impacted the ground.

It was fifteen feet down, but the angle and over a foot of snowfall blunted the impact. Court rose, found Andie brushing herself off, and he grabbed her and ran to the east, slipping quickly into thick pines.

No words were spoken for over a minute; the two of them just ran, coughing and hacking, wiping their eyes.

Andie Delaney in front, Court Gentry in back.

Thirty seconds after he opened the garage door, Pete Delaney exhausted the second can of bear spray. It had been his plan—a plan he did not communicate with the two CIA men—that he would then draw the pistol Hightower loaned him, brave the chemicals, and race in to try to help find his daughter.

But the bear spray was already wafting back into the garage, and he found it impossible to breathe.

Delaney drew the pistol, then began backing up, backing up more, then even more. Finally he was outside the garage, in the snow, exposed to the upper windows.

His eyes burned and tears rolled down his face.

Just then, the man Hightower just referred to as "his friend" broadcast over his AirPod.

"Got the kid! Dropped one enemy! He's not Lancer."

Delaney continued backing up; his eyes were watering even more heavily now, but he tried to keep them on the door.

Hightower broadcast, as well. "I smoked two enemy. Neither are Lancer."

Fuck, Delaney thought. The guy behind all this was still in there, but his daughter, according to some stranger he just met, was safe.

He began to turn away from the door, but just then, he saw movement. It was difficult to discern through his burning eyes, but eventually he realized it was a man holding a towel to the lower portion of his face, with an AR-15 rifle in his right hand.

Pete aimed as best he could, fired, fired again, fired again.

The man in the garage next to the parked Wagoneer fired back, and then Pete just emptied most of the magazine of Zack's gun into the area.

He saw Hightower running around from the front of the house. He waved Delaney off, telling him to stop shooting.

Hightower approached the side of the Wagoneer with his submachine gun at his shoulder, spun around the side, and found a man there on his knees, leaning against the wall of the garage, right next to the open fuse box door.

Hightower blasted the man with at least a dozen rounds.

Delaney fell to his knees into the snow, dropped the pistol, looked on.

Hightower kicked the body in the garage, flipping it over.

He turned to Delaney and gave a thumbs-down.

This wasn't Lancer, either.

Just then, another man came running around the back of the property, an AR-15 at his shoulder. Pete saw him before Zack, because Zack was still inside the garage.

Pete was far enough out of the light that the armed man hadn't seen him, but Pete picked up the pistol and fired once at the man at a distance of sixty feet.

The round missed, but the enemy raised his weapon and fired back into the trees, narrowly missing the deputy fire chief.

Zack couldn't see the man shooting to his left, but he was well aware of him now, so he raced out of the garage, onto the slick and steep driveway, and fired his submachine gun fully automatic, dumping round after round into the man.

When Zack's gun emptied, the man was dead just twenty feet away, but Zack was slow in his reload, because he dropped to a knee and began hacking the choking bear spray from his lungs.

Pete Delaney looked on and began walking towards him to try to help, but he'd made it only a few feet before yet another man appeared from the cabin.

Running out of the house, through the garage with a towel covering most of his face, the man staggered, slowed, and put a hand on the Bronco to steady himself. Whoever he was, Pete was sure the man was almost overcome with the chemicals, and when he began walking forward again, a pistol swinging in his left hand, the man rubbed his face and eyes with the towel.

Pete realized Zack didn't see the man approaching from behind, and the man approaching was unaware of Zack, just steps in front of him.

The fireman raised his pistol at the threat, but he couldn't be sure he wasn't going to shoot Zack in the process.

Ultimately, he did nothing, because the two men collided, fell to the ground, and Zack knocked the pistol out of the other man's hand and threw a reactive punch.

They fought there on the driveway on the slick surface, the empty submachine gun between them, and very quickly Pete got the impression Zack was battling the man called Kincaid, because even partially blinded and coughing uncontrollably, this individual was one hell of a ground fighter.

FORTY-SEVEN

Court felt like they'd been running a long time, but finally they made it to the utility road that Court had seen on Google Maps.

He called out to the girl, who was now twenty feet or so ahead. "Hang on."

She pulled up, Court pulled his neck gaiter back up to his nose, and then he put his hand to his AirPod. "Six for Night Train. You with me, brother?"

There was no response. The girl looked at him, so he motioned to her to follow the trail down the hill towards the two-lane road.

"Night Train?"

He heard coughing now; the signal here on the mountain was poor, but he thought he heard the sound of grunting.

Andie looked up at him. "Everything okay?"

He nodded, still listening to his earpiece for any news.

She said, "Who are you?"

"Me? I'm . . . I'm just a guy helping out."

Andie said, "Are you a cop?"

"Sure am."

"What's your name?"

Court thought a moment. Finally, he said, "Starsky."

"Starsky?" The young girl was clearly bewildered by the name.

Court said nothing.

"You don't look like a regular cop."

"That's because I'm *not* a regular cop. I'm an *awesome* cop. I'm also the kind of cop that doesn't like a ton of chitchat, so let's just walk for a few minutes, okay?"

"Okay," she said, and the teenager adhered to this agreement.

For about twenty seconds.

"Why did all this happen?"

Court sighed. Said, "A simple case of mistaken identity."

"You mean . . . like, they had the wrong kid?"

"They most *definitely* had the wrong kid."

"Are they dead? The guys that took me?"

"They're not going to bother you anymore."

She walked in the dark a moment, then looked at him. "Because they're dead?"

Their feet crunched the snow. "You can just go back to your life like nothing—"

"You can just say they're dead. I know they are."

A few more footsteps crunched. "Yeah. They're all extremely dead," he said, but he wasn't sure about that.

Into his earpiece he said, "Night Train. Go for Six?"

Zack Hightower's eyes didn't really clear up enough to see until he was moving down an icy slope on his back, skidding at high speed, with a man on top of him.

He knew he was fighting Lancer, he knew Lancer had been disarmed, but the man was under at least as much of the effects of the bear spray as Zack himself was. The man coughed as he rained punches down in those brief moments of contact while the two of them slid, rolled, and stumbled down the long and steep driveway.

Zack went airborne a moment, crashed down on his right shoulder, then rolled end over end, striking against Kincaid's similarly tumbling body right before hitting the ice again on his back. He tried a punch of his own as the two of them kept careening down, whiffed his swing, and then Kincaid landed an elbow into the side of Zack's head.

Zack had his knife on his belt, but his hands were too occupied trying to break his fall with each of his contacts with the ground or thwarting the blows from the man falling along with him.

For a moment both he and Kincaid were on their backs, next to each other and sliding as if down an Olympic luge track. He started to take the opportunity to go for his knife, because even though they were by no means at the end of the driveway, he expected this might be his only chance to get a lethal weapon in his hand for a moment.

But then it occurred to him. Lancer would have a blade of his own, and he was probably coming to the same conclusion.

Zack brought both hands up and crossed them into an X, just as Scott Kincaid flipped towards him in the air, a blade shining in the moonlight in his swinging hand.

Zack blocked it with both arms and grabbed the man by the wrists, and just then both struggling fighters' feet hit a snowbank as the driveway curved to the east.

The momentum slung them into the air. Zack kept his hold on Kincaid's wrists while they tumbled into trees and snow-covered brush.

Scott Kincaid ended up on top; he leaned onto his knife with all his might, but Zack brought a knee up into the man's hip, knocking him off balance.

Kincaid went into the air; Zack held on to the man's arms for dear life, and when the disgraced Navy SEAL slammed his back against a pine tree, the impact forced him to let go of the knife.

The blade fell and hit Zack in the shoulder, cutting him but doing no real damage that he could immediately feel.

Zack Hightower was utterly exhausted, but he rolled onto his side and grabbed the knife, and just as Kincaid leapt into the air towards him, Zack swung the big blade in a slashing motion in the air.

The knife swept across Kincaid's midsection, cut through his coat and his shirt and his stomach. Opened him up deeply, and the man rolled over and past Zack, then tried to climb up.

Zack lunged again, landed on top of the man, and stabbed him in his midsection.

Kincaid's wide eyes, shining in the moonlight like the bloody knife in Zack's hand, stared up at him in disbelief.

Zack straddled the wounded man, raised the knife high over his head. "That's my girl you fucked with, you son of a bitch!"

He dropped his full weight down onto the man, the blade leading the way, and it sank deep into Scott Kincaid's heart.

A noise off to Zack's right pulled him out of his rage. He looked to see Pete Delaney sliding down the driveway, moving quickly, but in a much more controlled fashion than Zack and Lancer had just done.

He climbed to his feet at the edge of the snowbank. Stared down at Zack through the broken bushes, took in the dead man lying on his back in the snow.

"That him?" was all he said.

"Yeah," Zack replied through gasps for air.

Delaney nodded. Then looked at Zack. "You hurt?"

Zack breathed heavily, staring back at Delaney. He knew he'd been cut on the shoulder, had taken blows all over his body, might even have broken bones during his dozen or so rough impacts with the driveway. But he said, "Never better, brother."

Pete moved through the snowbank, arrived at Zack, and extended a hand. Pulling him off the dead kidnapper, he said, "Nice work."

"Thanks."

With only a tiny hint of a smile, Delaney said, "Now . . . get out of my life."

Zack glanced down at the dead man, then back to Delaney. "Yeah. Will do."

Delaney pulled his earpiece out of his ear and handed it over. "Think you lost yours. Your guy has Andie; they're safe, she wasn't harmed at all. Your guy keeps asking for you to report your status."

Zack took the headset, spoke between labored breaths. "Night Train for Six. We're good here. Lancer's DRT. We're heading back to get the vehicles. Pete's gonna come grab her first; I'm going to police up the cabin we staged in and then follow."

Court had spent the last two minutes assuring Andie Delaney that everything was just perfect, when all the while, all he'd heard was her father telling him that Zack and Lancer had fallen down the sloping, iced driveway and disappeared while trying to rip each other's throats out.

He confirmed receipt of Zack's transmission, then he smiled now at the kid, and the kid looked back at him, but he knew she couldn't see much with his neck gaiter up.

He said, "Your dad is going to pick you up when we get down to the road."

She nodded, then, after another minute trudging through deep snow, she said, "I can't believe all those people got killed because they grabbed the wrong kid."

Court tried to think of words that could help. Over the crunching of boots in the snow, he said, "They got killed because they grabbed *a* kid. Listen carefully to me. None of this is on you. Shit like this happens. It most definitely shouldn't, but it does. Everything is okay now. I'm taking you to your dad, I'm dropping you off, and you need to forget that this happened."

She stopped and looked at him. "Bruh, what are you talking about? It's gonna be all over the news."

"No. Actually, it's not."

"Why not?"

Court shrugged. "There are things I can't explain. Somehow, a lot of the details of this are going to get covered up."

"Why?"

He'd said too much. "Let's just keep walking."

He moved on, and she followed.

Soon she was ahead of him again. Court had a hard time keeping up with her in the heavy snow; she was obviously more accustomed to this terrain and these conditions than he was.

Finally, she said, "Do you do stuff like this all the time?"

"Do I use ladders and bear spray to rescue kids from bad guys in the mountains all the time? Almost never, to tell you the truth."

"You . . . you kind of act like you do this all the time."

"Believe me, it's just an act."

"Not sure I *do* believe you," she said, but she did not pursue the matter further.

They made it to the road after another twenty minutes, and Pete Delaney was already there, standing in the flashing lights of his emergency vehicle, his arms wide. He took his daughter, and her snowboard boots were lifted off the ground as he hugged her.

He didn't put her down for some time, but when he did, she turned back to Court.

"Thanks, Starsky," Andie said. Court waved and nodded, his neck gaiter still shielding his face, and she climbed into the passenger seat of the vehicle.

Delaney stepped forward in the dark. "Hightower's five minutes behind me. He's really banged up, but he won't admit it. You need to work on that leg. He's got a hell of a gash, and he's basically ignored it for the past six or seven hours. He took a knife in the shoulder, too."

"That body of his has taken a lot worse. We'll get him seen to."

"They're all dead, right?" he asked.

Court said, "I just got one guy, then I got the girl out. I honestly think your bear spray might have saved the day." With a little chuckle, he said, "Although, in hindsight, maybe one can would have been plenty."

"No shit," Delaney said softly.

Court said, "The important thing is, that will never happen again."

"You're sure about that?"

Court was not. *How can anyone be sure about anything?* he thought. He just put a hand out, shook Delaney's, and said, "You guys get home safe."

The lights of the Boulder Fire and Rescue truck had just disappeared in the distance when Zack's F-150 pulled up along the utility road. Court opened the passenger-side door and looked in.

"How bad are you?"

He could see bruising on Zack's face. There was fresh blood on his leg. A compression bandage on his shoulder jutted out from under his open coat. But he smiled, his fat lower lip cracked, swollen, and bloody, "What did you think of that kid?"

"Rock star."

"Right?" Zack beamed.

"Reminded me of you. The same vibe."

"How so?"

"She told me she smacked one of the kidnappers with a toilet tank lid, damn near knocked him out a window."

"No shit?" he said, pride evident on his face. "Outstanding!"

"You okay to drive?" Court asked.

"I'm good to go."

The F-150 began rolling through the snowy conditions towards Boulder Municipal Airport.

FORTY-EIGHT

Court Gentry was the only passenger in the back of a five-passenger Cirrus Vision Jet flying south over Georgia at seven in the morning. He'd slept a little with his cabin chair reclined and his feet on his backpack. Mostly, however, he'd been making and taking encrypted phone calls.

He had landed with Zack at Hampton Roads around three a.m., helped him hobble down out of the Hawker that brought them from Colorado. He'd asked Zack if he could borrow his pistol, and then, while Zack was assisted by both Erin Childers and a nurse into the back of an SUV sent by Hanley, Court immediately boarded the waiting Vision to begin his flight down to Florida to pick up his father and bring him back to Virginia.

Court's dad knew nothing about this; Hanley and Court had agreed operational security was crucial, so Jim Gentry would only learn what was going on when his son showed up at his door. In the meantime, however, the man Hanley had watching over Court's dad down in northern Florida had been told to keep an even more careful eye out for strangers in the area.

Court was three hours into his second flight now; it was well past dawn outside, and the pilot announced they'd be landing soon.

Then Court's phone buzzed again, and again, it was Hanley.

"I have some news."

"Good news or bad?"

"Definitely bad if your name is Lewis Shaw."

"Somebody smoked him?"

"Affirmative. Murdered in his home overnight." This *was* big news, principally because, as the presumed leaker of intelligence product that had been getting people killed around the world, Court had assumed he'd be the one to kill him.

"Saves me the trouble," he said. "We know who did it?"

"A neighbor heard a gunshot, described a man wearing a British riding cap leaving in the back of an SUV driven by someone else. No other description."

"Sounds like Whetstone," Court said.

"Yep. I thought you'd want to know about it as soon as I did. Didn't want you to worry you were going to run into that bastard down there this morning."

"Well, just because he's still in D.C. doesn't mean he's not going to pose a threat to my dad."

"I agree, but I guess you have a little more time for the extraction." He then said, "You want me to go ahead and let my guy down there know you're coming? He lives a couple blocks away from your dad and has been having coffee with him most every morning."

"Better not. You don't know my dad. Old Jim might take some coaxing, and I don't want him planning on how he's going to tell me no. I'm going to just go there and sit with him and tell him as little about the danger as I can to get his ass moving. I'll text you when I'm just a couple minutes out from his house, and you can call your private detective off. Give him my sincere thanks, but I want him gone when I get there."

"I get it. You and your pop have some stuff to hash out before he gets in a car with you, I'm sure."

"Something like that." Switching the subject, Court said, "How's Night Train?"

"Thirty-three stitches in the leg, right down the center of his left quadricep. A dozen more in the shoulder. His body's beat to shit, but nothing he won't shake off. No square dancing for him for a bit, but otherwise, he's doing well. I haven't talked to him about why he never mentioned his daughter to me yet. I just told him I'm glad everything worked out in Boulder."

Court replied, "He blames himself for the enemy homing in on her. I get it. Maybe you don't say anything more right now; he feels bad enough as it is."

Hanley sighed a little. "Right. I'll have to find some other reason to chew him out."

"I'm confident you'll come up with something. How's Teddy doing?" Court asked.

"I told Teddy last night that the good news was that he was now officially the *second* worst injured Ghost Town asset. He's moving around fine. Not operational, but doing good, considering he took a bullet to the fucking neck."

"Good." Court hesitated a moment, then said, "I want him to go to Charlottesville."

Hanley was surprised. "To where Zoya, Irene, and Cathy are being kept safe by five armed guards?"

"Yes. I want him there, watching over the people who are watching over Zoya. You can put Night Train there, too, to convalesce. I want them both armed."

Hanley was confused. "There's no compromise or threat to Zoya. The people protecting her aren't Gauntlet employees. They aren't foreign hitters. They're former agency paramilitaries; I know each and every one of them. Night Train knows them all, and Teddy knows some of them, too."

"Good. Then Teddy and Night Train will have a nice time recuperating with their old pals. I just want more guns around Zoya, honestly. Even if Teddy's got a hole in his neck and Night Train's leg is messed up, they're still solid operators who won't let anything happen to her."

Hanley thought about it a moment, then said, "Okay. Granted." He then asked, "How long will it take you to get your dad to agree to come back with you?"

"That's a good question. I haven't talked to him in twenty years."

"You want to bring him to Charlottesville, too? Turn the facility into a boardinghouse?"

Court laughed a little. "That's okay. I can put him on my boat. I'll tell him to stay on board till this is all over." He thought a moment. "Why do you think Whetstone killed Shaw, if Shaw was the one leaking the information? Whetstone and the others were obviously benefiting from that information."

"Pace and Lacy are trying to figure that out. There have been fourteen killings in the intelligence community in the past four days, several more attempts. We're wondering if the people who ordered the operation have decided they've achieved enough, and Shaw was just a compromise at this point."

Court said, "Or maybe there's a whole other aspect to their operation, something they no longer needed Shaw for."

"Right," Hanley said. "Pace is tracking some leads; we'll see what he learns. Any way you look at it, though, it means our work probably isn't done, and even though you and the boys have done a good job eliminating assassins, our own attrition rate hasn't been that good."

"Well, boss," Court said, "strap on a .45 and get after it." He then chuckled. "My dad is a former Marine sniper. Maybe you could hire him when I get his ass up to Virginia. Is there an age ceiling at Ghost Town?"

"The way things are going, the Five Guys and Arnold are all going to be out on the streets shooting it out with Gauntlet before too long." Hanley sniffed. "Enjoy your personal time, but get your ass back up to us, put your dad in that boat, and get back to work."

"Right."

Just then, the copilot gave Court a wave, telling him to buckle up.

Seventy-five-year-old Jim Gentry poured another steaming mug of coffee, then carried it over to his kitchen table, passed it to the man sitting there, then sat down slowly in front of his own half-empty cup.

Gentry had a full head of silver hair, cut short like a Marine. He was five foot eight, did not carry an ounce of extra weight on his body, but that appeared to be mostly because of genetics and not exercise, because he looked even older than his years, like someone who didn't do much more than sit on his porch.

His eyes were bright, but he wore thick glasses. His shoulders were slight. His mouth hung in a permanent scowl, and his face showed the effects of living his life entirely in Florida and working a blue-collar job.

And Vietnam.

The effects of a stroke several years earlier were only evident to those who knew Gentry before it happened: the way his mouth hung, plus he walked and talked a little slow. Still, he moved no slower than many septuagenarians, and his dexterity seemed normal enough for a man his age.

The other man at the table was nearly a decade younger, barrel chested, bearded. He looked like he could have been a boxer in his younger days; a crooked nose held up his eyeglasses, but his easy smile shone under his thick brown mustache.

His name was Stanley Echols, but Jim Gentry, and everybody else who knew him, called him Skip.

James Gentry lived in a small two-bedroom home with aluminum siding next door to a large parcel of property he'd owned for decades, a disused farm and shuttered-up firearms training facility dozens of acres in size, just a couple of miles south of the Georgia state line in Glen St. Mary, Florida. The property was surrounded by farms, flatlands, and woods, a half hour west of Jacksonville. A massive solar power plant had gone up just down the road from Jim's place, and many of the farms in the area, and the buildings on them, were in a state of disrepair.

The men at the kitchen table had been chatting for thirty minutes; Skip had been a daily fixture here since he moved in a block away a few weeks earlier, and today's conversation was similar to that of other days. The weather was first and foremost; a heavy storm was due to hit the area later in the morning, and they argued for a time on exactly when. Then they talked politics for a while, but only until Jim said they should both run for president, only on opposite tickets.

Just then, Skip Echols looked down at his phone, then back up to the older man. "Jimbo, you okay if I take this outside?"

"You got a girlfriend you forgot to tell me about?"

"Would I be here listening to you jabber all morning if I did?" Echols went out back, stood in the grass, and looked back towards a thick line of tall Florida pines swaying in the growing wind. The sky was dark and growing darker; a door to an outbuilding on Gentry's vacant property next door banged open and shut in the breeze.

Skip said, "Mornin', Matt. How's it going up there?"

Stanley "Skip" Echols had known Matthew Hanley for a quarter century, from back when Hanley was a young U.S. Special Forces officer and Echols was a U.S. Army Ranger.

Hanley had gone into CIA, Echols had gone to Delta Force, and when Hanley became an exec at the Agency, he tried to get Echols to join him as a paramilitary.

Echols felt he'd done his time, though, so he took his retirement from the Army, moved back to Jacksonville, and became a private investigator.

Work had been spotty recently, till Hanley called him out of the blue a couple of months earlier and asked him to move to Glen St. Mary and begin clandestinely watching over a cantankerous old man named James Ray Gentry, for reasons of national security that had never been adequately explained by the former deputy director.

An airplane flew overhead now, getting out of the area before the storm, Echols guessed.

"Skip," Hanley replied. "How close are you to Mr. Gentry right now?"

"I'm standing in his backyard, as a matter of fact. Just dropped in for coffee."

"Anything out of the ordinary going on?"

"Not a damn thing. Some storms on the way, but other than that, nothing that I've seen. Something I need to know?"

"Nothing at all," Hanley said. Then, "Skip . . . I need you to clear out of there. ASAP."

"Uh, okay. Why?"

"No emergency, but someone's coming that you don't need to meet."

"Ah . . . this would be the son? The guy in the CIA."

"Shit," Hanley said. "Gentry told you that?"

"He said he had suspicions about his oldest boy being a spook. I played dumb, sure didn't tell him the former DDO himself sent me to watch over him."

"Thanks for that. Anyway, the son is coming to take his dad back home with him for a few weeks or so, and it's better if you're not around when he does it."

"Why?"

"He's shy."

Echols laughed. "Fuckin' spooks. No offense, Matt. You need me to stand off close by in case of trouble?"

"No. Gentry is going to be leaving Florida today, so you're relieved of duty. You're paid up for the month. I'll call you if I need you again."

"Fair enough. I'm just going to go back inside and make an excuse to—"

"Skip," Hanley said. "My guy is inbound, ETA five mikes. You need to be outbound in two. Understand?"

"Okay," Echols said, not hiding his disappointment. "I'll come on my own time when Jim gets back home."

The elder Gentry sat at the table, doom-scrolling an alternative news site on his phone, but then he was surprised to hear Skip's truck start out front. He'd just made it to the kitchen window when it drove off to the east, back in the direction of Skip's house.

It passed a Range Rover that was coming this way, and the Range Rover pulled straight up into Gentry's gravel drive.

Jim put his coffee down on the counter, walked through the living room and over to his door, and opened it with a slightly quivering hand.

Standing there on the tiny porch of his little house, the American flag on the pole out next to him whipping in the wind, Jim put his hands on his hips and faced the SUV.

A bearded man in a raincoat climbed out of the Range Rover and walked straight towards him, and their eyes locked. Ten feet away the man stopped, then looked around, left and right.

Finally, the man turned back Jim's way. "Hey, Dad."

"Courtland."

The two looked at each other for a while, and then Court said, "You don't seem all that surprised to see me."

"Well, I figured it was you that sent Skip here to watch over me. He never said that, but I'm pretty sharp, still. Nice guy, Skip. I'm guessing I won't be seeing him again."

Court said, "You can see him when this is all over." After a beat, he said, "I mean, that's up to Skip. Maybe he doesn't like you."

Jim smiled a little. With the smile still on his face, he said, "You're in some trouble?"

"I need to help you pack some things. You're coming with me. Hopefully for just a few days. Maybe a few weeks." He sighed. "Please don't make this difficult."

Again, Jim didn't seem terribly surprised. "We got time for coffee first?"

Court looked at the sky. "How long till this rain hits?"

"You've been gone so long you can't tell?"

Court scanned to the east, towards the coast. Thinking a moment, he said, "Could be any time now."

"Nah," Jim answered back. "We've got an hour."

Court shrugged. "Okay. I guess there's time for coffee."

Jim turned around, headed back inside. "When you're my age, son, there's *always* time for coffee."

Court followed him in.

This was not the house Court grew up in; that had been on the property next door. At some point that house had been damaged in a storm, long after Court moved away, and Jim tore it down and put up a double-wide trailer, and he lived there for a decade.

He'd just bought this home next door to his dilapidated trailer two years earlier. It wasn't any larger, but it was a little newer than his long-lost home and a lot nicer than the double-wide.

They sipped coffee at the table, Court in the seat just vacated by Skip, and it was awkward at first. Court watched his dad move, was taken by how old he seemed, but he was also taken by how little he seemed to have changed otherwise.

Court looked out the back window and caught a side view of the disused farm next door, where he grew up. He knew that back behind the row of pine trees some two hundred yards from the road, a row of gun ranges, a massive shoot house, and several bunkhouses and classroom buildings used to stand. His father had been a private firearms instructor to SWAT teams from all over the United States, and many from abroad, and they'd all come right here to Baker County to train under the great James Ray Gentry.

Court said, "Is the shoot house still standing?"

Jim sniffed. "It's teetering, for sure, but it's still there." With a smile he said, "Maybe the storm that's coming this morning will be the one that finally knocks it down. I go back there and walk around every now and then, just for old times' sake. Take my pistol back to the ranges, get a little practice in."

"Can you still shoot?"

"Yeah, but not like I could ten years ago." He pulled off his glasses and held them up. "Vision's gone to hell. I see double if I don't wear these." He put them back on. "Plus, I had a stroke."

"I heard. You okay?"

The father looked at the son a long time. Finally, he broke the staring contest, said, "Aboveground and upright. That's something."

"Yeah," Court said. "That's something."

"How 'bout you, son? Can you still shoot?"

"You were around for my upbringing, Dad. Why the hell would you think I would be good at *anything* else?"

The elder Gentry smiled at this. Court was being a little passive-aggressive with his dad, and he regretted it immediately; he was about to get to the reason for his visit, but then his dad said, "What are you carrying?"

Court drew Zack's pistol and handed it over without removing the magazine or clearing the weapon.

Jim Gentry's eyes widened as he took it. "A Staccato P4? Only seen 'em on the Internet. You made of money?" he asked his son. The pistols sold for upwards of three thousand dollars each.

Court laughed. "It's a buddy's gun, actually. I borrowed it. Be careful holding it."

"I know how to hold a damn pistol," Jim said as he looked through the holographic optic.

"No . . . I mean, you don't want to get spoiled."

"It's nice." Jim handed the gun back. "We should take it out back and—"

"We don't have the time for that, Dad."

"Okay."

Court said, "What are *you* carrying these days?"

Jim patted the front pocket of his old cargo pants under the table. "Six forty-two."

It was a tiny five-shot revolver that fired thirty-eight special rounds through a two-inch barrel, made by Smith and Wesson.

Court shrugged. "Not a lot of firepower."

"I'm a civilian, son. Three by three by three," Jim said.

Court spoke his father's language; he knew what the old man meant. Statistically speaking, the average defensive civilian gunfight involved three gunshots in three seconds at a distance of three yards. A five-shot gun with a short barrel was sufficient for the vast majority of violent encounters.

Statistically speaking.

Court said, "I guess my life has been something of an outlier."

"I'll bet," his father said. "Three magazines in three minutes at three hundred yards?"

"On a slow day."

Both men chuckled, and then Jim said, "I know you didn't love it all the time, but I sure miss shooting guns with my boys out back. Would have loved to have seen you over the years."

Court looked through the window. It was getting darker by the minute due to the coming storm; the tall grasses and spotty clusters of trees in the lot across the street swayed. He said, "I had reasons for not coming home. It was nothing personal."

"I'm sure you were busy," Jim said. He added, "I'll admit, though, I *did* expect to see you at your brother's funeral."

Now Court looked down at the table. "Yeah. I was out of the country when Chance died. I'm sorry I missed it."

Jim waved his hand. "Well . . . as it turns out, it didn't matter." The comment confused Court a little. Then the older man said, "You work in the government, right?"

"Not anymore. But yeah, I did."

"You weren't military, I know that much. The military had too many rules for a kid like you."

"No, I wasn't in the military. To be honest, after being your son, I kind of wanted a little freedom." He shrugged. "Then I got a little too much freedom, and I got sucked into government service anyway."

"You went into the CIA." It was a statement, not a question.

"Dad, the less I tell you about what I've been doing the past twenty-odd years, the better it's going to be for both of us."

Jim waved a hand in the air. "C'mon, Courtland. Who'm I gonna tell?"

"Whoever the happy hour bartender is at Henry's."

The older man smiled. "Haven't been to Henry's in years. I quit drinking after the stroke."

Court cocked his head. "Really?"

"Quit smokin', too."

Court said, "Who even *are* you?"

Jim laughed now. Then he said, "I saw you once. At the diner. The feds came to talk to me about you, I look up, and there you were. They never suspected you were twenty-five feet away."

Court nodded. "That was me. Just checking up on you."

"I don't need a babysitter."

Court sighed. "You're annoyed I haven't been home, and you're annoyed that I did come home. There's no winning with you."

Jim let out a raspy laugh. "Anyway, they said you were a traitor to your nation."

"What do you think?"

"I think it was all just an honest misunderstanding."

"Really?"

"Fuck no." Jim laughed again. "I figured you pissed off the wrong person, a person with some clout, and they were trying to use the levers of power to squash you like a bug."

Whoa, Court thought. "Yeah . . . pretty much exactly that."

"I've got the Internet, son. I know what's going on in the world."

Court suspected that whatever his dad looked at on the Internet did *not* tell him what was going on in the world, but he let it go.

Jim said, "Those G-men. I didn't tell them shit about you."

Court chuckled. "Probably helped that you didn't *know* shit about me."

"Well . . . yeah . . . that was a plus." He asked, "Ever settle the score with the boss man that came after you?"

"He's no longer a factor."

Jim looked at his son a long time. Finally, he said, "You send any flowers to his funeral?"

"I did not."

Jim said, "So . . . that was, what? Three years ago? I'm guessing by the fact that you're here, you're armed, and you're looking around all frosty-eyed, you must have pissed off someone else."

"Yep."

"And you think they might be coming here?"

"We have to move you, just to be sure."

"What did you do this time?"

Court hesitated; he didn't want to give his father too much information at first, but something told him this extraction would go better if he did talk. "There's a lot going on. Problems in Washington. Problems that aren't going away any time soon, I imagine. But this thing I'm worried about with you? These people I'm concerned about? This is about something personal."

"Personal?"

"Yeah. A Northern Irishman. He's an assassin. I killed his son."

Jim Gentry did not reply; he just looked at Court behind his coffee mug, his eyeglasses steaming from the heat.

"The son? He had it coming?"

"Depends on your point of view." Court shrugged. "I was going after a target. A legit bad guy, but somebody I just needed to silence for operational reasons. This Irishman's son was in the way. Just . . . a bodyguard. He shot me, I shot him. We fought. I knifed him. Moved on."

"Jesus, Court."

"I never thought about the guy again. A couple months later, suddenly I'm on the phone with the man whose boy I killed."

"What was that call like?"

"Which one? We've talked twice so far."

Gentry blew out a chestful of air. "That was a mistake."

Court sipped the coffee. "I thought I could get some operational intel. Maybe I did. But he also got in my head a little bit. The people you go through on the way . . . you never expect to hear from their parents."

"What's this Mick's plan?"

"A simple one. Kill me or die trying."

Jim Gentry nodded. "Make sure he dies trying. Vengeance is a powerful drug. It'll never leave his system."

"Thing is . . . he's not coming after me for vengeance. He's coming after me because he thinks someday his grandson is going to become addicted to that drug. He's doing this for a damn baby somewhere in Northern Ireland."

The older man surprised his son now. "The man's logic is . . . well, I can't say it doesn't make sense. You'd do the same, wouldn't you? Do the business yourself so your kin didn't have to worry about it?"

"Don't know. Never had kids."

Court thought Jim appeared a little disappointed. Then he said, "This Irishman. You're going to have to end him if you ever want peace."

"And if his grandson comes after me?"

"By then you'll be in your sixties. Younger than me, but not by much." Jim shrugged. "You might see the world very differently then. You might not. You might have to kill him—"

"Kill the *kid*?"

"No, Court. He'll be an adult. You might have to kill the *adult* coming after you for something that happened a long time ago."

Court's phone buzzed; he saw that it was Hanley and answered it in front of his dad. "What's up?"

"Six, we've got a *serious* fucking problem."

FORTY-NINE

Court leaned back in his chair. "Can't wait to hear it."

"From some camera footage near the incident, Jim Pace learned that the man who killed Lewis Shaw was at least six-foot-three; it was definitely a Gauntlet employee, *not* Whetstone. For some reason, though, the killer wore a hat and a coat similar to the images we have of Whetstone."

"*That* can't be good."

"There's more. A Gauntlet aircraft flew from D.C. to Jacksonville early this morning. Arrived at seven thirty a.m." Court rose from the table, his phone to his ear. He looked out the kitchen window towards the street. "Lacy checked cameras at the fixed-base operator there at the airport. Six men left at seven forty-five a.m., driving a pair of—"

Court interrupted. "Let me guess. Gray Chevy Suburbans?"

Hanley groaned, then said, "How did you know that?"

In a voice low and slow, Court said, "Because they just rolled past the house. There's a farm road a hundred yards up the street, figure they're going to access the empty property across the road here, park behind some trees. Then fan out, hit the house."

Thunder rumbled outside.

"Shit!" Hanley said. "I'll call the local sheriffs and—"

Court said, "No. Don't call them. There's a storm about to hit; it's going to be chaos around here. The deputies who show up will get slaughtered by a half dozen trained hitters."

"What do you need, then?"

Court shook his head before replying. "Whatever I need, it won't get here in time. I'll work with what I've got."

He hung up on Hanley, put his phone in his pocket, and turned to his father, still sitting at the table with his coffee in his hand, looking up at his son.

"Dad. When you said we had an hour before the storm hit. That was a lie, right?"

The older man nodded. "Yep."

"I could tell."

"Just wanted to enjoy a few minutes at the kitchen table with my oldest boy. Is that such a crime?"

"No crime. What do you think? Another ten minutes before it hits?"

Jim looked outside. "Five."

Court turned back to the window. "Okay. Here's the deal. You and I are about to get into a gunfight."

"With each other?" Jim said, and Court swiveled his head back to him. There was a glint in the old man's eye that showed he was joking. It also looked a little like excitement. "Quantity and quality of the enemy?" Jim then asked.

"I think there's six in all. Five of them . . . they're probably adequate. The other guy, well, I'm told he's one of the best in the world."

"And he's the one whose son you killed?"

"Afraid so."

Jim rose. Stood next to Court. Trash blew by on the street. Beyond it, past the tall grass on the barren property, he could see a pair of SUVs disappear behind some trees.

The elder Gentry said, "I've got an MP5, but it's disassembled. Needs a new bolt. A 700 in .308, but I took the scope off to repair it. Bought an old PPK off a guy, but the ejector's broke and I need to—"

Court said, "We don't have time to assemble your old junk guns, Dad. We're armed. We're gonna make do with what we've got."

Jim kept looking out the window, but he said, "And your plan is to just stand here and shoot it out with six jokers in a two-bedroom ranch-style, or is it to make a run for one of the vehicles and then get chased down by them on the road in a violent thunderstorm?"

Exasperated at his father, Court said, "I'm *totally* open to other ideas if you've got 'em."

"Well, son, seems to me that you and I have one hell of an advantage that you aren't considering."

"What's that?"

Jim tipped his head towards the back of the little home. "We get our asses out back, next door, past the pines, and into that damn shoot house. You, me, and your brother spent thousands of hours back there; we know every inch of every room. Every hall, every doorway, every step on every stair, every single angle and sightline."

Court put his hand on his dad's arm. "How fast can you move?"

"Had no reason to find out till right now. Let me grab a flashlight first, then let's get our asses back there."

Jim and Court Gentry moved through the scrubby property, past chicken coops that hadn't had chickens in them in a few years.

The older man couldn't run; he seemed to have an impairment in his back and legs, but he shuffled along quickly, and Court stayed just behind him, looking over his shoulder every few seconds to see if Coyle and his goons had figured out that Court was making a run for it across the acreage behind the house.

There was standing water here and there. Jim wore roper boots and cargo pants, a plain gray sweatshirt. The temperature was in the low fifties, but the wind made it feel considerably cooler.

Lightning pounded the sky, and the winds whipped all around them; the rain began to fall, and their clothes were already soaked when they still had one hundred yards to go to the tree line.

As they moved across the rough ground, Jim said, "We get lucky, those Micks are gonna get bit by snakes before they make it to us."

"I've never been that lucky," Court said.

"Me, either."

They had just made it to the pines when Court looked back over his shoulder and saw the two gray SUVs passing up the driveway, past his Range Rover, continuing off-road, into the backyard.

He said, "They've seen us. They're being careful, staying back, but they'll catch up."

Jim took his glasses off, wiped rain from them, and put them back on hurriedly. He said, "We had rain yesterday afternoon too, so there's going to be some puddles and some mud back here, so watch your step."

Three minutes later Court came out on the far side of the trees and stood next to his father as he looked at the massive shoot house, now almost surrounded by overgrown woods. The storm had kicked in full force, and rain poured from the tin roof, so the two men immediately stepped inside a dark sloppy hallway with overgrown vines on the wall and the smell of rotting lumber and mold prevalent in the humid air.

The last time Court had set foot in this building, he'd been eighteen years old. He'd spent thousands of days of his life working in here, mostly playing the role of opposition force, fighting the SWAT teams training under his father and his father's training cadre. Both Court and the law enforcement teams used real but modified rifles and pistols that fired marking cartridges, non-lethal rounds that blistered and tore skin when they hit.

By sixteen Court was doing the training himself, walking the catwalks above, shouting orders to SWAT teams facing other OPFOR role players.

Jim said, "Listen up, son. I wouldn't trust that catwalk. I damn near fell through it ten years ago, back when it didn't look so bad, so I'm guessing anybody going up there is gonna come down on their ass, or worse."

Court pulled out his flashlight, and Jim pulled his own; the lighting inside the area was spooky, even for Court. The dark gray sky barely filtered in through holes in the tin roof, water poured in with it, and many corners and smaller rooms were pitch black.

Jim said, "This is mixed lighting, especially with the storm. We get them in here, get them confused, get them lost."

Behind them they heard the sound of a vehicle struggling, and they turned to see a gray Suburban caught in mud along the tree line. Quickly three men bailed out of it and ran behind a rusted-out CONNEX shipping container outside the shoot house surrounded by dense foliage, a stack of rotten railroad ties, and a high pile of sand with vines all over it.

A long, low earthen berm ran along that, parallel with the shoot house.

All three men had been carrying pistols.

Both Gentrys knew those three men could have gone anywhere after they'd disappeared, including right up to the entrances of the shoot house.

They turned and saw the other SUV at the edge of the pine trees, but it immediately pulled past a berm that separated the shoot house from a nearby handgun range. The berm was so overgrown that, again, the three men in this vehicle could enter the other side of the shoot house without Court or his dad seeing them.

Court said, "They can come over both those berms, enter this space from any one of the twelve entrances."

Jim spoke softly, even though the roar of the rain on the roof drowned out their voices at distance. "There were twelve entrances when you used to work here. There's over twenty now with all the broken-down plywood walls where the railroad ties rotted out. We need to go deep into the structure, son. Let them come to us. They won't stand a chance."

Court liked the idea. There were thirty-two different rooms or hallways here, and Court could still walk this entire building with a blindfold on.

He looked to his dad and said, "King Tut's Tomb."

Jim nodded. "Yeah. Center of the shoot house. We go there, defend. Our fallback is the Speakeasy."

Every room and every hallway had a name; Jim's two sons came up with most of the names when they were just children. King Tut's Tomb was a closet-sized space off a center-fed room in the middle of the building, but there was a low crawl space out of it that led to a room they called the Speakeasy because of a makeshift wooden bar built there to resemble an actual pub. The Speakeasy had four exits to it, plus the crawl space entrance behind the bar, so if the two Gentrys were overrun, they could possibly escape out of there.

Together they began hustling through the nearly dark hallways, making lefts and rights without needing to employ their flashlights, except when they encountered plant life, large puddles, or fallen wooden beams from the catwalk above.

It occurred to Court that if he had time to think about it, he'd probably have a serious bout of PTSD from being back in this building. He'd spent some scary times as a child in here, often against his wishes, growing up working for his dad, being subjected to thousands of Simunition rounds fired by amped-up and big SWAT officers who saw young Court as their mortal enemy, lest they fail the course.

As if his father could read his mind, Jim said, "I'm sorry I was so hard on you back then, Court. I know I made a lot of mistakes. Especially considering you and your brother didn't have a mom around."

"Dad, let's not get into that right now. It's good to see you."

"You, too."

They made it to the Tomb; it was even smaller than Court remembered, just enough room for himself and his father, but they could look out on a larger room, a long hall, and several stretches of the wooden-beamed catwalk above.

There, Court said, "I'm really sorry I got you into this, Dad."

Jim was breathing hard. This had to have been the most arduous morning of the last ten years for him. Still, Court saw his dad's smile in the low light. He said, "If we get you out of this alive, maybe kill that man who's after you, then this will be the best fucking day of my life, boy." He pulled his revolver from his pocket, looked it over. "I mean, if I had an MP5 it would be better, but—"

This gave Court an idea. He drew his bigger weapon, turned it around, and extended it towards his father.

"Dad, give me your piece."

"What? I'm not giving you my—"

"Look, I'm going to need some help from you if we're going to get out of here. I was taught by the best instructor in the world. With your revolver I can put five rounds in five foreheads in four seconds if it comes to it. You'll do better with a bigger gun, a red dot sight, more ammo, and a flashlight on the rail. You *know* I'm right about this."

Jim Gentry said, "Are you sure? I've never even shot one of those—"

"It's just like an old 1911, but without the recoil. Plus, an eighteen-round magazine instead of just seven." He handed his dad two extra magazines. "Let 'em have it."

Jim passed his little stainless steel revolver over, along with a six-round strip clip, essentially a slim rubber holder for ammo that helped one reload a little faster than just fishing loose shells out of one's pocket.

When Court accepted the Smith and Wesson from his dad, Jim said, "Take care of my baby. I'm gonna want that back."

The two men tried to listen over the racket of the rain and near-constant thunder. Finally, Jim said, "Those guys we saw on the right. They moved in a gaggle. Disorganized. We can frustrate them, get them pissed off. They will lose discipline."

Court nodded. "They'll hit from the west and the east, groups of three, probably, but by the time they come through the maze of this building, they could be separated and might be approaching from any direction."

Jim said, "Watch for vertical threats. They're going to assume the catwalk is going to give them better visibility. They'll have problems up there, but they might get lucky and see you before they come crashing down."

"Will do."

To his surprise, his father put his hand on his back. "Whatever happens, Court. Just know . . . you did the right thing by coming here."

Court nodded.

Jim added, "Now that I've seen you both again . . . I can die a happy man."

"You're not going to die." Then Court turned to him. "What do you mean, you've seen us both?"

"You and your brother." He smiled a crooked smile. "I told myself I had to see you both, just once more, before I went to the Lord."

Court's brother had died seven years earlier.

"When did you see Chance, Dad?"

"Last year. Just like with you, I just saw him from a distance, standing in a field, and then he was gone."

Court wondered if his dad was suffering from dementia.

A shouted voice came from somewhere in front of them, refocusing their attention. Court recognized the Irish accent of Campbell Coyle.

"Hey, Court? I'm talkin' to you, chief! I know you can hear me! Send your da out. I'm not after him! Let's you and me fight, forget the rest!"

Jim squeezed his son's forearm, shook his head no.

Court spoke softly to his dad. "I send you out there and he'd have you up on that catwalk with one of those other assholes pointing a gun at your forehead in ten seconds."

Soon they saw a flashlight's beam coming up a hallway, ahead and to their left. It shone on thick vines hanging from the catwalk above; they glistened with rain, and lightning struck somewhere nearby.

The thunder sounded like a bomb going off. Jim aimed the Staccato at the light. To his son, he said, "Save your ammo."

The light grew brighter, but before they could see the origin of the beam, it stopped. Whoever was holding it was now stationary in the hall.

Court and Jim both knew this indicated someone was coming from a different direction, and the man with the light, or men if there were more than one behind the beam, had been ordered to hold position.

Court took a chance, stepped out of the little room they called King Tut's Tomb, looked to the left in the darkness, and saw a man coming around the threshold of another entrance. He fired once with the .38 Special, hitting the approaching figure just above his left eye.

The man dropped his weapon in a puddle and crumpled down on top of it.

Behind him, Jim fired three rounds. Court looked back to see that his dad hit the wall just to the left of where the beam of light had been coming from.

The Gentrys knew that was a plywood wall, not reinforced like some others were in this massive building.

Immediately, the flashlight in the hallway fell to the ground.

Court began to regress to the Tomb where his dad was, but instantly gunfire sparked nearby.

Someone was firing from the catwalk above; the flashes came from behind Court, so he raced forward, towards the entrance where he'd just shot the man, and in so doing, leaving his father behind.

FIFTY

Court had wanted to take the pistol off the man he killed, but he was chased out of the room by more gunfire.

Jim had said the catwalk wasn't structurally sound, but apparently one of the attackers didn't get the memo and had gone up there, giving him a decent overlook of this portion of the large structure.

Court entered the hallway the dead man had just come through and was surprised to find it empty. This gave him the impression that the six attackers had all split up, and this made for an even more chaotic situation.

One was dead, for sure; he didn't know if the man his dad had fired at had been hit or had only dropped his flashlight, and there was someone up above somewhere, as well.

Court knew his dad would make his way to the Speakeasy, and he planned on meeting up with him there. But before Court could get to the Speakeasy, he saw another glow of a light, farther up the hall, coming from a room they called the Boardroom, because a massive plywood table had been erected down the center of it as a role-playing aid. Court imagined the table was long rotted away, but he knew the shape of the room and knew people could find cover in there, so he ducked off to his right into a smaller room they called the Guest Bedroom, because it had once been used for an overflow housing area when people came to train.

In here, Court was immediately drenched with rain dripping from the leaking tin roof. The catwalk above him had collapsed, and rotten wood covered the floor. He had to pick his way carefully through the darkness, because he didn't want to shine his light and give his position away to anyone on the catwalk.

If he hadn't left his father behind, he would have never made it back to the Tomb without getting shot, and then the enemy would have simply just shot up the Tomb itself, probably killing his dad. He hadn't heard any more firing, so he imagined his father was right now making his way through the little tunnel to the Speakeasy. That meant—for a moment, anyway—the old man was safe.

But Court had to get to the Speakeasy himself, and that meant he had to face whoever was up on the catwalk behind him, and whoever was in the room or the hall in front of him.

He had four bullets in his revolver, and another six in his pocket.

Campbell Coyle knelt in a muddy and dark CONNEX box on the eastern side of the building and called over his earpiece, checking his team.

One by one, they called in. "This is Alfie, I'm on the catwalk. I can move forward, but it feels like this floor is going to fall in. Also, I don't want to use my light, so I'm not doing much up here, but I shot at movement below me a minute ago."

"This is Gavin. I'm shot in the hand. I lost my flashlight. I'm hiding back near the entrance we came in. I still have my gun, though. Anybody comes this way and I'll blast the fucker."

"Nolan here. I'm in a hall somewhere, going into a room. By myself, I can't see or hear anything since the shooting a minute ago."

"This is Barry. I'm moving through the room where the shooting came from. There's a little closet here. I smell gun smoke. Somebody was just here, probably the guy that shot Gav."

It was quiet for a moment, and then Campbell said, "Jack? Jack, are you with us?"

Barry spoke up again. "Jack is here, facedown. He's dead."

Campbell sighed. He was still outside, moving to one of the entrances on the east side. If Jack was dead, his brother Alfie, up on the catwalk, was probably about to do something stupid. He said, "Alfie. Concentrate on the job. Move carefully on that catwalk. I'm going to come up there with you and assist, yeah? Don't you bloody shoot me."

The Northern Irishman began moving into the massive dilapidated building.

He didn't know why he was here, what this location was to Court Gentry other than the building next door to and behind his da's home, but it was already sounding like Court and his father knew their way around.

That would give them an advantage, but Campbell Coyle had spent time in plenty of shoot houses doing training, so he wasn't worried.

He held his pistol high and moved through the darkness, as another burst of gunfire kicked off somewhere ahead of him.

Court heard fire around the structure. It was undisciplined, and he knew it wasn't his dad. More like one of the men with Coyle had seen a shadow and dumped rounds toward it.

He moved to a fortified wall that separated the Guest Bedroom, where he was, from the Boardroom, where he'd noticed a light from a doorway moments ago. He worried about someone on the catwalk, but they would have to be far behind him, because the upper level here seemed to be completely caved in.

And this cave-in had given him an idea. He found a fallen cluster of boards leaning against the fortified wall, and he slipped his revolver in the small of his back and then began climbing up.

He wasn't silent, but the rain beating down on the roof was so loud that he wasn't worried about making noise.

He made it to the top; he was on the wall now looking down into the Boardroom. It was too dark to see anything in there, but he drew his Smith and Wesson and his flashlight and got ready.

Well aware there was someone up high, maybe twenty-five yards or so behind him, he knew he'd have to act quickly.

He flipped on the light, and immediately saw a man in a raincoat below him. The man's gun was up and pointed towards the doorway that led across the hall and, ultimately, to the Speakeasy.

The man swung his pistol in the direction of the light. Court fired twice into him, spinning him around and out into the hall, and then Court quickly rolled over the top of the wall, off the felled piece of catwalk that he'd climbed to get here, and dropped down into the Boardroom.

A volley of at least ten gunshots followed. Someone on the catwalk was shooting at him, but he'd made it behind the fortified wall. Tires filled with dirt and railroad ties protected him from the bullets of the shooter, though he heard impacts on the other side.

Court had landed hard on a stack of timber, rolled down into the muck on the concrete floor, and found himself in some foliage here. He heard the sound of a skittering rodent taking off to find some other place to hide.

Court had two rounds in the revolver, and the enemy, an enemy that was no doubt in comms with each another, knew exactly what room he was in. The man up on the catwalk could direct others to either of the two entrances. On his right, a hallway led to the eastern side of the building, more halls and rooms, and to the left, he just had to cross a hall to get into the Speakeasy, where he assumed his dad was waiting for him.

He opened the cylinder of the pistol quickly, dropped all the shells into his hand in the darkness, then reloaded the two unspent cartridges, letting the spent shells fall to the floor. He pulled three more bullets from the strip clip in his pocket, slipped them into the cylinder, and slammed it shut with a hard flick of his right hand.

Then Court rose and moved towards the exit, in the direction of the Speakeasy, hoping he'd get lucky and find the gun of the dead man there so he would have a backup.

Campbell Coyle called over his earpiece, his voice as low as he could make it while still being heard over the thunderstorm that seemed to be beating the building apart around him.

"Alfie. What happened?"

"A man shined a light and fired, went over a wall. Twenty yards in front of me and to the right."

Coyle knew this would be Court; it didn't sound like an old man's maneuver, so he asked his four remaining team to call in.

"Alfie moving forward on the catwalk."

"Gavin still on the west side. Watching several exits."

"Barry here. I'm in the hall right behind where the last shooting happened. I'm taking cover. Waiting to hear someone tell me which way to go."

There was no response from Nolan Walsh.

Both sets of brothers had lost a member. Alfie Donnelly, Gavin Walsh, and Barry Walsh were all Campbell Coyle had left.

He considered pulling everyone back and out of the building, but the storm would end at some point, the police would arrive at some point, and Campbell knew that the fact that Court's dad was here could be used to his advantage.

He wanted to end this, right here, and then he wanted to go back home.

Coyle said, "Alfie, I'll come up the catwalk on your right. You keep going forward, try to see into that room the target went to."

Coyle found a broken wooden staircase and carefully began climbing.

Court gave up on finding the gun the man had dropped; it must have fallen out into the hallway, and there were eight access points with a view to that area, so Court wasn't about to hang out there in the hall with a flashlight.

Instead, he took a big breath, let it out, and then sprinted across the hall and into the Speakeasy.

Gunfire came from above and from up the hallway, two shooters, both on his left.

But he made it into the room, immediately covered the area with his gun, then raced around a faux wooden bar that ran along the left-hand wall, because that was where the access from King Tut's Tomb led.

He got back there, knelt, then quickly flashed his light. In front of him, he saw his dad sitting on his butt on the concrete, leaning against the bar and adjusting his glasses.

There was blood on his hand and smeared on his face. Court crawled to him through a puddle that was a couple inches deep. "You're hit?"

Jim said, "Put my hand through a fucking nail crawling through that damn tunnel." He held it up. It was his shooting hand, and the nail hole was bloody and ragged, but small.

"Shit," Court said. "Can you shoot?"

"Hell yeah. Hey, son. Remember when this place was a lot more fun?"

"When both it and *we* were twenty-five years younger, and the bullets weren't real? Yeah, I remember."

"The good ole days."

"Right." Court said, "I got two of them. You?"

"I know I hit one, don't know if I put him down."

Court said, "Dad, we have to move. They are going to converge on this room from different doorways."

"Yep."

"I'm going to cross back towards Jacob's Ladder, go up to the catwalk."

Jacob's Ladder was a ladder in a vertical CONNEX box on the northeastern part of the shoot house. It led up to the catwalk, but it was covered, unlike most of the staircases.

Jim reloaded the Staccato with a fresh eighteen-round magazine. Said, "We haven't done CQB together in a long time."

"It's okay," Court said to his father. "I'll lead. We'll keep it simple. We get to a doorway. We peek, pause, push. You stay on my back, you have 180 degrees of responsibility behind me."

"I can do that."

They began moving through the warren of rooms, sure there were three or four men around here gunning for them. At each entrance to a room they would stop, and Court would move across the threshold, flash his light while looking in, while his dad checked the hallway behind.

Once Court was reasonably sure there was no one behind, he would begin moving, and his dad would follow, his left hand on his son's shoulder but his eyes, and his bloody right hand, on the weapon pointed behind.

Court had done this exact form of close-quarters operating back when he was a kid, maybe five or six years old, with his dad at the lead and him in back with a squirt gun.

Now Court led his elderly father, and the stakes were considerably higher.

When they were one hallway away from the CONNEX box with the ladder, Jim flashed his light and saw movement at the other end. He fired the Staccato multiple times at a target there, then ducked into the metal shipping container Court had just entered.

Court had been focusing his attention on the way ahead; he leaned into his dad's ear. "What did you see?"

"I got one of the fuckers. He's dead at the end of the hall."

"He have an Irish cap on?"

"What? No. Just a raincoat."

"Okay," Court said. "I want you to stay here, but when I go up that ladder, I want you to fire an entire magazine to the south, shooting up towards the catwalk.

"Then I want you to reload, stay right here, and wait for me to come get you."

"Okay. Be careful, Court."

Court put the little revolver in the small of his back again, then began climbing the old ladder, and then Jim started shooting to the south towards the pitch-black catwalk.

Campbell Coyle and Alfie Donnelly had seen each other on the catwalk and had begun moving closer together in the dark, their eyes still on the rooms they could see around them.

A burst of gunfire from the northeast turned their heads, but they saw nothing but glowing in an area, no pinpricks of light indicating flashes, so they had no line of sight on the shooter.

Coyle and Donnelly moved closer together, and then Alfie turned, leading the way slowly and gingerly on loose and, in some places, rotten flooring, always keeping one hand on the rail, his eyes ahead and his gun swinging left and right.

Campbell was close behind, his own weapon up, his own light ready to turn on at the first indication of trouble.

Coyle spoke again to his team over his earpiece, and this time he didn't get a response from Barry.

The Northern Irishman assumed Barry Nolan had been a victim of the last volley of fire he heard.

Then a near-constant barrage came from nearby, sending both men kneeling, as bullets sparked off the tin roof just above them.

Alfie started to react to the panic of the shooting and the rage of losing his brother. He rose and began to run along the catwalk towards the north, though Coyle thought someone was just letting off some probing fire, and he wanted to just stay where he was. But Coyle believed strength in numbers was of value now, so he himself rose as soon as the shooting stopped, and he hurried to catch up with Alfie Donnelly.

Court Gentry came out of the CONNEX box on the catwalk level just as his father ran out of ammunition in his magazine below. He knew his dad would reload, and he hoped his dad would follow his orders and just wait there, but Court knew it was his own responsibility to end this now.

He expected to find someone on the catwalk as soon as he flashed his light, but he was patient; he probed along slowly, putting each foot down carefully, heeding his father's advice.

He came to a T junction, turned to the left, then began moving south, still in darkness.

The sound of the rain pounding the tin roof was amplified up here, because he was only six feet below the ceiling, so he thought there was little chance he'd hear much of anything, but then the slapping sound of footsteps came from directly in front of him. Someone was running up here; they weren't close, maybe thirty feet, but they were approaching quickly.

Court aimed the little Smith and Wesson with one hand, then hooked the back of his hand around the back of the other hand, which held a tactical flashlight.

He clicked on the beam and saw a big young man moving along the catwalk with a stainless steel automatic pistol in front of him.

The man seemed surprised to find an enemy up here in front of him; his weapon was oriented towards the rooms down below.

Court fired at the man and hit the gun with his first round, sending sparks into the air. With his second shot he caught the man in the face, and then with the third the big man's head snapped to the side, and he began to fall forward, still running.

A fourth shot from the little revolver hit the stumbling man in the shoulder, and Court was about to empty the gun into the body when he realized that a second man was running right behind the first.

Instantly Court recognized Campbell Coyle, just twenty-five feet away from him.

Both men had their guns up; Court had just one round left in the chamber of his revolver.

And then the big running man's falling body impacted the catwalk floor, right above a support beam that had been quietly rotting away for twenty years.

The beam snapped under the weight.

Court squeezed his trigger.

Coyle squeezed his trigger.

The floor fell out from under them both, and they disappeared in the darkness and the wreckage, their shots flying harmlessly into the trees around the shoot house.

FIFTY-ONE

Jim Gentry heard the blasts of gunfire, the crack of wood, the symphony of a multistage collapse that shattered a catwalk, crumpled staircases, snapped support beams, even pulled a portion of the tin roof down as old and unmaintained support cables popped.

Jim knew his son had been up there, in the fight, when it happened, so he rose from the shipping container he'd been hiding in, then bolted as fast as he could towards the center of the building. He used his flashlight along with his gun to clear the way, but he wasted no time closing on the area.

The crash had happened halfway down and on the western side of the building, and Jim thought about going out an exit and then entering back into the building near to where it happened, but he saw that the hallway down the middle of the shoot house was only partially blocked with fallen debris.

He moved through it quickly, passing a man covered in blood and faceup. He had several obvious bullet holes and he wasn't moving, so Jim didn't shoot him again and reveal his presence any more than his flashlight already did.

He'd just made it into a room they called the Ballroom because of nothing more than its size when he found Court lying there, half buried under moldy plywood and two-by-fours. Rain from an open hole in the roof the size of a minivan poured in on his son, and the hole gave some light to the scene.

He knelt over Court, then quickly looked up to a west-side exit door to the outside, where a man appeared, silhouetted by the light behind him.

The man raised a pistol, Jim raised his, and they both got off one shot before the man stumbled away, out of view. Jim didn't think he'd killed the enemy, but he heard footsteps slapping through the mud, and that told him the man was running away.

Below him, Court said, "Was that him?"

"Don't know. You okay?" Jim asked.

"I'm fine." He began pushing the wood off himself. "Coyle. Coyle was on the catwalk. Did you see him?"

"I saw one dead guy. I don't think it was—"

"Was he wearing a hat?"

"No."

"Fuck!" Court said, still struggling to push himself free and stand up.

Jim said, "The only guy I saw alive is running away."

"Let him go," Court said. "We have to find—"

"If that's him," Jim told his son, "then this is the best chance to end this shit."

Jim Gentry rose and moved quickly towards the exit, his Staccato up in front of him.

"Dad! Wait!" Court said, still trying to push free of all the debris.

The elder Gentry broke into a run, got to the doorway at full speed, then caught his foot on a cable that had snapped from above and now hung loose across the doorway. Jim stumbled a little, just enough to lose his balance, and his eyeglasses fell off his face.

He caught them as they tumbled down his body, then he looked up to see two men going over the top of the berm, running away in unison, back in the direction of the SUV they'd parked on the western side.

"Dammit!" Jim said as he fumbled to get his glasses back on, and then when he did, he watched while the SUV drove at high speed around a CONNEX, then through the stormy weather back south towards the tree line and the road beyond it.

He rushed back towards his son, who was now clear of the wreckage but struggling to find the little pistol in all the mess.

When his father got close, Court said, "Give me my piece."

Jim handed the Staccato over to his son, and while doing so, said, "It's a full mag. I just saw two of them drive away."

"You're sure?"

"Yeah. West side. That means we killed four."

Court found the 642 revolver, handed it back to his dad. He reached into his pocket and passed over the strip clip. "Reload and wait right here for me." He moved towards the exit, hobbling a little at first, suffering the effects of the fall and the crash of the old catwalk. As he walked, he called out to his dad. "You're *sure* you saw two drive off?"

Jim opened the cylinder of the pistol, began removing spent shells. "Yep. I saw two go over the berm. Then I saw the Suburban take off. I can't say for sure that . . ." He paused, looking away from the gun, then said, "I didn't see how many were in the vehicle. It was too far away."

As Jim spoke, he reloaded the pistol with his four remaining bullets, his eyes on his son as he ran through the door, leaping over the cable Jim himself had tripped on. Court then ran up onto the berm, his pistol out in front of him as he went.

Jim stood there a moment watching, he closed the cylinder, then looked down at his partially loaded revolver.

He decided he'd go back to the dead man he'd passed in the hall and look for his weapon, but only after putting an insurance round in the poor bastard, just to make sure he was dead.

If those two men in the SUV doubled back, Jim reasoned, then they might need more firepower than his little two-inch Smith could provide.

Campbell Coyle looked at the rain, at the sky, trying to make sense of it all. It had seemed like it would be so easy, at first. Go to an old man's house, take the old man, force his son to show up to get him.

Then kill the son and let the old man go.

But now . . . but now it was all such a bloody mess.

Now . . . now he lay on his back, watching the rain pour down on him, and he wondered how long he'd been knocked unconscious.

He'd looked right at the Gray Man; the killer of his boy, Charlie, had been a half dozen paces distant, no more, when he began to press the trigger on his pistol.

And then the world had turned upside down.

He remembered falling, remembered something hitting his head when he was in the air, and he did not remember anything else, not till now.

He lay on his back, wet and hurting, no doubt injured. He felt around with his right hand, realized his weapon was there, and he grabbed it, and then he recognized that there was something lying across his legs. He lifted his head and saw that it was just a bit of plywood, some rusty tin, a few pieces of rotten support beam.

But then, beyond that, he saw something else.

On the other end of the hall, illuminated from light coming from another hole in the roof, a man stood there, aiming a gun at something on the floor.

Coyle couldn't make him out in the heavy rain coming down, but when the man fired his pistol, the Northern Irishman rose quickly, pushing debris out of the way.

He extended his gun arm.

Coyle got a sight picture through the window of his optic, put it right on the target in the low light, and then he realized he wasn't looking at Court Gentry. The killer of his son.

No, he was looking at the old man.

Through his weapon's optic he saw the father—wet silver hair, eyeglasses, a scowl of a mouth—look up in his direction suddenly, and the eyes behind the thick eyeglasses widened for an instant.

Then they narrowed with resolve.

He raised his pistol towards Campbell.

"No!" Campbell Coyle shouted. It wasn't supposed to happen this way.

Jim Gentry squeezed the trigger on the Smith and Wesson revolver, and the hammer dropped on the one empty cylinder in the weapon.

The gun went *click*.

And then Jim Gentry saw the flash of the barrel of the gun in the other man's hand.

The seventy-five-year-old felt the blunt, forceful impact dead center in his chest.

Then he was falling, not flying. Down, not back, dropping to the wet ground, amid the trash and the mud of the catwalk.

He folded up, rolled over, and died.

One perfect gunshot through the heart.

Court Gentry had swept the area out behind the berm for more enemy, found nothing but the tire tracks of the retreating Suburban. He heard a shot inside the building; it sounded like his dad's .38, and he took it as his father putting an insurance round into one of the killers.

Another shot came just two seconds later.

It sounded similar enough to him out here, out in the rain, so he thought little of it other than the fact that he'd told his dad to stay right where he was.

He headed back towards the shoot house, looking up at the unceasing rain, and then, just before he made it back inside, he heard a new noise.

An engine firing on the opposite side of the building.

He ran back to the top of the berm just in time to see the other gray Suburban roll off towards the trees.

Court was far away, over fifty yards, and he couldn't see who was inside, so he knew better than to fire.

So, just as his dad had said, two men had gotten away, but they'd each taken a different vehicle.

Court climbed back down the berm, squinting in the rain, and then he went back inside the shoot house to find his father.

The Cirrus Vision Jet flew over the East Coast, halfway between Jacksonville and Norfolk, Virginia, over two hours into its journey, the first time Court Gentry considered answering his phone.

It was two p.m.; he'd made it back to the airport by eleven thirty, just after the storm ended, and then the jet waited its turn to take off. All the while the FibreNet app on his phone kept buzzing, every ten minutes or so.

Each time, he'd reject the call.

The Signal app rang a couple of times, as well, and this would be Hanley, who knew what had happened, or Zoya, who by now probably also knew, although he hadn't spoken with her. He'd called Hanley when he was still on the property, when the storm still raged, before any police or ambulance had arrived, and who knew who Hanley had told?

Hanley had agreed to contact Skip, to have him come back out to the scene as soon as the weather cleared a little, and to make sure the body of his friend, Court's father, was respected by local authorities. Court wanted to take his dad back home with him, but that was a no-go. Hanley insisted the locals had to process the scene, that Court's dad had to be there or the incident would grow in complexity and attention by five thousand percent, and Skip would be told just what to say and just what to do.

Court told himself that someday he'd come back down to Florida and shake Skip Echols's hand. The man had meant a lot to his dad in these last weeks of his life.

Court had sat here for most of the flight, looking out the portal at the Atlantic, but now, as he continued looking out the starboard side of the jet, probably somewhere along the North Carolina coast, FibreNet buzzed for perhaps the dozenth time since they'd taken off.

This time, he told himself, he was ready.

This time, he accepted the call.

But he did not speak.

After twenty seconds or so, he heard a familiar voice, but it was softer somehow. "You there, chief?"

Court said nothing.

"I hear you breathing. Look . . . that was a bloody brutal situation all around. Made worse by my associates, I'm sorry to say. We had a plan goin' in, and it certainly wasn't *that* shite."

The man alone in the back of the tiny jet finally spoke. "You killed my father."

"Aye. No words I say will make a difference, but I do want you to know, that was, in no way, my intention. It wasn't an 'eye for an eye' situation. Not at all. Your da was about to take me out, and I tried to stop him. Or . . ." He seemed to think a moment. "Or maybe it was just reflex. I keep playin' it back in me head . . . and I can't really tell you how it all happened, but I'm sorry it did.

"It was me or him . . . I did what I had to do."

"Where have I heard that before?"

"Out of your own mouth, yeah?"

"Yeah. You're right about one thing, though," Court said.

"What's that, chief?"

"You were right when you said, 'No words you say will make a difference.'"

Silence again. Then Coyle said, "That shoot house. More like a house of horrors. I don't get rattled, but I was bloody rattled this mornin'."

Court did not reply.

"Look at us," Coyle said. "You and me. Our wee talks. Our lives seem . . . intertwined, don't they? Well . . . they're even more so now, yeah?"

Court said, "You had a chance of surviving all this, Coyle. If you gave up, if you stopped chasing me, stopped working for Gauntlet. If you went home, if you went back into retirement. If you grieved the death of your son like a normal human.

"If you'd done *any* of that . . . you would have walked away.

"But now you have no chance."

The Northern Irishman said, "What happened to the bloke who told me vengeance was a fool's errand?"

"He's long gone."

"Yeah? What now, then?"

"Now you're left with me, and I won't rest until you're fucking dead."

"You're not hearing me, mate. I did not kill your da on purpose. He made me."

"And your son shot me in the fucking chest. The circumstances didn't matter to you, and they sure as hell don't matter to me."

After a time, Campbell Coyle said, "I suppose it's all the same. People like us are always going to suffer the same fate. Pledge allegiance to a flag, an idea, a value. Then we're killed for it, and we rot under the flag we died for."

Court replied, "I'm thinking this, what's happening to us, is about you and me. About fathers and sons. About the past and the present. It's got nothing to do with a flag. The flag is up there in D.C. for me, and it's in tatters right now, but I'm not blaming *it* for what happened down in Florida."

Coyle said, "Yeah, about that. I'm no longer in the employ of those in your government who, for some reason, seem to want to *destroy* your government, or help someone else do so. I'm goin' away. I won't be showing up at your door. Not now. You can grieve your da, because what happened shouldn't have happened, and that's not what I was trying to do.

"In a month. In a year. I don't know. Someday, maybe, I'll not be able to sleep thinkin' about what you did to my Charlie, and maybe I'll not be able to live knowin' what might happen to wee Ronan. If that happens, I'll come back, and I'll finish this. But not now. Not like this."

"You're going to run and hide, then?"

"No. I'm going to go reach out to Charlie's wife, the woman who hates me, blames me more than she does you, for what happened. I'm going to beg her to let me help her with Ronan.

"And then, Court, I'm going to go grieve at the grave of my boy. Probably at the exact same time you are standin' at yer da's funeral."

"What did I just say?" Coyle said. "You and me . . . cosmically intertwined, we are."

Court hung up the phone and stared out the window at the winter sun over the water.

The Vision was less than thirty minutes from touchdown at Hampton Roads when Court called Hanley. Erin Childers, code name Conductor, answered, and she gave her sincere condolences.

But Court wasn't in the mood for sympathy. "Thanks," was all he said. Then, "I need Matt."

"Here he is."

Hanley took the phone. "I'm talking to Skip. Feds are down there already, he can't tell what agency, they aren't talking, but it looks like Homeland Security Investigations."

"Why is Homeland involved?"

"All the dead are U.S. citizens. Not sure why HSI is there, but the only thing I can think of is that someone high in the government knows about you, knows Jim was your dad, and they're trying to find out where you are right now."

Court didn't really give a shit. He knew he should, but he didn't.

Hanley said, "I'm going to see that your father is buried at Arlington. Full honors. He deserved that for his service in the Marine Corps, even if he didn't have you as a son."

Court softened now. "Thanks, Matt. That means more than you can imagine."

"Don't thank me. In fact . . . you are about to be pissed at me."

"Why?"

"Because I can't let you go to the funeral. There could be surveillance. Assassins watching out for you."

"I don't want to go to the funeral. That's why I called."

Hanley was clearly gobsmacked by this. "You don't want to go to your father's . . . I mean, I expected pushback. Maybe I can put you in a blacked-out Tahoe, a couple hundred yards away with a lens so you could watch, pay your respects from a safe distance."

"No, thanks."

Matt said, "I don't understand. Why don't you want to go to the funeral?"

"Because I want to go to Northern Ireland."

Hanley just blew out an annoyed sigh. Court had been listening to this man make this sound for a long time, usually because of something Court had said or done.

"Why?"

"You know why. I want to get off this little jet and then get on a bigger Bellstar jet that can get me all the way to Belfast. That is the only resource from Ghost Town I'm asking for. If you don't have something that can go transatlantic at Hampton Roads, charter me something at Reagan or Dulles. I want to go immediately."

"Disallowed."

"I'm asking you for a jet, Matt. I'm not asking you for permission to go. I'm going. If I have to take the fucking *Queen Mary*, I'm going. You want me to do this in a few days, or do you want me to take longer? That's up to you."

"I need you back here. It's a fucking convalescent ward at Ghost Town, unless you've forgotten."

"I'll be back. Pace and Lacy will keep working; when I get back I'll go help kill some other motherfucker that has it coming, but right now, I'm going to Belfast."

Matt sighed. "Pace thinks Lewis Shaw was just a fucking errand boy. And when the heat got too high for the real culprit, meaning when Pace, along with Ghost Town, did what we did, then whoever is responsible killed Shaw to use him as a fall guy. Gauntlet is involved, but there is somebody very high in the intelligence community who is behind all this.

"In fact," Hanley said, his voice a little lower now, "Pace has suspicions about Trey Watkins himself. Seems he is one of only a few who could have gotten intelligence on both Zack's daughter and your father. He thinks Watkins is setting us up."

"Well," Court said, "you guys work on figuring that shit out, and when I get back, I'll deal with it."

Hanley breathed into the phone a moment. Finally, he said, "Do you even know where Whetstone is?"

"No, but I can find him. I just need some time, Matt."

Hanley's response came in a different tone. Harsher, less sympathetic. "Six, you are a fucking resource. I'm never going to lie to you about that, I'm never going to pretend otherwise. So don't *you* fucking forget it. I'll always do anything I can for you, unless and until it gets in the way of our mission, at which point, I have to do what *I* have to do.

"And right now, I need you at Ghost Town."

"I hate this fucking shit," Court mumbled.

"No, you don't," Hanley responded. "The job you do, you know it's crucial. I'm sorry your dad died this morning, but that dad of yours saved the life of America's most important human intelligence resource. Jim Gentry died a motherfucking hero, saving his son, protecting my asset, and from what Skip tells me about Jim, nothing on this earth would have made him prouder than exactly what happened today.

"Now . . . make him even prouder by helping us do what you were meant to do."

Court felt the plane descending. "You come at me with your fucking logic, it just makes me want to beat the shit out of you."

"Because I'm right."

After a pause, the man in the jet said, "I'm going to Northern Ireland."

"To kill a man who probably doesn't want anything to do with you anymore."

"He and I both have unfinished business."

"Only in your fucking minds, Court!"

"As long as it's in one of our minds, then it's got to be dealt with." Court sighed. "Am I getting that aircraft? Because if not, I need to go online and book a flight."

"You are *not* getting an aircraft."

Court thought a moment. "Okay, fine. Next question. Will you tell these pilots to divert to Dulles, or do I have to hijack this plane?"

"You're fucking serious right now?"

"I don't know, Matt. Do I *sound* serious? I've got Zack's piece and half a mag of hollow-points. This plane is going wherever I want it to."

"Dammit!" Hanley shouted. "Okay. Relax. Just relax." Then he hung up.

Less than five minutes later, the copilot came over the PA. "Sir . . . we've been ordered by the company to divert to Dulles."

Court nodded, pulled out his phone, and booked the first commercial flight he could. Dulles to Dublin, and then he'd take a train up to Belfast.

From there . . . he'd figure it out.

He wasn't thinking straight, but he *was* thinking, and he wasn't acting rational, but he *was* acting.

FIFTY-TWO

James Westwood and Michael Scardino jogged through a foggy morning; the woods were dark and the mist in the air made it almost impossible to see fifty feet ahead.

The pair arrived at the meeting point; they stopped, and Scardino began to check his watch, but before he could bring it up to his face, he saw the flashing lights burning through the vapor in the trees, indicating that the Chinese MSS assets were right on time, as usual.

After the wanding by both sides, Gracie Wu lowered her scarf down to her neck and asked J.W. and Big Mike to sit with her on the fallen log.

Once seated, she said, "Spiral is dead. Snare is dead. Lancer was killed in Colorado." She looked to Scardino specifically. "Ten Gauntlet men are dead, in all."

The Americans did not respond, so Gracie continued. "We expected to take losses, but we also expected that the five assets with support would be able to remove the targets, and there would be no comebacks on Operation Marigold. Matthew Hanley and his team have managed to protect the reporter Catherine King and witness Irene Ortega, and these are dangerous compromises."

Scardino said, "I killed Shaw myself yesterday morning."

"I am aware," Gracie replied.

J.W. spoke up now. "How fast will we be able to get the intelligence we need to continue the operations now that Shaw is off the table?"

Gracie said, "I have spoken to my superiors about that. I am assured you will continue to obtain all the intelligence you need even though Shaw is no longer part of the equation. The person or persons in the U.S. government who have been providing what we need understand the critical nature of the intelligence product and will make sure the flow continues."

"That's good to know," J.W. said.

"There is one small problem," Scardino said.

Gracie looked at him. "If there were only one small problem, I would be very happy."

J.W. said, "I guess I should say there is an *additional* small problem. Whetstone."

"What about Whetstone?"

"He is not responding. He's been paid for the work he and his team have done, but four of the five members of his team were killed yesterday in Florida."

She cocked her head. "The murders in northern Florida? The dead from Boston? They worked for Whetstone?"

Scardino nodded. "Those were his people. He was down there at the home of the father of one of Hanley's assets. When I killed Shaw, I made it look like Whetstone had committed the assassination, both to cover my ass and to make Hanley and his team think Whetstone was up in D.C. when he was actually on the way to Florida."

"And Hanley's asset in Florida survived?"

"Yes."

"Why isn't Whetstone responding?"

Big Mike said, "If he ever responds, I'll ask him that question."

"Do I detect insubordination?" the young woman asked, her eyes locked on Scardino.

"You detect frustration," J.W. said, speaking for Mike. "We have one active asset, and we still have targets to attend to."

Scardino said, "And I'm having Gauntlet units exposed in ways we never agreed to."

Gracie paused a beat, then said, "This has been a difficult operation, conducted under less-than-ideal circumstances. But do not be concerned. My superiors are extremely satisfied with the work you both have been doing for us."

J.W. said, "That's good to hear."

Gracie said, "We have decided to remove all the remaining names on the original list."

The two men looked at one another. Confused.

"Marigold is complete?" J.W. asked.

"Not entirely," she said. "The Russian cell in New York will be eliminated by Gauntlet. The Russians will be blamed for all the targets killed; Gauntlet will be lauded for its part in stopping the threats."

She added, "And we are assigning some new targets. Gauntlet will have to help with this, as well."

Scardino said, "Let's not get greedy, we've already accomplished a lot."

The young Chinese woman said, "Getting greedy is not necessarily a bad thing, when the result warrants it."

Westwood looked into the woman's eyes in the poor light. As usual, he could read nothing from them. "Who are the targets, then?"

Gracie turned to him. "One of the targets is Paula Kerr."

Westwood blinked once. Once again. Finally, softly, he said, "*Senator* Paula Kerr?"

Gracie said, "I shouldn't think I would need to specify. She is the junior senator from New Hampshire." Gracie added a little smile, which was incongruous with her personality. "*Your* home state, James. Her tragic death will lead to a major investigation, needless to say, but if your team executes the mission correctly, then her tragic death will also lead to something else, won't it?"

J.W. glanced to Scardino, whose own eyes were open wide. J.W. said, "Bill Farrelly, our governor, would appoint someone to take her place for the remaining five years of her term." He looked back to Gracie, fully understanding what she was inferring. "You think he will appoint me to the Senate?"

"I know he will."

"I mean . . . I have an excellent relationship with Bill, have since college. But there's no way to be certain that he would appoint—"

The young woman interrupted. "There *is* a way to be certain. Don't worry. If you execute the first half of the operation successfully, then I am told my organization and its contacts in the United States government will execute the rest of it. You will become a United States senator."

Chinese intelligence was telling James Westwood and Mike Scardino that the governor of New Hampshire was, or could be, under their control.

J.W. said, "Is there some tie between Paula and the intelligence community, some other reason besides installing me as a senator that—"

Gracie shrugged, a gesture that conveyed she neither knew nor cared. "I'm not told these things. Perhaps something will come out in the press afterwards, perhaps not. Obviously, if the death could be made to look like an accident, that would suppress a deep dive into any connections she might have had to Marigold, and that would only expedite your rise to the Senate seat."

Big Mike confirmed. "This target . . . you are giving it to us now."

"You are a green light for Paula Kerr. I was going to suggest you use Whetstone, but since you seem to have misplaced him, perhaps you should employ Masquerade."

"And the other new targets that you mentioned?"

"Not assigned yet, but you need to begin immediate preparations. If it happens, just know it will be in the D.C. area, it will be in the next few days, and it should be carried out by a plainclothes Gauntlet field team. It will require significant paramilitary skills, and military weaponry that we can help provide."

Scardino just nodded, unsure what any of this meant.

Gracie said, "You complete these tasks, and Marigold will be considered a great success. You both will be rewarded, and our collective interests will be furthered." She smiled. Neither of the Americans had ever seen her smile even once, and now she had done it twice in less than a minute. "We are so close, gentlemen. Let's get this done."

J.W., beaming with newfound exuberance, said, "Mike and I will get it done."

The meeting ended moments later, and Gracie jogged off into the fog with her team.

A minute after this, James Westwood ran through the dark and the fog, a verve in him he hadn't felt in thirty years. He had been ready to wait two years to become a United States senator; he was ready to wait over six to run for president of the United States, but the Chinese were offering to repay him for his hard work by shaving several years off his wait.

For a sixty-year-old man, this was significant.

Scardino ran alongside him. "When you get to the Senate, I hope you'll remember fondly your friends at Gauntlet."

J.W. laughed. "Tell you what. You get Masquerade up to New Hampshire to begin looking into how to do it, make it look like an accident, and Gauntlet will have my vote for any contract it wants."

Scardino said, "Will do. And regarding the still unsanctioned op she mentioned, I'll go ahead and put together a team of my most experienced Gauntlet men, guys who won't have a problem with a targeted killing. Who do you suppose the Chinese will send us after?"

J.W. said, "Somebody with some security, it would seem."

It was quiet between the two men, only the slapping of their feet on the unpaved trail. Then Scardino said, "Any way we can pick up the pace, boss? I've got a shit-ton of work to do."

J.W. smiled, then sped up considerably, and the younger man struggled to catch up.

Matthew Hanley hung up his phone; the fury he felt right now threatened to get the best of him, so he took some calming breaths there in his office, then he called his principals team in.

Travers and Hightower were on their way to Charlottesville, and Gentry was likely on his way to Europe, so it was just Conductor, Gumdrop, and Bricklayer who converged in his office, but at the last moment, he decided to conference in Angela Lacy. Even though she was a CIA employee and not a Ghost Town spook, Hanley wanted her to hear his take on the matter.

When it was all set up, he said, "I just talked to Trey Watkins. Angela? Do you know what I'm about to say?"

"I have no idea," the woman on the speakerphone replied.

"Well, Watkins has reassigned Jim Pace. Taken him off the investigation into the murders, the involvement of Gauntlet."

Angela spoke first. The shock in her tone couldn't have been more authentic. "I . . . I talked to Jim an hour ago. He didn't seem to know anything about—"

"This *just* happened. I demanded to know why, and he refused to answer me directly over the phone. He told me we are to stand down, effective immediately. To delete any files, destroy any papers, any information or images relating to the work we've been doing this past week.

"We've been ordered to continue day-to-day operations, training, et cetera, but we are also no longer involved with finding the culprits behind hiring the assassins and conducting the killings."

"Has someone gotten to Watkins?" Gumdrop was the one asking. "Is he tainted by this, somehow?"

Hanley said, "I don't know. Pace had his suspicions about Watkins since Night Train's daughter in Witness Protection and Six's father were ID'd by the opposition. He said there couldn't have been more than three or four people in the intelligence community who could have accessed both those pieces of information as quickly as it was apparently accessed."

Gumdrop said, "But if Watkins was one of the bad guys in all this, why did he have us out here targeting the killers?"

Hanley wiped his face with a hand. "I don't know. Maybe someone got to him. Maybe something changed. I asked him to explain himself, but he said he didn't want to say anything else over the phone."

"So," Conductor said, "you are going to talk in person?"

Hanley nodded. "He said I could go up to D.C. later in the week for a meeting. Not today. Not tomorrow. He said he'd let me know."

"Damn," Arnold said softly.

Hanley shook his head, still in disbelief. "When I have a face-to-face with Watkins, hopefully I'll get some answers. In the meantime, I was ordered not to reach out to Pace." Hanley looked to the phone now. "Angela, what do you think? Could Trey be one of them?"

There was a long pause on the other end. Hanley said, "Angela? Did I lose you?"

"I'm sorry," she replied. Her voice sounded distracted. "I'm very sorry. I just received a message. I have to report to the DDO's office. Right now. I'm going to have to hang up."

Hanley let out an exasperated sigh. "I'm sorry, Angela. I have a feeling you'll be reassigned, too."

"Shit," she mumbled. "I'll call you back after I talk to—"

Now Hanley was the one who interrupted. "No . . . you won't. Thank you for your help, but I guarantee Watkins is going to tell you, at a bare minimum, to steer clear of us."

"This makes no sense," Lacy said, her frustration evident, but then she said goodbye, presumably to report to her boss.

When it was just Hanley and his three employees, he said, "I'm going to get in Trey's face in a couple of days, and I'll get answers." After a little sigh, he said, "You all deserve that much."

"Be careful," Conductor said. "If he's working with the killers, confrontation might be dangerous."

Hanley shook his head. "There's a lot in this world that scares me. Trey Watkins does not."

"It won't be Trey himself you have to worry about," Gumdrop said. "There are still assassins out there that are unaccounted for."

The room cleared a minute later. Gumdrop, Conductor, and Bricklayer had files to delete and messes to clean up. Hanley just sat at his desk, enraged. He and his team had eliminated three top-tier assassins, had saved the lives of two women who could prove helpful in getting to the bottom of whatever conspiracy was infecting the U.S. intelligence community.

And now Trey was stopping them. Stopping Pace, no doubt stopping Lacy.

His fury grew, and the fact that he'd have to wait a few days to even confront Watkins only angered him more.

Court sat on the train from Dublin to Belfast, his eyes closed, his body rocking with the vibrations of the tracks. His headphones in his ears played a George Harrison tune from 1970. He wasn't really listening to the lyrics; he'd tuned them out to think of other things, or not to think at all, but then his Signal app buzzed, and he immediately sent the call to his headphones.

"Yeah?"

Sir Donald Fitzroy's voice was low and serious. "I did what you asked. Got you what you wanted."

"Give it to me." Court opened a notetaking app on his phone, prepared to type something in.

But the Englishman said, "Lad . . . what on earth are you doing?"

"It's *not* what you think."

"Then what *is* it?"

"I'm going to try to make things better."

"Better for who?"

Neither man spoke for several seconds. Then Court said, "I'm not really sure."

"I don't like this. Not one bit."

"Then just give it to me and forget I asked for it."

The older man let out a long sigh. "The thing that always made you different from the rest, it wasn't your skill, though lord knows you have that in spades. It was your humanity. If you lose that, then nothing you do will be worth anything. You'll just be another one of them."

Pleadingly, he said, "Don't be another one of them."

"I don't need a lecture right now. I need some guns, and I need an address."

"You need a bloody knock in the head if this is what I think this is."

"I told you. It's not that." Angrily, he said, "Give me what I fucking asked for, Fitz. You owe me, and you fucking know it!"

A head turned on the train. A woman stared at him. Court glared back at her until she turned away.

After a long moment, the Englishman said, "You're going to play that card? That I owe you this?"

"If I have to."

"Very well. Write this down, but I'm warning you, nothing good can come from it."

"'Good' left the chat a long time ago, Fitz."

FIFTY-THREE

No one on this side of the city called it Londonderry. Londonderry was the name the loyalists used, and there weren't many loyalists here in Bogside, a community just west of the River Foyle.

Tiny row house communities stretched for dozens of blocks in each direction; paint was chipped from the walls that surrounded every tiny back garden.

Someone had spray-painted "IRA" on a wall nearby—quite recently, it seemed—and a crafted stone sign at the head of the development read "End British Internment of Irish Republicans."

This was the heart of Derry; these people weren't pleased to be part of the United Kingdom, to put it mildly, and even though the vast majority of the IRA killing had stopped with the peace accords decades earlier, there was still dissent, and counterdissent, and some people here continued to suffer for their disloyalty to the Crown.

The skies were low and ashen gray; darker wisps of pasty clouds hung seemingly within reach, and the frigid wet air kept most people in their homes. Christmas decorations in windows did little to brighten the day.

Those who did walk the narrow pavements towards the few low-end shops here on the east bank of the River Foyle were all bundled up in coats and hats, many carrying umbrellas.

On Meenan Drive, the sixth tiny house on the left looked like all the others: flaked paint walls, a tile roof that needed repair, a wooden gate on rusty hinges that led to the car park.

The woman who lived in the sixth house on Meenan stood in her tiny back garden, arms across her chest to ward off the cold that her heavy coat couldn't keep out, and she stood there on a cracked patio watching her son crawl in his heavy jumper. He was eight months old and moving surprisingly well, his head up, his curly blond hair blowing in the wet breeze as he awkwardly played with an orange ball on the ground. Bumping it with an arm, a hand, his head.

It was silly, but he was having fun, and it made the woman smile.

Twenty-four-year-old Deirdre Coyle reached for her phone to take a video for her ma, but realized she'd left it inside on the kitchen table, so she darted in to fetch it.

Inside, she answered a quick text from a friend; it only took her a moment, and then she stepped back out into the back garden, tightening her jacket as she did so. She had her attention focused on the device in her hand, and it wasn't until she looked up towards little Ronan, still sitting there on the wet concrete with his ball, did she realize a man was there, in her garden, standing next to the wet linen hanging on the line, the wooden gate door shut behind him.

She lurched back when she saw him, and her phone dropped to the ground. He wore a coat with a hood, had a dark brown beard, and his hands were stuffed in his pockets.

He stood three steps away from her child.

Though instantly terrified, she manufactured a little strength in her voice when she spoke. "Who the feck are you?"

Her eyes flitted down to her son, and she saw him looking up at the man now.

The man put a gloved finger to his lips, indicating she should keep quiet.

He stepped a little closer, then surprised her by sitting down on a small chair by the table. "Can I talk to you for a moment? Then I'll go. I promise."

He was American. She sat down across from him; her eyes kept checking her son.

He said, "I'm not here for him."

"Why would you be here for him?"

The man did not respond for several seconds; he almost seemed confused by the comment. Finally, he said, "I'm not here for you, either."

"What you want, then?"

"I'm here for him. For your father-in-law. I know that *you* know where he is. And you know how to get in touch with him."

"You're the American. The killer."

The man nodded.

The chill in the air seemed to blow through her bones.

He said, "I've learned a lot about Charlie in the past several days. A lot I couldn't have known before our paths crossed. He was just a regular guy, but a guy in the wrong place at the wrong time, working the wrong job for the wrong employer when the wrong thing was done to the wrong person."

Softly, with apprehension and no small amount of confusion in her voice, she said, "Aye."

"*I'm* the wrong person," he said, confessing, it seemed, to the murder of her husband.

Deirdre did not speak. She could tell he wanted to talk, so she decided to let him. Still . . . her hands shook now. Her body shivered.

The American said, "He got me good." He touched his breast. "Right here. Any other day, he'd have been the one walking away from that encounter, not me." He shrugged. "I had a vest."

When he said nothing else, she finally found the words. "You had to kill him. That it? You *had* to fight it out with Bulgarian mobsters, couldn't have stayed home in America and watched the telly, gone to work in an office, paid yer taxes, and raised yer bloody children like the rest of the world? You'se sayin' it wasn't your fault, that you was forced to pick up a gun and go swinging it around a nightclub full of gangsters.

"You just *had* to. That yer story, yeah?"

A long exhale, nearly silent, came from the man; his body slowly deflated with it. He looked to Ronan, then back to Deirdre. He said, "It won't make any sense to you. It won't change a thing. But . . . yes. I went there with a purpose, a purpose I believed in. Still believe in. Everything after that, everything that happened to those men. To your Charlie . . . it wasn't my plan, but I know that what I did, in the end, did manage to make a—"

She shouted over him. "Why the feck are you here? You can't be so daft to think I'm gonna believe ya, gonna forgive ya. Sure, if you need me to beg for the life of me boy, for me own life, I'll get down on me bloody knees, but there's nothing else I have that you could possibly want, so why don't you feckin—"

"I told you I wouldn't hurt anyone. I just need to find your father-in-law."

She pulled swirling locks back over an ear. "I'd have thought it would've been *'im* tryin' to find *you*."

"That's already happened. He came to America. A lot of people have died because of it. I need to put an end to this."

"End it by killing Campbell Coyle, ya mean?"

The American shrugged. "End it, one way or the other."

"'One way or the other' won't bring my Charlie back."

The American shook his head now. "No. It won't do anything like that."

"And an old man's vengeance on you is not my problem, is it?"

"It's not about vengeance with your dad."

"He's not my da. He's my dead husband's da. He's Campbell bloody Coyle to me, when I'm not calling him 'that eejit son of a bitch.'"

She cocked her head. "But . . . if it's not about vengeance, what's it about, then? All the killin' you say he's done?"

The American said, "It's about this little innocent guy right here. Campbell has it in his head that someday, in eighteen years, maybe, your little boy is going to pick up a knife or a gun and come looking for the American who killed his father. I thought it was insane when Campbell told me this a few days ago. Now . . . now things have changed. Now I feel *exactly* what Ronan might someday feel."

Deirdre scoffed. "My Ronan won't be a Coyle. He'll be a McDermott, just like his ma, as soon as I get me maiden name back." She added, "He won't know about the legacy of murder and depravity and foolishness on his da's side."

The man said, "That's what I wanted to talk to you about. You raise that kid right, not the way I was raised, not the way Campbell was raised, Charlie was raised. You raise him pretty much any other way, and none of us have anything to worry about."

"I plan on raising him right."

"I have money. If you need—"

"I don't want yer money. I have a job now. I pay me bills."

"But I can help."

"You've done yer damage. There's no makin' up fer it."

The man with the beard looked down.

She said, "I can stop Ronan from coming fer ya in the future. He's not gonna have a fecked-up childhood where that's gonna make a lick of sense to him. I can promise ya that. But I *cannot* stop Campbell from coming fer you now."

Now the man looked back up. "I'm here because I *want* him to do that. We were close, he and I. Not much farther away than I am to that street out there, and we were armed, but it didn't happen, and then he left. I think he's come back to Northern Ireland to regroup.

"I just need you to tell me where he is."

She thought a long time, then said, "The second to last thing I want to do in this world is protect Campbell Coyle."

The man seemed to understand immediately. "And the *last* thing in the world you want to do is help the man who killed your husband."

"Ya may be a monster," Deirdre said. "But yer not bloody stupid."

She added, "'Ere's what I'll do. I'll call him. Campbell. I'll tell him to call ya. Tell him yer here. Ya didn't come for Ronan, though God knows ya could have done us both right here and there was nothing to stop ya."

The man shook his head. "That won't change anything. Coyle killed my father the other day. He and I are on a collision course. I'm not coming here to talk him out of anything. I'm here to kill him."

The young woman stared at the American for a very long time. Finally, she said, "I feel sorry for all you lot. You know no other way. But rest assured, Ronan will know another way. He won't grow up in your world."

The American said nothing.

"Charlie killed some people in Africa. He didn't talk much about it. But he drank, and he blamed himself fer something. I think he knew what he did was wrong."

"Even if what he did *wasn't* wrong, in this line of work, it's the *doing* it that gets to you."

He then said, "Please. Tell Campbell to give me a place to meet him. We'll end this. He doesn't do that, and I'll keep looking. Just like he did to me in America. Sooner or later, this will end. But we might as well settle it sooner."

She nodded; the wind blew her red hair in her face.

The American rose to his feet. "Thank you. I wish you both a long, peaceful life."

"I can't say the same for you, sir. God forgive me, I know I should . . . but I just can't. Charlie meant too much to me."

There was a sadness in his voice. "I get it."

The man turned away, stepped out through the gate, shut it behind him, and walked out onto the street, as Deirdre Coyle stood, hefted her son, and held him close, warming him from the cold.

Protecting him from the world.

FIFTY-FOUR

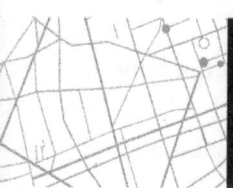

The town of Ballycastle in County Antrim, Northern Ireland, sits on the dramatic north coast of the island, and on this morning the cold breeze blew in from where the Irish Sea met the North Atlantic, making the prevalent sunshine all but irrelevant.

Campbell Coyle had driven up here the night before and taken lodgings, woken early, and had his tea and toast, then dressed in his Sunday best, though it was a Wednesday.

The last thing he did before he left the guest house was slide a long knife into a sheath on his belt, and a Makarov pistol into a holster on his hip.

His jacket came on over this; he positioned his cap on his head in the mirror, and he left his room, promptly at eight thirty in the morning, heading to a church nearby.

Thirty minutes later he knelt alone in a pew at the Church of St. Patrick and St. Brigid, prayed, took a moment to appreciate the beautiful building, and then he walked back to his car.

Fifteen minutes later he parked again, this time next to St. James Church. St. James was not Catholic, it was Church of Ireland, but Campbell was not here to pray.

He stood alone in the cold morning sunshine for a long time, still as the tombstones in the cemetery around him, and then, shortly after ten a.m., he walked back to his car.

It was time for an early lunch.

Matthew Hanley stepped out of Reagan National Airport into an overcast dawn, his coat already on and zipped. He'd not bothered with a tie; he didn't feel the need to offer that respect to the man he'd come to talk to today.

He only carried a shoulder bag; he had a feeling that, like the last time he'd come for a meeting with the deputy director for operations, this would be a quick affair.

He'd be picked up in a government vehicle, driven around Arlington for a few minutes, then deposited back at the airport.

He'd rehearsed his words on the flight up, and for the few days since he'd first heard the CIA was stopping its investigations into the leaks, into the murders.

A text came as he stood there in the frigid air; Watkins said he was two minutes out, and Hanley should be ready to shuffle into the vehicle.

Hanley sighed. His fingers were cold, but he checked the news on his phone. There'd been no more targeted killings in the past four days, and this was good news. A cell of Russian spies in Brooklyn, some of them known GRU assassins, had been eliminated in a shoot-out, and although the news was saying the FBI and Homeland Security had conducted the raid, Hanley had learned from others that it had been a team of twelve Gauntlet security operators who were contracting with Homeland. Men just working in the area who came upon the Russians coincidentally.

Hanley didn't believe this story for an instant, which meant he didn't believe the subsequent story, which was that these Russians had been responsible for all the killings.

He wondered if the killing of the Russian fall guys meant the immediate crisis was over, but it bothered him greatly that Lewis Shaw had been assassinated, and his concern was that the conventional wisdom in the government was going to be that Lewis Shaw of the Office of the Director of National Intelligence had been feeding the intel to the Russians, and everyone involved was conveniently dead.

Gauntlet Group, of course, had been lauded as American heroes by much of the press.

Scrolling the news for more information, he almost passed the breaking story on the *Washington Post*'s website. Paula Kerr, a Democratic senator from New Hampshire, had apparently been involved in a hit-and-run the night before after leaving a fundraiser. She was in critical condition up in Concord; other pedestrians had been hit by the same erratic driver, as well.

The damaged car was found overturned on a high school baseball diamond twenty minutes later, the driver inside it, his neck snapped. He was a twenty-four-year-old known user with two DUIs already, so no foul play was suspected.

The senator was not expected to survive.

Hanley didn't know Kerr. She'd been the CEO of a tech firm before entering politics, and in the Senate, she'd shown little interest in intelligence affairs. She wasn't on any committees Hanley paid attention to, so it didn't seem related to everything else going on.

Still, a U.S. senator hit by a car, fighting for her life.

Jesus, Matt thought.

Just then, three SUVs pulled up to arrivals, two Suburbans with a Navigator in the center. A back door of the Navigator opened, and Hanley climbed in.

The last time he'd met with Trey Watkins, Angela Lacy, Ghost Town's conduit to the DDO, had been in the vehicle and involved in the discussion.

This time, however, Watkins was alone, other than three security men in the vehicle with him, and that did not seem like good news to Hanley.

"Where's Angela?" Matt asked.

"Reassigned. Same as Pace." Watkins said nothing more.

"Where?"

"Undetermined, as of yet. For now, they're at Langley, but I've asked them not to communicate with you."

"What's going on, Trey?"

The DDO shrugged. "Not a lot I can tell you, to be honest. Basically, I was taken to the woodshed by the DNI when she found out Jim Pace had been involved in a clandestine investigation into Gauntlet Group. She ordered me to order him to stand down, and she now has HSI taking the lead on everything involving the killings."

"The DNI? Olivia Anthony? She has Homeland Security Investigations in charge?"

"Yeah. Says this is bigger than the CIA, the CIA shouldn't be operating domestically, so we're shut down."

Hanley was incredulous. "How did she even know Pace was working on this?"

"Because there are photos of Jim Pace in Georgetown climbing out of the BMW he later used to kill one of the assassins, and there's a photo of *you* circulating that has you driving through the crime scene in a minivan in Washington Circle."

"She knows about Ghost Town?"

"Yep," Watkins said, looking out the window now.

"Did Olivia Anthony fail to acknowledge the fact that Pace and I were involved with bringing down three of the assassins, when the rest of the intelligence community hasn't managed to accomplish a thing?"

Watkins turned back to Hanley. "Actually, she did acknowledge it. When she found out I was running an off-books op with the former DDO, she said, and I quote, 'I appreciate your initiative in all this, but I'll take over from here.'"

"Jesus Christ."

"Look. Anthony is okay. She's not the problem. But the president is very focused on bringing Gauntlet Group deeper into the community, especially after what they pulled off in Brooklyn, and Olivia Anthony is going to execute the president's wishes."

Hanley said, "Gauntlet Group, Trey, has been involved in this from the very start. Pace told you that, I'm sure. You don't think these guys just stumbled onto a Russian cell and saved America, do you?"

Watkins looked uncomfortable. "It's a bullshit story, but that's the story." He shrugged. "Gauntlet is a big company. Apparently some rogue operators might have been tricked into working with Russian intelligence assets here in America and—"

"Jesus Christ!" Hanley shouted it now. "You're talking like one of them! I mean, up until two months ago, I thought you *were* one of them, but I was starting to believe in you, Trey."

Watkins rolled his eyes. "Come on, Matt. I have a job to do. You do, as well. You are still my sub rosa outfit. We will just find some other tasks for you." He smiled a little. "This is all over. You should be proud. We aren't going to get the credit, but we won."

Hanley sighed. "We won? This is over? Bullshit! You don't believe the words coming out of your own mouth. But you sure as shit sound great when you say them, I'll give you that."

Watkins pounded on the glass behind him that separated the driver from the backseat. While looking at Hanley, he called out to the driver. "Back to Reagan! Matt has a plane to catch."

Campbell Coyle went to a chip shop at eleven a.m., ate his fish at a picnic table outside in the cold blowing in from the coast, and then he returned to St. James Church.

It was quiet here in southwest Ballycastle; the hustle and bustle was along the coastline a few miles to the north. A vehicle passed by on the road every few minutes, just as it had when he was here earlier in the morning. He walked the grounds, strolled around the nearly empty car park, even looked inside the church, but he did nothing to arouse any suspicion to himself.

He appeared to be just a middle-aged man with nothing to do. No place to be.

Just before noon, he returned to the spot among the tombstones where he'd stood earlier in the day, his face cold from the whipping sea wind, and he watched a car in the far distance on Novally Road roll slowly to a stop.

A lone man climbed out, and he began walking this way.

His hands were empty, but his gait was pure menace.

The man's coat was open in the frigid wind; his eyes were fixed ahead. Coyle knew how to check for every single tell that said someone meant trouble, and this man was doing nothing to hide the fact he imparted the gravest of danger.

Court Gentry left the road, passed through a little gate in a low stone wall, and then entered the cemetery.

The Northern Irishman held his ground until the man who had killed his son stopped, fifteen feet away, and stared him down.

Courtland Gentry faced off in front of the man who had killed his father.

He said, "You've had time to prepare the battlespace here. You have all the advantages, Coyle. Still . . . I came. That tell you anything?"

"It tells me yer feckin' mad. You had no right to go to the house of me grandson. I took that as a threat."

"It was anything but a threat. I spoke with Deirdre. She might not have liked it, but I could see in her that she knew that I didn't mean her or the boy any harm."

"Still. You shouldn't have done it."

"It put me right here, right now."

"Like I said . . . you shouldn't have done it."

Court said nothing. His hand was close to the Glock pistol on his hip. Even with the thick coat over it, he knew he could have it out and up in under five-tenths of a second.

His muscles were taut, his body ready for action.

"You know why I told you to meet me here?" Coyle asked.

Court looked around at the cemetery a moment. He gave a little shrug. "As good a place as any, I guess. You wanted to meet here at high noon. You've probably watched too many old Westerns, but whatever. I'll play along if it means your death."

When Campbell said nothing, Court said, "It's quiet. You and I can fight. Nobody is going to get in the way."

Still, Campbell did not speak.

A strong breeze blew Court's coat open a little, revealing the butt of a semiautomatic pistol. Campbell looked down at it.

He said, "That's an old-model Glock. You get that from an IRA cache?"

"Yep."

"You know an old Provo, do ya?"

"Nope," Court said. "I know somebody who knows where weapons are still hidden around here. He tried to talk me out of what's about to happen, but when I pressed him, he gave me your daughter-in-law's address, and then he told me where I could get this weapon."

A rumbling old farm tractor rolled by; neither man took his eyes off the other to look at it.

Finally, Campbell Coyle said, "I'll answer the question you can't answer. Why here?"

"What's to answer?" Court responded. "This is Church of Ireland. You and your family are Catholic. Your son isn't here. I don't know why the fuck we're . . ."

Court stopped talking when he saw a pair of large buses appear through some trees on Ramoan Road, far in the distance. They rolled this way slowly.

His eyes flitted back to the Northern Irishman, and he saw a little smile on the man's face.

Court brought his hand closer to his weapon, because Coyle's eyes looked confident now, and his smile looked like danger.

The three vehicles containing the deputy director for operations of the CIA, the former deputy director for operations, and ten bodyguards rolled along Potomac Avenue heading for the exit to Reagan National Airport. A plane passed by on the right, on final for Runway 1, flying just feet over the river.

Hanley had been looking at Watkins with mistrust for the past couple of minutes, wondering if Watkins could have somehow been sucked into a cabal in the American government responsible for the deaths of nearly two dozen in the past week. Surely, Trey couldn't have been with them from the beginning, but certainly, by his actions and by his words today, he'd implicated himself at the center of the conspiracy.

Hanley said, "Tell me one thing, Trey. Angela Lacy. If you were going to sell us out, why did you bring her into this?"

"I didn't sell you out. I didn't sell Angela out. I didn't sell Jim Pace out."

"Prove it."

Now the DDO gave an annoyed sigh, then put his hands up in the air. "How on earth can I possibly prove a negative? What will it take to convince you that I'm not part of whatever you think might be going on around—"

When it happened, it happened in an instant.

The light and the sound and the motion.

The heat and the pain.

It was all one sensation. One experience.

The Navigator was armored, but it came apart as if it had been made of nothing but rusty tin.

A roar of an explosion, then the vehicle launched into the sky, flipped onto its side; crashed down to the street. A flash fire erupted throughout the interior, then the screams of men, then the screeching of metal.

Matt Hanley was thrown through the open roof, as was the bodyguard traveling in the rear of the vehicle next to him, and the two men tumbled along the road together, then off the road, then down a grassy hill and into the trees at the bank of the Potomac River.

Neither of the other two vehicles suffered any damage at all, but the DDO's limo was completely destroyed, finally coming to rest in a ball of fire on the Potomac Yard Trail. Black smoke and yellow flames reached into the sky.

Hanley was forty yards away from the wreckage, on his back, on the wet ground in the trees. He was burned, broken, unconscious, unaware that anything had happened at all save for that first flash of light, that first roar of sound, and that first jarring motion.

Security men swarmed him and the other survivors of the vehicle; helicopters landed on the George Washington Parkway in minutes to begin life flights, and even the obviously dead were rushed to the hospital as if there was still some fleeting chance.

Later it would be said that something came out of the trees at the water's edge, and a search by Metro PD would find a spent tube from an AT4 antitank rocket left nearby.

...

Court watched the two buses roll ever closer, and he took a single step back, as if he were preparing to retreat to his car. There could be hundreds of people in the buses just ahead of him: Gauntlet operatives, a gang of football hooligans aligned with Coyle, ex–IRA Provo gunmen, bought-off heavies from a drug gang, a foreign entity of some sort.

Court had no idea what was heading his way, but of all the possibilities, what happened next came as a complete surprise.

As the buses stopped, the doors opened, and children in school uniforms under their heavy coats began pouring out, running through the little gate in the low stone wall of the cemetery, coming closer and closer.

Court looked back to Coyle for an explanation.

"They're late today. Gave me a wee bit of a scare, if I'm being honest, chief." As he nodded to some passing children, he looked back to Court. "The school kids come on Wednesdays for lunch if the weather isn't too bad. Then they tidy up the tombstones."

Now there had to have been one hundred kids on the church grounds, all in motion, moving around the older men, heading this way and that.

Court moved closer to Coyle. Spoke softly. "Then why the *fuck* did you set our showdown up for the same time?"

"You're not going to fight me in the middle of these weans, chief."

"These *what*?"

"Weans. Wee ones. *Children*, Gentry. I can't say I know ya well, but I *do* know *that*. So while we're standing here and *not* fighting, I ask ye to look down at yer feet, yeah?"

Court did as Coyle said. There, right in front of him, was a new tombstone in this forest of old markers.

And Court knew what it would say before he read it.

But he read it anyway.

"Charles Brendan Coyle." Court noted that the man had been born in March, and he'd died in October. The years of his birth and his death seemed so impossibly close.

Twenty-four years apart.

Court looked back up to his intended target now, unsure.

Coyle said, "Church of Ireland allows for Catholic burials. Catholic Church allows for burials in Church of Ireland cemeteries." He waved a hand. "All these here, they're Coyles. My da is just over there. I'll be laid between them and me boy, right here. Whether that's now, whether that's not now . . . I suppose that one's up to you."

"What are you saying?"

"An eye for an eye. That's some feudal shite, I think. I'm not for that. But I learned something in the death of me boy. I hope you learned something in the death of yer da.

"What I mean to say is, it doesn't have to be like all this. It *is* . . . but it shouldn't be. Now . . . these kids will be gone in an hour. The roads get busier in the afternoon, but at dusk, this place is empty. The light is good, we've ourselves a full moon comin'. You and I can get it on then, if yer so inclined. But for now, I want ye to just look down at me family, at the boy ya killed, and I want ya to know I don't blame ya anymore. If killin' me is yer wish, you can come back and 'ave at it. I'll give you a fight, I will. And we'll see what the future holds."

Coyle looked down at the open space between his son and his da. "If it's my time tonight, I've no problem resting right there." He sighed. "But I had a long talk on the phone with Deirdre when she called. I believe her. I believe she won't let her son, my grandson, turn into one of us. She won't let him be part of the hard line.

"He'll have a chance. You and I . . . maybe we have to fight. But now, that's on you."

Coyle began walking away, through children still moving about the cemetery, their lunch boxes swinging in their hands.

He called out as he walked. "I'll see ya tonight, chief. Or else I won't. Sound like a plan?"

He headed for the car park without another word.

Court Gentry walked back among the schoolkids, towards his rented car. It was twelve twenty in the afternoon, and he shuffled along, unsure where he'd go now, unsure where he'd be at six p.m.

He still wanted to kill, to avenge his father.

But somehow, he did not want to kill this man.

He thought about going to a bar, having a few drinks, letting the whiskey tell him what to do.

As he drove off to the south, leaving the church and the man he'd sworn to kill, and the grave of a boy he had killed, he looked down at his phone.

He'd gotten several calls—he didn't check them—and several texts on Signal. He ignored them all.

He was putting his phone away when he saw that he had one text that came through unencrypted. He looked down and saw it was from Zoya.

This was strange. Zoya never sent texts.

He opened it.

Call me. Now!!

He switched to Signal and dialed her number.

EPILOGUE

Bellstar Aviation chartered the Hawker 800 at Derry Airport, and Court boarded three hours and ten minutes before his scheduled fight to the death with Campbell Coyle over the Northern Irishman's son's grave.

He was rushing back to America because of what had happened just hours earlier in D.C., and he wondered if Campbell would ever wonder why he wasn't there at the appointed time.

Court put the Northern Irishman out of his mind when his phone rang. It was Signal, and it was Lacy.

"Hey," he said. "How's Matt?"

"He's stable. It's an absolute miracle. There were five men in that car. Matt and a thirty-three-year-old Agency bodyguard survived. Both have broken bones and burns. Matt's going to need a few surgeries, but he *will* live."

"And Trey Watkins?"

Lacy took a moment. Said, "Dead. Presumably he and Hanley were both the intended targets. You know, I thought Watkins might have been somehow involved in all this."

"You weren't the only one."

"Well, he's dead, so I have a feeling he was just another victim, and not the culprit."

Court said, "Matt's not safe. Even in the hospital."

Lacy replied, "I know. I spoke with Conductor. She's got the Five Guys watching over him there."

"Good."

Lacy said, "I've been reassigned overseas, but I don't leave for a few days. I'd like to talk to you when you get home."

"I'll meet you in the morning," Court said.

"Let's do it in Charlottesville. That safe house is secure. Anthem and Catherine and Irene are there, Teddy and Night Train are there, we have plenty of security, too."

"Okay," Court replied, happy that he was going to get to see Zoya. "I'll talk to you tomorrow."

"Six?" Lacy said.

"Yeah?"

"Um . . . Something else happened this morning."

Court cocked his head. "What?"

"In Arlington?" She said it as if she was prompting him to remember.

It took a second, and then Court closed his eyes and sighed. "Shit. My father's funeral. Of course." He was embarrassed. Said, "I'm just a little overwhelmed by events, I guess."

"Totally understand. But they did full military honors. It was very moving."

"Very moving?" Court was confused by this. "Did you go?"

"Well . . . no. I wanted to stay away in case there were people there looking for you. I didn't want to be associated . . . I mean . . . I don't mean that in a bad way."

Court chuckled a little. "I get it. I'm something of a hot potato these days."

"Right. Anyway . . . Skip Echols flew up from Florida to be there. I asked him to take video of the ceremony."

"That's great. I appreciate your kindness. And his."

"Yeah," Angela said, "that's not why I did it. I did it for intelligence purposes. Wanted to see if Gauntlet or Homeland or someone else was there. It could give us an indication of the threat against you."

"Good thinking."

"Skip sent the video. I watched it myself just now."

"Was the cemetery crawling with jackbooted thugs?" Court joked.

"Not at all. There was no one. Well, not no one, just one attendee, but of course it wasn't announced, and you said your dad didn't stay close with anyone in Washington."

"Well, I'm glad Skip was there, so somebody could be witness to—"

Angela interrupted. "No . . . I mean . . . one more person other than Skip."

"Really?" Court was surprised, and suspicious. "Who was it?"

"Oh, I have no idea. He stayed back, out of the way. Kind of watched from a distance, but he didn't film or anything. I don't think he was there conducting surveillance. He looked like he gave a damn about the funeral, I mean."

"That's nice," Court said, but he had no idea what this meant.

Lacy said, "I took an image from the recording, sending it to you now. Just thought you might recognize someone who knew your dad."

Court highly doubted it. The image came through and Court clicked on it.

He enlarged it, then enlarged it again.

And again.

He looked at the man standing on a hill not far from the gravesite, but not close, either.

A black raincoat, sunglasses, brown hair lifted by the breeze.

"Six?" Angela said. "Did you get it?"

Court didn't answer; his eyes were so fixed on the screen in front of him, he didn't even blink for twenty seconds.

"Hello?"

Still he did not respond.

"Okay," Angela said. "I think we lost signal. I'll give you a call later, Six, hope you have a good flight."

"Hey," Court finally said. He blinked. "Yeah . . . uh . . . I got the picture . . . I don't know him. Must have just been there and wanted to see a funeral." He added, "Military honors and all. I look forward to watching the whole thing when I get home.

"Thanks, Angela. I appreciate it."

"Sure," she said. "Anyway . . . Skip was happy to do it. I've got to run. I'm here at the hospital, heading in to check on Matt again."

"See you tomorrow," Court said.

"See you tomorrow," Angela echoed.

Court disconnected the call, but he continued looking at the picture on his phone a little while longer.

Then he put his phone back in his pocket and closed his eyes.

Nothing in this world made sense anymore. The government leaks. The rash of assassinations. The death of his father. Hanley's injury.

Watkins's murder.

A fight to the death that didn't happen in a cemetery where one of Court's victims lay in a fresh grave.

A victim Court hadn't even wanted to kill.

It was all just too much.

And now this.

This.

On the long list of all the things in this world that Court Gentry could not quite wrap his head around right now, at the very top was the fact that he'd just seen a picture of his dead brother, very much alive, attending the funeral of their father.

He looked out the window, at the sky around him, at the ocean below him.

And he wondered what the hell was going on.

ACKNOWLEDGMENTS

I'd like to thank Joshua Hood, Mike Cowan, Jon Harvey, Barbara Peters, "the real" Trey Watkins, and Dr. Tony Casper.

I'd also like to thank Allison Greaney, Trey Greaney, Kristin Greaney, Barbara Guy, and Ava, Sophie, and Kemmons Wilson.

Thank you to my literary agent, Robert Gottlieb of Trident Media Group, and my film agent, Jon Cassir of CAA.

A very special thanks to my editor, Tom Colgan, and the incredible team at Berkley, including Naira Mirza, Jin Yu, Loren Jaggers, Bridget O'Toole, Elise Tecco, Anna Venckus, Jeanne-Marie Hudson, Craig Burke, Ivan Held, Christine Ball, and Claire Zion.

And lastly, thank you to my longtime agent, Scott Miller. May you rest in peace.

RAISING READERS
Books Build Bright Futures

Dear Reader,

We'd love your attention for one more page to tell you about the crisis in children's reading, and what we can all do.

Studies have shown that reading for fun is the **single biggest predictor of a child's future life chances** – more than family circumstance, parents' educational background or income. It improves academic results, mental health, wealth, communication skills, ambition and happiness.[1]

The number of children reading for fun is in rapid decline. Young people have a lot of competition for their time. In 2024, 1 in 10 children and young people in the UK aged 5 to 18 did not own a single book at home.[2]

Hachette works extensively with schools, libraries and literacy charities, but here are some ways we can all raise more readers:

- Reading to children for just 10 minutes a day makes a difference
- Don't give up if children aren't regular readers – there will be books for them!
- Visit bookshops and libraries to get recommendations
- Encourage them to listen to audiobooks
- Support school libraries
- Give books as gifts

There's a lot more information about how to encourage children to read on our website: **www.RaisingReaders.co.uk**

Thank you for reading.

---

[1] OECD, '21st-Century Readers: Developing Literacy Skills in a Digital World', 2021, https://www.oecd.org/en/publications/21st-century-readers_a83d84cb-en.html

[2] National Literacy Trust, 'Book Ownership in 2024', November 2024, https://literacytrust.org.uk/research-services/research-reports/book-ownership-in-2024